THE FOOL OF VENUS

THE FOOL OF VENUS

The Story of Peire Vidal

BY GEORGE CRONYN

COVICI-FRIEDE, PUBLISHERS

NEW YORK · MCMXXXIV

Foreword

TWO hundred years before Froissart glorified the Age of Chivalry, and so identified it thenceforth in the popular mind with romance, the histrionic exploits of Richard the Lion had been faithfully set down by clerical correspondents in his train, who plainly admired that warrior though they did not gloss over the ambiguities of his character. A few years later, Villehardouin, greatest of all historiographers and crusader as well, recounted with matchless vigor the colorful if sordid happenings of the Fourth Crusade, further particularized by the Grand Logothete, Nicetas, who suffered in the sack of New Rome from being on the losing side.

These candid and generally scrupulous chroniclers have provided the groundwork for the present narrative insofar as it treats of military matters. But though the importance of the troubadours in the conduct of the crusades was recognized at the time, they fare obscurely in the annals, wherein deeds, rather than songs, are recorded. Fortunately for our knowledge of twelfth-century manners and customs when not at war, the world's most accomplished groups of singers, the jongleurs and troubadours of Provence, were self-revealing in their songs. And of these none was more autobiographical than Peire Vidal, who has left to the speculation of posterity some forty-eight songs which compose a sort of lyrical diary, though addressed mostly to lovely ladies or generous patrons. In the very words of the distinguished troubadour are to be found the sources of the curious legends that cluster about his name; and from them his story is largely drawn.

The other persons of this chronicle have been subjected to no more fictitious interpretation than may be justified on the basis of extant historical records.

G. C.

SOME HISTORICAL PERSONS OF THE CHRONICLE

TIME: from the battle of Tiberias (1187) to shortly after the battle of Muret (1213).

Richard I, known in the North as Cœur de Lion and in the South as the Lion, third son of King Henry II and Queen Eleanor; and himself king of England, mostly absent, from 1189 to 1199.

Enrico Dandolo, born about 1120, became doge of Venice in 1193, and in 1202 led the Fourth Crusade, diverting it from the Holy Land to the capture of New Rome.

Innocent III, born Lotario de' Conti, elected pope at the age of 37, while still a layman.

Philip II or Philip Augustus, king of France from 1180 to 1223; one of the greatest of the Capetian dynasty. To the Messinians, however, he was Philip the Lamb.

Alexis III, Angelus, emperor of New Rome and brother of Isaac II, Angelus, whose throne he usurped in 1195. He fled when New Rome was taken by the Latins and died in exile.

Alexis IV, Angelus, the Young Alexis, son of Isaac II, Angelus, with whom he was associated as puppet emperor in 1204, to be deposed and put to death by Mourtzuphlos.

Alexis V, Dukas, or Mourtzuphlos, briefly emperor of New Rome in 1204. After the sack of the city by the Latins he was captured in the Morea and cast from the top of the Pillar of Theodosius.

Baldwin I, born about 1171, the son of Baldwin VIII, count of Flanders and Hainaut; he joined the Fourth Crusade in 1200 and on May 9, 1204, was crowned emperor of New Rome as Baldwin I.

Simon de Montfort (l' Amauri), born about 1160; he became the father of the more famous Simon de Montfort, Earl of Leicester. In 1209 he led the Albigensian Crusade, for which service he received the possessions and titles of the count of Toulouse.

Villehardouin, Geoffroy or Geoffroi, marshal at the court of Thibaut of Champagne; he joined the Fourth Crusade and became one of its leaders as well as historiographer of the campaign, contributing to the French language its first great historical classic in the vernacular.

Bonifaz (Boniface), count of Montferrat (Monferrato), son of Guilhem III, a famous crusader; he reigned jointly with his brother Conrat until

1187 when he ruled Montferrat alone and headed the Imperial party in Italy.

Raimon V, the "Good," count of Toulouse, overlord of vast demesnes that stretched from his capital to the Rhône. Feudal overlord of Peire Vidal.

Raimon VI (son of Raimon V), count of Toulouse, reigned from 1194 to 1222; alternately leading the Albigensian party of Provence and suffering excommunication and humbling at the hands of Rome.

Barrale or Barral, viscount of Marseille, one of the most respected lords of old Provence, patron and friend of Peire Vidal; in his native city he held only the office of podestat, or chief magistrate, a position long peculiar to the reigning members of his house. He married the famous Adélasie, countess of Les Baux, but separated from her some time before his death in 1194.

Adélasie des Baux, or Alazais of Roca Martina, the most famous beauty of her time, sister of the Counts Hugues and Guillaume des Baux. The names of many troubadours are associated with hers.

Guillaume des Baux, brother of Adélasie, espoused the cause of Rome against the heretics and was caught and flayed alive by the dissenters of Avignon. He held the title of Prince of Orange, which passed by devious ways to the royal house of England.

Louve de Penaultier, or Loba de Puegnautier, wife of Count Jordan Roger, brother of Raimon Roger, viscount of Béziers. She brought misfortune to several troubadours, notably Raimon of Miravals and to Raimon Roger, with whom she was connected in a scandal.

Raimon Roger, viscount of Béziers and husband of Alazais, countess of Burlatz, the daughter of the Good Count Raimon.

Beatriz of Montferrat, daughter of Count Bonifaz, for her feats of prowess came to be known as La Bel Cavelier. Married at 12 to Enrico del Carreto the Younger, she accepted the love of Raimbaut of Vacqueiras.

Of the **Countess Rambauda of Biolh,** or Bueil, and the **Lady Estefania de Berga** little is known beyond their connection with troubadours.

TROUBADOURS

Besides **Peire Vidal,** the more famous troubadours were:

Gaucelm Faidit, born about 1156; he sang badly but left about 70 pieces, of which the most beautiful is the *Lament* for Richard's death.

Folquet of Marseille, troubadour, who became Archbishop Fulk of Toulouse.

Aimeric de Peguilha, born about 1170, the son of a draper of Toulouse; he lived until 1245 and left some 50 pieces.

The Monk of Montauban, or Montaudon; after leaving the abbey of Orlac he became famous for his songs, largely satirical, amorous, and profane, of which 18 survive.

Peire Cardinal of Le Puy, the foremost moral and didactic poet among the troubadours, of whose 70 pieces only three treat of love, and even these are not amatory. He castigated the viciousness of his age in biting sirventes, served as secretary to Raimon VI, and lived to be a centenarian.

Raimon of Miravals, a troubadour of large estates, most of which were lost through unfortunate love affairs.

Pons de Capduelh, a troubadour of grace and feeling, known for his devotion to Alazais of Mercœur; his songs number about thirty.

Bernart of Ventadorn, a famous troubadour of an earlier generation, wooer of Eleanor of Aquitaine, Henry II's queen; he spent his later life at Toulouse.

Raimbaut of Vacqueiras, son of a poor knight related to the noble house of Orange. He had many patrons but served Bonifaz of Montferrat the longest and was rewarded by the latter with a princely title. His 40 or more songs are difficult to understand, save the beautiful *Carros,* written to Beatriz of Montferrat, a piece that strongly influenced later Italian poets.

Peyrols, or Peirol, of Vodable left 35 pieces of varying quality.

Izarn, better known as an Inquisitor, defended orthodoxy in song against the Albigenses.

Gui of Cavaillon, baron and partisan of Toulouse, has left half a dozen good songs.

Arnaut de Maruelh, or Mareuil, scribe and notary, became famous for his devotion to the wife of Raimon Roger, Alazais, countess of Burlatz, and for his poignant love songs.

Arnaut Daniel in his "close and difficult" style marked the decadence of Provençal lyricism and won the admiration of Dante.

Provence, strictly speaking, was a triangular region lying east of the Rhône and extending from Avignon to the Maritime Alps. By common usage at the time of this chronicle, the term was extended to include all the territory where the *langue d'Oc* was spoken, Provence, Languedoc, and the coast of Aragon fronting the Gulf of Lyon.

The association of the troubadours with the Albigenses was accidental, as they had little in common except the patronage and protection of the dissident lords of Provence and Larguedoc. The Albigenses, as well as other unorthodox sects of Southern Europe, represent an early movement directed against the Roman Catholic Church, with the emphasis upon simplicity of doctrine and living. Troubadour culture perished in the Albigensian Crusade and was never successfully revived.

A Glossary of the more unfamiliar terms will be found at the back of the book.

THE FOOL OF VENUS

Chapter One

IN 1187 ANNO DOMINI Salâh-ed-din Yussuf ibn Ayub, called
Saladin by the Christians, drove the Latin armies in headlong
flight and took the Holy City. This same year in Provence,
during the calends of May, the goddess Venus, who had long
been absent from the haunts of men, returned and made herself
visible to Peire Vidal, a troubadour, son of a well-to-do furrier of
Toulouse.

Peire Vidal, at the age of twenty, had spent a term at the college
of law at Monpeslier, to which his sole parent had despatched him
in the hope that what he plainly lacked in natural judgment he
might by degrees gather into his large misshapen head from the
weighty discourse of the learned Placentinus. The hope was vain.
The collegium, having experienced his wayward and riotous disposition, dismissed him with a stern warning, and he returned to
Toulouse in disgrace carrying, instead of a headful of learning, an
abominable instrument, a tongue tripping with rhymes, and a
throat ever uttering albas, canzos, and other vagrant tunes. He soon
displayed an aversion toward priests, an inclination to wenching, an
inability to bear up under tippling, a leaning toward heretical argument, and an indifference to the sterner duties of life that boded
no good for his future.

When Messer Pons Vidal, furrier, had stood all he could of his son's twangling and scraping on his viol and of his yawping of love ditties, he summoned the hulking lad to him, gave into his hands a wallet stuffed with silver sols and deniers, bestowed a casual blessing, and commended him to the protection of Sant Julian, patron of singers and outcasts.

"My son," he said at the parting, "I am putting you out because you are good for nothing. You are lazy, which is a hindrance to getting on in trade; and you are stubborn, a quality commendable only in a sprig of nobility. You know more of what a maid is good for than you do of reckoning profits, and since you have given yourself to the filthy trade of song, it behooves you to master the tricks of the jongleur—such as they are!"

"The art of the jongleur is not held low in estimation," said Peire Vidal haughtily. "Many great troubadours began as jongleurs and audiarts!"

"Many oaks have acorns, but the thistle seed does not become a cedar. You are choosing a way of life that has little to commend it and much in its disfavor. Henceforth, since this wallet is your inheritance, you will be dependent upon the bounty of lords, whom you are bound to enrage with your impertinence, and of ladies whose favor you will lose through indiscretion. You will compete with others of greater talents and sounder principles—"

"None shall surpass me in the practice of the Joyous Craft!" cried Peire Vidal hotly.

"I have noticed," said the furrier, stroking his beard complacently, "how much you resemble your sainted mother, who died in the belief that she was the most richly endowed and virtuous of females. But you, my son, will discover in due time what is in store for you from the stinging of your tail. I bear you no malice, for I am now relieved of the burden of your maintenance and the ill repute coming of your follies. Sant Julian keep you from the gallows!"

"You shall hear of me when my name is on all men's lips!" shouted the son in a fury; but his sire had re-entered his place of business without looking back.

That night Peire Vidal dined below the salt at the table of his lordship, the Good Count Raimon of Toulouse, by whom the greater part of Provence was held in fief. When the squire of the table passed about, holding a silver ewer of scented water and a basin, the furrier's son stared goggle-eyed at the utensils until he was nudged, then he dipped his over-large hands into the ewer, splashing the water on the trestles. Jongleurs and squires grinned, for the proper thing was to hold the hands gracefully above the basin as the lackey poured from the ewer. He dropped gobbets of larks upon the board, audibly munched his oaten bread, and choked on a half-ripe medlar, evoking the whisper, "Who is the keeper of this bear? Do they let such beasts go about unchained?"

But when the carvers could do no more and the trenchers had been well polished by the guests down to the last dripping, and when spices, sweetmeats, and hot spiced wine had taken their place, there followed an evening of song, during the course of which the Lady Constance, wife to the lord of Toulouse, commanded Peire Vidal to sing, for she had already heard of his voice in the city. He rose awkwardly from his place at the board, took his viol, brushed the bow across the strings, and began to sing an alba he had made for the fair daughter of a cook, a wench whose shapely breasts beneath her fustian bliaut had cost him several sleepless nights. He sang: *Li doutz consire, quem don amors soven*—— "Sweet reveries that passion often brings"—a lyric of greater sweetness than the object of it, as is sometimes the case with songs. Though untrained, his voice was rich, deep, and full-throated, and as the air rang through the great hall no other sound was heard save the fluttering and hissing of torches in the wall brackets, and the flapping of arras bellied by the wind.

"He can fashion a good song, for all his boorishness," they said. And, "This lout has the making of a jongleur, perhaps a troubadour!"

But the countess, being English, said, "Senher Vidal, the song is somewhat too much of the earth and flesh; still, it was well done." Greatly flattered to be called senher, he stumbled back to his seat.

Before the company retired to their pallets to sleep naked between coverlets of silk or on sacks of straw, as the case might be, the Good Count Raimon bade his steward deliver "to Senher Vidal, jongleur, twelve oboles in silver, a hood and cape of russet, and his name is to be entered on the rolls of Castle Bargarde as a squire of the menie, or household."

The next day the newly created squire sent word to his father: "Having moved them all to tears of ecstasy by the power of my singing, I have been taken into the service of the Good Count Raimon and they name me Senher Vidal, which should be a cause of gratification to you. Also, the count's lady was so charmed by my presence, there is no telling where it will end."

The furrier grunted, scowling at the script. "I can tell you where it will end, you egotistical jackanapes! It will end in such a cudgeling as will bring you back crawling to this shop. Senher indeed! By Sant Marti, you'll soon be calling yourself monsenher, you dog!"

In his two years at the court of Toulouse Peire Vidal learned the manifold arts of the jongleur and the more warlike discipline of a squire in arms. As jongleur he learned to be dextrous and nimble, a difficult thing for one of his cumbrous build; to be a mime and an acrobat; to toss a naked sword and catch it; to play on six or seven instruments, such as the lute, flute, gigue, harpe, symphonie, and organistrum, besides his favorite viol; and to sing all the many kinds of songs—an alba for the morning, a serena for the evening, a sirvente, sharp and satirical, a planh of grief or melancholy, a dancing balada, a gallant canzo, and the like. Moreover, he learned to modulate his voice to the narrow limits of a lady's chamber, to stand a bit more gracefully, and to manage his arms less like flails. He learned chess, rackets, tennis, tables or backgammon, and the art of casting dice; but he took little interest in the subtleties of falconry. He came to washing his face and neck once a week, and found how to kneel before a lord or lady without bruising his shins; yet he remained inexpert and fumbling in the courtier's art of adulation. In speech he was somewhat witless, so that the ladies of the court took him for a fool, gifted with song.

In the spring of that fateful year when the Holy Land was overrun by the hosts of Saladin, the countess of Toulouse decreed for the last week of April a Court of Love, to be held at Castle Bargarde, and this was to be a part of a great festival, concluding with a *tornimen* of song. Having held counsel with her court ladies, the countess despatched messengers to the troubadours and jongleurs in all parts of Provence, from Aix to Carcassonne and from Arles to Valence. She also invited twelve ladies of known judgment and discretion to sit as judges in the Court. Soon, in small companies and large, afoot and on horseback, they came trooping across the wooden bridge over the Garonne, past the church of Saint Sernin, where the Albigensian heretic, Peire Valdo, was preaching, and out beyond the massive walls of arrogant Toulouse to the Castle Bargarde, warden and protector of the city against the Frankish lords of the north. Toulouse, rich and noble, proud and stiff-necked toward all but the Good Count Raimon, sheltering heretics and contentious sects, welcomed the illustrious singers, fêted them, and delivered them to its beloved overlord.

There were troubadours of the rank of squires, humbly furnished, and troubadours who were knights, lords, and barons; and there were jongleurs little better than mimes and buffoons, and others of noble birth who were undergoing their apprenticeship in the Joyous Craft as audiarts to renowned singers. Some of the troubadours composed and delivered all their own songs, but others delegated the execution of their pieces to their audiarts. And each troubadour, in his songs, proclaimed his fidelity and devotion to some fair lady, the wife of a knight or lord, for this was the custom.

Among the eminent singers was Gaucelm Faidit, a mountain of flesh and a despoiler of many larders, who, though he was no more than a squire, having dissipated his patrimony in gaming, could count three kings and lesser notables among his friends. He had with him his wanton, Guilhelma Monjo, a being whose virtues consisted in ample breasts, bold eyes, a complexion built of saffron, quicksilver, and mare's milk, lips of brightest vermilion, braids that hung long and sleek to her voluptuous thighs, and in certain natural tendencies that best expressed themselves when her lord was deep in his cups.

When Peire Vidal set eyes upon the pursy troubadour he thought at once, "This is my friend!"

Said Gaucelm Faidit, "So you are the Messer Vidal they say is witless, yet has a voice? I should have taken you for a swineherd, for you could throw a boar with those feelers of yours, and outrun a deer on those shanks! Well, your face is honest, which is more than can be said for this wench of mine!"

Guilhelma Monjo came close to Peire Vidal, so close that the scent of musk was strong in his nostrils. "My lord abuses me," she said, her bosom less than a hand's breadth from him. "He is a besotted creature that makes lovely songs to the great ladies, such as Maria of Ventadorn. They had him in his prime, but I must take what is left of him—a poor remnant of a man, mostly appetite!"

"Slut!" said her lord amiably. "You are already trying to seduce this young man, shame to you!"

"I have heard some of your songs, monsenher," said Peire Vidal eagerly, "and indeed I know a few of them, the alba 'Hark, the watchman on the tower,' the retroensa, 'If I might know you love me still'."

"Your memory flatters me, young man," said Gaucelm Faidit, "but let's have no monsenhering. My father was a good knight, but I am only a poor squire, rich in my knowledge of wines. Let us go and discover some vintage of Toulouse. You shall sing to us, and I warrant my alley cat will be fondling you before we have drained the second flagon!"

As they passed through the crowded hall, Peire Vidal observed two singers whose looks and apparel afforded a singular contrast. One was clad in a dirty cassock, drawn up and held by a scarlet girdle; his beard hung long and unclipped and his face wore an unctuous leer as of one relating a tale of special lubricity. His companion was richly clad in silken tunic and satin cloak, lined with costly fur. He was clean shaven, his hair hung smooth and silky to his shoulders, and his expression, haughty and at the moment faintly amused, was that of a young lord.

"The Monk of Montauban," said Gaucelm Faidit, jerking his thumb toward the pair, "boasts he has not changed his cassock since he abandoned his monastery twenty years ago, while the Senher Folquet of Marseille, the son of a merchant of Genoa, boasts that he changes his garments thrice a day. As for myself, I change when needful."

"He changes," said the wanton, "when I threaten to leave him!" She looked scornfully at the retreating backs of the troubadours. "Those two have this much in common: they have both made me offers of their bounty; to one I returned a box on the ear, and to

16

the other, laughter. The one is hot as an old bull, and the other, though he be as amorous as a young rake, keeps his heart in ice. Let him take himself back to the countess of Les Baux, I'll have none of him!"

"Folquet of Marseille," explained the fat troubadour, "gives himself out as the lover of the incomparable Alazais of Roca Martina, better known by her French name, Adélasie des Baux— though she is no more French than am I. She is the wife of the viscount of Marseille, Barrale, and if you ask me, Who is Barrale? I shall tell you he is one of the three great men walking this earth, the other two being our Good Count Raimon and the Saracen, Saladin. Viscount Barrale, I say, is of nature's elect, and his wife— when I think of her I regret my age and obesity!"

Guilhelma Monjo pursed her red lips maliciously. "You forget them, my lord, whenever a sly minx casts dove's eyes in your direction! Ah, that Folquet. There is something strange about him. As the Monk is well out of the Church, he would be well in it." The wanton smoothed her silken bliaut. "Folquet's life runs by calculation. He makes an investment of loving and when he finds a better return, be sure he will give up the Joyous Craft. His songs are as well made as glass of Poitiers, yet they give out a hollow note."

Peire Vidal looked down at the glossy hair brushing his knee, where Guilhelma Monjo, squatting at his feet, had let it rest. She turned her head and gazed full upon him, little lights burning in her slightly almond eyes, as she took his hand and examined it.

"My wanton," said Gaucelm Faidit, "is not only an admirable critic, she is an astrologer and can foretell the future."

"Well?" Peire Vidal asked, as she remained silent.

At length she spoke in a constrained voice. "I do not understand. It is all very curious. You are to move among vast happenings, and yet you do not seem to be a part of them. You desire goodness and justice, and you cause villainy and injustice. You love, and you escape love. You . . . you are wed, always, to one who is not your wife. You—— No, nothing more, Peire Vidal!" she cried shrilly.

During the first two days of the festival, while the cases in the equity of love were being prepared by the plaintiffs and their counselors, the singing advocates, there were almost continuous exhibitions of skill in the Joyous Craft, but in these the jongleur Peire Vidal took no part. He listened and observed, watching the fingering of the instruments by the masters of the craft, noted their gestures and delivery, and marveled at the ease with which any one of them could improvise on a theme set by the countess or one of the ladies.

Peire Vidal was not only obscure and untried, he was without an amorous attachment to put spurs to his imagination. He might, it is true, have dallied with the lesser damsels of the castle, but his mind was set on higher affairs; aspiring to greatness, he would have a paragon or nothing. From the corners of her feline eyes the Monjo glanced at him betimes, noting his diffidence and morose unrest.

On the third day, while the first cases were being presented before the Court of Love, Peire Vidal sought out Gaucelm Faidit for a game of backgammon. They retired to a small chamber, remote from the singing, where, as the dice clicked, they sipped red wine from cups of chastened silver which no sooner were emptied than they were filled again by Guilhelma Monjo. She chattered incessantly.

"There are to be some pretty trials. There is one I know of where a lady forbade her lover to praise her in public no matter what the circumstances. Well, her knight is in the company of those who begin to speak ill of her. He can contain himself no longer, defends her with passion, and challenges her detractor to a passage at arms to the uttermost. The lady then throws him over. Myself, I think she's a viper!"

"Think as you like, but keep your tongue still," said her master. "You spoil our play."

"And there is another, how a knight was pricked by a pin while his lady was kissing him——"

The dice in Gaucelm Faidit's box rattled violently. "Doublet!" he cried angrily, and shook again. "*Six, quatre*! I have borne my men!"

"You have left a *blot*, Messer Faidit," said Peire Vidal and, throwing, he added, "It is gammon for me!"

18

"And there is another case," began the wanton, shaking her gown of crimson cisclaton and tapping her slippers of purple brocade as she leaned above Peire Vidal, "of a troubadour who——"

"Be still, harridan!" shouted Gaucelm Faidit, flushing scarlet as her dress. "I've already lost seven sols through your gabbling! I would have you know, Messer Vidal, that when I first laid eyes on this baggage, the provost of Arles was about to have her whipped naked through the streets. A punishment they reserve for——"

"In wine," said she, tossing the thick braids from her forehead, "my lord suffers loss of memory. It was in Arles I found him, in the market place at dawn, stripped to his shirt and senseless as a dead owl. It was I got him hose and tunic, filled his wallet, and procured him lodging, from whence, newly refurbished, he shortly issued to ensnare——"

"Peace! Peace! Fill our cups, my sweet!" said the troubadour, wiping the beads of sweat from his face.

So they played through the waning afternoon, and still Guilhelma Monjo brimmed their cups, until the players found it not easy to read the dice and their tongues tripped in the calling of the plays. The water clock distantly announced the hour of nones. Gaucelm Faidit began to sing hoarsely, "When praising her whom I adore . . ." but he could manage no more than one verse when he sagged across the board, scattering the pieces.

"Let us leave him, Peire Vidal," said the wanton, bending over his shoulder and slipping her hands down his tunic.

"Sleep," said Peire Vidal thickly. "I must sleep."

"Sleep you shall, my darling!" she whispered, steadying him as he rose.

To a scented chamber where the coverlets were of cloth of Champagne set with jacinths to induce slumber she guided him, and there he cast himself down upon a pallet of luxurious softness, craving oblivion. He became aware that he was being shaken. His fumbling hands touched cool, silken flesh, and he felt himself trembling violently.

"Tomorrow, my love," she breathed, "you will sing before them all. . . ."

Chapter Two

THE jongleur Peyrols came to Castle Bargarde in the train of Folquet of Marseille, whose retinue was as imposing as that of a petty lord. Peyrols of Roquefort, according to Gaucelm Faidit, had once been a knight and a troubadour, but he had the misfortune to conceive a passion for Sail of Claustra, wife of the Baron Beraut of Mercoeur and sister of Robert the Dalfin, prince of Auvergne. The Dalfin was not fond of his brother-in-law, the latter having espoused the cause of Duke Richard (before he won the appellation of Lion) in the matter of a certain town of Issoire under dispute. Therefore the prince of Auvergne countenanced the liaison of his sister and her troubadour. The affair would have passed unnoticed save that, unhappily, the baron's bailiff, a man of finicky morals, came upon the lovers in their extremity and reported what he saw to his lord. When the case was brought before the prince, he could do nothing but pronounce the accused knight guilty of adultery with one of higher station.

The culprit, exposed before the people of Vodable on a scaffold, in nothing but his shirt, beheld his coat of mail torn apart and broken at his feet, his spurs cast upon a dunghill, and his shield fastened to the croup of a cart-horse and dragged through the dust. Then a herald cried loudly three times the name of "Peyrols of Roquefort, knight"; but as he was bound and gagged he could not

20

answer and was solemnly pronounced dead, and his estates were forfeited to the injured party. Carried thence to church on a litter, the nameless man heard the liturgy for the dead delivered over his living flesh, and he was then placed in the tomb of his fathers. At midnight the door of the tomb opened and, seeing no one, he crept forth and left Vodable for all time. Thereafter, dispossessed of his knighthood and title of troubadour, he was known as Peyrols the jongleur, and was under the necessity of acquiring the acrobatic tricks of a common mountebank. By degrees he came to have something of a reputation as an advocate in the Courts of Love, and was so employed by troubadours who did not wish to plead their own cases.

On the third day, when the Court was in full session, Peyrols appeared before the fair judges and declared that he had come to represent a certain troubadour who had experienced ill treatment and cruelty at the hands of his lady love; and he said further that the appellant desired to remain anonymous since his impeachment touched a very great lady.

After some whispering among the members of the court, Lady Constance said, "Messer Peyrols, your request is unusual. If we grant it, we shall be enabled merely to invoke a general principle of justice, for if we decide upon the guilt of the accused, we have no means of enforcing our decision, either by pronouncing a penalty or by publicly censoring the culprit."

"Mesdames," said Peyrols, bowing low before the silk-clad arbiters, "my plaintiff well recognizes the limitations of judgment in this instance, but he pleads for a hearing in order that the justice of his claims may be admitted wherever love and its principles obtain. He does not urge redress or punishment, but vindication in the eyes of his beloved. And he trusts rather to the scourging of her own conscience than to the infliction of chastening correction by this honorable tribunal."

The countess frowned. "Your reasoning, Messer Peyrols, is specious. How can we be assured that the defendant will receive adequate counsel before the court? Or that she will learn the tenor of our decision when it is made?" Again she consulted with her advisers and after a moment said, "It is our opinion that the indictment be presented; then, if a champion appear to take the case

21

for the defendant, it shall proceed; otherwise we will require you to name your principal."

Peyrols now gave himself the air of a learned advocate as he began the presentation of his suit. His plea, in substance, was that a troubadour had entreated a lady for her love, but was unable to overcome her reluctance to grant it to him. In the course of a full year he had bestowed upon the object of his passion numerous presents, to the value of twenty gold marks; but at the expiration of this period he found himself no better off; worse, in fact, for he was considerably out of pocket and more distraught than ever. "And so," concluded Peyrols in his peroration, "my noble gentleman, kept ever on tiptoe of expectancy, finds that his harvest is meager enough after sowing innumerable canzos of endearment, a mantle of ermine, a needlecase bought from the Moors of Famagosta, scents and soaps from Grass, a necklace of pearls———"

"Enough!" cried the countess with asperity. "Before you leave your gentleman a beggar, who will champion the cause of the unknown lady?"

The judges rustled in silken bliauts, the jewels of the gold bands clasping their long braids sparkled, and they looked inquiringly toward the attendant knights, squires, troubadours, and jongleurs, the silent witnesses of the court's proceedings. Then from the midst of the latter a voice said, "I will take up the cause of the defendant!" And upon those about him giving way, Peire Vidal stepped forth and stood facing the tribunal, his large head slowly wagging and his long arms pendant at his side. At the sight of the ungainly jongleur a faint ripple of mirth passed through the assemblage, which was instantly hushed as the countess delivered herself in measured words.

"Peire Vidal, squire and jongleur, has offered to defend the honor of the unknown lady. The Court accepts the champion and enjoins both advocates to observe all usages and courtesies proper to the occasion. Counselor for the defendant, Senher Vidal, is permitted to set the form and mode of the tenson, and it must be similarly answered by his opponent. The judges of this court shall be mindful of their great and serious obligations to the principles of love in rendering their decision. May God and the Blessed Virgin grant us wisdom and discernment!"

22

Peire Vidal unslung his viol from about his shoulders and, after playing several measures at random, fixed upon a simple air well suited to the nature of the argument, and the tenson, briefly, went somewhat as follows:

PEIRE VIDAL
You have said your master loved profoundly,
Gave generously, but received nothing?

PEYROLS
He did indeed offer a noble love
And many gifts, to the value of twenty marks.

PEIRE VIDAL
Was he in expectation to be paid in kind?

PEYROLS
Your question hardly deserves an answer!

PEIRE VIDAL
As I understand, he was a year at this business.

PEYROLS
You defame love to name it a business!

PEIRE VIDAL
You have declared his investment paid nothing.

PEYROLS
Only great discomfort and anguish of spirit.

PEIRE VIDAL
Was he not well entertained at the castle?

PEYROLS
The lady's husband knows what is due a gentleman!

PEIRE VIDAL
Does your master go alone or well attended?

PEYROLS
His train is numbered at more than twenty!

PEIRE VIDAL
Twenty, and these were given food and lodgings—
Twenty marks would hardly cover the outlay!

PEYROLS
What manner of reasoning is this, fool?
Is love a matter of price and reckoning?

PEIRE VIDAL
Your master would have it so, Messer Advocate.
He has made love a thing of the market-place!

PEYROLS
Then what of the creature who dickers, a miser
Of love; who accepts and gives naught in return?

PEIRE VIDAL
She gave, I doubt not, plenty—her presence,
Her beauty, and radiant graciousness!

PEYROLS
Those are cheaply had, says my master,
And need not be purchased so dearly!

PEIRE VIDAL
Then I swear, on my faith as a lover,
Your troubadour loves like a trader'
Who measures his cloth on the counter!

The voice of Peire Vidal echoed through the great hall and fell
silent. Peyrols plucked the strings of his lute, preparing his final
rebuttal, but before he could make answer there came another voice
from the throng, arrogant and cold. "False! False as the face of
Lucifer! I challenge the maker of these feeble verses to something
more than words, for he seems a vaunting lackey!" It was Folquet
of Marseille, the merchant's son, who spoke.

Peire Vidal placed the cord of his viol about his shoulders.
"Messer Folquet of Marseille," he said mildly, "I do not pretend
to measure my singing against yours, for you are a gentleman and
a troubadour, but if you will match me at arms——"

"No!" said the countess sharply. "The Court of Love forbids
any recourse to arms. I command the participants in this case to
await judgment!"

During the retirement of the judges for discussion the Good
Count Raimon approached Peire Vidal. "Well sung," he said.
"But you must watch your strings during these lengthy tensons.
The warmth soon puts them out of tune. And, messer, preserve
more harmony in your *voltas* and *tornadas*. With a song it is all
in the phrasing. It is your old fault of the tilting ground—a too
great eagerness that defeats its own end. Smoothness and dexterity,

my lad, with both the lance and the canzo are desirable. Still, you are learning. I doubt not you will make a troubadour, though you are a good deal of a natural fool!"

That was the Good Count Raimon. At the barriers he was ever observant of defects in horsemanship and in the handling of weapons. In the hall he missed no slighting of a note. He had been a doughty warrior and a troubadour of no inconsiderable merit. Peire Vidal revered him.

The judges were re-entering the hall, the whispers subsided, and in the hush of expectancy there was plainly heard Gaucelm Faidit hawking and spitting.

Said the Lady Constance, "The judges having carefully weighed the accusation and evidence as presented by Messer Peyrols, and the defence as presented by Messer Vidal, pronounce it as their verdict that the anonymous plaintiff has no case whatsoever in the equity of love; and that his reflections upon the integrity of the unknown defendant are to be condemned. Furthermore, the Court considers that the ungracious act of Messer Folquet of Marseille, troubadour, in impugning the good faith and ability of the defending advocate is highly censorable; and since he manifests a not impersonal interest in the case, our curiosity concerning the parties to the suit is amply satisfied."

The decision was greeted with a burst of applause by the audience, who had been won over to Peire Vidal principally by the quality and resonance of his voice. It is certain, however, that they little suspected the cause of his assurance in making his first appearance in public. Nor would they have credited Guilhelma Monjo with greater understanding than she seemed to possess. If conscience pricked him at the remembrance of his recent encounter with the wanton, Peire Vidal took comfort from the access of tenderness she displayed toward her lord.

Of all the questions debated in the Parlement of Love the one most hotly and eloquently argued was: "Whether or not real love may exist between married persons." It had been the theme of numerous tensons and the subject of many tornimens of song. In the present instance, after the case had been skilfully presented by several noted troubadours from various angles, the Court withdrew to weigh the arguments, and its absence was so prolonged that

25

much good wine had been dispensed before the countess, attended by only three members of the council, reappeared. It seems that the others had been unwilling to pass judgment upon a matter affecting their own domestic relations.

Said the countess: "We declare and affirm that love cannot exercise its powers on married people, for the examples adduced have proved conclusively that, whereas lovers grant everything mutually and gratuitously, without being constrained by motives of obligation or necessity, married persons, on the contrary, are compelled as a duty to submit to one another. For this reason, therefore, if for no other, it is evident that true love cannot exercise its power on those lawfully wedded. Let this decision, which we have arrived at with great deliberation, and after taking counsel of the ladies of the Court, be held henceforth as a confirmed and indisputable truth."

This decision was received by all the jongleurs and troubadours, and by certain husbands and wives, with applause. But a few appeared to suffer from doubt and confusion of mind; while from the throat of the Good Count Raimon there issued a sound near to a snort.

The sixth day of the festival was reserved for the tornimen of song, and the contending knights and squires of the Joyous Craft, in preparation for entering the vocal jousts, sought inspiration from their several ladies. Even the humbler jongleurs made bold to seek the response of well tended hands and of eyes whose lashes, deftly darkened, added luster to complexions the natural fairness of which was enhanced by rare cosmetics. But in this dalliance and concourse of love Peire Vidal took no part. Notwithstanding his recent triumph, on the eve of the tornimen he was far from tranquil. He wandered restlessly through the castle, pursued and tormented by the secret vision of his night with the mistress of his friend, a circumstance he resolved never to repeat, even though it had lent him some temporary confidence in the face of all those acknowledged lovers. He hoped, yet feared to find her; but Guilhelma Monjo was nowhere to be seen, and Gaucelm Faidit, deep in his cups, was none the less jocular. At length the jongleur found himself in the refectory where certain bachelor squires were engaged in eating, drinking, and making merry. With sudden zest for clamor and fellowship, he thrust himself into their midst, and they hailed him riotously.

"Ha! Messer advocate! Sant Julian was with you!"

"Will you sing us a comjat or a carros? A farewell or a paeon of joy?"

"Sing us the descort, 'I thought, alas! that as her beauty glows, there must be warmth within'!"

"Nothing, friends, till I've drunk and fed!"

They plied him with a roast leg of mutton, a handful of dried sorb apples, and tankards of mulled wine, and by degrees his spirits grew expansive and he regaled them with snatches of such character as will not bear repeating. Among the jocund company was one in the habit of a crusader knight, who sat apart, nursing his bile, and was no ways moved by the general mirth.

"Of what has he eaten," asked Peire Vidal of a squire, "that the taste is so bitter?"

"He is the knight of St. Gilles, lately made stone deaf by a blow on the headpiece, and he's the most jealous of husbands over his lady, the fair Yolanz."

"I will restore the hearing of this knight," said Peire Vidal. He rose tipsily and taking his viol, he began to sing:

> In the springtime's gentle fire
> Lark and nightingale conspire
> To destroy a lover's peace;
> With their songs that never cease
> Night and day, they bring to mind
> Golden hours that fret and bind
> His poor heart to fair Yolanz.

He paused, but the dolorous knight of St. Gilles remained of the same visage, as though he looked upon a death's head. So Peire Vidal began again:

> When the wind in vagrant whim
> Whirls the leaf and shakes the limb,
> Seems its ardor matches his
> Nomad heart; but when it is

27

Tranquil, then his agitation
Sinks in quiet contemplation
Of his bountiful Yolanz.

" 'Bountiful' ", said the squire slyly. "To be bountiful is to be prodigal, that is, to bestow favors. Go on, Peire Vidal!"

And as the jongleur placed his bow against the strings of his instrument the rueful knight raised his eyes and they shone, as it were, with a certain malignancy. But Peire Vidal with much fervor sang:

Love whose fretful humors keep
Rest away and banish sleep—
Love, that drives the lover daft,
Opens doors with stealthy craft—
When the watchman on the tower
Cries 'God's peace!' at midnight's hour,
Bring me to my fair Yolanz!

With the ending of the last phrase the knight of St. Gilles puckered his brow, a short breath whistled between his teeth, and his eyes flamed dull red. But the bachelor squires had risen and were shouting, "Wine! Wine for the votary of the fair Yolanz!"

Abruptly the dour crusader rose, gazing blackly upon them.

"Peace to this jargon!" he said in the silence, touching his dagger's hilt.

"A miracle!" quoth the squire at Peire Vidal's elbow. "His hearing is restored!"

The crusader, however, let fall his hand, drew his mantle about him so that the ruddy cross was concealed by its folds, and without another word or look, passed from among them. It was close to the hour of lauds and the hubbub in the refectory was at its height when the jongleur, tranced with the fumes of wine, felt someone pluck the sleeve of his tunic, and a voice whispered in his ear, "Senher Vidal, I bear a message for you."

"Deliver it forthwith!" said Peire Vidal, maudlin in his haughtiness. He had just been picturing himself as the most honored and esteemed of all troubadours; the lady he adored was the fairest and wisest in all Christendom, and she had inherited a throne which, with modest yet respectful insistence, she invited him to share with her. He was filled with a sense of infinite superiority, of omniscient wisdom. From the throne he would dispense justice throughout his kingdom. . . .

"The Lady Yolanz, messer," said the voice with insinuating softness, "whom you have honored in song, greatly desires to hold speech with you, for she would make her beauty manifest to one who has sung so well of it."

"Lead me to her," said Peire Vidal, finding his legs somewhat unsteadily, "and I will promise her more songs to come."

The messenger, who seemed to the uncertain gaze of the jongleur to be a squire of sorts, took him by the arm and steered him by many devious passages and dark corridors through the mazes of the castle. They spoke not at all. Sometimes they passed beneath torches that hissed from wall brackets, and again they descended a flight of circular steps, and seemed to cross an open court for the singer felt cold air upon his humid face. The chill of it momentarily cleared his head. He was aware that he stood in utter blackness and alone—at least there was no hand upon his elbow. Strange . . . and sudden caution made him feel for his dagger. But there was no blade in its accustomed sheath.

Then came a scuffling sound, and hands in the darkness seized upon him. They caught his arms, writhed about his neck, sought to pinion him. He flung them off and heard curses: "Sant Dalmatz! Hold the swine!" He plunged away, toward a beam of light showing from a distant wall. Again they had him, this time with greater violence. He stumbled on a flagstone and fell backward, the pack falling upon him; and they all went writhing, cursing, and clawing over and over, like dogs on a fox. He felt a hand about his throat, twisted his head and sank his teeth into it. A yell followed. But they had whipped cords about his legs and ankles, and another cord, as they drew his arms backward, lashed his wrists. In a moment he was trussed, gagged, and blindfolded. Then they dragged him away, heaved him across the back of some beast of burden, and, with the dull clanking of mail in his ears, he was jounced and jolted, like a sack of grain, for some leagues, or so it seemed.

Again, like a sack of grain, they dumped him off, and he fell upon soft earth, striking his head on a rock. There were whisperings among them and torchlight flickered on his eyelids, tightly swathed. Hands groped about his face. A blunt object, wood or steel, touched his lips, and his teeth were pried apart. He felt fingers in his mouth, ruthless and obscene. The fingers were pulling at his tongue. Then, with a bright flash of pain, a fiery agony that burnt to the very center of his being, his mouth closed again.

From a remote distance, engulfed in a molten sea of pain, he heard a voice of satanic malevolence: "The Lady Yolanz bestows her last favor on her paramour!"

He was fast losing his senses; but he felt them unbinding him, heard a low command, and the jangling of chain mail growing softer. Then silence, and the mewing of a nightbird; a beetle crawled across his neck; he swooned.

Chapter Three

THE taste was salt. He choked and, putting his hand to his lips, found his fingers were moist and red. The infernal fire of his tongue seemed to extend deep into his throat from whence, against his will, issued groan upon groan. It was partly pain but more, a deep fury at the unexpected violence done him by his unknown assailants. He could not well remember the events of the preceding night; he had drunk much, had sung a song, had been led somewhere, and here he was, in torment, in some strange spot.

As he raised his head a single bright ray of sunlight, darting through the foliage of young trees, smote his eyelids. A hillside lay below him. Through an opening in the covert he beheld at a little distance the ramparts of Bargarde and more distantly the crenelated walls and many towers of Toulouse. He sat up, resting on unsteady hands, and saw his tunic all torn and begrimed, his cloak ripped to shreds, and—oh blessed Mary!—the fragments of what had been his precious viol scattered about on the sod. Again a wild rage possessed him and he rolled over on his face, clutching the grass and biting the black loam beneath. Thus he lay for a long space of time, inert as a dead man and devoid of any feeling save extreme anguish. But by degrees he became aware of a song. It mounted on the morning air, thin and sweet, from far below him, and as it penetrated his afflicted senses it soothed and healed like balm of Gilead. The pain in his mouth was no less, but wrath and dismay passed from his spirit; and so he lay quiet as the singing neared.

"Hola!" cried a voice, a young man's voice. "Hola, dead man! Or, if you be living, who has assassinated you?"

Hands—they were soft as a woman's—raised up his head, turned him over. The youth wore the long, loose tunic of a jongleur and carried a lute slung about his shoulder by a silken ribbon. His green cap with its silken tassel hung rakishly over his left ear and beneath it was a face of angelic comeliness; but something about his lips might have inspired caution in the more skeptical; a sly devil lurked there, a graceless imp.

"Brother," said the jongleur, bending over to scan his fellow craftsman, "I see that you are not entirely extinct. Pray, relate the circumstances of your martyrdom! Have you been attacked by routiers? They have broken your viol—may Sant Julian curse them!—and that's infamous. But, my friend, though the viol be smashed, there's still hope while the heart is whole!"

As Peire Vidal made no reply to these reassuring advances but only stared dully about him and spat a mouthful of blood, the jongleur knelt beside him and with gentlest touch examined his mouth.

"By Sant Dalmatz! they have done you a double wrong, brother, for they not only have destroyed your instrument, they have dug through your tongue with a knife or an augur—a villainous deed to a singer! Plague on them for unchristian knaves!" He was feeling the cavity. "Yet they have left enough to sing with, praise the Virgin! Yea, brother, give thanks! Though you'll croak like a magpie for a time, your voice is undamaged! And I have no doubt your songpiece is curable. So, friend, be of good cheer; all is not lost! Behold me, brother. Last night I killed a man and lost a lady. But do I lament? Not Aimeric de Peguilha!"

Peire Vidal looked at the jongleur with a gleam of recognition. He had heard of the scapegrace son of the draper of Toulouse.

"If you have any throat left, friend, let us have your name."

"Vidal," croaked the stricken jongleur.

"Peire Vidal!" cried the other, and his face became suddenly worshipful. "Peire Vidal, the best singer of Toulouse! Ah—the hellish rascals, what have they done to you, master!" And he leaped up and went racing down the hill.

It is true, thought Peire Vidal, I should give thanks that my tongue was spared. And this youth calls me master. Indeed, he thought, I have earned that title, for I have won a case in the Court of Love. This jongleur shall be my audiart. I will improve his talents and he shall do me honor in attending me. Sant Julian, perhaps, is more mindful of my welfare than I imagined. For there is a saying, "Whoever in the world would live, must oft endure chagrin and pain."

Aimeric de Peguilha had returned with his cap brimming. The cold spring water eased the ache of Peire Vidal's burning throat and when the clotted gore had been wiped from his lips and his tongue cleansed he felt, if somewhat sick and dizzy, a newly created man.

"Come," said Aimeric de Peguilha, "lean on me, dear master. Let us find help for you, food and lodging, and suitable apparel for troubadour and jongleur, for master and audiart! But I must tell you, master, that since there is likely a price on my head for the slaying of a certain burgess of Toulouse—may the worms soon devour his carcass!—we had best avoid the castle of Bargarde and the city—that is, unless you are resolved to return and avenge your injury."

Peire Vidal shook his head. In his condition, and smarting under humiliation, he had no desire to be the laughing stock of that gay and indifferent throng. As for his lord, the Good Count Raimon, when he learned the cause of his squire's downfall, he would probably censure his folly in having invited it.

Skirting Toulouse by devious ways, they fared toward Carcassonne, the audiart babbling the while of his adventure with the wife of the burgess, from whom, besides other favors, he had received sundry additions to his wardrobe, including new silk breeches, white silk stockings, and enameled shoes.

"Ah!" said Aimeric de Peguilha regretfully, "What a bosom! What honey lips! What an angel when her pursy money-bags was away! She had an ear for songs, too, and I may say that I sang my best for her. For a time I lived in paradise, supping on cates and dainties and enjoying the sweets of stolen interviews—and

33

plenty of deniers jingling in my wallet. In return, I gave her songs, love, and certain items abstracted from my sire's stock. But the old cuckold was a sly varlet. He tells my amiable madomna that he has a fortnight's business in Marseille. No sooner had he galloped over the bridge on the Roman road south than there was I, knocking at the little barred gate, in a fever of expectation. Sweet, sweet moment as I held her again in my arms, singing, 'When my heart answers to your call.'! And so, as you might say, we were at very pretty sport when of a sudden the door creaks, and in he comes, snarling like a wolf, holding a naked blade before him.

"When he lunged I dodged, laying hands on a brass candlestick, and as he drew back I let him have it on the pate. Down he topples, without so much as a grunt, swimming in his gore. Now, master, would you believe what my bountiful mistress does? Leaps at me, clawing like a desert pard, and shrieking murderer! Out of the house I flew, with murderer! ringing in my ears and a clatter and stir of folk at my heels, and never stopped until I was well hid in a certain hovel that had been my home since my sire—the devil take his miserly soul!—showed me the door, and all over a piece of green sarcenet, and a wench named Marote!"

They fell in with a company of chapmen coming from Spain with an escort of men-at-arms, their sumpter mules laden with Moorish brocades and cisclatons, Cordoban leather, Castilian swords and pieces of armor, Spanish wool, and other commodities. While the cavalcade proceeded amid the cheerful jingling of the mules' silver bells, Aimeric de Peguilha tuned his lute and sang, "Triflers and fools I call you all, that fall in meek surrender," and when he had finished, they demanded, in their several tongues, more songs, which he gave them in return for a handful of silver coins and several ells of silk and velvet. Nor did he cease to extol the superior genius of his celebrated master "who has been crossed in love, messers, and is sworn to silence until the wrong he suffered at the hands of the countess be righted. But she has sent for him, and soon all will be well. Ah! Thank you, noble sir! And you, sir, are to be recommended to the saints! My noble master, the eminent troubadour—whose name I dare not divulge—will remember you all in his next sirvente, when his vow of silence is removed. Alas, he must likewise wear the poor

34

garments you see him in until love crowns him once more! But I pray you, do not let it be known that you have met this renowned troubadour on the highway, for he wishes to remain, for the present, unknown."

The merchants rode on, distinctly impressed and duly reported that a celebrity was traveling in their wake. It was scarcely surprising, therefore, that when the master and his audiart had passed Carcassonne and come to an inn near Cabaretz, the Countess Louve de Penaultier, mistress of that demesne, despatched a messenger to find them and bring them to her castle. The innkeeper, who had eyed them with distrust as a pair of vagrants, was no little astonished when a scented lackey inquired concerning the presence of a great troubadour and his audiart at the tavern.

"Tell your gracious lady," said Aimeric de Peguilha, "that my famous master is honored by the attention of your countess, but he cannot, because of the nature of a certain vow, present himself before her."

"My lady," said the squire haughtily, "desires to know the name and station of this troubadour."

"Unhappily," quoth the jongleur, gazing at the ceiling, "it is not permitted to divulge that information. However, my master is the bearer of greetings to your lady from the Good Count Raimon, count of Toulouse, marquis of Provence, master of Quercy, Rouergue, Vivarais, Agenois, Gevaudan, Béziers, and Uzès, as well as suzerain of Foix and Comminges, and duke of Narbonne!" And before the astonished lackey could recover, Aimeric had pressed into his hands the cloth he had received from the merchants. "You will be good enough to deliver to your noble mistress these slight tokens of my master's esteem!"

The squire bowed deeply and retired. Peire Vidal raised his eyes from the bowl of soup, the consumption of which, with his constricted throat, had been causing him considerable misery. "What——?" he grunted.

"More wine! And let it be your best, fellow!" said the jongleur to the innkeeper.

"Ay, messers! Very good! Whatever you wish and it shall be the best!" And mine host bobbed himself out, with all the deference of an inferior before gentry.

"Pardon, master," said Aimeric de Peguilha, "if I arrange these details. Often-times a small venture brings a large return."

They slept on the best pallets the inn provided and the audiart secured from the host an ointment of great potency in curing saddle galls, stones in the spleen, dark humors of the blood, and all other distempers that afflict mankind. This, when applied to the tongue of Peire Vidal, produced an instant result, for he straightway cast up his morning meal. But they were not disappointed in the investment of the silks and velvet. Scarcely had they issued from the inn—the jongleur having paid the account in the currency of song—when they saw the messenger of the countess leading a Breton palfrey, saddled, bridled, and decently caparisoned.

"My lady, the countess," said the squire, "desires that the troubadour, Peire Vidal, accept this slight token of her estimation of his great gift of song. She urges, when his vow has been fulfilled, that he return to sing at the castle of Cabaretz, and she prays the blessing of Sant Julian on his journeying!"

And Aimeric de Peguilha returned thanks in a speech of such length, magniloquence, and gallantry that it was evident the squire's memory would be sorely taxed to deliver it.

When the squire had gone, Aimeric de Peguilha grinned. "What did I say, master? Bread upon the waters, eh? And she has taken pains to discover your name. Marvelous, the ingenuity of women! You shall soon see how well we travel!"

For ten sols he purchased of the innkeeper a mouse-colored ass which he named Blancaflor after the heroine of a popular romance. She was galled, spavined, and had lived beyond her prime, but she was gentle and dutiful, and she loved the sound of the lute. Five sols got him a frayed Moorish saddle, and from some cast-off leather thongs he fashioned a bridle of sorts. Altogether, the pair of them, mounted, were not unimpressive. And though the wound in his tongue still troubled him, Peire Vidal's spirits began to respond to the enticements of the spring season. The smell of thyme was sweet on the air, and the fields were bestrewn with yellow roses, eglantine, joy flowers, the *flor de gaug,* and the flowers of the brier, plantagenet, which were to be the symbol of a royal house; for Duke Richard had fiefs in Languedoc and at one time would have traded London for Arles, which he loved better.

They passed through Narbonne, where they saw many Moors and Jews, the latter with a circle of saffron on the breasts of their tunics. Here the singing of the audiart procured victuals, and pence for their wallets. As they left the city they fell in with a knight, attended by a modest train, one Antoine Beaujeu, marquis of Sorgues, a vassal of the Good Count Raimon, who recognized Peire Vidal, for he had attended the Court of Love at Castle Bargarde.

"Sant Laurent!" he exclaimed. "I was right! You are not murdered but merely transfigured! Let me tell you, Messer Vidal, you have left all Toulouse in a fine stew of apprehension as to your safety! We had all expected you would try for the peacock crown of the tornimen. When your broken viol was discovered, following your mysterious disappearance, it was concluded you had been waylaid by routiers. Our good count had the whole countryside combed for you. When word was brought of the ruined instrument, my lord swore that someone would hang for it. Messer Gaucelm Faidit gave himself to grief and composed an excellent planh for your demise. The buxom Monjo threatened to enter a convent. Even the Lady Constance, in her British fashion, expressed concern. But I argued that had you been murdered, you would be found murdered. And I was right! Halting at the castle of Cabaretz, there comes word of a troubadour traveling that way in disguise, together with his audiart. Ha! say I: 'tis the missing man himself, and so I told the Lady Louve de Penaultier. You, messer, have missed a great beauty in refusing to attend her court."

"It is better to win in silver than to lose in gold," said Aimeric de Peguilha.

The knight's gray eyes twinkled above his sandy beard. "You have acquired a perspicacious audiart, Messer Vidal," he said.

"Sir Antoine Beaujeu," said Aimeric de Peguilha, his voice trembling slightly, "did you perchance hear of an atrocious murder done upon an honest burgess of Toulouse?"

"No, that I did not. But I heard rumors of some merchant who caught a rascally knave seeking to tempt his virtuous wife and thereupon drubbed the fellow from his house."

"The moldy liar!" cried the jongleur. "Sant Laurent be praised, he still lives! As for his dame, her virtue is no more than a cat's!"

But so cheered was the youth at being no longer under the ban of the provost of Toulouse that he let fall the bridle of patient Blancaflor, and unslinging his lute, began to sing:

Volages sunt et poi estaules
Et sans mesure enfin canjaules. . . .

"They are giddy and inconstant; wayward without measure; and not to be trusted. 'Twixt virtue and persuasion they will always be wavering. Truly, to find a woman artless, good, loyal, and submissive is to discover one of the wonders of the world!"

The marquis of Sorgues, being a man of discretion as well as a troubadour of some merit, made no inquiries of his fellow singers as to the singular affair in which Peire Vidal had been involved, nor did he seem to take notice of the latter's silence, which had been attributed to a solemn vow. He merely suggested that, as his squires bore with them far too many changes of apparel, he would be eager to bestow one of these upon his fellow craftsman. The offer was accepted, and at the next tavern Peire Vidal found himself being arrayed in the following articles: crimson shoes, with the points long, as was the fashion; stockings of white silk; a tunic of garnet-colored samite; a Phrygian mantle of dark green brocade, lined with taffeta, and a belt of crimson leather. With his face again clean shaven, his hair combed down smoothly to his shoulders, and a silver-embroidered cap set jauntily on his head, he looked rather the titled troubadour than the son of the furrier of Toulouse. Strangely enough, in this resplendent garb, his uncouth figure and strongly marked features took on a certain charm, for it was plain he was no ordinary singer.

At Béziers the cavalcade was well received by its viscount, Raimon Roger, nephew of the Good Count Raimon, a young man of fiery eyes and firm persuasions. He favored the Albigensian heretics because they were simple folk, entertained wandering singers lavishly, and often contributed good songs of his own composition. He was outspoken, wielded a strong lance in battle, gave generous largesse to the poor and to widows, and promoted the arts and trades of his vassals. Indeed, he was more than usually thoughtful of the citizens of Béziers; for his sire, Roger of the

Bloody Hands, during an unfortunate uprising, had slain every male of the city, and had replenished it with Spanish auxiliaries. The younger generation were notably dark of complexion.

Here the travelers found the troubadours, Peire Cardinal of the bitter tongue, Raimbaut of Vacqueiras, and Arnaut de Maruelh. The latter was then enjoying one of his periodic intimacies with the viscount's wife, the changeable Alazais, countess of Burlatz. The viscount was in high good humor, as he always was during the sojourns of his wife's lover, since it relieved him of the necessity of entertaining her.

"Messer Vidal," said Raimbaut of Vacqueiras that night over their wine, "we have heard that you worsted Peyrols, the advocate of Folquet of Marseille, before the Court of Love at Toulouse. It serves Folquet right for not presenting his own case, which he might very well have done, seeing that he is one of the best singers in Provence."

"A strange man," mused the viscount. "A good deal of the trader in him. I doubt not that his natural course would have been to follow his father, and to run a great fleet of merchant galleys, plying the Mediterranean. But no, he must make himself a figure of romance, dress like a prince, woo the greatest beauty of Christendom, and having lost her favor, seek to belittle her!"

Arnaut de Maruelh raised his somber eyes. "There is indeed something unaccountable about Folquet, and you will laugh if I tell you what I think it is."

"We will not laugh, Messer Arnaut," said the Marquis Beaujeu, "but give us leave to wonder at your instinct."

"I think," said the troubadour, "he intends at some time to seek the consolation of the church, for he will never be satisfied in love. He expects too much for the little he gives."

"Hah!" laughed the viscount. "You may be right. And if he does, mark my words, he'll rise to a bishopric!"

Curious, thought Peire Vidal, how two persons, so unlike as the wanton and the learned notary, had arrived at an identical conclusion.

"They say," said Raimbaut of Vacqueiras, "that where balsam is gathered, it is guarded by a most poisonous serpent, called the aspic, which has two tails and breathes out fire that sears the flesh.

This monster can be put to sleep only with the sound of a lute, and that is how they get the balsam. But when the creature sees it has been tricked, it stops its ear with one tail and rubs the other on the ground; and the balsam-gatherers then become afflicted with cankers and ulcers, and in time they die of a loathsome malady."

"What," said Antoine Beaujeu, "has that to do with Folquet of Marseille?"

Raimbaut laughed, saying, "I am thankful he is *not* an archbishop!"

The talk turned to politics, of the emperor, Frederick Barbarossa, and Philip Augustus, king of France, and of Duke Richard, not yet king of England.

"Mark me," said the viscount, "there will soon be a new crusade. With St. Jean d'Acre, Ascalon, and Jerusalem taken, our Latin friends in the Holy Land will find themselves in difficulties. This new pope, Innocent, has great projects in mind, and so, I think, has the fox of the Adriatic, old Dandolo, who has his eye on the eastern empire, Romania. Constantinople, or New Rome, is a nest of intrigue. Ah, these ceaseless wars, for which we have to pay so dearly!"

"Ho!" laughed Aimeric de Peguilha. "You and your brother crusaders will pay, my lord! We jongleurs and troubadours will fight with you, and sing for you in battle and out, but pay for your exploits? Only in the currency of song! With us, one beautiful woman is worth two crusades!"

"There is only one such," said Raimbaut of Vacqueiras, musingly, "and her name is Adélasie des Baux. She is like a crusade, for she raises hopes that cannot be fulfilled, and though many strive to conquer her, none succeed!"

Said Arnaut de Maruelh, "To me she is as a monument of the ancient Romans—marvelous, imperishable, but beyond human comprehension!"

Peire Vidal leaned forward. His face was flaming, for he had been drinking heavily to ease his throat.

"Speak more of her!" he uttered thickly.

"In verse or in prose?" grinned Raimbaut.

40

"Any way! Any way!" growled the troubadour, pouring himself another cup of mulled wine.

Raimbaut began to sing:

> In one white and tapered hand
> She held a carven comb
> That slid silver through
> The gold of unbound hair.
> There, before her mirror,
> None come near her;
> They adore and fear her
> When she does her tiring. . . .

"Enough!" shouted Peire Vidal. "Give her to me in plain speech!"

"Ah!" quoth Raimbaut. "You will have to take her yourself. But if you must have her in words, she is one of these dazzling beings, all gold and alabaster, fair as the witch Herodias, and dangerous—yes! for you would think there was nothing under that shimmer of silken tresses, nothing but milky softness. But she is glacial, my friend, impervious to persuasion as the ice of Mount Ventoux! You may offer her glowing canzos, for she has an ear tuned to melody, and you may kiss her fingers, for she loves it, but if you reach to her pomegranate lips, you are more a man than Saladin!"

"What of the viscount, her husband?" demanded Peire Vidal hoarsely.

"Ho!" laughed Raimbaut. "He is the best of hosts, Barrale of Marseille! He'll lead you to her, place you at her feet—and go a-hawking! If you fail to sing passionately to her, he'll inquire of your state of health, and urge you to eat more heartily of warm, sweet, and savory dishes, to increase the warmth of your blood. He asks daily concerning the progress of your courtship, and will recommend wearing a beryl for success in love. Indeed, there is nothing the jovial viscount will not do to further your suit!"

"I do not like such a man," said Peire Vidal morosely.

"You have never seen such a man!" Raimbaut retorted. "Nor such a woman!" He studied Peire Vidal with half-closed eyes,

41

speculatively. "Messer Vidal," he said, "when you downed the advocate of Folquet of Marseille at Toulouse, you did something more than win a case."

"I know that," said the troubadour between his heavy shoulders, "I made my first essay in the form of the tenson. It was an excellent tenson!"

"No, Peire Vidal, more important, you won the case for Adélasie des Baux! You have been the first to do something for her that she could not better do herself. She will be grateful."

Peire Vidal pulled himself to his feet. He leaned on his long arms. "If I were emperor of Romania my consort would bear the name of Adélasie . . . if I were emperor!"

Raimbaut's beard was agitated by smothered laughter. He spoke gravely.

"There are countries without moon and sun, where the men have skins harder than iron, and some are born with lions' claws on their hands and feet. In the land of Bucion the people wear horns like sheep, and in Buridane they bay like mastiffs. There are known to be fauns, mermaids, griffins, satyrs, and the phœnix who rises from fiery death. But there never yet has been emperor of the city of Constantine, who was a troubadour!"

"Whosoever kneeleth to the Golden God, he shall lose the power of song," said Peire Cardinal with a thin, cryptic smile.

"Why do not you yourself become the lover of this golden beauty, Senher Raimbaut?" asked Peire Vidal thickly.

"Though I do not hold myself a coward," answered Raimbaut of Vacqueiras, "there are certain hazards I would willingly forego —one of them being to become this lady's lover."

"Then you are indeed a coward!" Peire Vidal retorted. "I myself have no such fears!"

"Monsenher Emperor of Romania and Buridane," quoth Raimbaut sardonically, "I resign my amorous claims to Adélasie des Baux in your favor! May you prosper in your suit!"

Chapter Four

THAT night, sleeping under the viscount's roof on sheets of Champagne, embroidered intricately in thread of gold, Peire Vidal had a strange dream. He seemed to be in some sacred edifice devoted to the worship of a great witch or goddess, and he had come to the very sanctuary of the witch herself. It was a statue he saw, all of purest and whitest marble, but the hair of the goddess was of gold and hung below her waist. The statue stirred, saying, "Come, Vidal!" and he came to her and knelt down and kissed the hem of her garment and then kissed her marble feet. With that, she bent over and her golden hair fell tinkling about him, and the touch of the marble was warm as flesh. He was overcome with a great desire so that his heart beat almost to suffocation, but when he sought to clasp her, she straightened and returned to marble again.

The next morning, upon awaking, he resolved to set out for Les Baux.

This plan, so instantly conceived, seemed to offer a favorable solution to the uncertainty of mind under which he had been laboring. For, as the successful defendant of the lady, might he not expect well of her? And, too, upon its announcement, he learned that the amiable marquis was also journeying in that direction. So, upon the promise to the viscount of an early return to Béziers to sing to his fickle lady, the Countess Alazais of Burlatz, he set out with the gay company in the cool of the morning when larks were uttering canzos in the flowery meads.

They did not tarry long at Nismes, for there was a great tumult in the city. They learned that a struggle was impending between the Knights of the Arena, who held the great fortress in its midst and owed allegiance to the emperor, and the forces of the free city surrounding it. Heedless of this internecine quarrel, the marquis took them to view a Roman relic, a wide, still pool, enclosed in weathered marble. When Peire Vidal had gazed upon this ancient spring, and had passed through the nearby portico, a moldering ruin, with its columns carved in figures, flowers, and fruit out of the unremembered past, he experienced a strange, uneasy feeling . . . something familiar, intimate, and yet long dead . . . a dream, half a foreboding. He turned away.

"It is said to have been dedicated to the worship of the witch Diane," said Antoine Beaujeu. "The Romans were a mighty people. Their blood is in the veins of most of us, and their dust under our feet. And before them were the Greeks, through much of Provence. And before them a wild race that raised up pillars of stone. They say that the powerful witch Venus has been seen in the mountains near Les Baux, long after she was driven from the Arena of Arles by Sant Trophimus. I do not know if that be so or not, but there are rites still held in her honor, I am told, among the idolatrous and superstitious peasants of that region. It may be that the ancient gods wander at times among us, touching the threads of human destiny as they once did in the time of Prince Caesar."

"They say," said Aimeric de Peguilha gaily, "that the women of Arles are all daughters of Venus, and the most beautiful in the world!"

Said Antoine Beaujeu, "If you go on to Les Baux, you will find there a living image of the heathen goddess, and I warrant her spell to be no less potent!"

In the castle at Beaucaire, a fief of the Good Count Raimon, they were well entertained, but Peire Vidal awoke on the day following afflicted with a severe chill. He had lain all night with the fierce wind from the north, the mistral, blowing upon him, and its cold seemed to have entered into his very marrow. His tongue ached and his throat was again a channel of fire, but he desired with an urgency that was inexplicable, to push on to Les Baux. They crossed the river Rhône, turbulent with its spring flood, and passed through Tarascon, where the marquis must leave them to take the road north to Avignon and Sorgues. "Messers," he said at the parting of the ways, "I trust Sant Julian will befriend you." But privately he said to Peire Vidal, clasping his hand warmly, "Senher Vidal, having heard your singing at Bargarde, I expect great things of you. When you use your voice again, it will be to better effect. God be with you!" And Peire Vidal nodded dizzily.

They were sorry to see the marquis ride away, for his company had been agreeable, and his store of information inexhaustible, while his escort of armed men was not unwelcome in a country still occasionally visited by wandering bands of routiers. The Camin Aurélien took them to St. Remy and a valley jeweled with all the flowers of spring, yellow primroses, narcissus, and hyacinth, asphodel and hawthorne; but of these and the ancient monuments and relics scattered through the flowery meads Peire Vidal took no heed. He was a sick man, scarcely able to keep his saddle. Beyond St. Remy they passed by many windings and turnings through upland reaches, covered with purple clouds of wild thyme, tufts of lavender, rosemary, and blooming box, where the air was heavy with mingled scents that seemed to eddy through the fevered head of the troubadour in gusts of fragrance, borne upon the mistral. Higher yet, among sculptured crags and pinnacles and odd fantastic shapes of stone, the wind ceased. If the sorceress Tavèn and wizard Merlin of old legends had conspired to fashion in rock the likeness of deserted cities, broken temples, shadowy avenues, and monsters never seen by man, then was their magic well wrought on the road that climbed to the citadel of Les Baux.

The setting of the sun and the full moon just rising gave the place to fantasy and weird illusion. The creatures of stone seemed to breathe and tremble, while the abysses on either side of the rough road appeared fathomless. Aimeric de Peguilha essayed to sing loudly, but his voice failed him under the spell of utter silence.

"Hasten, sweet Blancaflor!" he urged. "You shall be well bedded soon, and you shall not lack provender; for I would not be caught

45

over night in this demon-haunted fastness for all the gold of Charlemagne! Ha, ha! Stones cannot come to life, can they, master? The learned Erigena does not attribute souls to rocks, does he?"

But Peire Vidal said nothing. He rode stiffly, leaning sideways in his saddle, and his eyes glared fixedly.

"My poor friend," said the audiart uneasily, "the mistral has got into your bones and given you a fever. Master! What is it you are seeing?" His voice trembled. "They say the fairies inhabit these rocky rookeries, and flutter forth at night, seeking to snatch the souls of new-born babes, but I doubt——"

"Do you see how beautiful she is?" croaked the troubadour, pointing to the glittering road before them. "Ah, Venus, fairest witch, goddess and destroyer of my soul——!"

Then it was that the great goddess, who had long been absent from the haunts of men, returned and made herself visible to the furrier's son.

Some hours later, arriving at the high summit where a fortress had been carved from solid rock by the Ligurian chieftains, Pons and Profecta, when the Arab corsairs were sweeping the Mediterranean, the audiart delivered to the senechal of Les Baux a madman who called himself "Emperor Vidal!"

Barrale, viscount of Marseille, laughed. His laughter always came without warning, a sudden shout that ceased as quickly as it began, and all the while his eyes remained cool and sober. He was a man of middle age, gray before his time. His movements were deliberate and unhurried, yet with slight effort he accomplished more than most men. At Les Baux, the demesne of his wife and her brothers, he was in especial good humor, both because of the mountain air and the release from his arduous duties as podestat of Marseille.

"Ho!" laughed Barrale. "You ventured greatly in defending my lady, sight unseen, Senher Vidal!"

"When I espoused her cause," said the troubadour, who was lying on a richly damasked couch, "it was in the name of common justice. Had I seen her before then, I might not have done so well, for the advocate should not be swayed by personal feeling. That much I learned at Monpeslier."

"Law was not lost on you, Peire Vidal," said Adélasie des Baux, countess of Saluza. "If the collegium failed to reward you for your efforts, we shall not be so remiss." And she smiled upon him, her gray eyes enigmatic. They were neither veiled nor shrouded, yet their meaning remained unrevealed, like an inscription in an unknown tongue. Peire Cardinal of the bitter tongue, whom the countess had long held in leash, affirms: "The mystery of a woman is more often that of an empty place, endowed with the qualities given to it by the beholder." But Peire Cardinal, it is said, had suffered at her hands.

Her bliaut, a loose over-dress of écru silk, half concealed a samite robe of Tyrian purple, lined with flame-colored silk and trimmed with ermine. Below her waist her robe was bound by a girdle made of heavy braided cord of silk, studded with pearls, and having a carbuncle at each end. Her tapering fingers held a fan of ostrich tips, its gold handle set with rubies. The bronze gold of her hair was restrained by a circlet of gold, set on the crown of her head, and worked into the shape of eglantines, a diamond at the center of each well wrought flower. Her closely plaited braids fell below her knees and were something of a weight for her bower women to lift. Her voice was soft and expressed the whole gamut of thought and feeling, or so Peire Vidal believed. But then, she was the first living soul he saw coming out of his delirium after many days. And he conceived of her as a being almost supernatural in beauty and wisdom.

It was Hugues of Les Baux, brother to the Lady Adélasie, who summoned a leech from Arles to cure the singer, whose prowess before the Court of Love had made him known to all at Les Baux. This medico concocted a potion of powdered scorpions, the beak of a vulture, wormwood, the eyes of a cockatrice, and other baleful ingredients, on the principle that one virus expels another. But the tough constitution of the furrier's son survived the treatment.

When one looked from the countess to her brother Hugues, it seemed improbable they had come from the same womb, for his visage was as hard and battle-scarred and unlovely as hers was fair. Their sire, Prince Bertrand, was the son of Princess Stéphanette and

Raymon des Baux, she famous for her beauty and charity, as he for his courage. This Count Raymon had defied his feudal lord, the count of Barcelona and, being defeated, died; and his sons, Bertrand and Hugues, had rebelled in turn, and Les Baux and all its fiefs were scourged by fire and sword, the great fortress of Trinquetaille was taken and leveled. Hugues left Les Baux to Bertrand and founded another line in Sardinia, and soon after Bertrand was assassinated. The younger Hugues became lord of Les Baux; the younger Bertrand, of Berre; and the third son, Guillaume, of Orange. Thereafter, for many generations, the strong blood of Les Baux infused itself through all the courts of Europe. A tough brood nested among these crags!

The warm air of early May came in through open casements, and daily came the Countess Adélasie des Baux, now with some cate or delicacy, or again bringing her Book of Hours, or some oak-bound romance, from which she read in her soft, slightly inflected voice. But the viscount, Barrale of Marseille, was impatient of the troubadour's weakness. "Come, come!" he admonished. "You shall not lie here to be petted into a lap-dog! Let's hear the timbre of your voice!"

"One needs a weapon in the lists, my lord," said Peire Vidal.

Then secretly Aimeric de Peguilha was despatched by the viscount to Arles with a bag of silver deniers, and in three days he returned, wearing the smile of an amorous angel. In his hands he bore a viol of such superlative polish, tone, and workmanship as Peire Vidal had never known. He leaped from his pallet, and took the instrument reverently to him, placing the bow upon the strings, and at the first sound he was again a whole man.

That night he sang, before them all:

> Lark and nightingale I choose
> Over other birds that sing,
> For they first divulge the news
> Of the birth of infant spring;
> And I, too, with equal zest,
> When my fellows still are mute,
> Bow the viol or pluck the lute

48

While my song, above the rest,
Tells of love for Na Vierna.

By her favor I confess
Openly my secret mission,
Which I know is nothing less
Than perpetual submission
To her will; and I foresee
Servitude must be my part,
For the gaoler of my heart
Holds it under lock and key,
Bound by love to Na Vierna!

They praised his song, especially Barrale of Marseille. They assured him that the lady of his heart should feel highly complimented, though all were aware that the piece was addressed, under the convention of the day, to the wife of the viscount, Lady Adélasie des Baux. And that lady herself, to indicate her acceptance of its message, showed him special favor for the remainder of the evening.

But on the following morning he became party to an agreement that amounted to a great triumph. Shortly after the morning meal the viscount drew him aside. "Messer Peire Vidal," he said paternally. "I would that you were my own squire, but since you are still bound by oath to your lord of Toulouse, I desire that we two execute a certain covenant approved by ancient custom in Provence. So long as we bear good-will toward each other, whenever we ride together you shall wear a livery identical with mine; and we will be known to each other by a common name, Rainier. Would you wish it so?"

For answer, Peire Vidal fell on his knees and kissed the viscount's hand.

Thereafter, privately, they addressed each other as "Rainier"— "chosen friend"; and thereafter the songs of Peire Vidal breathed as great a fervor for "dear Rainier" as for "Na Vierna."

It was mid-May and through the open casements came the sound of maidens singing in the court below. As they sang they danced, holding in their arms bundles of last year's corn husks.

A l'entrada del tems clar, eya,
Per joya recommencar, eya,
E per jelos irritar, eya,
Vol la regina mostrar
Qu'el es si amoroza.

A la via, a la via, jelos,
Laissez nos, laissez nos
Ballar entre nos, entre nos!

When days grow fair and bright, heigh-ho!
Awakening delight, heigh-ho!
The queen, to irk and spite, heigh-ho!
The jealous king, her spouse,
Young lovers doth arouse.

On your way, on your way, lads;
Give us leave, give us leave, jealous ones,
To dance among ourselves!

The dancers formed a circle, taking hands, and swaying like
aspens as they sang:

From all parts of the land
She calls the amorous band
And gives each lad her hand;
But the old king, all unseen,
Burns, jealous of his queen.

On your way, on your way, lads;
Give us leave, give us leave, jealous ones,
To dance our dance of joy!

Hugues des Baux, peering from the window, said, "The six
virgins, Amelot, Doette, Aiglantine, Clarette, Doulce, and Rix-
ende, are going down to the well of Venus. At the time of the full
moon in May when the first grain is sprouting they make figures
of last year's corn husks and take them to the well of Venus, where
they burn them. They will let no man look upon the ceremony

50

lest they have bad luck in love. They have gathered their husks, and they will make them into little men, and tonight they will commit them to the flames. I am told they dance naked in pagan fashion. The priests are set against this ancient custom, but I see no more harm in it than superstitious silliness."

Barrale's laughter boomed. "The enchantment is surely effective," he said, "for the virgins who go to the well of Venus do not long remain such!"

"It may be silliness or not," said the Countess Adélasie, "but the witch Venus is still believed to linger about Les Baux, and she is sometimes reported to have been seen by those whose thoughts are turned toward her."

"I myself have beheld her!" cried Peire Vidal stoutly. "Has she no comfort for bachelors?"

"Truly she has," the Lady Adélasie replied. "If a bachelor greatly desire that which seems unattainable, he need only perform the following: let him find a strong young boar, one that has not yet begotten a farrow, and let him ride this beast thrice about the well of Venus. Without question your bachelor will achieve what he most covets!"

Peire Vidal stared at her with moon eyes, a strange idea taking shape in his mind.

Some days later they heard horns sounding in the town and saw a company winding up through the precipitous lanes of Les Baux toward the emerald green pleasance near its summit. Shortly the voice of Peyrols, raised in song, announced the advent of his patron, Folquet of Marseille.

"Ha!" said the viscount. "I wager he has won the peacock-feather crown in the tornimen at Toulouse and now comes to offer it to my lady, for he's a better singer than pleader." He observed Peire Vidal's disgruntled expression and added, "You, Senher Vidal, and he must compose your differences in the interest of good fellowship and for the bettering of the Joyous Craft. A little competition—" his eyes twinkled—"should spur you to greater efforts in the winning of my lady's regard."

"Come with me, Peire Vidal," said the viscount's lady, "while the new guests are being bestowed in their quarters. Senher Folquet hardly need expect me to welcome him in person!"

Barrale smiled placidly. "Go with her, and you will return a full-fledged nightingale!"

The troubadour wondered how many ardent wooers this lord of Marseille had seen discomfited. As if under a spell, scarcely knowing how his legs carried him, he followed after his lady, who trailed the scent of jasmine where she walked. Seated at her feet in the chamber with its richly figured arras, his mind was confused; alone with her, he felt awkward and embarrassed.

"Peire Vidal, when you first arrived at Les Baux, stricken with fever, you proclaimed yourself emperor. What would you do, were you an emperor?"

"I would seek not to destroy but to create happiness for all, both high and low; and I would desire to dispense justice rather than to demand submission."

"And if you were a favored lover?"

"I should wish to be pleasing to my lady, and never to cause her pain."

"That is not in the nature of love, my friend. One lover suffers or the other. Do you know the story of the troubadour, Raimon of Miravals, and how, for the love of Louve de Penaultier he lost his wife, his fortune, and his castle?"

"Louve de Penaultier!" Peire Vidal raised his head sharply, and the countess said, "You know her?"

"No, madomna, I do not. But I have heard of her." There was that in the eyes of the countess which drew out the truth unwillingly. "In fact, she gave me my Breton palfrey, and some day I shall return it to her, and repay her in song."

"If you remain with us, Peire Vidal, you need not lack for a palfrey, nor for a destrier. And as for repaying her—" Adélasie des Baux half closed her eyes—"that may wait. She has taken ample payment from her other lovers!"

The amber light of afternoon shone full upon a mosaic above the hooded fireplace, revealing the knights Eteocles and Polynices before Thebes. The city resembled Arles, and its crenelated walls were lined with knights in armor and their ladies in wimples and bliauts.

"Your song for Na Vierna pleased me, senher," she said, fingering a Byzantine casket intricately wrought in silver filigree, set

52

with lozenges of turquoise. She opened the casket and the gems within glowed and sparkled like the embers of a brazier. From the midst of them she plucked a signet ring and laid it in the hand of the troubadour. It was of dull gold set with a single carnelian, engraved with two griffins facing a trident, and on its inner surface were characters in Greek.

"When Andronicus, son of Isaac, emperor of Romania, was banished from New Rome by his cousin Manuel, who was then emperor, he fled to Jerusalem to take refuge with Amalric, the Latin king, whose son Baldwin became king, though he was a leper. There Andronicus seduced Theodora, the niece of Manuel, known to the Greeks as the Empress Xene, and by her he had two children, a boy and a girl. Andronicus Comnenus later became emperor of New Rome, but he soon lost his throne to Isaac the Angel, who delivered him to his enemies to be tortured to death. His ring came into the hands of the Châtelain de Coucy, a knight and troubadour, and he sent it to me from New Rome."

Peire Vidal examined the ring curiously. "What do the strange letters mean? Are they a charm?"

"They are Greek, and they spell the name of Andronicus, emperor of Romania. He ruled briefly, but he exercised justice. I give you this ring, Peire Vidal, because you also desire justice." She laughed. "But mostly because you fancied yourself an emperor, and because God has given you a voice that is better than a throne!"

Peire Vidal flung himself upon both knees, seized her hand, and kissed it. For a moment the breath of the countess warmed his neck, and there came into his mind a passage from an old and well thumbed volume belonging to the Good Count Raimon. It was known as the "Laws of Love" and the Sixteenth Article reads: "At the sudden and unexpected prospect of his lady-love, the heart of the true lover invariably beats." His heart beat to suffocation.

Folquet of Marseille entered the chamber with the jongleur Peyrols and Arnaut de Maruelh, exiled from Béziers by his capricious countess.

Peyrols took three short leaping steps and spun until he was all a whirl of colors, then he stopped short, balanced on pointed toe, and held out a silver hoop. A small man-like creature clinging to his

53

neck leaped through the hoop and back. Three silver balls glittered in the air, tossed between the points of daggers held in the jongleur's right and left hands. The balls and daggers vanished, and he knelt before the countess, unclasping a silver chain from his scarlet leather belt. The furry imp sprang into her lap, buried its head under her arm, and uttered plaintive squeaks.

"Gracious lady," said Peyrols, "my little Mischief begs to be accepted as a gift from the humble jongleur, Peyrols of Roquefort in Auvergne, who brings a greater gift from the eminent troubadour, Folquet of Marseille, for her whose beauty has been the inspiration of unnumbered songs, the anguish of lonely nights, and the often-sung object of perpetual devotion!" And from beneath his cloak he drew a wreath of peacock feathers which he laid at her feet.

Folquet of Marseille stood with bowed head, but his furtive look sideways at Peire Vidal had been that of an enemy. His eyes were small, set close together, his nose pinched, his lips had the lines of secret cruelty, and his dress was rich as a lord's.

The countess closed the Book of Hours and said, "*Your* gift is welcome, Messer Peyrols!" She took the peacock crown in her tapering fingers. "The gift of the eminent troubadour. . . ." She paused, and the eyes of Folquet glowed and died in his white face. ". . . is—shall we say it, Senher Vidal?—acceptable as a trophy of skill in the Joyous Craft, even though we may be led to doubt the strength of a devotion that must be tested in a suit brought before a Court of Love!"

The head of the proud troubadour sank lower. "Pardon, my lady! I. . . ."

"There is naught to pardon, messer" (she names him only messer, thought Peire Vidal) "since you have already got justice from the judges of your case." Her voice whipped him, cold as the lashing mistral, and, like a beggar, he crept slowly nearer to her. Arnaut de Maruelh, who knew too well the purgatorial aspect of love, turned his head away.

"Pardon, pardon, sweet lady!" Folquet's voice broke in a sob and he sank down before her.

At this sight Peire Vidal cried vehemently, "Have mercy, madomna, for the love of Christ!"

54

"Rise, Senher Folquet of Marseille!" she said, with a quick laugh. "Emperor Vidal has pardoned you!"

The discomfited troubadour rose and, by the dark malignancy of his glance, Peire Vidal knew that he had made an enemy for life.

That night he dreamed he stood before the smoldering throne of Satan who was condemning him to the lowest depths of Purgatory. He woke, sweating with terror.

Chapter Five

WHEN midsummer heat veiled the distant lagoons and stagnant étangs along the sea's edge, and pestilential vapors overhung the Crau and the Camargue at the mouth of Father Rhône, Peire Vidal took thought of a project that had long simmered in his mind. The more he considered the well of Venus, the more certain he became that the witch who had pointed the way from St. Remy to Les Baux had guided him to the place of his destiny. But that destiny, as it touched his relation to "Na Vierna," remained unfulfilled. When he was with her he felt great happiness, yet, as he never knew for certain what she thought of him, his pleasure in her company was troubled by doubt. She accepted and praised his songs; she seemed to desire his presence—particularly if Folquet of Marseille were about—and she allowed him at times to press her fingers to his lips. But all the while she gave no assurance of further favors.

He determined, therefore, to essay the riding of a boar about the well in order to propitiate the potent goddess who, it was said, haunted the green, still depths of its water. The securing of a likely beast was no easy matter. It needed several expeditions to surrounding hamlets before he found a two-year-old swine of robust and aggressive bearing, for which noble steed he paid two deniers, and an obole a day for maintenance until he should be needed. The swineherd was pledged to secrecy. In the town of Les Baux he discovered a saddler expert in the making of harness, and ordered a saddle, bridle, and caparison, the bridle to be fastened to the ring in the boar's nose. There lacked only stirrups, their usefulness under the circumstances being doubtful. The boar he named Destrier, the designation for a charger.

Aimeric de Peguilha had been overcome by a longing to visit his native city, where he was no longer—if he ever had been—an outlaw. In a sirvente composed at this time he sang, "Give room for impulse, and allow a holiday to prudence. Discretion may be overdone; and too much wisdom often makes a man against all rules of commonsense rebel." He rode off on patient Blancaflor, singing a gay balada, and bearing an epistle from his master to Ser Pons Vidal, furrier, of the Street of the Seven Angels.

One day, early in September, when the wind broke in mighty surges over the crest of Les Baux, Peire Vidal, whose mood was strongly affected by the weather, wandered through the corridors of the castle, filled with a more than usual disquietude. Under the rough fingering of the gale the trophies of the barons of that house shook on the walls. Rusty hauberks of chain mail rattled and dented helmets clinked. Ailettes smote against gambesons, and everywhere the figured arras flapped. Climbing by stone stairways and passing through round-vaulted galleries, he came at length to the topmost part of the keep and, buffeted by the wind, he struggled along the sentinels' walk below the parapets.

Suddenly he came upon the Lady Adélasie, where she leaned against the parapet, her silk-clad arms resting on one of its embrasures and her face turned toward the distant sea that showed a slender scimitar of light on the far horizon. As he stood watching with thumping heart, her fingers slipped down the plaits of hair hanging below her waist, undid them, and spread the shining stuff abroad, to be lifted by the wind about her until it shone lustrous as an aureole in the afternoon sun. With trembling hands he unslung his polished viol from about his neck, put his bow to the strings, and began to sing:

Atressi co.l perilans
Que sus en' laiga balansa,

57

Que non a conort de vida,
Tan sofre greu escarida. . . .

As a mariner, sea-tossed,
Capsized in desperate plight,
Gives himself up for lost,
Yielding to craven fright,
Then sees a sudden light
And feels a rescuing hand
Drawing him safe to land;
So I, distraught, downcast
By heavy doubt, and long
Love-hungry, find at last
A splendid theme for song.

If she heard the splendid theme for the new song, she gave no sign. There had been times, when he was with her, that his mind went searching for a melody to fit an alba or sirvente, or the air came, but not the words, and then he became silent, forgot his lady completely, and his face wore a vacant expression. At such times she would recall him to herself by some movement of her arm, laying its sensuous modeling bare, or by some slight turning of her seemly body she would make the shadows play along the white curves of her breasts, half-glimpsed above her flowing tunic, a garment cut low in the neck and long in the sleeves. And then words and music dissolved in his brain, as mists under a bright sun, and they did not reappear until he was again alone. But on this occasion it was she who was possessed, oblivious of his presence; it seemed the wind was her lover. In booming thunder it died among the crags of Les Baux, and again he touched his viol.

Beneath her beauty's mask
If I could know her mind
I'd have no need to ask,
Is she no more than kind,
And am I somewhat blind,
To steer my passion's bark
Through the uncharted dark,

58

Trusting to her regard
Without assurance? Dear
Lady, be not so hard,
But make the sailing clear!

The wind was returning. Like a great long wave, breaking at the base of Les Baux, where it is said the sea itself once broke, it gathered volume as it thundered nearer. Rocks were snatched loose to hurtle clattering into echoing gorges. The air was all tumult, whipped to fury. It took the countess of Saluza in a whirling eddy, lifted the soft folds of her pelisse and raised her loosened hair straight above her head in the likeness of Gorgon locks, until she looked a golden demon.

She uttered a strange cry—"Au hazard, Balthasar!"—the battle cry of the house of Les Baux—Les Baux, with its emblem of the sixteen-pointed star seen on almost every battlefield of Christendom. As the troubadour stared at her aghast, she turned in a fury and shrilled, "Are you no more than a tinkling rhymester, like the rest? Leave me! Go!"

Peire Vidal, bewildered by his lady's inexplicable mood, retreated hastily to the hall below. There he found the troubadours drinking spiced piment while they ate sweet and pungent spices from silver vessels with covers of wax sugar. But he remained so forlorn and crestfallen that the Countess Adélasie, entering sedately, was moved to pity and showed uncommon gentleness toward her troubadour all that evening.

The eve of the feast-day of Saint Remy fell on the last of September, and this night Peire Vidal chose for his exploit, for had it not been on the road from St. Remy that the fair vision had appeared to him? The riding gear had been finished, the saddler had been paid, and Destrier, subdued and corpulent with weeks of feeding, had become sleek as a charger groomed for the lists. Peire Vidal that day had saved his strength; he ate sparingly, drank little, and refused a game of tennis with the squire, Bertran d'Aurenga, who would have wagered ten sols on a match. It happened that the evening meal was composed of some of his favorite dishes: veal, with sour wine, a roast young kid dressed with an acid grape

59

sauce, cucumbers, pomegranates, and the first tart apples of the harvest; but he only eyed the courses ruefully, as one who has cast off the sin of gluttony.

"For the love of Sant Miquel!" cried Barrale of Marseille, observing the meager servings of his troubadour. "What melancholy afflicts you, Rainier? Is it the pangs of love, or a toothache?"

Peire Vidal quickly swallowed the crust of manchet bread he was chewing and answered, "Neither, Rainier. But I was considering the briefness and uncertainty of this our life. I had in mind the cobla of Guiraut of Borneil, in which he says: 'All things hasten to decay, all fall, all perish, all things come to an end. Man dies, iron is consumed, wood decays. Towers crumble. Strong walls fall down'."

"And food that is eaten once cannot be eaten again!" said Barrale, with his sudden laugh. "Also, a kiss on the mouth leaves no mark, unless there is vermilion in it, and that is soon erased! What! Must we be melancholy over the spectacle of decay? The Romans builded well but they died, too, and being pagans they must live in hell. Give thanks, Rainier, that we are living Christians!"

"It is fortunate for the world," said Arnaut de Maruelh, "that the world is Christian in part only, for if it were wholly so, the seas would be as bloody as the rivers that flow through Christian lands!"

"That smells of the Albigensian heresy, Messer Arnaut," said Folquet of Marseille, with a frigid smile; "or do you hold with the Poor Men of Lyons that purgatory is in the soul and not a place of torment for sinners?"

"Purgatory," said Arnaut de Maruelh, "is a conflict in the soul; and it is that place where there are lacking *joi,* or gladness of heart, *joven,* or young-heartedness, *mesura,* or equanimity, and *cortesia,* or grace of behavior!" He looked directly at Folquet. "Perhaps, Senher Folquet of Marseille, you have better knowledge of purgatory?"

Folquet of Marseille answered impatiently: "Since these admirable qualities are never for long present in any individual and are entirely wanting in the mass of men, it would follow from your

60

premise, Messer Arnaut, that most of mankind spend their lives suffering the pangs of purgatory!"

"I am convinced that such is the case," said Arnaut de Maruelh. "Guillaume of Champeaux has said that the same thing or substance is present in its entirety in each individual, and individuals differ no whit in their essence but only in the variety of their experiences, or accidents. Thus, that person whom I know as Arnaut of Maruelh is merely an accident of the substance 'humanity.' And as I conceive purgatory to be an essential condition of the species *homo,* it is lodged necessarily in each and every member of the species. And not all the prayers of sinners nor the chanting of priests will remove it from our lives."

"God save us!" cried the Lady Adélasie. "You offer us slight promise of salvation, Messer Arnaut!"

"Salvation," said Arnaut de Maruelh, "is the overcoming of evil desires. And evil desires are those desires which do not conform to our natural character. Therefore, to live according to the true dictates of one's inmost essence is to achieve salvation."

"That doctrine should give comfort to usurers and murderers!" said the jongleur Peyrols; and, taking out a little silver ball, he made it roll across the back of his hand, up his arm, and into the neck of his tunic.

"Murderers and usurers are not evil by nature but are made so by circumstance," continued Arnaut de Maruelh. "They have the conviction that their iniquities are justifiable. Lovers, on the contrary, are usually in a state of doubt or uncertainty. As Peire Abelard has said, 'Doubt is the road to inquiry, and by inquiry we perceive the truth.'"

The soft melancholy tone of Arnaut's speech seemed to inflame Folquet. He flung his words across the narrow board as one tosses dice: "Rhetoric to cloak cursed heresies! Inquiry, doubt, uncertainty —they are the promptings of Lucifer, and they will be expiated by blood!"

"Very likely," said Arnaut de Maruelh. "For beliefs have always begotten bloodshed: I trust, when that time comes in Provence, Senher Folquet, you will be safe in the arms of Rome!"

"I shall not be among those whose offences against God include schism and heresy!" sneered Folquet.

61

The Lady Adélasie, seeing by Folquet's expression that more bitter words might follow his speech, proposed a tenson.

"Messers troubadours," she said, "I offer you a choice of two subjects for a tenson: 'By what qualities a lover may render himself worthy' or 'Whether it be greater grief to lose a lover by death or infidelity.'" Upon a vote they chose the first subject to debate in song.

It was well for Peire Vidal that the discourse on doctrines had been broken off, for he had fallen asleep with his mouth open—a position that never displays a lover to best advantage before his lady. When Peyrols wakened him to join in the tenson, Peire Vidal mumbled something about Destrier, which they took to mean he had been dreaming of his Breton palfrey.

At the hour of lauds, when the watchman on his lonely rounds had sounded his last cheery note from the castle parapet, Les Baux fell into quietness. Peire Vidal slipped through a postern gate and made his way toward the swineherd's hut. The galaxies shone with the strange fervor that precedes the dawn. The full moon hung low in the west and beneath her gleamed the silver shield of the Étang of Vaccarès. Peire Vidal thought of the line of Master Ovid, the Ancient: *Immensum gloria calcar habet,* and his heart was uplifted in hope.

Destrier, roused from his slumbers, blinked at the torchlight but responded eagerly to the proffered bowl of mast, and by this means the beast was saddled, bridled, and led to the well of Venus. Here, when the swine had munched his fill, and while the shepherd held him by the nose-ring, the troubadour leaped suddenly upon his broad back and took the bridle firmly in his hands. It was fortunate that Peire Vidal had been schooled in hard riding in the lists of Toulouse, for Destrier, with a nimbleness unknown to other steeds, and with a speed that would have been admirable in an Arab courser, took to flight.

In all his care for practical details Peire Vidal had neglected one item, to wit, the muffling of the voice of Destrier; and this voice was now raised in a sound so piercing, shrill, and heart-rending as to wake and utterly to terrify every citizen of the town of Les Baux, and all the menie of the castle. They listened, but they dared not move, for it was well known that in ancient times a Roman general, as a sacrifice to his gods, had more than ten score barbarians flung headlong into the black abyss of the Val d'Enfer, or Valley of Hell, whence, on the anniversary of the slaughter, their souls issued as demons and whirled, screaming, about Les Baux. Peire Vidal, although he would have given his hand to have stopped that cry, kept his seat, and by exerting his full strength, turned the beast, and turned him still again. So, in zigzag fashion, he drove him, ever protesting to the moon, about the well—once, twice, and thrice! At the completion of the third round and with victory assured, the troubadour flung up both his hands with a shout of exultation, but Destrier, taking advantage of a loose bridle, dashed straight toward the castle midden. On its oozy brink the flying boar came to a halt, with such abruptness that his rider, taken unawares, pursued his course with unabated velocity. His impact, after describing a precipitate arc, was signalized by a splash and a single curse, issuing from its putrid depths: "Christ Jesu!"

Though he had fulfilled to the letter the requirements of the spell, the great witch during the ensuing days seemed little inclined to promote the interests of her votary. If anything, his lady treated him with coolness and a slight lifting of her penciled eyebrows, as of incredulity. Lord Hugues, however, let fall a casual remark one day to the effect that "the conjunction of Saint Remy and Venus is unlucky, since the goddess of virgins is most jealous of male divinities!" And Barrale uttered his shout of laughter. Abashed, Peire Vidal crept away to his chamber to compose a lament for the harshness of love and its scant rewards.

The month of October turned unseasonably hot. In the castle preparations for an important event were on foot. Barrale, son of Lord Hugues, a personable young man, was to receive knighthood. The initial steps of the lengthy ritual were to be conducted at the castle, but inasmuch as Lord Hugues was a consul of the free city of Arles, he felt it both honorable and politic to have his son perform the Vigil of the Sword, and receive the accolade in the church of Saint Trophime.

The night was spent by young Barrale with the chaplain in confession. At dawn of the next day the squire, accompanied by Lord Hugues, Viscount Barrale, squires, troubadours, and even jongleurs, with many gay songs and jests, set out for Arles where on the coming night, alone in the church, saying endless orisons, he would watch his armor until break of day.

This great occasion had thrown Peire Vidal into a fever of excitement. He composed in rapid succession an alba, to be sung on the morning after the Vigil, a canson redonda, celebrating the house of Les Baux, for the conclusion of the ceremony, and a balada for the torch dance to be held at the castle after the return of the whole menie. But—such was the muddle of his brain—when the splendid procession had descended through the town of Les Baux and was headed toward the fair city beloved of emperors, the troubadour, to his dismay, discovered that his precious viol had been left behind. Overcome with mortification and without a word to his companions, he wheeled his palfrey about and urged her, all unwilling, back up the steep ascent to the citadel.

The castle seemed deserted, and indeed, save for a scattering of men-at-arms, sentinels, minor attendants, servants, and the women folk of the count's menie, so it was.

Through halls melancholy with emptiness he wandered, searching for his beloved instrument. Not an arras stirred. Through narrow windows bright bolts of sunlight fell, illuminating rich stuffs, patterns in thread of gold, scarlet, azure, leaving the rest to somber shadow. Then he remembered how, on the night before, he had sung a last even-song to his lady in her chamber, and so he mounted the little stairway with a glad heart.

He drew the arras aside and looked within. At first, in the dimness lit by a single square of light high on a wall, he saw only the priedieu and crucifix, the corner of my lady's carved oaken wardrobe chest, and the outlines of the rug of Poitiers, on which was thrown the skin of a fox or wolf. The sweet scents of thyme and wild rosemary, mingled with musk, aloes, and amber, assailed his nostrils. Then he saw her.

On a low couch covered with a blood-red velvet cloth embroidered in gold of Cyprus, she lay pillowed, clad only in her shift of fine white linen worked with gold thread. One breast, like an ivory-tinted fruit hanging from a basket, had escaped the confining cloth, revealing itself to his astonished vision. Her long braids, dull gold in shadow, drooped over the edge of the couch to the floor. Behind them he saw the polished handle of his viol. With infinite softness, as if to counteract the thumping of his heart, he strode across the room. Slowly and stealthily he slipped his hand beneath the viol, drew it down and out from under the weight of silky hair, at the touch of which his fingers seemed to burn. He hesitated, his gaze fixed irresistibly upon that white fullness tipped with coral bud, and, at a step, he bent and kissed—her forehead; kissed, kneeling. The half-parted lips moved.

"My lord. . . ."

The words were whispers, struggling out of sleep.

"—Beloved!"

Her eyes opened, yet he could scarce have told when the lids drew back. Her eyes, unseeing, smiled. Then she recognized him, kneeling abashed, and her expression changed, like a sudden gust upon still water—darkened to chagrin that instantly became anger. In another instant she gave voice—a sound so piercing, harsh, and horrible that the terrified troubadour came near to falling over backward. Again she shrieked her wrath, and Peire Vidal, in an access of pure terror at this inhuman outcry, scrambled to his feet, his viol clutched under his arm, and fled. Down the corridor the dreadful caterwauling pursued him, headlong in flight; pursued him through the castle, and over the drawbridge as, mounted upon his palfrey, he kicked and goaded the frantic beast into a wild gallop, down, down, down. . . .

Lord Barrale was holding his hand warmly, bidding him adieu. "Yes, it's absurd, Rainier; ridiculous! When she told me, it put me into stitches of laughter—not at you, my dear friend, but at the whole idea. All that hullabaloo over a kiss! What's a kiss more or less, among friends? Fifty stolen kisses would not have been worth the loss of your voice to me! Banish you? I laughed again. Why publish to all Provence the details of a little private scene?—not that I doubt your own discretion in this matter! The point is, everyone will assume the occasion of your dismissal to have been far more serious; though, for that matter, so far as I am concerned, no behavior—outside of downright boorishness—toward my wife would merit your exile. Sant Marti preserve us from the ways of women, that they should ever come between good friends, Rainier!

"In the end, however, I had to yield to her slightly mad insistence. You wonder? Because, Senher Vidal, women with child must be humored! It is her first, so we must pardon her . . . one owes it to one's heir presumptive. Let us hope—ha! ha!—that it resembles its sire, and does not at once begin to squeal for a lute! My regret is that Senher Folquet should not have been in your place. I'd miss him infinitely less! But don't take this too much to heart. When her condition will have become normal 'twill all blow over, and you'll be with us again, with many new canzos and sirventes! Farewell, Rainier! Sant Julian keep you, and may the Blessed Virgin give you better luck in your next love!"

The viscount kissed him on both cheeks. Peire Vidal rode over the drawbridge. The winches clanked as it was drawn up. The portcullis clanged into place. That was all. He was an exile from Les Baux.

Chapter Six

BEFORE the lately finished portal of the church of St. Trophime at Arles, stood Peire Vidal studying the carving that enriched the sacred edifice. Fresh from the last deft touches of the Comacine masters, Creation, from its beginning to the trumpeted end, was fashioned in immaculate and living stone. The Serpent, coiled round the tree of Life, has plucked the forbidden fruit and given it to Domna Eve, who urges Senher Adam to share it with her. Beneath the throne of God the Father marches the Procession of the Just; among the lost souls of Purgatory are two bishops in their miters. Beneath the frieze of the Last Judgment are unrolled the Dream of Joseph; the Annunciation; the Nativity. The Three Wise Kings, sleeping in the same bed with their crowns on, hear the voice of the Angel. Among these figures Peire Vidal discerned those of a man and a woman, whom he guessed to be Samson and Delilah. She bares her naked breasts, inviting him to gaze, and so be lost.

"As it was with Senher Samson, so with me," he muttered, and turned away, for the artful carving of that hard bosom made him remember too intensely another and fairer one.

The gay, populous, and mysterious city, with its busy life of the quays, its veiled women who walked with such easy grace and assurance, the lively marts, and the strange garb of foreign traders, all disturbed him.

In the market place the torches of the hucksters of cloth, venders of spice, and food purveyors still flickered above lengths of cheap fustian, drugget, and diaspre; above heaps of nutmegs, cinnamon, dates, figs, and liquorice, grains of paradise, sorb apples, brown medlars, pomegranates, plucked geese, skinned hares, and the occasional carcass of a young kid or goat. There was a great clamor of wares being hawked, the usual torrent of oaths—"by Sant Marti, I swear!"—"Sant Dalmatz give you understanding, domna!" Two merchants were ceremoniously shaking hands to clinch a bargain and make it legal. A juggler was performing tricks with a sword. The trumpets of a wedding procession bound for St. Trophime blared, a procession which was without torches or open candles, pursuant to the law. Behind the bride and groom, who were simply and plainly arrayed, as the statutes prescribed, danced a jongleur, singing a gay devinalh to the accompaniment of an organistrum.

The mind of Peire Vidal, absorbed in melancholy reflection, was startled into sudden awareness by a commotion in the wedding party. Against the contrabass of men's voices rose the shrill treble of a woman's screeching, and this discordant strain modulated to a general and confused hubbub, punctuated by most unnuptial curses. In the center of a ring of scowling faces and clenched fists stood another jongleur, who was explaining somewhat incoherently that he had not—he swore by Sant Maximin, Santa Marcelle, Sant Sidonius, and Santa Marie the Magdalene—he had not pinched the bride on the buttocks. The bridegroom and the jongleur with the organistrum swore by all the saints they could remember that he had, and that he was a lecherous-fingered fornicating varlet. The consul's bailiff, wearing his badge of office, the Lion of Arles, opened a way through the crowd with his staff, and Peire Vidal followed. Before the officer could take further action, the troubadour spoke with an air of authority he had acquired by observing Lord Hugues des Baux.

"Messer Bailiff," he said, "I will be surety for this man."

"You, sir!" said the bailiff fussily. "And who may you be?"

"Peire Vidal, troubadour of the court of Les Baux!"

The bailiff was impressed, as were the onlookers. Few of them had not heard of Peire Vidal; luckily, none knew yet of his banishment.

"Why, senher troubadour," was the surly question, "do you take upon yourself the warranty of good conduct for this filthy fellow that has such itching fingers for ladies' buttocks?"

"Why? Because he is my audiart, Aimeric de Peguilha, of Toulouse—an excellent song-maker and a vassal of the Good Count Raimon!"

At mention of the jongleur's prowess the temper of the crowd changed at once to approval. They demanded a song to prove his worth, and the jongleur, with a becoming nonchalance, took his lute in hand and sang a retroensa of such ingenuity as to win applause even from the bridegroom. But while they fumbled in their wallets for sols and deniers, crying out for more songs, Peire Vidal quickly steered his audiart from the press of listeners.

"Largesse!" protested Aimeric de Peguilha. "Must we leave a little harvest of silver behind?"

"With me, yes!" thundered Peire Vidal. "I have witnessed your concupiscence but I will not stay for your cupidity! Besides, it isn't fitting for a troubadour and squire to seem to angle for common gratuities in the public thoroughfares! And now, my dear friend, let me have the news of Toulouse—and of your châtelaine of the shops!" And the reprimand ended with a slap on the back.

Aimeric de Peguilha needed little encouragement to set his tongue clacking. In the middle of an endless tale of love among the linens he broke off with—"You, master—a billet, a legal document—give me the itch if I can't find it! Here!" And from under his tunic he produced a roll of parchment addressed "to Messer Peire Vidal, at Les Baux or wherever he may be." In this communication it was set forth that "Messer Pons Vidal, furrier of Toulouse, having been deceased on Lord's Day, in the year 1188, Anno Domini, all of said Pons Vidal's goods, chattels, moneys, and lands——"

"Lands!" cried Peire Vidal. "Ah, my poor father! I did not know—what grief!—and I so far away at his passing! . . . *What lands?*" He read further: " ' . . . including the estate known as

69

Belgueil on the banks of the river Orbiel, in Aude, Languedoc . . .' "

"Estate!" shouted Aimeric de Peguilha. "Master! You are a lord, a baron, or at least a knight! The castle of Belgueil! *Sir* Peire Vidal of Belgueil! Praise God the Father for your good fortune!"

"Silence!" commanded the newly created knight in a voice that would have suited Lord Hugues des Baux. " '. . . are bequeathed to his sole heir, Peire Vidal, whilome squire to Count Raimon of Toulouse.' " And so of other matters pertaining to the last testament of Pons Vidal; of expenses incurred in the furrier's burial, carefully itemized, "to wit: ten sols for the choir boys singing a dirge; one mark, three deniers, for candles at the church of Sant Sernin and for a Mass to be said for his soul . . ." and the like. The epistle was signed "Gantelme Boso, notary and clerk, district of Margues, Toulouse."

The knighting of Peire Vidal, like his ascension from jongleur to troubadour, was somewhat unusual. It occurred without previous solemnities other than the quaffing of countless flagons of mulled wine on the part of himself and certain boon companions who had come to share his good fortune at Belgueil. These included Gaucelm Faidit and his wanton, Guilhelma Monjo, the Monk of Montauban, Aimeric de Peguilha, and two damsels of uncertain lineage and occupation, known as Jusserande of Ventabren and Mabille of Vodable. They had with them several ill favored varlets and house servants, under a villainous castellan, one Jehan Porcelet, who had been flogged from a neighboring castle for thieving.

An inspection of his estates revealed to the new lord a dilapidated manor house, empty stables and piggeries in a state of extreme disrepair, and two aged vassals, man and wife, who held a tiny plot of soil for an annual fee of three sols and a goose "well hung." However, Ser Pons Vidal's establishment, now in charge of his master furrier, was a profitable business.

It was November. The wind whistled through open casements, whirling the smoke of their hearth fires through the desolate halls, obscuring the dingy and tattered arras. The rain dripped from the ceilings and an unpleasant odor rose from the heaps of filth on the littered floors. But the four troubadours and their wenches made merry and took no heed of the weather or of the condition of "castle" Belgueil.

"You must be made a knight," said Gaucelm Faidit on the eve of the third day of carousing, "and I am the one to do it, for although I am but a squire, my father was a knight, and made me, in an hour of indulgence. Fill our tankards, sluts!" They drank to the dregs, and the fat troubadour got to his feet as best he could. "Stand by and turn the next round bottoms-up, brothers of the Joyous Craft, for we are to have one lord among us!"

They put their lips to replenished cups and drained them at one long draught. "For the love of Sant Julian, and the honor of Peire Vidal!"

But Peire Vidal, for whom this signal honor was intended, had grown so fiery of visage it seemed he might at once burst into flame, and his eyes bulged like carbuncles from under his shaggy brows. No sooner had he quaffed the last trickle of red steaming liquor than he reeled and sank to his knees like one smitten in the thick of battle. At this moment Gaucelm Faidit, lifting a great fist, let it descend sharply on the neck of the troubadour.

"What are you doing?" cried Peire Vidal, smarting under the blow.

"It is the custom, it is the act that makes you knight," said Gaucelm Faidit, striking him again. "By the grace of my grandsire and the knightly heritage of my sire, I dub you Knight of Song and of Belgueil, Peire Vidal!" And he smote him once again, until Peire Vidal was like to bury his nose in the offal on the floor. Then they helped him to his feet and offered him respectful salutation, and as he was still dazed, Gaucelm Faidit began to sing lustily in French:

> Bele Aliz matin leva
> Sun cors vesti et para
> Ens un vergier s'en entra
> Cinq fleurettes y truva

"Fair Alice rose in the morning, clothed and adorned her body, entered an orchard and found there five little flowers. She made

71

herself a wreath of fair flourishing roses. God has drawn you there, you who love not."

And as Peire Vidal recovered his senses, he knew himself for a knight in truth. He was, however, ill at ease for he had begun to retch, but soon he was relieved of his distress, while Aimeric de Peguilha held his master's head and let him cast up the burden in his belly.

"Sant Laurent!" gasped the troubadour. "This knighting is difficult!"

"It is only the beginning!" cried Gaucelm Faidit cheerfully. "The Bath! The Bath of Purification for Monsenher Vidal!"

In the moldering kitchens of the manor house they found a huge vat or caldron that had been used for rendering fat and tallow. Though the vessel gave off a rancid odor and was none too clean, the varlets filled it with warm water and carried it, at the command of Gaucelm Faidit, up to the chamber where the three maidens had retired. Leaning on the arms of the Monk of Montauban and Aimeric de Peguilha, the newly made knight followed after. Here they bestowed him, after removing every garment, down to his tunic and hose.

"It is the custom," said Gaucelm Faidit, "for the postulant to have the service of only one lady at his bathing, but as our monsenher is already a knight, he will be allowed a threefold honor. I commend his lordship to your offices, Domna Guilhelma, Domna Jusserande, and Domna Mabille! And may he be thrice purified!"

That night, till cockcrow, he watched his sword. It was an ancient weapon and rusty, but it was all they could find; and the chapel itself was partly in ruins. One trembling taper lighted feebly the gloomy recesses of the crypt. Aloft the inky darkness was alive with squeakings and the ghostly flitterings of innumerable wings. He tried hard to keep his mind on his orisons, but recalled, instead, fragments of old songs and odd snatches of those still unborn.

He must have fallen asleep again, for his eyes were staring at a figure behind the altar, in the niche that once had held a statue of the Blessed Virgin. It was a half-naked woman—a figure that bent and swayed with the inviting gestures of unveiled harlots of Arles; the breasts of Delilah, the voluptuous hips of Jezebel! Even as he stared in horror at this seizure of his wits, another form slid up beside the first; and then another, one to the right and one to the left, moving in unison, in a kind of dance, lascivious as the wanton images of a dream.

His fingers clenched upon his sword, his brain swirled in an agony of disgust and apprehension.

"Begone!" he cried. "Avaunt, foul spirits that tempt the soul! You have come out of Gehenna to destroy my knightliness! O God and Holy Mary and great witch Venus, keep me true to Love!"

The laughter was that of Guilhelma, Jusserande, Mabille.

With a hoarse bellow, like a wild beast, he leaped up, gripping his rusty blade, and sprang toward them. It was well, perhaps for their safety that, as they ran shrieking, his foot caught in a heap of rubble and he fell headlong.

One jest of Gaucelm Faidit had gone awry.

Chapter Seven

JEHAN PORCELET of the unsavory past combined in his person not only the offices of castellan and seneschal; he was bailiff of the estate of Belgueil as well. As overseer he contracted for the restoration of its works and defences, for the refurbishing of its halls and chambers, even for the reclaiming from desert and wilderness of its fields, vineyards, tangled meads and pleasances. Though his master delivered to him, without further thought, certain moneys for this mighty work, the erstwhile rogue was more painstaking in his accounting of each obole, denier, and mark than the most finicky clerk. More than that: out of a pack of slovenly, quarrelsome, knavish, slippery, and surly rascals he fashioned, not without the accompaniment of howls and curses, a menie that would have done credit to the most exacting of senhers. Nursing sundry welts and bruises, the varlets came to respect authority; under the bastinado they acknowledged the desirability of being honest. Or at least, of not getting caught.

The Nineteenth Article of the *Laws of Love* states that "if love once begins to diminish, it quickly fades away as a rule, and rarely recovers itself." The absence of many months from his countess of Les Baux, combined with the duties and activities of his position as a knight, rendered less sharp to the troubadour the image of that unreasonable lady. During the winter, however, he composed a number of graceful songs for Rainier and Na Vierna, and in early spring despatched Aimeric de Peguilha, with a full wallet and new apparel, to sing them at Les Baux. And since it is set down in the Seventeenth Article that "a new love affair banishes the old one completely," at the coming-on of the fresh and flowery season Peire Vidal's thoughts turned often to the countess of Cabaretz, Louve de Penaultier, or, in Provençal, Loba de Puegnautier, who was the wife of Count Jordan Roger, a brother to Raimon Roger, viscount of Béziers. It was she who had bestowed upon him the palfrey, and he was mindful of his promise to return and favor her in song.

The troubadour, pondering the best mode of introducing himself to his unseen benefactress, conceived of a project that would redound to her credit throughout Provence, and at the same time would prove his chivalric intentions. He proposed to take the name of "Loba" or Wolf, and go to her as Monsenher Loba or, as one would say, Sir Wolf. In essence, the enterprise was no less unusual than that of an earlier troubadour, Jaufie Rudel, prince of Blaia, who, on hearing of the remarkable beauty and charm of a certain Mélisset of Tripoli, set out across the sea to find her. But he fell sick unto death during the passage and lived only long enough to die in the lady's arms, and she took the veil and became a nun.

To his castellan Peire Vidal said one day, "Jehan Porcelet, I must have a wolf."

The factor showed no surprise at this strange request, for he believed that a touch of madness accompanied greatness. "Yes, sire," he said. "But should it be a pup, a bitch, or a dog-wolf?" He always addressed his master as "sire" and spoke of Belgueil as "the castle."

"It must be a male, full grown and in his prime."

"Yes, master," said the castellan doubtfully, "but it is not so easy to get one living. Our curs and mastiffs are not bred for the chase, and it is unlikely they could raise a wolf from cover. A baited pit is the best way to take them, but to get them out of it they must be half dead."

"A dead wolf will do," said the troubadour, "but let him have a good, thick, and handsome coat, a proud bearing, and a sturdy tail, for I have in mind to make a banner for the House of Vidal,

75

sable with a silver wolf rampant, crowned with fine gold. When you have the wolf, let him be skinned and the hide dressed soft and pliant. And have no false eyes put in the sockets, for that would be an indignity to Monsenher Loba."

In due time a villein was brought in with a badly bitten hand, and somewhat later a wolf hide of wondrous proportions, with fur of surpassing luxuriousness, was proudly presented to the monsenher by his castellan.

"It is a noble beast, Monsenher Vidal," said Jehan Porcelet, "and the catching and killing of him came to only two sols three deniers. I gave the varlet that lost a thumb to Master Wolf three oboles. Was it too much?"

"Give him a bezant, poor fellow!"

"A bezant? Sant Marti! what would he do with a bezant? If you please, twenty oboles, in a sack; the chink of it will make him think he's richer than a bishop!"

At this time Peire Vidal made his first song for Loba de Puegnautier. That spring was late and reluctant. Icy blasts swept out of the barbarous northland of the Franks. Old snow clung to the shadow sides of the dark clefts in the Black Mountains above Belgueil. While great logs cracked in the hooded fireplace and Gaucelm Faidit played betimes at dice, chess, and tables or backgammon with the Monk of Montauban, Peire Vidal tuned his viol to this song:

Neus ni gels ni ploja ni fanh
No.m tolon deport ni solatz . . .
Que.l temps escurs mi par clartatz
Pel novel gaug en que.m refranh;
Quar joves domna ma'a conques,
E s'eu leis conquerre pogues
Quan la remir tant bela.m par,
Que de gaug cugera volar.

Neither snow, ice, tempest, nor the mire
Of frozen tracks dampen my joy and mirth;
For this bleak season darkening the earth
Seems as the clarity of heaven's fire

76

To me, basking in secret joys and made
Rich by her youthful beauty; I have prayed
Before her image, hoping to overbear
Her who, possessed, would seem more fair.

Love. What is love, he thought? Not the antics of infatuation,
nor the groveling of blind devotion. It is something that looks
through the outward aspect to the intrinsic nature and beneath
the superficies discovers the essence. Love is grace and proportion.
Love is the grain of understanding left after the winnowing of
passion. But the lover? he is forever the fool and witling, a clumsy
apprentice at the *gai saber d'Amors*. Even the best of lovers! Thus
he sang:

Nobly to love a noble lady needs,
In the lover, wisdom, an understanding mind,
Courtesy, and such discretion as will bind
Herself to him; for no wise lover feeds
On brooding and self-pity; in such fashion
Doubts enter through the breaches of a passion;
So, lover, if you would love rightly,
Keep all your loving fair and sightly!

Carving out the song by bits and phrases, now blocking out
roughly a new canzo, and again chiseling at an old one, he finally
fitted its many parts together and ground them fine. After he
had instructed in the singing of it a newly arrived jongleur by the
name of Aimonet, he sent him to Castle Cabaretz, richly liveried,
and with a message that he was come as the emissary of Monsenher
Loba of Belgueil to deliver the love and respect of his master for
the Countess Loba de Puegnautier, in whose honor this song had
been made. Upon the jongleur's return at the end of three days
he had little of consequence to report: he had been graciously received, had fed well, was listened to attentively by the count and
countess. They had applauded the song and tendered him a handful of deniers which he (as he had been commanded) refused. But
there was no message.

"This stripling," thought Peire Vidal, "is unseasoned in courtly

77

ways. He may have sung badly. And a bungling delivery spoils a good song. I should have waited for Aimeric de Peguilha. Still, they liked it. Perhaps the husband has the bad taste to be jealous; but such incivility is unlikely. No, my lady is expecting a plainer demonstration of my passion. Well, I will not disappoint her!"

When Jehan Porcelet learned of the reception of Monsenher's song his choler knew no bounds. "Sant Dalmatz!" he cried to the warden. "Who are these people of Cabaretz to spurn our master's honest avowals? The great Marcabru was right when he said in a sirvente: 'The young people are becoming false and treacherous. Generosity is no more. It is a settled thing that propriety is disappearing and the mother and daughter alike are governed by base motives!'"

It occurred neither to the troubadour nor to his bailiff that the cause of the Countess Loba's silence was her knowledge of the episode of the kiss at Les Baux and the subsequent banishment, which by now were the common property of all Provence. A lover may be eccentric, but he should not be ridiculous!

As he made circumspect preparations for the quest on which he was about to embark, Peire Vidal called to mind constantly the First Article of the *Laws of Love:* "Marriage cannot be pleaded as an excuse for refusing love"; and the Fifth, that seemed to complement it: "Favors which are yielded unwillingly are tasteless."

One night, for lack of other amusement, the tables laid on trestles were removed and to the gay music of lute, gigue, and symphonie, the troubadours, Gaucelm Faidit and the Monk of Montauban, and the jongleur Aimonet danced with the three damsels, treading many merry measures, the Dance au Virelet (wherein each in turn sang a verse), the Pas de Brabant, and the Dance au Chapelet. This last, because of the kissing at the end, pleased them all so well that it was often repeated. Peire Vidal, in the midst of the merrymaking, stole away in secret to the chapel which had been wholly restored, adorned with an image of the Virgin, and made fragrant with rushes, green twigs, and early blossoms. To the chapel he brought his sword that was now, thanks to Jehan Porcelet, as bright and shining as any blade of Damascus. He had named it Durandal, after the mighty sword of Orlando, reputed to have split rocks and severed tree trunks. Advancing to the shrine of the Virgin, he knelt and laid the sword at her feet, saying:

"Madomna, Gracious Lady, rose without thorn, sweet above all flowers, dry rod bearing fruit, earth bringing forth fruit without toil, star, Mother of the Sun, in the world no woman is like to Thee, neither far nor near! To Thee, virgin pure and fair, I dedicate my sword Durandal, in the cause of justice and love; laying it humbly at Thy feet and giving oath, by all the fair saints of Heaven, that I will neither rest nor sleep, eat nor drink, make music on my viol nor raise my voice in song until, by Thy favor, in my wolf-skin, I have looked upon the face and beheld the beauty of my lady! Lady! Star of the sea, brighter than all other stars, the sea and the wind buffet us; show us Thou the right way: for if Thou wilt bring us to a fair haven, secure in the esteem and warm regard of our beloved, ship nor helmsman fears not tempest nor tide lest it trouble us!" The Virgin appeared to smile upon him and he went away with a confident heart.

In the great chamber they were dancing the old, paganish, and wild estampida, the dance of ancient Provence, the men with bloodshot eyes and faces streaming sweat, the damsels with blousy hair, quivering breasts, and jerking hips, lascivious, half-naked.

It was a night of moon and stars, of breathless silence, unstirring calm; a night of the beginning of the season of joy, giving out scents of opening buds and of hyacinth, narcissus, and the joy flower, the flor de gaug. In the luminous stillness the waters of the river Orbiel sang albas and sirventes for the pleasure they had of running fresh and full; and all the little streams added liquid canzos celebrating the night in its beauty.

Unencumbered by ought but his wolf-hide cloak, Peire Vidal strode rapidly through the valley, following shepherd tracks, for he wished to avoid any chance traveler on the road to Carcassonne. There was danger in such a meeting. His garb was not reassuring, and he had only his poniard for defence. From a distance he saw a village with its crofts and sheep byres huddled about a moated castle; then came the dense gloom of a forest where the track was hard to follow, spattered with moonlight, and he held his dagger ready, should he come face to face with Monsenher Loba in the flesh. He kept his course by the light of one bright star he knew

79

hung above the citadel, for he had once ridden that way, even to the foot of the crag. It was not easy going now. The vagrant track wound among boulders, plunged into the black depths, and several times he lost it. But after some wandering up and down the hillside, he found it again—by the aid, he was sure, of blessed Sant Julian and the Holy Virgin.

There came to him a canzo from the song of Prince Jaufie Rudel when he sailed to find his unknown love, Mélisset of Tripoli:

> Not happiness nor any rest
> Shall be my guerdon if I fail
> To know the curving of her breast
> And secret beauties, only guessed,
> In the telling of a pilgrim's tale,
> By me, a listener, doubly blessed!

Though Rudel had died in the arms of his beloved, Peire Vidal had no great desire for a similar ending to his present quest. Therefore he pursued his darkling way with a certain caution. A flaming star sprang suddenly from the depths of the night sky, and hurtled, like the gonfalon of a Saracen warrior, across the zenith, to vanish behind the forest-crested summits of the Black Mountains. The star of his destiny! A sign of good omen promising the power and glory of earthly things.

> Ah! sweetest lady, might it chance
> My love should shelter in your heart,
> Whatever hour or circumstance
> Conspire to keep us still apart. . . .

He stopped, listened . . . danger!

It was not a sound. There were no sounds. It was not a movement; no living thing was to be seen in all that world of night, profound in its secrecy, potent in sorcery. But still, danger! It whispered in his ear, touched his spine, prickled his skin, urged at the roots of his hair—something whose ominous presence made itself felt by the sense of fear. And that was curious, for Peire Vidal could remember few occasions in his life when he had known fear.

Then far below him, above the sheep byres, a dog barked; howled. Another answered, and another, in a demoniac chorus the eager ferocity of which was more than a warning against intruders. It was the hunting cry of the pack.

"There are, likely, wolves about," he muttered, tightening his grip on the handle of the poniard. "But who am I to fear a wolf or two—I, who have taken the name Loba the Wolf myself! It is not winter, they'll have no lean bellies, and they'll not attack a man armed. Sant Dalmatz, what a zany to take fright at naught!" And he laughed to hearten his quaking knees. Still, he was in no mood for lagging.

It was not long before he heard the baying again, and this time nearer. By the sound there must be five or six of them. "Good beasts," he thought, "to watch their master's folds so well! No wolf will stay when the dogs bay!" But at the very moment of this reassurance a thought leaped like a blazing brand into his mind, burning its way through: "There is no wolf. *I* am the wolf they seek!"

Peire Vidal quickened his steps. It was not far, now, to Cabaretz. Through a curtain of young leaves he could see the vast dark mass of it looming above him, rock and citadel all in one. A thousand paces to safety, but all upward in steep ascent, and with his long trudging even his great strength was by no means fresh. And so, as the baying hung ever closer at his heels, he began to run. Clad in the wolf hide, he found it no easy matter. For a moment he was tempted to cast off the skin whose scent the pursuing beasts were following, but it was the badge of his high emprise and a part of his vow to the Blessed Virgin to appear before Loba of Puegnautier in the guise of Monsenher Loba of Belgueil. "Perhaps Our Lady of Heaven has set this trial of my fortitude," he thought, panting up the slope. "I will not fail her, even though it bring me to a bloody end! Good saints, look upon me and give me succor, for I am in sore need! Most blessed Sant Julian, lend me thine aid, I pray! Help me, Sant Marti! Sant Dalmatz! Sant Peire! Sant Honorat! Sant Trophime! Sant Lazarus!" With every leap he uttered the name of a saint, in the hope that of the holy multitude there would be one whose business in heaven would not prevent ministrations to a suffering mortal.

Once he tripped and fell sprawling. As he raised himself, dazed, to his knees, the pack, in a huddle of flying forms, leaped from cover below him, caught fresh wind of their quarry, and gave voice in horrid unison. Again he fled on, with bursting lungs and heart that could no longer find room to beat. Then, at length, he could do no more; winded and faint, the fierce stars whirling in blackness before his eyes, he stood backed against a rock, poniard in hand, awaiting the onslaught.

The first dog to reach him was a small one. It leaped, making no sound, and moonlight silvered his dagger as it flashed, finding the furry neck. Before he could withdraw his weapon, however, a great mastiff had overborne him by the sheer weight of its impact; down he went, in the midst of the snarling, snapping crew.

Two shepherds toiled up the slope. They were armed with whips and cudgels, hoping to be in at the kill and save the pelt for the two deniers bounty offered by their lord. But also from Cabaretz had issued three men-at-arms, curious of this midnight hunt.

As the whips fell, the dogs drew away, yelping. The cudgels were raised, as well as the guisarmes of the soldiery, to despatch the animal that lay in a heap, not quivering.

"By the Bloody Christ, the game is ours!" cried one watcher of flocks.

"You lie, vermin!" shouted a pikeman. "The kill belongs to the land, and this is Cabaretz—no place for dunghill serfs! Back to your midden, scum!"

Further debate was stayed by a very human groan that came, to their horror, from the wolf-like creature stretched at their feet.

"Saints defend us!" whispered the shepherd, hoarse with terror. "They have run a werwolf to earth!" But the pikeman, less given to superstition, knelt and gingerly undid the shaggy covering.

"It is a man," he said. "A madman, but yet a man, and nothing more!"

In the great hall of Cabaretz, to the sound of citole, mandore, psaltry, and rote, there was singing and dancing, which ceased as they brought in, on a dark-gray, shaggy hide, a form whose tunic had been white and was now carmined, and they laid it down before Loba of Puegnautier and the Count Jordan Roger. The count and his lady stared. She had black eyes, the eyebrows thin

82

and delicately arched. Her mouth was small, proud, disdainful; her beauty was hard and bright as a diamond.

"What is this?" she asked of the seneschal, an old man who stood beside his henchmen, biting his nails. "Do you cast your carrion before us, to spoil our revelry?" Her voice was steel, her smile fiery-cold.

"He it is, my lady," he stammered, "a madman that has been brought down by shepherds' dogs, and he would die in my lady's arms!"

"Is the man known to you?" said Count Jordan Roger in a not unkindly voice.

"He wears the livery of Belgueil," said the seneschal. "And I doubt not it is the mad troubadour, Peire Vidal!"

The jongleurs and troubadours stirred with sudden interest. The lips of Peire Vidal, crusted with blood and earth, moved. "Monsenher Loba . . . of Belgueil . . . by your favor . . . my lady!"

And then the laughter of Loba of Puegnautier broke the silence, rose in a gush of shrill derisive merriment, peal upon peal, ringing through the vast chamber with uncontrollable and infernal zest.

When it subsided the count spoke curtly: "Let his wounds be dressed, and send to Carcassonne for the chemist and a balm against infection!"

Though he remained at Cabaretz until he was healed of his wounds, and paid for the Breton palfrey in songs to the countess, Peire Vidal was not wholly happy in the citadel. His songs of this period are his least felicitous, and they contain certain phrases that might be construed as irony. The arms of Belgueil, granted later by Count Raimon, are azure, two viols saltire-wise, the dexter over the sinister, between four saltires argent. There is nowhere in the troubadour's armorial bearings a wolf rampant.

It is possible that the Countess Loba detected beneath the complaisant attendance and slightly formal songs of gallantry of the knight of Belgueil a mere perfunctory recognition of her place as a noble lady, rather than her desirability as a woman. It is certain that after her first outburst of derision she tried none of her tricks on him. She listened attentively to his albas and serenas, his chanzos and sirventes; praised them tactfully, commended his performance on the viol, even gave respectful ear to his political tirades and his tedious disquisitions on the strategy of war in the Holy Land. This last maneuver almost drew him into her toils, for the troubadour knight-errant was exceedingly vainglorious of his tactical genius.

"On the next crusade," he was wont to say, "Richard the Lion will need me!"

"I am sure he will," said the countess, "for, despite his courage, English Richard's a blundering fool. He took issue with our Good Count Raimon, who should have been his best friend here in the South, let himself be hoodwinked by that sneak, Philip of France, and laid his own father in his grave. A bad friend and a vicious son, for all his brawn and lion tawniness!"

"That was the doing of a trouble-maker, the troubadour, Bertrand de Born, viscount of Hautefort," said Count Jordan Roger. "Richard in battle is a lion. In intrigue, he's a foolish lamb, led by any shrewd meddler. The brains are lacking!"

"For all that, he makes good sirventes!" Peire Vidal declared stubbornly.

"Good songs do not always come from wisdom." It was Raimon of Miravals speaking. "For the wisdom of the singer is achieved at the expense of his actions. From defeats and misfortunes he learns—but not how to avert future ones. He mounts from failure to understanding, and so, to further failure, and greater understanding; until death, his last frustration, leaves him without final enlightenment."

The words of this man fell upon their ears like the tolling of a bell. The countess clapped her hands.

"Music!" she cried almost angrily. "Enough of dirges! Let your playing be as merry as the mating of birds on the wing! Senher Vidal, tune your viol to a tenson with the tabor of Messer Brunenc—nay! we will make it a joc-partitz and the subject will be: How best may a lover make known his love to his beloved, when there is still nothing between them, and they are always in the public view? Now I give you a moment's leave to consider."

Peire Cadenet began by singing the praises of the foot. He maintained that the foot, being more hidden from observation and having, so to speak, a language all its own, was capable of transmitting ardent messages without difficulty and with unmistakable meaning. His whimsical fancy and his description, with appropriate illustrations, of the best usage of the pat, the tap, the lingering touch, and the slow, gentle pressure received the applause of a delighted audience.

The mood of the tornimen having thus been set in so sprightly a fashion, Hugues Brunenc took his stand for the superiority of the hand. The foot, he declared, was an accurate but not a subtle means of communication. For the responses of love should be direct, and unless the foot were entirely naked—which would be, God save us! an immodest thing—its covering of silk or leather will always interpose a material barrier to the advances of love. The hand, however, is not only the servant of desire in its early stages, it is the master of the ultimate ceremonies.

The judges, with approving smiles, looked at their hands as if there had been revealed to them a new meaning in those white and tapering fingers.

Raimon of Miravals, in a more melancholy key, was an advocate for the eyes. "They are," he sang, "removed by their very nature from the deceit and corruption of the flesh. Eyes cannot lie; if there is falsehood in their owner, it looks out of them; and if there is goodness, and warmth of feeling, the eyes declare it. Glances are messengers of the heart, for the eyes reveal to lovers what fear keeps back; but hands can be hypocritical, and often a lady presses the foot by accident."

The earnestness and sincerity of his declaration and the grace of its delivery moved all the judges save the countess, who betrayed a slight impatience by the tapping of her tiny scarlet slipper.

The field by this time had been so well covered that there was nothing left for Peire Vidal to defend but the voice; however, he was, by the lapse of time, the better prepared, and he launched into a fervent eulogy of Monsenher the Tongue.

"The Land of Scobellum was a very fruitful land, but the inhabitants exceeded the Persians for pride, the Egyptians for luxury, the Cretans for lying, the Germans for drunkenness, and all nations together for the generality of vices. In vengeance the gods changed all the people into beasts: drunkards into swine, the lecherous into goats, the proud into peacocks, scolds into magpies, idle women into milch-cows, jesters into monkeys, dancers into squirrels, and misers into moles. There were no troubadours in Scobellum else they would have become song-birds; and there were no true lovers, for they would have become doves. The tongue, when it speaks, cannot deny love; and before all the world, the voice of the lover betrays, by its tone, by its tenderness, its trembling reticence, or by its dove-like cooing, the presence of desire and of passion. And, mark you, the words do not matter; love flows from the tongue as water from a clear spring! It will not be denied! For in the end the tongue finds greatest delight in loving, both in kisses and in the words of ecstasy, and in other ways."

After a period of deliberation the judges, whose spokesman was the Countess Loba, declared Peire Vidal victor in the lyrical debate, and he received at her hands an embroidered cordon as a token of his triumph. As the three other troubadours concurred heartily in the judgment, Peire Vidal felt that the Blessed Virgin had at last taken an active interest in his affairs and that his strange introduction to Cabaretz had received divine sanction.

The remainder of that night was given to tumultuous revelry.

The floor being cleared of its trestled tables, dames, troubadours, and squires joined in a torch-dance, in which each couple bore a lighted taper, endeavoring to blow out the tapers of the others while keeping their own lighted. In this dance the countess chose Peire Vidal for her partner; and it seemed, by the frequent pressure of her hand in his and the touching of her foot, as well as by the boldness of her glances, that she accorded him more than the customary favors of this diversion.

As the night wore on, the gay assembly became less of a single gathering. It suffered by partition and diminution as each senher found a domna compliant to his whisperings and withdrew with her to some secluded nook. Spring, heavy with a multitude of flower scents, came in at the open casements and mingled its sweet breath with the fumes of wine, while the jongleurs kept up their endless strumming and the wavering flames of torches sank slowly in the brackets.

"Monsenher Vidal," said the countess, laying her head against his shoulder, "you do not talk to me."

86

"I do not talk because I am thinking," said the troubadour, stretching out his legs that were numb with the weight of her body against them.

"Are you thinking of something of which you dare not speak?"

"Yes, my lady," he said, scratching his nose where one of her stray black locks was tickling it. "I dare not speak of it."

"I give you permission to speak of anything, Peire Vidal!"

After a portentous silence he spoke: "This tale of the knight Monsenher Samson and his domna, the Lady Delilah—they say he was shorn of his long hair by that witch and so lost his strength. I do not believe it, Madomna!"

She drew herself away sharply. "Oh! You do not believe the tale! Well, what does that matter?"

"I believe that Monsenher Samson became weak after he had lain with this Delilah and found that she was only a common slut, and so he cut off his own hair in mourning for the loss of his love, and let himself be taken!"

"Monsenher Vidal," she said, "you are a good singer, but a curious sort of fool!" And rising quickly, she left the hall.

Peire Vidal stumbled away to seek his couch. He felt desirous of something, yet empty of any known desire. . . . Yes, he wished to be among men. At Cabaretz he would not long remain, he thought, as he lay tossing restlessly on the silken coverlets. He was startled by a sound in his chamber—the rustle of arras drawn aside, then dropping into place.

"I have come," she said, standing in the whiteness of her samite mantle, "to know if you are as much a lover as your songs declare, Peire Vidal!"

He turned slowly and looked upon her with much the same interest and curiosity with which he had studied the carvings of the church of St. Trophime, but with less reverence.

"You are daring, my lady, to make trial of my—" he could not utter the word love; he said—"strength?"

She twitched her mantle from her and stood white as a nightshade blossom. Peire Vidal plucked the single torch from its socket and flung it sputtering into the encroaching darkness without. Then he strode toward her.

87

"Take me, Peire Vidal!" she cried softly. "You are so ugly; hurt me!"

In the morning he awoke, alone, and heard the larks singing distantly, far below, and desired only to be out among them. Across his chest lay a girdle woven of silver threads. He stared at it without touching it. To the Countess Loba of Puegnautier he gave no more than a passing thought—whether she would miss her girdle, or whether it was a gift, and if so, what could he do with it? Wear it into battle as the livery of love? He laughed aloud.

"My lady's favors! I have already enjoyed them; there is no need to carry them about!" In truth, he had drunk the wine and had found it savorless. And now he wished to be away, but he knew not how to accomplish a decent departure.

But the guiding hand of his destiny was again evident, for that very morning there arrived the jongleur, Aimeric de Peguilha, fresh and fair as a daffodil, with the amazing intelligence that King Richard of England, at the behest of his troubadour, Messer Arnaut Daniel, and upon the high estimation of Barrale, viscount of Marseille, desired the troubadour, Peire Vidal, to accompany him on a holy crusade to rescue the True Cross from the infidels!

"And, master," cried the audiart, dancing for joy, "we are to meet His Christian Majesty at Genoa, where will assemble a great host of good knights and troubadours, and all the bolder spirits of Provence are going!"

"He will need me," said Peire Vidal, "for his strategy is vile, and his English singers have the voices of ravens!"

He stayed only long enough to compose a sirvente, dedicated to the countess of Cabaretz, and written, to please her, in the French tongue. It began:

> *Je m'en voiz, dame, à Dieu le creator*
> *Commant vo cors, en quel lieu que je soie. . . .*

"I must go, my lady; to God, the Creator, I entrust your fair body. I do not know if you will ever hear of my return; it is doubtful that I will see you again. My heart remains in your keeping; do with it what you wish! My sweet lady, I commend you to Jesus. It is not my fault, surely, that I must desert you."

As a knight and troubadour he was expected to practise, among other virtues, *cortesia;* and therefore he went mournfully from her presence and often looked back until the castle was hidden by rocks. Then he spurred his horse into a gallop, shouting his exultation.

The Sixth Article of the *Laws of Love* states: "A person of the male sex cannot be considered a lover until he has passed out of boyhood."

Chapter Eight

YOU will not," said Jehan Porcelet, "put Belgueil in pawn for any crusade, my lord."

"Do you think I am coming to Richard the Lion empty-handed, and without a following well liveried and suitably armed?"

"Sire, you will not go empty-handed. You will have your viol, which is worth more than any of his draughty English castles. For a following you will have Messer Gaucelm Faidit, and Aimeric de Peguilha, and Aimonet."

"And Jusserande and Mabille, and Guilhelma Monjo!" grunted Gaucelm Faidit, who was industriously polishing the links of his hauberk. "Which will hearten English Richard more than three companies of Norman witlings."

"A knight must have a respectable train and not a pack of ruffianly tinklers and their drabs!"

"Ha!" growled Gaucelm Faidit. "Little you know of crusading, Monsenher Vidal! I've seen high-and-mighty nobles gnawing the bones of rats and crows, and riding scrawny jackasses—when they didn't walk. But I've never seen a soldier of Provence go hungry. In the last holy campaign there were times when I'd sell some oaf his goat or sheep before he knew he'd lost it—and get it back, too, by nightfall, without paying an obole. Give me half a score of lean, thieving varlets from hereabouts and I'll guarantee to starve out a stronghold of the infidels."

As Gaucelm Faidit had said, the soldiery of Provence were the bane of all the captains of Christendom. Where a legion of them had passed, the countryside was left as the land of Egypt after the plague of locusts. As auxiliaries on a campaign they were impudent, tricky, unreliable. Held in reserve on a battlefield, they were sure to be found at the critical moment, safely sheltered from arrow showers or charging horse, casting dice or clustered about their jongleurs and troubadours, listening to some romans or sirvente. And the sweating courier who flung himself into their midst, delivering a command to advance, found them singularly unresponsive. They would, belike, commend him to the Fiend—and go on with their play. But if, as frequently happened in the Holy Land, the lines of the crusaders were placed in jeopardy by the thundering charge of Islam's warriors, and the Provençals were caught in the thick of it, they stood their ground with a certain commendable obstinacy, and with their singers chanting their loudest, the knights, squires, and men-at-arms held the line until the last voice had been silenced.

In the end it was the establishment of Ser Pons Vidal in Toulouse that paid for the equipment and service of twenty lusty varlets for Peire Vidal. In the hands of his father's journeyman furrier the business had prospered mightily, and the troubadour had little difficulty in giving its income as security for a loan (at a handsome rate of interest) of twenty gold marks.

At the head of the brave company that set out one June morning to take ship for Marseille rode Monsenher Vidal, in the green surtout of the knight-errant, his viol slung across his back and his good sword Durandal hanging at his side. Beside him rode Aimeric de Peguilha, his tongue never still for an instant, and the jongleur, Aimonet who, as the knight's squire, carried his lord's new coat of armor across his horse's saddlebow and held the black-and-silver banner of Vidal. Then came the foot soldiers wearing, in ill-fitted assortment, the liveries of the house of Vidal, and looking a merry troop of cut-throats. There followed sumpter mules laden with pillows, sheets, sacks of chaff covered with velvet for bedding, pots, pans, kettles, skins of wine, and all the household gear demanded by the provident Monjo. Somewhat in the rear, Gaucelm Faidit ambled comfortably in the company of the three damsels. At the front of the cavalcade there were decorum and music; at its rear, sallies of ribaldry and sharp retorts, mingled with lewd laughter.

"My Lord Barrale," said Peire Vidal to Aimeric, "he is at Marseille?"

"Waiting there for the Lion, master. The English cattle and the French vermin are coming down together from Chinon, and there are enough fat bishops and pursy archbishops with them to fill a two-tier galley! They say that when Richard, as count of Poitou, took the pilgrim's staff and wallet from Guillaume, archbishop of Tours, the staff cracked as he leaned on it. 'Thus,' says my lord the king coolly, 'is evident God's will that this crusade trust rather to the sword than to the staff!' He and God are never in the wrong! They say he sets up his court of justice every night and hangs evildoers before vespers. He doesn't sleep well unless he's been at a hanging! God give him good slumbers without the help of my carcass!"

"It is harsh," said the troubadour thoughtfully, "but it is justice; and there are few enough kings that care for justice. Is my lord's lady with him?"

"The French princess?"

"I mean," said Peire Vidal, "my Lord Barrale's not the king's." It was curious that before his audiart he felt such embarrassment he could not speak her name.

Aimeric de Peguilha said, "The Lady Adélasie, so the seneschal told me, bides at Les Baux and is close to the time of her lying-in. And he says she is of such prodigious size that——"

"Silence!" cried Peire Vidal angrily. "It is not for a stripling squire to discuss the condition of a lady!"

"But master," protested the jongleur, "it is considered an excellent sign when a noble lady's belly is——"

"Another word and I'll beat you!" shouted the master.

For a long while they rode gloomily in silence, the jongleur subdued beyond the plucking of his lute. He eyed his master sideways and at length ventured, "Richard the Lion heard of you, master, even in England."

"Why not in England?" said the troubadour in his lordliest manner.

"True," said the jongleur, "why not? And it is likely King Richard will give you a castle for a good song or two."

"I do not want his castles. But if he is a just king and desires to establish the kingdom of justice on earth, I will follow him to the last trumpet call!"

"Justice," said Aimeric de Peguilha, "is good enough for those that are dispensing it, but I'd rather have a castle!"

"You have many good songs in you, Aimeric de Peguilha," said Peire Vidal, "but no philosophy."

"My philosophy," said the audiart, "I keep inside my breeches." And Peire Vidal laughed then, for he loved his jongleur's whoreson impudence.

Narbonne hummed with the business and bustle of the new crusade. Among the motley multitude that thronged the city, the most were well-born youths eager to join the two kings and the emperor on the high enterprise of winning back the True Cross from Salâh-ed-Din al Malec an-Nasr Abu'l Modaffer Yussuf. There were also a few seasoned veterans wearing the white mantle and red cross of crusaders. Their faces held no illusion of adventurous dreams. In some the lines were covetous and rapacious; others had the baffled look of aging younger sons whose only heritage was the sword; and there were certain ones among them whose leaden features reflected the heavy burdens of their existence. To such as these the words of the Bishop of Puy were addressed: "For each of you who shall die, shall a bed be prepared with the Holy Innocents. In spacious Paradise your places are all prepared."

To the tumult of embarking Gaucelm Faidit was oblivious. Dragged bodily from a tavern where he was seeking a cure for sea-sickness, and stowed safely in the cramped quarters of a coasting esnecca, he had sunk at once into the pleasant lethe of his cups. There issued from his slowly heaving bulk only the mellow sounds that are the truest hymns to Bacchus. Down the river Aude, with pennons, banners, and gonfalons fluttering gaily in the breeze, to the accompaniment of viols, lutes, and voices raised in song, the oars of the esnecca beat their way.

The jongleurs were singing together. The rhythm of the song was that of lashing blades churning flowing water into flashing foam. The esnecca rocked as the lusty voices rose in thundering chorus, knights, squires, and soldiers joining in a mighty paeon—

> Parti de mal e à bien aturné
> Voil ma chançun a la gent fair oïr. . . .

> Cherish the good; drive sin away
> You who hearken to our good song,
> For it is God who maketh this lay
> Ripe for the hearts of the valiant and strong,
> To whom the Cross and Kingdom belong;
> Thus in His service may we repay
> Some of His debt, owing today!

> Counts and dukes and kings delay
> Penitence, but it is not for long
> They will enjoy their earthly sway,
> Amassing treasure by right or wrong—
> Death comes to bind them with his thong,
> Casts their crowns and their jewels away,
> And dungeons them until Judgment Day!

So it rang out on the clear air, canzo after canzo, until they sang, with a certain mournfulness:

> God give His blessing to all this throng
> Of gentle knights, loving they say
> Each other;—forget not His love, I pray!

At the conclusion of the chant there fell upon the ship a silence that was broken by a great bellow out of its bowels: "Christ's love! Is there no more to drink a-board?" It was Gaucelm Faidit awakening from his slumber.

At the palace of Viscount Barrale in Marseille the great hall was crowded with crusaders assembled to do honor to a singer and hom-

94

age to a king. Bernart of Ventadorn, the most famous living troubadour of his time, with his scant white hair and his deepset melancholy eyes, looked to be an old man; his hands trembled as they held the bow against his vielle. He was playing the air of a song known from Marseille to London Town, from Seville to Jerusalem: "Whene'er the lark's glad wings I see"; but he did not sing it. Henceforth others would sing his songs, for he was on his way to the abbey of Dalon in Perigord, there to end his days repeating aves and benedicites in the gray silence of monastic walls. This is the man, thought Peire Vidal, for love of whom the Lady Margarida of Eble was shut up in a tower by her husband; and long ago he was the lover of a queen, Eleanore of Aquitaine, whose son, Richard of the Lion Heart, now sits listening to his playing.

Richard, ignoring the singing, rose suddenly to his feet. He seemed a blond giant among the throng of courtly dwarfs who filled the palace of Barrale of Marseille.

"God's blood!" he said loudly, interrupting the audiart of Bernart. "There are naught but thieves in Provence! Fifty horses must I have, and do you know the price these rascal chapmen ask? Twelve pounds for a common palfrey! Four pounds for a scrawny sumpter mule! One greasy varlet has a pair of sorrels—bless you— at ten pounds each! In England, senhers, I paid but two marks for my own gallant lyard, and a mark each for thirty chargers in a mixed lot, but all of the best breeds!" He glared about him challenging an answer from his courtiers; but these, endeavoring to express at the same moment indignation and assent, succeeded merely in looking vacuous.

The white-haired troubadour rose quietly and, looking neither to right nor left, passed from the great hall.

"Is it to be endured," said Richard, "that God's holy work should be hindered by a pack of——?"

"My lord king," said the viscount suavely, "will have his horses —and at his own price. And, sire, may I urge that you do not give over to your agents the purchasing of necessities in Provence? Our traders, sire, have a keen scent for profit, unless their sensibilities are appealed to."

"Sensibilities!" snorted the king. "The king of England has no need to consider sensibilities!"

95

"Not in England, sire," said Barrale with faint irony. He glanced, as it were by accident, at Ranulf de Glanville, chief justiciar of England. That great man's face was stony, fixed in resignation or despair. "In England, Lord Ranulf," he continued gently, "I have heard that your customs and manners are different from our own?"

"They are, my Lord Barrale," said the justiciar briefly.

Hubert, Bishop of Salisbury, stole a sly look at his superior, the Archbishop of Canterbury, but the Most Reverend Baldwin dared not commit himself by so much as a smile. Nevertheless, the worthy prelates enjoyed the discomfiture of their lay compatriot who had so lately tendered, not without reluctance, some fifteen thousand pounds of English coin to the uses of the crusade.

"In England," said Richard, seating himself again, "there is everywhere a spirit of justice and of largesse, save among the filthy Hebrews—God's malison upon the lot of them!"

"Amen!" said the bishops soulfully, and "amen!" echoed the court heartily.

"In Provence, sire, the Jews supply all the tapers for our great festivals, and all our churches are lighted by their candles." The voice of Barrale was bland. "Indeed, were it not for the trade they bring us, we would be in a miserable state of barbarism, like our cousins of the north—I mean, the Germans!"

"The unbelieving dogs know well how to turn goods into treasure!"

"Aye, sire, as our troubadours turn catgut into heavenly music!"

To Peire Vidal it seemed that these simple speeches were like a passage at arms; and that every violent thrust and lunge of the English king was deftly turned aside by the viscount. All the more he loved Rainier! Yet there was something in the tawny Lion, with his youthful bulk and vigor, that caught the fancy: an open, bluff countenance that showed no guile or subterfuge; the blue, unfaltering Norman eyes begged no man's pardon for their arrogance; the lips a little scornful, as though impatient of all human weakness— seal of majesty!—and the large kingly ears. But it was a restless Lion. He neither sat, stood, nor lingered long in one place. When others spoke, he seemed not to hear, his words came without regard to what had been said, and Peire Vidal felt that any moment he might open his mouth and roar!

The knight of Belgueil wished mightily to speak to Barrale of his countess, but there was scant opportunity. The palace was in a continual turmoil. Couriers arrived hourly on the king's business; from Philip Augustus who—because of his distaste for the sea— was taking the land route to Genoa; from the English captains still struggling to get the vanguard of the host across the Rhône at Lyons, where a bridge had crashed, dropping an unfortunate company into rushing waters; from his mother, Queen Eleanore, who was reaching after him in this venture as in all others. A German landknecht came as envoy of the Emperor Frederick and convulsed the court by his uncouth manners and outlandish jargon. Emissaries came from Genoa, offering ships and convoy—at a stiff price —and Richard raged, cursing them for brigands and pirates, cursing his great fleet that had sailed so magnificently from England, and was nowhere to be seen, and casting special maledictions on the head of its constable, Richard de Camville. In the end he hired two large busses, or transports, the Pumbone and the Rustancri, for his own menie, and twenty well-armed galleys for his knights, to make the voyage to Cyprus.

On the day before the Assumption of the Virgin Mary, Peire Vidal had escaped with Gaucelm Faidit from the tumult of the court into the palace-close where Barrale of Marseille, who loved flowers and fruits as he did songs, had laid out a pleasant garden. Below them lay the cramped and crooked streets of Marseille, thronged with the soldiery, upon whose mail, pikes, spears, and shields the sun glinted. In the roadstead of the harbor red and bronze sails of busses, huge tub-like ursers and dromonds, beaked galleys at anchor, their tiers of oars drawn in, made a Jacob's coat of colors; skiffs laden with gear and baggage plied back and forth; cries and shouts, and an occasional trumpet call came up faintly to them. But in this little pleasance, watered by an artificial stream, were green cool alleys, clipped lawns, and beds of flowers, among pomegranates and nutmeg trees.

Gaucelm Faidit had spread his bulk in the shade of a plane tree and was sucking a plum. "Well," he said, spitting out the pit, "I have seen a great sight—the king of England and his tub!"

97

"Tub?" said Peire Vidal.

"A silver basin, and the bishops and the justiciar and the higher officers have wooden ones. They are all taking their tubs to the Holy Land. I would to God that Saladin might come upon them being scrubbed! There is one knight, Humphrey of Eugene, who must wash the king's feet and his neck and ears once a week. And he has a lord to shave him every Thursday before Mass! He has offered me a place as Marshal of the Whores, but nobody shall say I've been a king's pander! Our damozels—plague on these Englishmen!—have been approached with money to serve their barons, but the sweet wenches properly cast it in their faces! Can they not tell a wanton from a whore? If any of the swine lays a hand on my Guilhelma he shall feel my steel, if he be the constable of England! They will have it that money buys everything. It buys not me, senher! Have you seen our silken Folquet of Marseille pattering after the Lion?"

"I did not know he was here!"

Gaucelm Faidit leaned over, lowering his voice. "On business. His overweening ambition to be up in the world has so set him off, that now he aims at being an archbishop, no less! And with this bee in his cap, he crawls after Richard—this I have direct from a squire of the king's menie—and makes an offer of so-and-so much in gold marks and bezants for the office."

"Did not the king upbraid him for such impudence?"

"Not he! The Lion looks down upon him from his height of brawn and says coolly, 'To be a bishop will cost you twenty thousand pounds sterling, senher. An archbishop comes to thirty.' 'Jesu!' cries our troubadour. 'How should I have such sums?' 'That's not my affair,' says the king. 'You may buy in a county sheriff's tenure at five thousand.' 'My lord king,' says Folquet, 'surely you do not put up everything in England at auction?' 'I would sell London if I could find a buyer for it,' says the Lion. And now, since the merchant's son refused the dignity of sheriff, I think the king is sending him on a mission to the pope to get the Holy Father's blessing for the crusade, and I doubt not Brother Folquet will soon be rising toward holiness. God shrivel me if ever I must listen to his hymns!"

98

"Folquet . . ." mused Peire Vidal. "There is more venom in that man than music."

A squire in the livery of Richard's menie stood before them.

"Messer Vidal," he said curtly, "to attend His Majesty, the king of England. At once!"

As the troubadour rose his friend called out to the squire, "Say to your master, the king, if he wants Gaucelm Faidit, troubadour of Provence, he may come and find him emptying his bowels in the garden of Viscount Barrale, of Marseille!" To Peire Vidal he said, "Sant Julian be with you, my son! And forget not that every good troubadour of Provence is the equal of a king!"

With Richard the Lion was a smallish bearded man in faded green surcoat whose polished viol proclaimed him a troubadour. Though he had not the clerkly look of Arnaut de Maruelh nor the scholarly forehead of bitter-tongued Peire Cardinal, he was of their kinship in a certain aloofness from the world. Perhaps, thought Peire Vidal, looking at him curiously, he is a philosopher or an alchemist.

Without prelude the king said abruptly, "Messer Vidal, we must have a crusading song—a good ringing chant that will set them all in motion and keep them at it when they are weary and saddle-sore."

"Sire," said Peire Vidal, "there is an excellent old chant beginning, 'Cherish the good; drive sin away.' "

"I know that song," said Richard impatiently, "but it won't do for this crusade. There is too much mention of debts and penitence and the like! And it is in French, which my English common soldiers speak very ill, though of course it is the only tongue of all well-bred Englishmen. Do you, therefore, make us a new song and put into it plenty of rousing hatred of the Saracens. Let it be in the Provençal, or *langue d'Oc,* and Messer Arnaut Daniel, our court singer here, will turn it into barbarous Saxon for the common soldiers."

"Should not a version be made for the French, sire?" asked Arnaut Daniel.

"No!" cried the king testily. "Let the whoreson rascals make their own songs, if they have any troubadours—which they haven't! And, Messer Vidal, you will be good enough to have the chant ready tomorrow, for we weigh anchor the day following and my knights should be practising the piece on shipboard."

"I will do what I can, sire," said Peire Vidal uncertainly, "but I have not broken my muse to utter obedience. She comes as she lists."

"It's time you trained her to the spur, messer! Tomorrow at the hour of nones we shall hear the chant." Turning to Arnaut Daniel he said, "The matter of the Princess Aloysia will need your greatest skill. There are many things between the king, her father, and myself still to be settled before I wear the pledge of our late troth openly. I would have the song you send in my name in the form of a *novas,* or letter, the substance of it to the effect that I . . . hum . . . that I am at the present time dedicated to holiness and have turned my thoughts from the ways of the flesh, though of course I consider her tenderly as my sister in Christ, and so forth. Having put the matter in this seemly fashion it will be easy to close the song without compromising endearments."

Arnaut Daniel bowed as though he were used to such commissions. "Shall I be the bearer of your song, sire, or one of my jongleurs?" he asked.

Richard frowned, "Go yourself, my Arnaut, for if perchance my later dealings with wily Philip put me out of mind to marry her, I would have you at the French court for her consolation."

"Your wish is my command, sire!"

Peire Vidal left the audience chamber somewhat bewildered by the high diplomacies of love and song. It had never before occurred to him that a song could be served up, at instant notice, like a roast peacock on a silver trencher! He passed through the corridors of the palace, oblivious of the throng, seeking his stout friend and the wanton. Under the plane tree Gaucelm Faidit lay sleeping on his back. Guilhelma Monjo, in a bliaut of blue watered silk, sat fanning the flies from her lord's face. She wore a wreath of joy flowers in her dark, musky hair and her white breasts were dabbled with gold lights like some rare cloth of Champagne broidered in thread of gold. Her face was virginal as a maid's.

"This city of Marseille," she said in her soft husky voice to Peire Vidal, "is so filthy the flies are very bad. One cannot walk the streets for the refuse. The sailors are pretty, though. They wear caps and blouses of a hundred colors and they speak fifty strange tongues. There was one tall fellow, Edward Monthermer by name, who wore a fine coat of mail and said he was one of the king's butlers. He persuaded me to bed but Jesu! he was so clumsy I fled from him in my shift!" So her tongue rattled on. When her gossip ceased, Peire Vidal, to take his mind from the pleasant sight of her bosom, told of his interview with the king, and of Arnaut Daniel and their commissions.

"Richard the Lion," she said, "is too busy with projects to understand people. He is only clever in getting what he wants. And that Arnaut Daniel, I have heard him sing, and may you believe it, when he had finished I no more knew what his song was about than if he had sung in Moorish! Gaucelm Faidit, though he has a high opinion of Arnaut Daniel's craft in song, says he is more of a magician of words than a true singer." She looked down tenderly upon her master, as though he were a child, and said softly, "Gaucelm Faidit is like no other man on earth; I could poison all the women he has loved, and he knows it, and still he abides me. And I have a great inclination to every fine fellow I see, and he knows that, too, and says never a word of it. Though he is silly in his cups, he understands more than all the kings in their glory and the popes in their pomp!"

Two men were approaching down one of the green alleys. One was a knight in armor and the other Peire Vidal recognized, with a thump of the heart, was the Viscount Barrale. He was about to spring to his feet and salute Rainier when the viscount, turning abruptly on his heel, passed into the shrubbery. Peire Vidal felt the earth sway beneath him: it could not be that Lord Barrale . . . Christ Jesu! he saw me surely, and yet he would see no more of me . . . recognition, and dismissal . . . wherefore, and what . . . ? His thoughts groped blindly and desperately for enlightenment.

"My Lord Barrale," Guilhelma Monjo was saying, "has not yet made his peace with you? My friend! You are death-white!"

"Why," said Peire Vidal hoarsely, "should there be anything but peace between us?"

The wanton looked at him in astonishment. "You—you do not know, Peire Vidal?"

"I know nothing, save that my dear lord looked upon me with

stony eyes and turned away!" said the troubadour miserably. Suddenly his eyes were blazing. "Tell me! How have I angered him? Surely not that wretched kiss—why, that was all over and erased almost a year ago! He laughed, himself, as he spoke of it!"

"Since then, Peire Vidal, others have spoken of it."

"What of that? Is my Rainier one to take heed of idle tongues? Sant Dalmatz! tell me!"

He was on both knees, kneeling before her. Gaucelm Faidit stirred in his sleep. "Sh!" she whispered. "Do not wake my lord, and I will tell you, though I swore to him I'd not do it. He feared you'd take it very ill, and at the right time, he said, it would all be smoothed out."

"Tell me!" groaned the troubadour.

She laid her hand on his head and gently smoothed his hair, as a mother smooths the hair of a fretful child.

"There have been going about certain curious sayings concerning the reason for your leaving Les Baux. The kiss, they said, was nothing——"

"Nothing! Who said, and what——?"

She laid her hand upon his knee. "Sh! Listen, and do not twist your brows so fiercely. Well, there were odd kinds of tales spread abroad, and just lately a certain person retailed to the viscount a story that you had got the countess with child, and had stolen into her chamber and would have had her yet again, and that then she made a fearful outcry, to protect the unborn babe——"

"Oh Blessed Virgin! be merciful!"

Peire Vidal had sunk to the ground. He was pressing his face into the loam, biting at it, and his mouth was filled with dust.

"God's blood!" cried Gaucelm Faidit, sitting bolt upright. "What's this? Has the man gone mad?" He turned fiercely on his wanton. "Speak, hussy! Have you denied my friend your love and made him mad?"

"No, my lord! I swear, he has not sought it of me!" she quavered; "I did but tell him what is known to everyone——"

"Oh, you blabbing strumpet! You piece of erring female flesh!" He put his arm under his friend's neck, raised him up, and wiped off the smear of dirt about his lips. The knight of Belgueil seemed as one daft; his eyes rolled, tears streamed from them, sobbing shook his body. "Quick! you fornicating wench! Fetch us a stoup of strong wine!"

Guilhelma Monjo ran with the swiftness of one pursued by a demon. Her wreath of joy flowers fell off; for once she was in mortal dread of a beating at the hands of her lord and master.

Peire Vidal, touching his viol, was staring vacantly into the night. The restless sea stirred about the quays where torches flickered. The evil-smelling streets of Marseille seethed with soldiery and sailors, rollicking on the eve of departure for the crusade; there were brawls, bloodshed, shrieks and laughter in the brothels; taverns reeked with riotous throngs; cobbles echoed to the tread of men in mail. But of all these things Peire Vidal took no heed. He was finding surcease for his humiliation in his beloved viol. Soon he began to sing, softly, to himself:

> Friend, fair and gracious lady, chief among
> Things dear to me, my heart's humility brings
> A joy so keen, hearing your praises sung,
> Birds feel none sweeter when the new nest swings
> Gaily amid fresh green; and such sweet savor
> Love has for me that wakeful visions waver
> Nightlong about me, promising my lady's favor.
>
> My love, Domna Vierna, wisely taught
> My heart to find comfort and courage, savory
> Lessons of joy; and though some would have brought
> Our high devotion to a loathsome slavery,
> That evil will soon mend. Dear friend, my thought
> Makes you my comrade; for God gives you bravery
> For both of us, to make an end of knavery!

When he had made this song he was once more at peace and fell instantly and dreamlessly asleep.

At the hour of nones on the following day, the king held a great council of his lords, bishops, and captains. After a perfunctory benediction, Ranulf de Glanville began to read from a lengthy script:

103

"From our lord, the king of England's charter, given under his hand and seal at Chinon, in France. . . ." The bishops yawned, for it was secular business, but the captains listened attentively. ". . . to enforce the discipline necessary to the conduct of this most holy and righteous crusade. . . . And the seventh article of these regulations: let a convicted thief be shorn like a professional pugilist, his body covered with hot tar, and feathers applied to every part . . . and there shall not be allowed at any time in the course of this crusade cursing, nor dicing by sergeants, mariners, or servants. For knights and clerks the limit of play in any one day shall be twenty soldi, but the kings of England and France may play for any stakes. . . ."

Gaucelm Faidit, at Peire Vidal's elbow, grunted. "A plague upon their crusade! I'll not be mulcted by an Englishman for gaming! Twenty soldi! Let him stick them——"

"Hush!" said a knight in the livery of Toulouse. "The king's informers are all about us!"

"If they have the ears of a jackass and nose of wolf, I care not!" growled the paunchy singer. "God's blood! We may not dice above twenty beggarly soldi nor curse a comrade! How then shall we pass the time when we are not killing infidels?"

"Beware the Lion's claws, friend!" the knight whispered sharply. "He is speaking!"

The king's voice was high and penetrating; like a mime's, thought Peire Vidal, in the vulgar street shows of Arles, and quite humorless.

". . . and to right this great injustice against God and my sister, Joan, who was the lawful queen of Sicily, and has been basely robbed of her dowry and hereditaments by the nefarious usurper, Tancred, we are minded now to turn our course toward Sicily, firm in the conviction that God and the saints will favor an enterprise so laudable. . . ."

"Sicily!" muttered Gaucelm Faidit. "Breath of Christ! May I be hung if they find me in Sicily among the Lombards and Griffons!"

"There's much gold and treasure in Sicily," said the knight of Toulouse, "and we'll not come away empty-handed!"

Gaucelm Faidit made an uncivil noise. "If I want gold, senher,
I need not fight Greeks for it!"

There was other business, interminable and tedious, then at
length the justiciar dismissed the formal council, bidding the lords
and bishops remain, at the king's pleasure, for further entertainment. Peire Vidal's heart sank as the time for his singing neared;
he would have fled but Gaucelm Faidit had him by the arm.
"Courage, my friend! Remember, no troubadour of Provence need
duck to a king!"

The knight of Toulouse was quoting in their ears:

> "He that will in Court dwell
> Must curry Favel;
> And he that will in Court abide
> Must curry Favel back and side!"

"Let the king's groom curry the king's horse, not we!" said Gaucelm Faidit gruffly.

After the departure of the captains, clerks, and lesser knights,
an officer of the court announced that the assemblage would hear a
chant, composed especially for this crusade, by the troubadour,
Peire Vidal, attached to the king's household. There was some
whispering among the courtiers. The king was deep in conversation with the archbishop of Canterbury. At length, as Peire Vidal
was not to be seen, he raised his head, saying, "Where is this
Vidal?"

"Where is Vidal?" repeated the officer, looking about the hall.

"I am here," said Peire Vidal.

"Come forward and sing your piece, at the king's command!"
said the officer testily.

"I have made no chant, monsenher!"

The king's voice, astonished and annoyed, split the silence.
"What! No chant?"

Gaucelm Faidit shoved his stout bulk to the fore.

"Sire," he said, " if I may be so bold, among these gentlemen
and knights and lords, and the reverend bishops, my good friend,
Monsenher Peire Vidal of Belgueil and Toulouse, howbeit he is
most dutifully and worshipfully inclined toward your gracious and

noble self, was put in a quandary at the very moment of beginning the composition of the chant by—I dare not reveal the precise nature of it, since a very great lady is involved—a choice between the dictates of love and conscience. And, sire and noble gentleman, as a knight of love, he had no alternative! He has written, therefore, a song of no mean quality which, if you are so disposed, he will sing to you, and he resigns its merit to your worthy judgment!"

King Richard frowned, then he smiled, as though putting aside the pettiness of lesser men and kings. "Gaucelm Faidit," he said, "we approve your able defence of the Monsenher Vidal, and we command him to sing his song, on condition that, when love is not so importunate, he shall give himself to the chant!"

"Sire," said Peire Vidal in confusion, "I will do so, if it will please you."

So then he took his viol and placed his bow against the strings, and began to sing. By degrees the court ceased to whisper and even the king gave up talking to the archbishop.

"... for God gives you bravery
For both of us, to make an end of knavery!"

He had never sung so well, with such fullness of heart. The courtiers smiled politely and a little uncomfortably, as though they deprecated the utterance of such simple and forthright emotions, and they gave the song the proper measure of applause—light, and quickly ended.

"Monsenher Vidal," said the king graciously, "you have done so well by this lady that we expect much more of you when you sing for Christ's sake."

As the troubadour was making his way toward the door, someone touched him on the shoulder. It was the knight of Toulouse, and he was with the Viscount Barrale.

"Peire Vidal," said the knight, "you have gained great mastery of your craft. When you are done with crusading, may we hear more of your singing at Bargarde!"

"My Lord Rai——" cried Peire Vidal.

"Silence! I am here as a knight—observing my enemy. . ."

And Barrale said, "You have made a good song, Peire Vidal!"

That was all, but the way he said it made the tears start in the eyes of Peire Vidal; and he seized the viscount's hand and kissed it.

"Rainier, I——" he could say no more.

"Enough, Rainier. We understand each other!"

Gaucelm Faidit dragged him off. "Now, my knight of love, for a tun of the best wine of Marseille—and we'll drink to the discomfiting of that son of Satan, that miscreant, Folquet!"

Then Peire Vidal knew the bearer of the tale.

Chapter Nine

To the singing of the old crusading chant, "Cherish the good; drive sin away," the little fleet of dromonds and galleys sailed leisurely along the coast of Italy as far as Pisa. There Richard, fretful at the handling of the Pumbone, removed himself and his staff to the Rustancri. A delegation waited on him to urge a visit to Rome, but without reason he bluntly refused their proffers of entertainment. "He was on God's urgent business, that gave no time for dallying!" However, at Naples they lingered a full fortnight, during which time the king made many trips to observe the wonders and curiosities of this region. And here he changed to the Pumbone again, for the Rustancri had a torn sail whose flapping disturbed his meditations. At Salerno they put in and the king announced that the cursed Genoese vessels were no better than tubs; he would ride by horseback down the coast the rest of the way. The justiciar and others of the nobles remonstrated, urging that part of Italy, especially Calabria, was dangerous to a small body of men; it was torn by petty wars and overrun by brigands, and to disembark the entire force would be no small undertaking. The Lion roared at them, they were base cowards, fearful of peasants! He would go alone—by the saints!—yes, alone, without guard or menie of any kind. He would show them that a king was no such weakling as his courtiers! "And God Himself will be my bodyguard!"

Peire Vidal, stirred to his depths at this display of kingly courage, cried, "Sant Dalmatz! That's a brave speech, my lord king! Take me with you!"

"You shall go with me, Peire Vidal," said the king, "and until we reach Messina, God willing, you shall be my lord high chancellor!"

It was a high-sounding title but the duties of the office were, the troubadour discovered, not a little onerous. They consisted chiefly in securing lodging and victuals—such as they were—at the few wretched inns and miserable monkish hospices on their journey, and in listening respectfully to the fitful and erratic speeches of the king.

The king and his chancellor met with no adventures of any kind on their way. There were neither brigands nor robber knights, and little worse than churlish and niggardly hospitality to irk them. Then they left Mileto and, with the end of their journeying close at hand, an incident occurred that almost deprived England of its king, and Provence of its most notable troubadour. They were passing through a small walled town whose appearance seemed especially unprepossessing when they heard a strange piercing cry from a house that fronted on the narrow street, scarce wide enough for the passage of their two horses. Instantly the king leaped from his destrier, tossed the bridle to Peire Vidal, and strode through an open doorway into the dark interior. In a moment he emerged, bearing on his wrist a falcon. The bird was still uttering its savage and doleful lamentation as the king sprang into the saddle.

"A falcon!" he said complacently. "And mine died on the way from England, thanks to the stupidity of my falconer!"

"You made a happy purchase, sire," said Peire Vidal. "They must not have haggled over it."

"The king's bargain!" said Richard the Lion briefly. "Let us make all speed from this moldy rookery. It has a plague stink!"

At the very moment of putting spurs to his horse there issued from the wooden pile behind them two strapping knaves who, with surprising agility, leaped at the horses' bridles, shouting the while, "Thieves! Robbers!" and other maledictions in Italian. Peire

Vidal's horse, a mettlesome favel, lunged sideways, throwing his assailant to the ground, but the citizen on the king's side, hanging stoutly to his bridle, continued to bellow imprecations. This clamor in an instant emptied the surrounding nests of their creatures. Out they came tumbling, like black ants from a hill, while the king sought to wrest his mount free. The troubadour, meanwhile, had drawn his sword from its scabbard. The blade flashed through the air and descended flat, with a resounding thwack, on the bare arm of the hardy scullion, who let go his hold, uttering a howl of rage and pain. By now the dark alley was in pandemonium.

In a quick glance, looking toward escape, Peire Vidal glimpsed the dull sheen of scythe-like guisarmes and of deadly fauchards. Luckily the space was too confined for the free use of these weapons. In the confusion, however, the two riders had got completely turned about, and though, for the moment, they had thrust their way out of the throng, the lanes on every side seemed blocked. Then Peire Vidal saw a way clear and cried, "Back, sire! We must ride through them! Follow me and shout as I shout!"

He pulled his favel up on its haunches, wheeled, and pressed his spurs into the horse's flanks, shouting at the top of his lungs, "Au hazard, Balthasar!"

"Au hazard, Balthasar!" shouted the king as they bore down on the huddled rabble. The pack, with screams of fright, scattered like partridges, seeking the walls, and they drove through them in a whirl of hoofbeats, their swords fanning either side. At full gallop they traversed the little town, clattered over its drawbridge where men-at-arms stared goggle-eyed, and headed, still galloping, toward the sea. When the walls of the town were hidden, the king drew rein. "Well conceived, that bit of strategy of yours, Peire Vidal!" he panted. "It is a plan I have often used in battle—when outnumbered, attack!" He was examining the falcon tenderly. As he smoothed its ruffled feathers, the bird, whose fierce eyes showed a sly intelligence, nestled peacefully within the royal fist. "A ger-falcon!" said the king triumphantly. "I did well to snatch it from its base confinement among churlish serfs! In England they would be well punished for possessing the noble bird. We let none below the grade of knight have them." From a metal collar about the falcon's neck hung a broken chain. Peire Vidal now understood what was meant by a "king's bargain"; it was, to take forcibly, and without payment, what the king desired to have.

"Sire!" he cried suddenly. "We are followed!"

From behind a clump of gnarled oaks, across a salt meadow, a group of horsemen had emerged—five, six, a dozen. They wore hauberks of chain mail, and carried lances and croquepois, which were like fish spears.

"The provost's guard!" growled the king. "I'll tell the filthy knaves——"

He had turned his horse toward the company that was cantering toward them and had his hand on his sword's pommel.

"Tell them nothing!" said Peire Vidal in alarm. "We can't stay to argue with those wolves. They've smelled blood and plunder!"

"Then let them come and try our steel," said the king stubbornly. "Two knights are a match for a dozen cowardly thralls!"

"Not if they get one of their beastly hooks into you, my lord king!"

"It shall not be said, the Lion turned tail!"

"A lion caught in the toils of the hunters loses his skin, sire! I have no mind to be flayed alive!" pleaded the troubadour. As he spoke another body of horsemen swung into view. They were waving flails and shouting, and they came from a direction that would cut off retreat.

"God's blood, sire, we must run for it—down, down to the sea-shore!"

They broke through clumps of furze and tangled sea-grass, plunged headlong over slippery boulders, and, their horses snorting terror, gained the pebbly strand. Here the riding was easier but the footing treacherous among slimy rocks and quaking sands. Hot on their flanks rode their pursuers, yelling like demons. Their own horses, better bred by far than those of the motley soldiery, were nevertheless in poor condition after more than a week's riding and soon gave signs of being winded. Their flanks heaved, the slaver from their foaming bits was tossed back and flecked the armor of the two riders.

Their way was barred now by a jutting cliff that threw its beak sheer into the sea. Indolent billows creamed at its base, the sheen of silver sand ceased in that darkling shadow, and death rode close at their heels. Without a thought more than, "It is the end, but better drowning than disemboweling!" Peire Vidal spurred his gallant beast straight into the sea, forgetting, for the first time, Richard, the king of England; and Richard followed. The horses staggered. A wave took them up and let them down. There was still ground beneath. And suddenly they had rounded the headland and were stepping slowly through the sucking tide toward dry land. Overhead loomed the sheer walls of a great fortress, to which a crooked path wound up from the beach.

It was not a castle but the fortified priory of La Bagnara. The Griffon monks spoke only Greek but Peire Vidal, recalling what scraps he could of the little learning he had got at Monpeslier, gathered that they were near the Far of Messina. That night, after a meager refection of lentils and black bread, the king and his chancellor lay side by side on thin pallets stuffed with straw, and as they fell asleep they heard the chanting of the cenobites engaged in endless liturgies.

The king, tossing restlessly on his hard bed, murmured:

> *Chevaliers en ce monde-cy*
> *Ne peuvent vivre sans soucy;*
> *Ils doivent le peuple defendre*
> *Et leur sang pour la Foi espandre.*

> Knights, in this world of theirs,
> Cannot live without cares;
> They defend the folk with their sword
> And give their blood for the Word.

But this philosophic comfort was lost to Peire Vidal, who was already trumpeting through his nose.

The next day at dawn, having enjoyed the hospitality of the bearded monks and procuring from them a little esnecca, they were rowed across the Far of Meschines and put in at a stone beacon tower at its entrance, which was called the Pharos. There were no signs, on all that blue and placid sea, of the galleys or of the English fleet, and the king, pacing with restless lion strides, fumed and fretted, talking to himself and to the troubadour. But Peire

Vidal, content with safety, flat on his belly, gazed at the quivering languor of the sea, and at the rocky outlines of those two promontories that once, they said, in the days of the ancients, had been devouring monsters, Scylla and Charybdis. The voice of the Lion was raised in fulminations against his justiciars of the navy, and against the fourteen captains of his hired fleet; against the bargaining of Philip Augustus; against the usurper, Tancred, who had defrauded his sister of her dowry; and, strangely, against the Greek monks who had given them shelter.

"It is a great and a wicked misprision of justice," he said, "that these false priests, worshiping idols and obeying the anti-pope at New Rome, should be allowed the name of Christian, and that they should spread their foul and carnal gospels even upon the soil of Italy! I am not sure but that it would be an action welcome to God and the Holy Spirit if we should at once destroy and wholly extirpate all the abodes of these vile worshipers of Abaddon, and swell the loathsome hosts of purgatory with the souls of the diabolical Griffon friars!"

Peire Vidal said nothing, for there is little to be gained in argument with one who has not slept well, particularly if he be a king. Below them, on the shore, the boatmen of the monks, in faded red blouses, lounged against the thwarts of the esnecca. From a door in a tower nearby three men emerged, wearing leather gambesons and armed with short curved swords. They might have been Griffons or even Saracens, so dark they were, and Peire Vidal loosed his sword. But the tenders of the beacon, or men-at-arms, made no motion to molest the armed knights. Suddenly one of them raised an arm and shouted, pointing to the entrance of Le Far, and there the English sails blossomed on the sea. It was a gallant sight they made as they bore in, warping toward the shore with the rhythmical beat of oars, the larger vessels in two and three tiers, and the swifter, single-tiered smacks in the lead, plowing the blue with foaming beaks, a hundred ships, in squadrons, decked with pennons and gonfalons, hung so thick along the bulwarks there was not a hand's space between them, and each bearing the blazon of a lord or knight!

The king sprang to his feet, his eyes gleamed, and his thin, well-formed lips were drawn in a tense smile of exultant triumph.

Horses could be heard stamping and neighing in the holds of the great ursers. "Forty steeds in each!" cried the king. "And forty footmen, with their arms and gear. Fourteen sailors to a ship, and they have, each, thirteen anchors, thirty oars, two sails, and triple ropes of every kind!" He smote his mailed hands together gleefully. "Provisions for a year! There are fourteen treasure ships, laden with a king's ransom in each bottom!"

Blood of the Cross, thought Peire Vidal, he's an inspired clerk, as well as a crusading king!

"With such a fleet, and my stout English churls and a few good captains, I could carve out an empire in the East that would dwarf New Rome!" the king was communing half aloud, "and need never again set eyes on foggy England!"

Peire Vidal took him by the arm and they went down together to the boat. As they rowed toward the nearest ship, that had laid to and was dropping its anchors, the monastic seamen began to sing in Greek, and the troubadour, intent upon the strange melody, for the moment forgot all else. There was something curiously familiar in the air, or rather, in the mode of the song. Then he remembered the chant of the six virgins as they went down to the well of Venus:

> *A l'entrada del tems clar, eya,*
> *Per joya recommencer, eya,*
> *E per jelos irritar, eya,*
> *Vol la regina mostrar*
> *Qu' el es si amoroza.*
>
> *A la via, a la via, gelos,*
> *Laissez nos, laissez nos*
> *Ballar entre nos, entre nos!*

The words had been in Provençal, but the air was an ancient one, likely, pagan. And these Greek sailors were more than half pagan. They made a sign upon their foreheads, looking fearfully toward Scylla and Charybdis. Peire Vidal looked, too, and it seemed to him that he saw, rising from the crinkly foam, the image of that great goddess who had accompanied him on his fevered first journey to Les Baux. Her face was dim and inscrutable, and her head was turned in the direction of distant Cyprus.

It was this image, and not one of the True Cross, that later held him to the crusade, even when he was weary to death of its futilities.

Throughout the fleet there was great rejoicing at the safe return of the king. The main squadron had put in at Marseille and finding their lord gone, had coasted down the shores of Italy until they overhauled the dromonds and galleys. When the captains were informed of the king's extraordinary excursion, they were not greatly surprised; most of them had served on campaigns with him before. That day of the congregation of the great fleet was a busy one. Besides the celebration in honor of the king, a Mass was said and a dirge sung for the soul of the Emperor Frederick Barbarossa, tidings having just been brought that he had drowned on his way to Acre, more than three months before; and these liturgies concluded, elaborate preparations were made for a landing at Messina the day following.

As for the incident of the gerfalcon, since the king never at that time or later made mention of it, Peire Vidal also kept his silence. But the boatmen of the Griffon friars, who had got the tale from the baffled members of the provost's guard, blabbed to sailors of the fleet, and by the time it was borne to the ears of the officers the exploit had undergone such magnification as that the king had fought single-handed with thirty armed horsemen, had slain five of them, and had put the rest to flight. The troubadour's part remained a matter of conjecture. It was supposed that he had conducted himself honorably by singing during the affray. Peire Vidal himself was glad to be once more at ease and not unwilling to have the king off his hands. The great of this world, he thought, are better at a distance, for they make poor company on a journey. What a difference, if his companion had been Rainier! There had been no lack, then, of good fellowship!

At the hour of nones, when he was sunning himself contentedly on top of the chart-house of one of the dromonds, there came to him a minor officer of the king's menie with a message from no less a personage than Sir Richard de Camville, commander of the great fleet. "Messer Vidal," said this emissary, "my lord the Admiral has heard you well spoken of by our great king, and out of consideration for your talent, intends to employ you in a most signal service."

"I hope it is no great labor he will have of me for I am truly weary," said Vidal. "After ten days' hard riding my bones are all of an ache!"

"On a crusade one does not speak of weariness!" said the other curtly.

"Very well," said the troubadour. "I am not weary, but I am mightily fatigued!"

"The king's business brooks no light answers! You are urged—*commanded*, Messer Vidal—to prepare a suitable song or chant for the great occasion of the king's entrance into Messina on the morrow."

"H'm. . . ."

"Let there be no humming!" said the officer tartly. "And be good enough to arouse yourself to the magnitude of this honor. You are to go in the king's own ship, and as it enters the harbor of Messina, and before all the French, Lombards and Griffons——"

"And Jews and Saracens, monsenher! Don't forget them!"

"——before all the assembled multitude of the city, you will sing of the king's largesse and nobility toward his friends, and of his unrelenting severity toward his enemies, recounting, as is suitable, the tally of his brave and astonishing deeds."

"When he was at war with his father?"

The officer paused and stared fiercely at the troubadour. "Messer troubadour," he said bitingly, "you have little talent for politics!"

"True," said Peire Vidal, "for I do not like the nature of this song. I have never yet made a good romance."

"You refuse this commission?" cried the officer angrily.

Peire Vidal raised his head and said blandly, "I am not in the mood of singing. Seek elsewhere!"

The officer swung on outraged heel. His mail clinked spitefully across the deck. Peire Vidal closed his eyes blissfully and fell asleep. As he did so there floated through his head the first phrase of a new song:

"After long absence, when
I come again to you. . . ."

The citizens of Messina were in expectation of seeing the simultaneous arrival of the two greatest monarchs of Christendom, Their Majesties of France and England. Mindful of a long-standing hatred of former Norman conquerors, they swarmed about the quays and perched like flies on the walls, and in their eyes shone hostility mingled with curiosity. But Philip of France was already in the city. He had put in at the harbor the previous evening in a borrowed Milanese galley (having delayed sailing as long as possible because of his queasy stomach) and scuttled ashore in the dark, preferring to let the English king receive the city's welcome, such as it might be, for he well knew the Sicilians' ancient grudge against all Northern invaders.

The king of England, though he publicly berated "that scurvy turntail, France," was not wholly displeased at the defection of his ally. It left the stage clear for his entrance. And nothing was lacking to make that entry effective. The great fleet filled the strait of Le Far, spread out fanwise, the swift, two-tiered esneccas in the lead, followed by slower ursers, all in even formation, and brought up in the rear by the more unwieldy busses and dromonds that came in under half-sails—huge tub-like vessels constantly losing way in the vexing currents. The ships were crowded with hardy looking warriors and knights in glittering mail, and they were decked with countless pennons and banners. At the apex of the formation moved the king's ship. It had neither gonfalons nor escutcheons but, standing at the prow, was the king himself, holding his shield that bore two lions passant gardant in pale. His coat of mail gleamed silver and was partly covered by a surcoat richly embroidered in small silver stars, a garment of Saracen manufacture, with the white cross of an English crusader sewn on the left shoulder. His helm was down and his right hand held his great double-edged sword, made in Toledo by the Moors. Behind him were grouped the royal body-guard of arbalestiers, their heavy cross-bows wound taut and charged with deadly quarrels. "So came the king to the shore amid such blowing of horns and trumpets that all the city was alarmed at the sound."

This pageant passed all unnoticed by Peire Vidal, who, by order of the king, had been placed in durance within the ill-smelling hold of one of the dromonds because of his failure to contribute an appropriate song for the occasion. He was not, however, without pleasant company, for he found there the greater part of his Provençal troop. They had gambled, cursed each other vilely, had even come to blows, until the ship's guard, smothering their own hearty oaths at such a pack of seasoned knaves, had thrown them all together and left them to rats and bilge water. By the light of a holy candle stolen from a church in Genoa they made merry, and when the knight of Belgueil, their captain, was cast among them, they hailed him with joyous and bawdy imprecations. At once they demanded a song, and Peire Vidal having luckily secured his precious viol, was nothing loth to please them with several ribald pieces.

Following these merry catches, he tuned his viol to his latest air in a more serious vein.

Tant ai longamen cercat
So qu' obs no m' avia
Qu' enaissi o ai trobat
Com eu o queria

Blessings I have paid for dearly
All these long years (hungered nightly,
Victim of my longings, clearly
Little valued!) now come lightly
At my summons. Friends have wondered,
Seeing how my gains were scattered—
How I fumbled, stumbled, blundered—
Nothing gained that really mattered!
Oh spendthrift life! A fool at folly's wooing
Feeds on delusions, blind to his undoing!
From all the uses of sweet pleasure and insistent
Honor, I am cut off; Love, too, seems strangely distant.
Body of mine, and my too ardent boldness
In love, consume my heart; but hers, the coldness!

There were many stanzas, but they listened with glowing eyes, tasting the words to themselves and savoring them. When the song ceased they were silent, until one heavy-browed rascal with a scarred and pock-marked visage said, "Monsenher Vidal, I swear by Sant Dalmatz and Sant Julian and the Heart of the Blessed Virgin, you make better songs than did ever Cercamon, who saw the world, or his audiart, Panperdut, the Lost Rag, who was slain by the nobles for his singing—may the Fiend keep them still in hell!"

And the whole company, with hearty oaths, approved the statement. Thus, while below decks they talked and sang and spoke of love, God, the ways of false priests, and whether there was any truth in the Albigensian creed, the dromond bore into the harbor of Messina amid such blaring of trumpets as had not been heard in that place since the coming of the Romans to the island, and that was long lost to the memory of men.

Early the next day Richard the Lion set up a gallows for thieves just outside the English camp. His judges delegate spared neither age nor sex. For the subjects of the English king there was scourging or branding, and for the subjects of Tancred, hanging. Even the French malefactors were seized upon by Richard's men. In a short while the Sicilians had begun to think ill of the English. As for Philip the Lamb, he secretly cursed the zeal of his ally.

Chapter Ten

Just a week after the king of England entered the harbor of Messina with his fleet, he recrossed Le Far and, with a body of soldiers, took the monastery of La Bagnara, turned out the Griffon friars, and installed his sister, the deposed Queen Joan, whom Tancred of Sicily had permitted to depart with her bed-gear and one million terrins of expense money. Leaving her there with a guard, the Lion next seized the "Griffons' Minster," a tower on an island in Le Far, put its garrison to death, and made it a storehouse for the fleet.

All this came to the ears of Peire Vidal through the Lady Rambauda, lately wife and now widow of Sir Rostaala of Biolh, or Beuil. This knight had led a dissipated and violent life, and, being heavily burdened with debts, desired to clear his conscience and his material obligations by taking the cross. At the moment of setting out on the crusade, however, he fell grievously ill, and on his death-bed commissioned his lady, whom he had greatly wronged and loved, to be his deputy on the pilgrimage, and thus rescue his soul from everlasting torment. He gave the cross into her hands—fair and dainty they were, too!—and entreated her to bear it to Jerusalem for him.

So, to release her husband's soul from its burden of mortal sin, the Lady Rambauda took staff and script and assumed the gray woolen robe of a pilgrim, which agreeably set off the paleness of her face, the redness of her full lips, and her eyes that had the gray of vair. She had the sign of the cross pricked upon her left breast. The great flowing wealth of her reddish hair was clipped and tucked under the pilgrim hat. Yet even that gave her a provoking air of piety that would afford her protection among the rougher element of the crusade and would hardly discountenance the interest of the more courteous. It was this lady who discovered the troubadour in the dark belly of the dromond on which she had embarked at Marseille.

On the day following the debarkation of the English army at Messina one of Peire Vidal's followers was stricken suddenly with a mysterious malady and it soon became evident that his condition was serious. The ship's commander, Sir William de Forz of Oléron, being well disposed toward his Provençal prisoners and also fearful of a visitation of the plague, sent at once to Messina for Gilles de Corbeil, court physician to Philip Augustus. This learned medico arrived shortly and after examining the victim, began to deliver a Latin poem of his own composition having to do, presumably, with the proper treatment of the case.

"You, Messer Vidal, are out of Provence, where the art of medicine is little practised," he said pompously, turning to the troubadour at the conclusion of the sonorous recitation.

"There is a very good school of medicine at Monpeslier," said the troubadour. "I know, for I studied law there."

"Faugh!" said the physician. "Jews that got their quackeries from the infidel Moors! There is no true school but that of Salerno, which has given us the great Copho, the illustrious Platearius, and the *Antidotarium* of Nicolaus Prepositus, a work of stupendous learning!"

"That may well be," said Peire Vidal, "but will you give this poor fellow something to ease him of his extreme pain?"

"Nay," said the doctor solemnly, "for it is now approaching ebb tide, and whatever he takes into him will only be drawn out by the efflux of the waters about him. I understand the nature of this man's affliction; the essences of his heart and of his liver have held unlawful congress and it will need a heavy purge to draw them apart. In a few hours, when I have compounded the necessary ingredients, I will send my apprentice with the powders and instructions how to administer them." So saying, he recited another verse in Latin and took his departure.

In a short time, with the ebbing of daylight, it was plain that Ugo of the Wood, as he was known, would not live to see another dawn upon Le Far. The captain would have summoned a priest for him but there was none left on any of the ships and it was night and the waters filled with terrors of the unknown, so he thought of the fair pilgrim and sent her down to ease the sufferer in his last moments. She descended into the dimly lit hold of the vessel where she found Peire Vidal singing in a low sweet voice to the dying man. He sang of the golden land, a song composed for the golden lady of Les Baux:

> When the wind rides over-seas
> From Provence, I taste its savor
> Eager-breath'd, and count a favor
> Any crumbs of news; they please
> Me, my Queen's devoted slave,
> So entirely that I crave
> Endlessly to have them spoken.

> Should one think of her an hour
> One would cease to be forlorn
> All that day; for she was born—
> Yes! and lives in pleasure's bower
> Joyously. None may overpraise
> Her beauty and her gracious ways,
> Her spirit, lofty and unbroken!

The pilgrim knelt beside the sack of chaff on which the stricken soldier lay. She held in her hand a consecrated wafer and a small taper that had been blessed; gently forcing open the stiffening fingers, she placed the taper within them, and lighted it; this was to ward off demons who were hovering about, eager to snatch the wavering soul. She held up the cross, but Ugo of the Wood did not open his eyes, and she said, "Our true Father, who never speaks falsely, who raised from the dead Sant Lazarus, and protected

122

Daniel among the lions, deliver the soul of this being from all perils that through his sins he has in life contracted". "Amen!" said Peire Vidal. So, as they prayed together, the man Ugo died. She laid the wafer on his heart, and all night the two of them watched and prayed beside the body. At dawn of the next day Ugo of the Wood was taken to the headland of the Pharos and buried there, with his feet and face pointing toward Provence.

"It would be more Christian," said Peire Vidal to the Lady Rambauda, "to let him face the Holy Land, but I am sure his spirit would rather return to Provence."

The dromond was emptied of its prisoners when the captain of the fleet was ordered to release all fighting men and send them to join the English; but, since the troubadour was in no temper to see the Lion soon, he let it be known to Sir William that he was more of a singer than fighter, and a better hand at a bout of wine than either. The knight-commander readily overlooked the tarrying of his most distinguished prisoner and, moreover, made no inquiries about the fair pilgrim. Daily, a steward was despatched to the hold bearing cates and delicacies and bottles of the best wine provided for the crusaders.

Peire Vidal's confinement on the dromond was now not only lightened, it was made miraculously sweet. Of all the days of his life, these few were the most singular—for, enclosed in a darkness lit only by a single taper, they knew neither day-time nor night-time, and moments became years, and hours, in turn, were moments. He enjoyed converse with her even more than the pleasure of their bodies joined together—and that was curious, seeing that their speech was tranquil and quite lacking in the tremulous fury of love. Thus, when she was closest to him and their limbs so entwined that he knew not whose flesh were whose, it might be that she would say, "Peire Vidal, how do your songs come to you?"

He, startled, said, "How? I do not know . . . . They come. Like wind or rain. Out of the deserts and forests of the soul perhaps."

"And how large is the soul?"

"Sometimes it is no bigger than the wing of a gnat; and sometimes it will not be contained within the bounds of oceans. Madomna Rambauda, now with my eyes closed, I see ships and fleets sailing through your body, and cities standing with many towers! You have a large soul, madomna!"

"Do you love me, Peire Vidal?" she asked suddenly.

Again he was perplexed. He had not thought to ask himself that question.

"Why are you silent?" She snatched her cross and placed it in his hands. "Answer!" she cried peremptorily. "On God's holy relic!"

He thought quickly of the thirty-one articles of the *Laws of Love,* and there seemed not one that applied to this situation unless it might be the Twenty-sixth: "Love can deny nothing to love."

But how can one measure denial until it has been tested? Perhaps he would deny her in something; very likely.

Finally he said, very slowly, as though fumbling for words, "You are dear to me, madomna, and I thank God and King Richard for having brought you to me, and will pray for the soul of Ugo for that same reason. But love? . . ."

She laid her finger on his lips.

"Enough! I would not have you foreswear yourself. If you loved me, even by the tiniest fraction, it would be a sin to deny it!"

She sat up on the rough pallet that was stuffed with straw and drew about her white nakedness the coarse cloak of drugget.

"Some day," she said reflectively, "I shall have returned from the Holy Land and so assuaged the eternal torment of my sinful husband. . . . Biolh is a pleasant place, with many rich fiefs, and I shall want," she said firmly, "someone to be lord of them."

But he bethought himself of the Eleventh Article— "It is not becoming to love those ladies who only come with a view to marriage"—and he said, "Madomna, I do not know what way my life will run, but though you are fair, noble, and precious, you are not the lady of my love. She is Madomna Adélasie des Baux, wife to Lord Barrale."

She rose abruptly and passed from him, nor did he see her again for three days and nights. But he was not greatly concerned, for a new song had slipped into his mind and was plucking at the strings of his viol. Yet it was an obdurate song and refused to show more than glimpses of its configuration; it was wilful as a haughty courtesan who reveals much, but not all of her charms.

"Knowest thou the reason of my measureless love for her? Verily, because in all my life I have seen none so fair, so matchless, so angelic; therefore I hold myself possessed of great bounty, rich in the friendship of her valorous spirit!"

Though his new song was for his old love, he was not sorry to see his new love when she reappeared. She was quiet and submissive, surrendering herself to his caresses with a kind of finality, as one who looks upon the brightness of the world before entering a convent. His heart flowed out to her, he was enraptured, and he said, "I do believe, madonna, that I could find it in my heart to love you, you are so gracious, kind, and debonair!"

She said, "I came to tell you that you must now return to the king."

"What is that you are saying?"

"Richard the Lion has need of you."

"To celebrate his deeds? Let him find someone else more gifted for that business!"

"No, not for that reason. It is because the spirit of the English soldiers is badly shaken."

"Impossible! Are they not Englishmen?"

"Listen, Peire Vidal. The king began by dispensing justice."

"Then he has no need of me, for all men love a just king!"

She went on without heeding his irony, "The French king took no notice of any ill-doing on the part of his own men, nor of any evil done to them, but Richard has not cared whose subject the criminal might be, considering every man as his own. So then the Lombards and Griffons began to say that the English were demons and wore tails——"

Peire Vidal laughed uproariously. "Tailed Englishmen! And have they slunk away with their tails between their legs?"

"It has been very bad for the soldiers of Richard. First, the Messinians have tried to starve them by refusing to sell them food; then they have fallen upon them and slain them in small parties— every day they find the mutilated bodies of sentinels, outposts, and scouting parties. And the walls of the city have been raised higher."

"And what has the Lion done in retaliation?"

She told him of the taking of La Bagnara and of the Griffons' Minster.

"The devil take this king and his cursed justice!" he cried. "I will not go to him! I have no quarrel with these Griffons and Lombards!"

"One of your men would speak with you, Peire Vidal," she said quietly. "The king sent him."

She went to the ladder and called. A man tumbled down, crept to his captain, and fell upon his knees, sobbing. By the light of the taper the troubadour could see that his nose was cut in twain and there were only bloody splotches where his ears should have been.

"Master!" he moaned. "You see what they have done to us— the foul Griffons! There were six taken out of our company, and only I returned alive. The rest——" He choked, groveling. "Vengeance!"

Peire Vidal reached for his sword. "Not out of desire for vengeance," he said, "but because in war one folly invites others! Madomna," he said gently, "may I wear your favor or enseigne?"

"Besides my cloak I have only my shift," she said, and she took it off her fair white body and gave it to him. "If you will wear it against your own flesh, monsenher!" So he stripped to the waist and drew the shift down as far as it would go, and put on his leathern hauberk, that was sewn all over with rings of steel and its bottom edge scalloped and gilded. Over his nether limbs he drew chausses of chain mail. His sword was long and straight with quillons drooping toward the blade and a circular pommel enriched with Moorish designs. His coif he carried in his hand, until there should be some need for its protection. He wore no surcoat, for that was little more than vanity. Clad all in shining mail, his uncouth bear-like figure had the dignity of strength that is without malice or ferocity.

"Madomna Rambauda," he said, "I promise to God in Paradise and to His Sweet Mother by whom He was nursed, that no shame shall come to your enseigne by my doing!"

"I believe you, Peire Vidal," she said, "and in the name of Jesus Christ, and with all the love of my heart, I pray for you, for my body has felt the whole force of your body, and we have had great gladness together!"

In the boat that took him to shore were three men-at-arms. They were not of his company but they were Provençals and therefore knew his songs well and, very likely, much of his private history.

"It is a bad business at Messina," said one. "The English are jumpy as deer. They have seen too many of their dead and those cut to ribbons. Also, they do not know if the French, who are snug inside the walls, may not be standing in with the Griffons and Lombards. But worst of all, there's not a jongleur in the whole camp has a decent tune in his head; those who sing you would think were cats miauling, and little wonder we have all lost heart!" He looked hopefully at Peire Vidal's polished viol. "Monsenher Vidal, they say you have a voice will make the angels clap their wings together for joy. It would be a taste of paradise if you'd favor us with an alba or a serena, to take us back to Provence and put this filthy crusade out of mind!"

"It would indeed be a blessing!" said another; and the third added, "Amen!"

So the troubadour laid his sword in the bottom of the boat and tuned his viol to a gay and pleasing balada, but all the while another song was working in his head. Suddenly he broke off, rose from his seat, and cried to the oarsmen: "Hold your blades!" The oars were suspended, dripping silver. "Now as I sing, do you smite the water all together, and with right good will!"

His bow flickered above the viol; the air sprang forth from the strings, like a spirit released from bondage; he flung back his head, the cords of his thick neck swelling as the sounds leaped from his throat and rolled across the water. It was a chant for the crusade; not for this halting, mistaken, miserable expedition in pursuit of dowries and tribute, but for the great crusade for justice and fair dealing among men, and for the recapture of the Holy City of their dreams, where Jesus, the Good Knight, had lived and suffered. Keeping time to the rhythm of the chant, the oarsmen whipped the little waves to bubbling whirlpools that fled back and became foamy in the wake of the sharp-beaked vessel as it bit the glancing spray.

Baros Jezus, qu' en crotz fo mes
Per salvar crestiana gen. . . .

Jesus our Lord, who gave His breath
Making us Christian, doth command
Our hosts to win the Holy Land
Where He resigned Himself to death
For us; now, if our spirits are
Faint in this war to banish war,
Let all the ages hence unroll
The ignoble records of each recreant soul!

The fleet craft rose on a billow, urged by the redoubled efforts
of the oarsmen, and Peire Vidal caught one brief glimpse of the
fertile fields and terraces of Sicily—like Paradise itself—each rood
of soil won by unremitting labor from the mountain slopes. Ah,
even so would the bold-hearted crusaders win their heritage in
heaven!

And though He promises to all
Warriors of God who cross the sea
Perpetual and tribute-free
Fiefs in sweet Paradise, whoso fall
Victims of cowardice, brown or blond
Be they—bachelors or lovers fond—
They shall not get a tittle's worth
Of Heaven, but only their small plot of earth!

Behold our times! The closer scanned,
Greater the evils and the ills unfold
Of greed unbridled and fraud grown bold
And each one fearing other's hand
In knavery; yet, since all our trying
To flee from Death ends but in dying,
Only the fool will seek to hoard
His years, and not die gloriously for the Lord!

By the time they landed his companions had learned the song.

Skirting the bastioned walls of the city, they picked up others from Provence and Languedoc, and a few English, and they all sang lustily, gathering heart and numbers as they went.

While city and camp were in a state of ferment and tension, a peace conference had been called, which was attended by Richard and Philip, the governors of Messina, Margarit and Jordan du Pin, the justices of Sicily, and the archbishops of Messina, Montreale, and Reggio. As they fenced with words and veiled their several hostilities in courteous phrases, a messenger crept to Richard's side and whispered that the English were being attacked; but the king merely frowned at this repetition of a daily story. Shortly came a second, with pale face, who stuttered out that the English were being worsted. "It will do them good!" growled the Lion, tapping his sword. "Let the rabble pull their tails till it do anger them!" And somewhat later a third squire, dazed with fright, groveled before his king, crying, "Sire! they are killing us within and without the walls!" The king rose and kicked the man into a heap, took up his sword, and hurling a great oath in the teeth of the assembled dignitaries, hastened from the hall. Buckling on his armor, he gave orders to assault the city by land and sea.

The Messinians had closed their gates and a strong party outside were attacking the quarters of one of the king's Aquitanian followers, Hugh the Brown, of Lusignan. These Griffons were readily dispersed, but the high walls of the great city reared impregnable ramparts above the English host, and they soon learned that their fleet, on whose support they had counted, had been stopped at the entrance to the inner harbor by command of Philip of France. Who, then, they questioned doubtfully, is our ally? The walls were densely packed with archers, and they could hear the clanking of mangonels and espringales being wound up and loaded. They themselves had no engines of war, not a single truye, or "sow." The men at arms thought, with sullen satisfaction, that at least the grand seigneurs, in their glittering armor, made better targets for the enemy.

Richard came out of his tent and looked at the city and at the steep hills back of it, where a strong body of Lombards was posted. There was one eminence that commanded all the rest, a hill so high and steep that no one would have thought it could be climbed, yet it was black with armed men. A narrow ridge connected it with a postern gate, on the west side of the city toward Palermo. The king's blue eyes were cold and speculative.

Then he began to speak to his men. His high, penetrating voice reached to the furthest ranks and his words flicked them like a whip. He asked them how they hoped to overpower Turks and Arabs and restore the kingdom of Israel if they now showed cowardice before effeminate Griffons. Thus conquered on the very borders of their own land, would not the sluggishness of the English be a proverb to the world's end? They must avenge themselves or old women and children would mock them over the sea. His sword flashed in a blazing arc and came to rest, pointing at the sheer-walled crag. "That must be taken first!" he cried. "I go to take it, and any who are minded to follow, do so!"

The soldiers fidgeted and were silent, their eyes turning this way and that, but mostly to the ground.

At this moment they heard the chanting of Peire Vidal and his disorderly following.

> *Baros Jezus, qu'en crotz fo mes*
> *Per salvar crestiana gen. . . .*

There were hundreds singing. Those that knew not the words hummed the tune, for it had a good swinging pace and marched itself quickly into memory.

> "Only the fool will seek to hoard
> His years, and not die gloriously for the Lord!"

Peire Vidal stood before the king. He bowed, saying, "Sire, we are here for any use you may put us to!"

The king let his finger travel toward the precipitous escarpment.

"That is our goal, Monsenher Vidal!" he said. It was the first time he had spoken to the troubadour as "monsenher."

"Sire," said Peire Vidal, "if you will move your eyebrow, the whole of Sicily shall be yours; aye, if you wish it, the whole host

130

will go even to the Columns of Hercules!" And he began unlacing his armor. There was no lack of hands to help him.

The king called his captains to him and said, "Throw a ring of arbalestiers about the city in ranks three deep. Let them be set four paces apart and let them load and fire by ranks, taking aim deliberately and without haste, and let them not cease shooting until the city is taken!" Then he told off certain companies of soldiers and knights to attack the gates. The chronicler, Richard of Devizes, who was there that day, wrote that the Sicilians had to leave their walls unmanned, "because no one could look abroad but he would have an arrow in his eye before he could shut it."

Peire Vidal was standing at the head of his company clad in his breeches and the shift of Lady Rambauda. His men, too, were naked to the waist. The king of England was wearing a leather jerkin. There were less than two score of the party, but when, a short time later, they appeared in the midst of the astonished Lombards on the hill's summit, their swords and their nakedness were terrible. They drove the enemy down in headlong flight all the way to the postern gate and were in time to join the English main body that had forced the western gate. The rest of the day was spent in looting one of the richest cities of the Mediterranean.

From the bloody business of butchering, raping, and frenzied plundering, Peire Vidal was glad to escape. The white shift was splotched with red stains and cut to tatters, but he had suffered only flesh wounds which, beyond smarting, mattered little. In the cool of evening, in a vineyard where the vines showed a few dried clusters still unharvested, he sat alone, weary and gloomy, and saw above the battlements of Messina the slowly coiling clouds of smoke.

Chapter Eleven

THOUGH his part in the taking of Messina—more especially the composition of the crusading chant—had brought him into good repute with the soldiery and had even induced a mild interest in Philip Augustus, Peire Vidal found Sicily, what with intrigues and counter-intrigues, little to his liking. From the moment of the city's capture, when Richard's banners were set up on the walls and Philip, as the English king's feudal lord, straightway demanded that they be taken down and replaced by his own, there were constant bickerings between the two monarchs, lasting all of that dreary autumn. There was also much bargaining amongst the principals. Philip the Lamb (as the Griffons named him) held out for his share of the booty, and got it. Tancred, perceiving Richard's tactical advantage, reluctantly delivered forty thousand ounces of gold in exchange for a promised union between his daughter and Richard's nephew, Arthur of Brittany. Richard, in one of his generous moods, gave away a considerable amount of treasure to his nobles and largesse to his men. He even bestowed upon Peire Vidal a richly embroidered green satin surtout, with the Plantagenet arms worked upon it in gold thread, and a pair of gilded spurs; and so among the skeptical and lofty English courtiers there was no further question of the troubadour's right to knighthood. Then the Lion set himself to build a great wooden fortress on a hill overlooking Messina, which he called Mategriffon, or Kill-Greek. At times he showed a quaint sense of humor.

But all of this, except the spurs and surcoat, held little interest for the knight of Belgueil. The fleet, having missed the fall passage to the Holy Land, must lay to until March, and who, beside kings, would choose Sicily to winter in? Only one dromond had sailed east with despatches for Guy of Lusignan, still engaged in the siege of St. Jean d'Acre, and it bore the fair pilgrim of Biolh. She was gone before ever Peire Vidal could show her how fairly he had borne her enseigne. For weeks he was silent, his viol unused, while he moped, hungering for Provence. Then, on the eve of All Saints' Day, when the whole city and the English camp were given up to festivities, came word that an urser had arrived from Marseille. Scarcely had its sails been lowered and its anchors dropped when Peire Vidal, perched on a quay among the throngs of onlookers, heard the clear sweet voice of Aimeric de Peguilha.

The jongleur was gay, voluble, and insouciant as ever, fresh as the orange blossoms of the Provençal ajoncs, and his loquacious tongue spilled gossip like a chattering magpie. Over flagons of choice Sicilian wines they held night-long converse in Peire Vidal's quarters.

"They say—or a very flood of rumors have it—that you, Monsenher Vidal, have followed the Lion up hill and down dale to glory! Is it true," he asked with a sly grimace, "that the English would rather ravish a falcon than a virgin?"

Peire Vidal related the story of the falcon.

"Ha!" said Aimeric de Peguilha at its conclusion. "I like this king. He is not above petty larceny! Is it true, master, that you remained at the bottom of a dromond seven days, saying prayers for the good of your soul?" And Peire Vidal told, in part, of his captivity, but he refrained from mentioning Rambauda of Biolh.

"And now, Monsenher Vidal, let me hear how you and Richard, stark naked, took the city of Messina!"

Aimeric de Peguilha in his turn described the doings of troubadours and their ladies, of jongleurs and their mistresses, of seigneurs and their marital misadventures. Arnaut de Maruelh had been summoned back to Béziers by the Countess Alazais. Peyrols the jongleur was dangling at the beck of Loba of Puegnautier, "and she has made him madder than ever!" Peire Cadenet had abandoned her, after much fruitless singing, for the Viscountess Agnes of Monpeslier. Aimonet, the scamp, had set himself up for a troubadour and had gone to the court of King Amfos where they didn't know an alba from a capon! Gaucelm Faidit had taken himself and his wanton to Monferrato, to be with Rambaut of Vacqueiras, and they were well tended by the Marquis Bonifaz and the beautiful black-browed Beatriz, "whom they say would draw the angel Gabriel himself to earth, if he could be her lover!" All the while, during this discourse, Peire Vidal listened, his heart beating with impatience, for some word of his golden lady, but the rogue must keep him on tenterhooks till suddenly—"and as for the goddess of Les Baux——" Ha! thought Peire Vidal, blessed saints! it is coming! "—she is in good health and the child as well."

"Did she send me no message?" He trembled to hear the answer.

"Not she. But our very noble Viscount of Marseille sends you most heart-felt greetings and urges your speedy return, in the event that you do not at once go crusading. He assures you, master, that not only will you be well received by himself but by his lady as well, since he has secured from her your full and free pardon in your undeserved exile!"

Peire Vidal leaped up, laid his huge arms about his audiart, and kissed him on both cheeks. The next day he went with Aimeric de Peguilha to ask King Richard if he might have a furlough at Marseille over the winter.

The king, luckily, was in an agreeably exalted frame of mind, for he had lately summoned all the bishops to come together and when they had assembled he came before them, standing as a naked penitent with three scourges in his hand. Then he knelt and openly confessed a secret vice and, declaring that "the thorns of his evil life had grown higher than his head, and there was no hand to root them up," he besought absolution of his sins. The bishops, gratified at the king's humility and after satisfying themselves fully as to the nature and details of his trespass, laid upon him as penance three days of fasting, sackcloth and ashes, light flagellation, and final lustration. This atonement, with its purifying bodily effects, quickly restored him to his usual mundane energy and he had six malefactors hung with great despatch. He was further elated on All Saints' Day by a long session with the diviner and soothsayer, Abbot Joachim who, having consulted certain friendly spirits raised by magical formulas, assured the king not only of ultimate victory in the crusade but that his star would rise higher than that of Alexander the Greek. The unkempt monk left the royal presence laden with alms.

"Monsenher Vidal," said the king, "you wish to leave me? Well, do not these dark-skinned damsels of Messina tempt you?" Then, with a tinge of sarcasm: "Your Viscount of Marseille, I know, sets a good table." He glanced at the troubadour's audiart. "Who is this fair young man?"

"Aimeric de Peguilha, sire, and a very good singer."

The king looked upon the flowery beauty of the jongleur and said, "You have permission to go to Provence for the winter, Peire Vidal, if you leave me this young man to sing in your stead. Without my Arnaut Daniel and you, we shall be sorely in need of troubadours these tedious evenings."

"I am only a humble jongleur, sire," said Aimeric de Peguilha, "audiart to my master, Monsenher Vidal, who schooled me in the Joyous Craft."

"If you do well in Messina, you shall be named a troubadour, Messer Aimeric de Peguilha."

The jongleur seized the king's hand and kissed it. "What I may do, I will do as well as I may!" he said fervently.

"And I release him from his apprenticeship, sire, for indeed he is already an accomplished master," said Peire Vidal. Aimeric's eyes filled with tears of joy; he saw himself become the lover of a countess, of several noble ladies. The king smiled one of his rare wintry smiles. In his menie there were a number of milk-skinned, well-born youths, slender and delicately featured as girls and proud as falcons. The Lion was no passionate lover of women.

So the urser, round-bellied and cumbersome, difficult to handle in its lack of oars, sailed back to Marseille carrying Peire Vidal. As one who, after long absence, goes to meet a friend and in endeared anticipation visions him more clearly than ever seen in the flesh, he saw Provence, both the separate items and the great sum of her. He saw her many flowers, the little white bells of the brière,

135

the yellow blossoms of the wild broom, plantagenet, that gave its name to a line of kings; yellow roses, purple clouds of thyme, tufts of lavender, wild rosemary, jasmine, eglantine, flowers of the thorny acacia, and the flor de gaug, giver of joy. He saw her many small rivers and little streams quick with life and garrulous as her people; and suzerain of them all, Father Rhône. He envisaged the mysterious interminable étangs, with their salt wastes and clouds of rose-winged flamingoes, cormorants, and bustards, and sea-birds mewing in the dusk; the rocky desert of le Crau and the fertile tilth of the Camargue; and the all-enclosing ramparts of crenelated mountains, the Cévennes and Alps, God's battlements against the Northern barbarians.

Many kings had claimed her, but none possessed Provence; and if her free cities bickered among themselves, they only hated intruders the more whole-heartedly. A land of little intrigue and much song and laughter, where there was more care for living and loving than for believing, or achieving, or persecuting.

Peire Vidal's song that he made on this voyage was for Adélasie des Baux; unknowingly, he made it for Provence, too, his equally beloved.

> Friend, whose generous gifts are tendered
> Without guile or subtle malice,
> Fair your soul is, as a palace
> Where my heart dwells, self-surrendered
> Willing captive; hear my story—
> Not in pride nor in vainglory,
> I'd prefer this high romance
> To all Lombardy or France.

In this way occupied, he saw, after days of wind and scudding foam that perilously rocked the bobbing urser, Marseille, its gray roofs overlooked by the vast and formidable Château Babon and the dark battlements of the Abbey of Sant Victor. And the thought of his beloved made a conflagration in his brain.

She wore an overdress of ermine and a mantle of gray fur, ornamented with sable. Because of the chill—it was the middle of

November—her robe had been replaced by a pelisse. Her wimple of gray silk concealed the burnished glory of her hair. In gray Marseille she was all gray. When he knelt and kissed her hand, her smile burned for a moment like a lighted candle. He pressed between her taper fingers a needlecase, artfully embroidered in the Griffon style with nymphs and satyrs among heads of angels, all in thread of gold.

"Monsenher Vidal," she said, "you come glittering from the foam!" He was wearing his mail and the Plantagenet surtout. She studied his face. "But you have witnessed bloodshed."

"To see men die is nothing new," he said, "but to look upon your face, madomna, is to anticipate the glory of paradise!" She said nothing but her eyes thanked him.

"Rainier, we have missed you!"

It was Viscount Barrale. Seeing him, Peire Vidal thought, this podestat of the free city of Marseille has more of the emperor in him than Richard has of kingliness. His manner was easy and genial, he could talk familiarly with his butlers and pantlers, and they would pass him a jest to hear his sudden booming laugh. He went on no crusades, fought no wars, gained no rood of land that was not his own, but emperor and pope and many kings were glad to have his ear. When asked it, he gave counsel; otherwise he mixed in no man's business.

"And I have missed you, Rainier, and your lady more than I have words to tell. Sicily is a witches' cauldron. They brew the devil's potion there. Ah, I thank God for Provence!" said Peire Vidal fervently.

"The vintage was good this year. Trade flourishes, thanks to the crusade. We are all prospering." Barrale was smiling but his cold clear eyes were weighing distant matters. He said, "An astrologer once told me to beware the turn of a century. What is tilth will lie idle, and what is fallow will know fresh seed. Men count for little in God's calendar." He spoke low to a lackey and the man went to a doorway hung with figured arras. Then genially, "But still we sing well in Provence. You will be glad to know, Monsenher Vidal, that Arnaut de Maruelh is with us, and the fair Albigensian, Lady Ermengarde de Castras, and her devoted knight, Raimon

137

of Miravals, and others. So we are assured rare entertainment in singing. I trust fighting has not made you hoarse, my friend?"

"It needs more than five hours of that to crack my voice, sire!"

The arras parted. A little group advanced into the hall. The first of these was Folquet of Marseille. Peire Vidal's heart leaped and his throat became thick. He remembered a Lombard he had run through with his sword; the man twisted and fell sideways, leering, and Peire Vidal had cursed God who permitted wars. Now he thought: not in this house; I cannot kill him here!

Barrale was saying, "Monsenhers and madomnas, we are welcoming a troubadour who has been proved a knight on the field of battle. My lady lately sent him into exile for a kiss. Now she returns him the kiss, together with her love—and my own."

Before he knew it, Adélasie des Baux had laid her hands, one on either shoulder, and then, raising her face to his, she kissed him full on the lips. He came near to swooning, not so much from ecstasy as from amazement.

She said, "I give this kiss freely and accept Monsenher Vidal as my true and loyal knight, as he has always been."

Folquet had come near, unwillingly it seemed, as by some compulsion of magic. His face was gray and fixed like a sleep-walker's. She barely turned her head, saying to him, "Messer Folquet, you have been often a guest in our house. That is no more." She had called him Messer; had spoken as one well-born to a varlet.

There was silence. They heard the footsteps of Folquet of Marseille, the merchant's son of Genoa, as he walked rigidly from the room. At the doorway he paused. He took his lute from about his shoulder and, taking it in his hands, he broke it in twain. The polished wood cracked and the strings snapped, each with a little cry like a dying child. Then the arras hid him.

He had been a great craftsman, one of the best of the troubadours.

Though many good songs were heard in his brief stay at the palace of Barrale, and in spite of the nearness of his lady and of her gentleness toward him, Peire Vidal was not wholly happy there. In the garden of the castle the leaves had fallen from the vines, the flowers were only denuded stalks, the grass was thick and tangled like an old beggar's hair, and the pale sunlight distilled the essence of autumn. Blowing from southeast, the sirocco whipped the waters of the gulf against the quays and churned among swaying masts of dromonds and esneccas. Sheltered from its violence, in a nook of the castle wall, the child of the house was tended by a bower-woman. Though the countess listened to the words of the troubadour, her eyes were ever on her infant's crib lest, by some momentary inattention on the part of the nurse, a fairy should lay some spell upon his sleeping innocence. Looking at her face, Peire Vidal felt it fitting that she had left Les Baux to dwell in Marseille. But Adélasie's tenderness toward him made her more distant than the moon of misty nights; she gave off a veiled radiance that moved his heart and left his passion dry. When she bared her breast, now sculptured to full perfection, to suckle the lusty feeder, he turned his head away, as a prisoner, freed from a dark dungeon after long years, avoids the glare of day.

"My lady," said Viscount Barrale, "will let the little rat gnaw at her, though I could have got her a gentlewoman for wet-nurse. This maternal milking is a peasant virtue." The reproof, though lightly spoken, carried some hint of deeper import—one of many signs, barely perceptible, of a growing rift between these two. Beneath his host's mask of equanimity, Peire Vidal sensed some secret malady of the soul that tinged his patron's jests with gall.

Once, at the fall of day, Peire Vidal wandered through the mazes of the vast establishment until he lost himself completely, immersed in the first lines of a serena, or even-song, that he intended singing to the countess. It was a long passageway, closed at the end by an arras and in the center of the arras, where it had torn or raveled, a single beam of light filtered through. Walking slowly and softly in the confusion of his wits, he reached the arras and peered through the little aperture, hoping to see a chamber that he knew. It seemed empty. He smelled the sweet odor of balsam twigs covering the floor, and another scent, sweeter and headier. Then he saw Adélasie des Baux. She had no bower-women in attendance, and alone she unclasped the gold bands of her braided hair that fell luxuriantly below her knees. As he watched through the slit, she undid the woven plaits with nimble fingers, unfastened her overdress, and one by one, silken bliaut, chemise, and shift

139

floated to the floor in a soft, richly-colored heap. Then, unclothed, she lifted the child from his crib, stripped him of his fleecy coverings and swaddling bands, and held him, naked-pink, against her breasts, while about him she made a golden canopy of her hair. Peire Vidal was awed, as one who has witnessed forbidden mysteries, yet his senses were not so much quickened as was his spirit overwhelmed by the beauty in this sight.

There was a step in the chamber. Barrale entered, carrying in his hand a small rod of pine, the symbol of his office as podestat of Marseille, for he had just come from a meeting of the city council. His face was stern and magisterial. This was a different Rainier. He looked upon his wife. "Clothe yourself!" he said harshly. "Where are your tiring women?"

She did not answer. There was no change in her and no movement save the slightest tightening of her arms about the child. The viscount took three steps: "Did you hear?"

In that moment of silence Peire Vidal's heart died in him.

Then Barrale of Marseille raised the mace and brought it down across her shoulder; she did not flinch. There would be a mark. . . .

Peire Vidal, stifling a cry, whirled and stumbled back into the hall's darkness and groped his way through many turnings and windings. He started to run and lunged blindly into an armed man, who filled the air with curses, but the troubadour ran on. At last he found his way out and ran along walks and under bushes, and plunged into a thicket, where he fell, face down, and bit the earth as he had done at Castle Bargarde.

Chapter Twelve

M Y NOBLE patron," wrote Gaucelm Faidit in his fine, almost undecipherable script, "has heard your merits so diligently recited by myself and Monsenher Raimbaut of Vacqueiras that he desires mightily to test our judgment of the quality of your singing. They say you have fought side by side with the Lion; it seems your knighting was not in vain and you have well used the sword Durandal. And 'tis said, the hold of a vessel may have certain compensations as a prison; truth, the witch Venus has you in her keeping! Our Marquis of Montferrat has had a father and a brother who were kings, and is himself no mean composer of vers in our Roman tongue—excellent reasons for you to take heed of his earnest invitation. But a better reason lies in the Bel Cavalier. As her sire rules Monferrat with wisdom, so the imperious Beatriz rules him with love. So firm is she in her fourteen summers, that, though she wedded Enrico del Caretto, lord of Finale, these two years gone, her husband, I am told, has not laid a finger on her. They have given her the name of Fair Knight for her prowess in arms, which is a strange accomplishment in a woman, but this poor world is being given into their ruthless hands. Witness myself, who am no more than a pet mastiff to my faithless wanton! She, by the way, leads my lord's brother-in-law, Albert of Malespina—a malicious, cross-grained cur!—by the nose. Hanging over my shoulder at this writing, the lewd wench plants kisses for you on the parchment. So, torn between jealousy and affection, I am still your comrade in the Joyous Craft and brother in the great order of Bacchus."

When Peire Vidal told Adélasie des Baux that he had been summoned to Chivasso by the Marquis of Montferrat, she raised her eyes from her needlework and said, "That is good news for you."

He would have offered passionate denial—would have affirmed his perpetual delight in her company, but her calm eyes had the power of destroying ambiguity and falsehood. He kept silent and she continued, "Peire Vidal, I have caused you too much pain to desire you to keep me tangled in your heart out of gratitude. It is I who am grateful—so grateful that I would willingly yield you the pleasure of my body if I thought it would be to your great advantage." She paused and spoke low. "But it would not be so. You are restless and eager for further life; my own lies now within the compass of a cradle. You have been good to me, and for that I shall always hold you dear in my thoughts. Make songs for me, if it please you, but let not too tender memories hold you in their chains."

The troubadour knelt at her feet, laying his head between her knees, but she did not touch it, fearing by so slight an act to hold him captive. It was the last temptation of her great loneliness.

When he left the palace he was glad the viscount was away on business at Avignon, for he did not wish to see Rainier again.

The city of Marseille was celebrating Candlemas in honor of the Purification of the Virgin Mary. There were processions and burning candles and an air of festivity that made the dingy port seem entirely happy and gay. So, too, was Peire Vidal; something had set him free, in a manner he had not ever known before. He felt kindly toward all men, and somewhat superior, as though he stood upon an invisible elevation. He would never again look up to kings, or blindly worship women, but he would continue to seek the Kingdom of Justice.

On board the coasting esnecca from Marseille to Genoa was the Châtelain de Coucy, a brave gentleman who had been of the scaling party at Messina. He was returning to Sicily from a hasty journey to England on a secret mission. They talked of Richard and the crusade.

"A great soldier," said the seigneur warmly; "the greatest of our times, except for Saladin; but my lord the king has one defect: he will turn from a boar hunt to prick a mouse!"

At least, thought Peire Vidal, the Lion would not strike a woman!

Genoa; and then, after following a good road north, bustling Turin, and many quaint and peaceful towns of the duchy of Montferrat; and then Chivasso, set in a little garden of paradise watered by the river Po, the castle high and looking toward the gleaming battlements of the Alps, north and west, and west and southerly, the gulf of Genoa.

The hoarse voice of Gaucelm Faidit bellowed, "God's blood, it's our naked knight, dressed like the emperor!" There were Guilhelma Monjo, hanging about his neck and rubbing her pendant breasts against his mail. Raimbaut of Vacqueiras, with large kingly ears and blond graying hair, smiling and saying, "A challenge to a tenson, and no mercy to be shown, monsenher!" And the marquis, of medium height, stout and muscular, with full, rosy face like that of his sire, the old crusader. And Beatriz of Montferrat, who had straight, heavy, black eyebrows, meeting above warm, imperious eyes, the nose of a falcon, and the figure of a stripling squire. She said, with a grave smile, "Most welcome! You are not as ugly as they described you, monsenher of Belgueil. I had thought to see a walking bear, but I am sure you are good at dicing and tennis and chess!" What she thought, she said, always. And a sourish man, with a crabbed visage of great haughtiness, was the Marquis Albert of Malespina. There were many others, who all seemed happier than people usually are, thought Peire Vidal. One could hardly be other than gay, apparently, in the presence of this Bel Cavalier.

It was Italy, but the countryside had the air of beloved Provence, gracious and smiling and fertile, as though there were no wars in the world. That night, however, he learned that Raimbaut and the marquis had lately seen arduous fighting. The former still carried his arm in a sling, for on the very borders of Montferrat they had fallen in with twelve robber knights, from whom they escaped whole with difficulty. Italy, with all its many cities and duchies and petty dominions, was a hornets' nest of brigandage, betrayals, and other deviltry. In this seething turmoil Montferrat, with its *bellisimo* Chivasso, like a fair oasis, offered security and the fruits of culture.

For Peire Vidal there never was a happier month than that one spent at Chivasso. The days were given to sports and amusements, contests in the tilting-yard, falconry and deer hunting, tennis and other games. The nights were for feasting, dancing, dicing, and singing. In all these pastimes, whether difficult or diverting, the Bel Cavalier took an active part. At dice, in which he was a master, Gaucelm Faidit found her an able opponent, for she had acquired her skill from a member of the Dicers' Gild, who had learned the art at a scoladeciorum, or dicing school. She rode, armed in mail, in the tilting-yard and gave the young squires blow for blow, sometimes unseating one, to his great discomfiture, by her swift charge and a thrust of lance, judiciously timed.

When the weather without became unseasonable, she invited Peire Vidal to her bower for chess. For a long afternoon they bent over the carved ivory pieces, her large serious eyes fixed so intently on the board that the troubadour saw only the silken fringe of her eyelashes resting closed, it seemed, upon cheeks whose color was not heightened by cosmetics. Since he held it no courtesy to let himself be worsted, when the first game proved to be a stalemate he gave up stealing glances at her face, but it did him no good, for some time later he was surprised to hear her say, "Checkmate!"

"Madomna Beatriz," he said, "you have vanquished me in fair encounter. I had not thought to concede victory to a woman!"

"Have you never before been beaten by a woman?" she asked. He thought: Guilhelma Monjo; Adélasie des Baux; Louve de Peinaultier; and Rambauda of Biolh. By whom of them had he suffered defeat? . . . By all, perhaps, and yet, by none. Each of them in her way (but this he did not know) still loved him more than he loved her; he had songs for any of them, but his singing loosened his heart from them. After a moment he said, "In the ninth article of the *Laws of Love* it declares: 'No one can love, unless the soft persuasion of love itself compel him.' Therefore, madomna, while I have been overcome by the power of love, there is no woman who has caused me lasting grief."

"That is specious reasoning, Peire Vidal," she said gravely; "as if a knight were to argue that since he still lives, he has not been overcome in the tilting-yard! Still, though I doubt not you have had some tumbles, your bruises only strengthen your arms and lend encouragement to your spirit. Luckily you have been spared the affliction of ambition."

"Why luckily, madomna?"

"Because your judgment is inferior to your understanding."

"But madomna, I am the most ambitious man in the world! I desire to excel all others in the Joyous Craft!"

"The desire for excellence is not ambition. No more than holiness. Ambition is of grosser composition. It must have an eye open for intrigue and an ear deaf to suffering. My father is ambitious."

"Madomna! He seems the kindest of men."

"And so he is, unless crossed in policy; then he becomes harder of heart than the Saracen sultans. Your Richard is ambitious, so he let the Jews be burnt in England to fill his treasure ships for this crusade! And many thousands will give their blood to his desires."

He was about to reply hotly that the report of the burning of the Jews might have been a malicious canard when he recalled that Richard the Lion had a curious appetite for certain cruelties. He let it pass. At the same time he marveled at the wisdom of this child.

"Is Raimbaut of Vacqueiras ambitious?" he asked.

"Adventurous," she said instantly, "but with princely tastes that give him no peace. He was born poor and his reckless tongue has kept him poor. If he follows the fortunes of our house he will not remain so. Yet if I told him that, he would at once desert me!" She laughed, as though enjoying some secret jest. No one would have thought that she and Raimbaut of Vacqueiras were lovers. From that afternoon Peire Vidal found himself more and more desirous of holding speech with the girl. More than her beauty he admired the quickness and agility of her mind. He often flung an idle question to her to get her response, as one unhoods a gerfalcon to watch its swift unerring flight.

"What is love?" he asked once.

145

"Ask me, what are people?" she retorted. "Love is a motion in a soul. It may be like a running brook, or like a river. It may be a vagrant wind or an airy cloud, soon dissolved. Or it may be like a tide of the sea, rising and falling, yet never losing itself. It may be a whirlpool that sucks and draws down whatever floats within its reach. It is distinct in each and every human body, and the laws of it are different for each person."

Peire Vidal had been turning over in his head a certain question ever since the afternoon of the chess game. Now he asked it.

"Madomna, do you hold with the third article of the *Laws of Love,* that no one can really love two people at the same time?"

For once she was perplexed. "By really is meant passionately," she mused. "I do not know, Peire Vidal. With lesser loves, yes! But with a greater love, I do not know. There are moments when two loves seem equal in the heart, but it may be that neither is deeply held. Or it may be that then one is slipping, even though one does not know it, from one love to another . . . I do not know."

They were silent. From the tilting-yard came the clang of metal and the shouts of squires urging on their fellows. Hoof-beats clattered on the stone flags. Fine dust made bands of golden motes where a shaft of sunlight pierced the window of her bower. The fresh smell of green growth filled the air, for an early spring was beginning.

She rose suddenly. "Peire Vidal, you are fonder of questions than anyone I know. But you should not ask things that make one sad!" Though she had not dismissed him, he knew that he should leave her—and as he passed from her chamber she was still standing, motionless, gazing at an arras figured in nymphs and satyrs.

On the north side of the castle, in a high tower, he found a casement opening toward the Alps. The four peaks of Monte Rosa were hidden by veils of cloud and falling snow. Nearer ridges, like the backs of fabulous beasts, were sharp and black, bristling with forests. Glittering sunlight flung wheeling spears of light into the distant murk, striving to pierce it. A furious battle raged in the heavens between the forces of light and darkness. It seemed a prelude to chaos.

Before the marquis and his guests that night he sang a new song:

Ges pel temps fer e brau
Qu' adutz tempiers e vens . . .

When sullen winter vents
Its dark and savage spite
On earth, and mad winds fight
All other elements,
It seems they set alight
Old passions, and incite
My tongue to honeyed phrase
And voice to eager praise
Of the fresh, snowy garlands on the heights,
Whose icy flowers renew outworn delights.

When the song was finished and the applause had subsided, the Marquis Bonifaz drew Peire Vidal aside.

"Monsenher Vidal, you have fully lived up to our expectations of your gifts—acquirements, I should say, for I perceive that such mastery is not attained without rigorous discipline of one's talents. I hope you will find it within your power to remain long with us. My daughter who, at times, is a bit headstrong, could profit by companionship with one of your caliber—experienced, yet prudent. The excellent Viscount Barrale of Marseille speaks as highly of your discretion as of your singing, and the Good Count Raimon of Toulouse holds you in high esteem. Italy is chaos. Piedmont, thank God, stands outside the universal brawling. I would like to establish here a school and a tradition of the Gay Science that would shed light in the darkness of this land. Monsenher Vidal, I am looking to you to perform prodigies!"

"My lord!" Peire Vidal stammered. "I only sing as I know how. Still, it is very lovely here, and when I have done with the crusade——"

"Monsenher," said the marquis with a touch of acerbity, "why smear your hand with that pitch?"

"I have given my oath, my lord."

"Many have broken theirs, since they have seen the course it is running."

"I do not take back my words, sire!"

"Then you have more conscience than your royal leader. The Lion has never been bound by such paltry scruples!"

"It is not my place to question his integrity. I have accepted a commission and I am under orders. Until I am released I have no other course to follow."

"Your fidelity, I hope, will be rewarded. But whether it is or is not, we have a place for you here." He changed the subject at once, inquired in detail concerning the composition of the king's army and of his tactics at the taking of Messina.

"Arbalestiers! Attack under concentrated fire? Yes! The English are good bowmen. They shoot like devils! Massed fire by foot soldiers . . . some day that will mean the end of our galloping knights. If only the Lion were more of a strategist he would be a master soldier. But he cannot conceive a large design. He wastes his tactics in petty fighting!"

"Oh, sire, and he cannot see that the way to the Holy Land is through Egypt!" cried Peire Vidal eagerly. "He could take Saladin in the rear with half the trouble. And the Saracens would be through for a generation!"

The marquis contemplated the troubadour through half-closed eyes.

"Someone said you were a fool, Monsenher Vidal," he said, "but I can tell them better!"

Peire Vidal saw little of his host during the ensuing days. He found, however, that by accident or design he was thrown much in the company of the Bel Cavalier. Raimbaut of Vacqueiras had been despatched on an urgent mission to the city of Casale, to offer the aid of Montferrat in its revolt against Vercelli. It was only February, yet the violet and narcissus showed their heads. Small birds began their stealthy business of weaving and plaiting rubbish in secret places. The heart of the troubadour bubbled like a fresh spring with joy that flowed forth in song.

The Lady Beatriz wished to ride. The company should be four: herself and Peire Vidal and two stout esquires. The latter rode chestnut roncins, and for the Lady Beatriz there was a white palfrey, with trappings of white and silver, figured with the arms of Montferrat in azure, and with many tinkling bells on the bridle. There was also a dapple-gray palfrey, caparisoned in scarlet and vair, hung with a hundred bells, for Peire Vidal.

"Monsenher Vidal," said the varlet, "the noble lord, the marquis of Malespina, begs you to accept this gift, in token of his pleasure in your singing."

The troubadour was bewildered. Albert of Malespina! He had scarcely spoken to the man; in fact, had felt an immediate distaste for that lord's hauteur and consciousness of his lineage. He looked his amazement at Beatriz as he stuttered words of thanks. She laughed.

"Beware the generosity of our house, Peire Vidal! He is going to ask you take a city for him. If you and the Lion and a few other naked gentlemen could take Messina, you could surely secure Pavia, alone, in armor!"

The air held the zest of the season of joy. They galloped over fields in flower, where birds circled and sang. Rabbits scattered before them in little leaps. A doe stood transfixed with curiosity in a covert, then bounded airily away. Hawks slipped across the blue sky above, dropping hoarse, plaintive cries. The peaks of distant Monte Rosa glistened like the gates of paradise.

The Lady Beatriz' dress was the color of daffodils and his was the green of the knight-errant. They sat in a little glade of the forest where there was a natural greensward, dotted with yellow violets; and the esquires, having furnished them with cates and wine, withdrew to a discreet distance. There Peire Vidal related the story of Charlemagne and his nephew, Orlando, and of Farragus, whose body was rendered invulnerable by enchantment, and of the traitor, Ganelon, who prevented the great king from coming to the rescue of Orlando at Roncevalles. And how Orlando, despairing of succor, and fearing that his sword, Durandal, would fall into the hands of the Moors, tried to break it against rocks and trees, but being a magic sword, it cut through trees and splintered rocks. And so he blew the terrible horn that could be heard six leagues, and his veins burst and he died.

Beatriz was interested in the telling but skeptical of the truth of this tale. She listened with greater interest, however, to the story—

vouched for as authentic—of the lady of Limousin whom the envoys of a French king came to interview for their master, with a tentative proposal of marriage, conditional upon the perfection of her charms. And how she removed, one by one, her garments, until she stood before them naked, and they approved and reported favorably to the king, who married her.

"That rings true," she said, "for that French king may have been as cautious as Philip Augustus. His legates no doubt would greatly relish such a mission, and any lady would consent to such immodesty in so proper a cause!" Her laugh chimed like the silvery bells of the palfrey's harness. She leaped up suddenly and vanished into a thicket. Peire Vidal was startled. He followed, for this was an unknown country and there were wolves in dark rough places.

Pushing through a leafy tangle, he heard running water. It was soft footing, and a thick, humid mat of moss sank beneath his tread. He slipped on a stone and soon there were many stones, and then a purl of waters, and a jutting crag that let the brook down in a splashing sheet into a round still pool. There she stood, reft of her coverings, white flesh glistening wet and dappled with flakes of light, laughing from under straight black brows—a sylvan creature such as the pagans envisaged and pious monks still dreaded to behold.

"What will you tell the king, monsenher?" she called gayly.

"I shall not return to tell him anything! Let him come and see for himself!"

"He will cut off your head if he ever takes you!"

"It's no matter. To lose one's head is a common misfortune. But I think he'll never lay hands on me!"

She bent over, cupping water in her hands.

"They say you are a madman, monsenher, and madmen know no fear," she said from under her long black braids. "Are you afraid of water?" And with that, he felt a cold douse in his face. He leaped into the pool, took her in his long arms, all wet and cold, and carried her to the bank where the mossy turf was like velvet of Amiens in triple ply.

In the quiet of an azure twilight lanterned by a slim new moon they rode back to the castle, the esquires hardly visible behind them.

"To whom do you belong, my lady?" he asked, out of a long silence.

"To myself," she said soberly. "And to whomever I choose to give myself. But giving is not being possessed, monsenher."

"I do not understand, madomna."

"Stay here with me and be my friend, and you will understand, Peire Vidal."

It was all very strange, he thought.

Albert of Malespina was the younger son of a great Piedmontese house, allied with Tortona against Genoa. The marquis showed in every lineament the breeding of five hundred years of nobility, a line in no way enfeebled by the exercise of power or the indulgence of luxury. He rose, holding out his hand to Peire Vidal, and the troubadour, reading disdain in his smile, remembered that his lordship was, withal, a troubadour of parts, could compose an acceptable sirvente or enter readily into a tenson. It was not disdain, merely the family cast of his features. His voice was friendly.

"Monsenher Vidal, you have come to tender me your thanks, and being an honest troubadour, you are going to declare that you cannot accept a gift unless you know the terms of it."

Peire Vidal was astonished. It was true, he wished to give formal thanks and return the palfrey. "My lord, you have read my thoughts. I am grateful to you, but I cannot bargain with my gratitude. My songs are given freely."

The marquis waved him to a chair. The table between them was of polished oak from the trees of Monte Rosa, carved skilfully with a device of running vine along the edges. A servitor poured wine into silver flagons.

"We are not buying your songs with a horse, monsenher," he said, with light irony. "You have already well deserved this gift, for a signal service of which you are unaware—not to speak of the great pleasure we have had in your excellent singing, and the honor it does the Lady Beatriz to be so celebrated!"

The troubadour waited, sipping his wine. Association with worldly greatness had taught him to hold his tongue and to let power cautiously reveal its demands; for power, he had learned, condescends to the humble only when in need of service.

151

"Your friend, monsenher of Vacqueiras," said the marquis irrelevantly, "has many knightly qualities."

"He is an excellent troubadour," said Peire Vidal warmly.

"But he is quite ignorant of the art of diplomacy. They say his father was more than a bit cracked!"

"That is the common report, my lord marquis."

"I can well believe it, if the son resembles his sire. Has he ever told you how he came to this castle?"

"No, my lord, I am not in the confidence of Monsenher Raimbaut."

The lips of the marquis tightened.

"*I* brought him here, monsenher; and for that he hates me! When this talented young man was booted from the court of Orange for insulting his patron, Guilhem des Baux, he went over to the court of Aimar, Count of Die and Valence, to try his luck with the count's wife, the Countess Philippa. Again he was turned out, and came hot-foot to Italy where he assiduously cultivated a certain wealthy lady of Tortona. Here his suit did not prosper, for there was a more engaging rival." Peire Vidal knew that—the successful rival had been the marquis himself. Details of this incident flitted through his mind. Gaucelm Faidit had once told him that the house of Malespina had wished to ally itself with Tortona against Genoa, and a part of that tortuous statecraft no doubt had been the ardent wooing of the lady.

"Nor did he himself greatly prosper," added the marquis. "Having laid out his last sol in amorous expenditures, the ambitious jongleur found himself roaming the streets of Genoa with nothing but a lute to comfort him. But not dismayed, our gay young man turned once more to the fair sex for support. He found himself a trader's blowsy dame—one who smelled of her husband's spice and condiments, no doubt. Unluckily the merchant was a crafty fox who came upon them at their pleasure——"

"Pardon, my lord marquis," said Peire Vidal, "my lack of interest in Monsenher Raimbaut's history."

"Of course. I understand, monsenher. In brief, when I picked him up in Pavia some months later he was threadbare and in debt to his landlord. I paid his bill, bought him clothes, brought him to Chivasso, and you know the rest! That is," he corrected, "you know that he became the lover of my niece, the Lady Beatriz."

He ceased speaking, looked directly at Peire Vidal as though expecting comment. The troubadour took his time; he was trying to follow the clue to this discourse.

"I know very little," said Peire Vidal, "except that Monsenher Raimbaut has seen a good deal of fighting as squire, then knight, of my lord the Marquis Bonifaz. At Rondasso he acquitted himself well. He showed valor at Paterno, Palermo, Catagiro, Azaistrigo . . . at Quarto——"

"Yes! Yes!" the marquis interrupted. "No one doubts his courage!"

True, thought Peire Vidal, for at Quarto he saved your life, noble Malespina! And he wondered idly if saving a person's life squared all other accounts. Does the saving of a life cancel a money debt or a moral obligation like becoming a lady's lover, or——

The Marquis was still talking. "I had to thank him for my life at Quarto," he said. The man was a noble; not petty in acknowledgments. "But that does not alter the fact that he has ill repaid the many benefactions he has received at the hands of his patron."

Peire Vidal asked abruptly, "Why do you need to tell me these things, my lord?"

The voice of the marquis was suave. "Because, my dear monsenher, they touch your own fortunes very closely!"

The troubadour got up quickly. "They do not! I wish to hear nothing more of Raimbaut of Vacqueiras!"

"Finish your wine, monsenher," said the marquis pleasantly. The troubadour sat down reluctantly. "As you may know, we are divided here in Italy between those cities that are still loyal to the emperor——"

"The emperor is dead, my lord. He was drowned in the river Salef, in Armenia."

"Ah! but the empire is not dead! When these impudent towns of Lombardy, fretting against the grand unity of empire and desiring their silly and insolent independence, instituted their cursed league, only Pavia and Monferrat stood firm for the Holy Roman Empire that has come down from the great Caesars. But after the peace of Constance we were joined by Genoa, Alba, Cremona,

Como, Tortona, Asti, and Alessandria—a goodly company! All that was the doing of this house of Monferrat. The emperor is dead, it is true, but my lord, the Marquis Bonifaz, who is a great man, still lives!" He spoke these last words with singular impressiveness, as though their implication might be clear to the initiated. Peire Vidal looked blank. What had all this to do with Raimbaut and Beatriz and himself?

"Bonifaz, my good wife's brother, is great and politic, but he is not invulnerable. There are mutterings and stirrings among his allies. Safety for the grand plan of unity depends largely on Enrico del Carreto, lord of Finale, the Lady Beatriz' lawful husband. He is prevented by my headstrong niece both from enjoying his marital rights and from visiting the castle of his father-in-law. It is an unheard-of situation! A chit of a girl and an upstart troubadour threaten the very existence of Monferrat! Mind you," he said, with scarcely controlled animosity, "my lord of Carreto is a reasonable man. He, no more than any of us, would stand against the wooing of his wife by a distinguished troubadour; but there must be discretion! Peire Vidal, it came to this: my lord Bonifaz enters his daughter's chamber, finds them sleeping there——"

"Stop, my lord!"

"You shall hear! He lays his cloak upon the bed, covering them, and the next day your monsenher of Vacqueiras must kneel before his liege in public assemblage and pray forgiveness for, as he said, *having stolen a precious possession!* I ask you, sir, would not many a father have had the fellow hung, drawn, and quartered?"

"I do not know," muttered Peire Vidal. Sant Julian and all saints preserve him from such revelations! "What do you expect me to do? What do you want of me? Let me go away, I pray you, my lord! I have no heart to remain here longer!"

"By remaining, monsenher, you may save an infinite amount of strife and bloodshed. By remaining you will be serving the great and holy cause of justice!"

Justice! . . . Perhaps there was something in that. Perhaps the cause of justice would be better served here at Montferrat than with Richard the Lion. Perhaps the great witch Venus had led him to this spot and had granted him an unexpected and delicious experience as assurance of her interest in his destiny, a supposition he

154

had little reason to doubt, for she had surely, at strange times, bestowed rare favors upon him!

"But I am committed to the crusade, my lord," he faltered.

The marquis smiled outright. "So have been many good knights, Peire Vidal. But they have been glad to pay the Saladin-tithe to get out of it—and not for lack of courage, either! We, monsenher Bonifaz and I will pay your Saladin-tithe, and to Richard himself!"

"Sir, I will consider it, but I cannot promise. Now what do you wish of me? No meddling between lovers, that's understood!"

"Certainly. You are a knight and a gentleman. Now, give heed. Milan and Pavia have fallen out. They are bellowing threats of war. Pavia is of our imperial persuasion. Milan is not. We do not want war; we want peace and amity between these fine cities. We should be happy to act as mediator between them but Milan distrusts us. For that reason we may not send one of our troubadours as an ambassador of conciliation. But Milan would have no reason to suspect a known adherent of our antagonist, the Lion. Milan knows that Conrat of Monferrat inaugurated this crusade by placards in color, posted in all the courts of Europe, showing the Holy Sepulcher defiled by horses of the Saracens—and then this Richard stole his thunder! If you, in the interests of peaceful negotiations, should compose a sirvente urging Milan to be reconciled with Pavia, great credit would accrue to yourself, and many brave lads would be spared an early death before the walls of one of those cities! You would be speaking to them as Richard's man, not as ours." The marquis rose. "It is not a command, monsenher. It is a request. You are free to choose, and we shall not hold it against you if your reply is in the negative. In any case, the palfrey is yours, because you have pleased my excellent brother-in-law's heart by pleasing his daughter."

He spoke so earnestly and held the troubadour's hand with such warmth of feeling that the latter was at last moved to believe in the generosity and good faith of the proposal. Peire Vidal, neglecting the Bel Cavalier for a day or two, at once set himself to the composition of a ringing political exhortation, a type of song in which henceforth he was to indulge frequently.

In the meantime Raimbaut of Vacqueiras returned to Chivasso. His mission had been successful but he did not have the look of one upon whom fortune smiles. He was taciturn, dispirited, and quite unlike his old reckless self. He was not seen in the company of the Lady Beatriz and rumor had it they had quarreled. She kept to her chamber. Pastimes and gayety flagged at the castle. Only the busy emissaries of petty states came and went secretively, wearing the aspect of men who carry heavy destinies and threats of war in their portfolios.

In all that vast establishment Gaucelm Faidit alone kept his jollity, for the wine and the fare were good, dicing prevailed, and the marquis was generous in largesse.

One evening Gaucelm Faidit, jovial and potulent as usual, came to persuade his friend to attend a joc partitz between the Marquis Albert of Malespina and Raimbaut of Vacqueiras in the great hall. Peire Vidal remonstrated that it would distract him from his own composition.

"Sant Dalmatz!" protested the pursy troubadour. "Is there not stimulation in concert? I promise you some pretty unearthing of old scores by those two. They will puncture each other with pithy couplets and try for mortal wounds with words! If music has poison —and I think at times it has—they will pour it in each other's ears. Come, you are losing your curiosity as well as your deviltry, my good friend. Guilhelma, the brazen Circe! plagues me that you no longer buss her. Have you ceased to love the wench? One might think you were bitten by ambition; beware that drug, boy! It drags good men down. Let politics and virtue alone; the one is the invention of Beelzebub and the other the vice that makes martyrs. I'll not dirty my fingers with court intrigue no more than I'll wear the hair shirts of the Cathari and Albigenses and Poor Men of Lyons! They're all at variance with the true nature of the gay science!"

In the crowded hall were court dignitaries, ladies in many-colored gowns, knights, troubadours, squires, jongleurs, and a few burgesses from neighboring towns. After several preliminary exhibitions of musical skill by the more distinguished troubadours, the two contestants took their places, the Marquis Albert set the form of the composition, and Raimbaut, with the ease of long experience, answered the challenge in the same measure. Truly, it was a bitter bout. Each recalled in detail the iniquities, misprisions, fornications,

and other enormities of his opponent. They accused each other of
highway robberies, the betrayal of allies, forswearing of oaths, the
deflowering of virgins, the deceiving of friends, and of lesser pecca-
dillos. Little was left unsaid, and the audience listened with
gusto. But always, being gentlemen, they kept within the forms
prescribed by courtesy, and it would have been difficult to have laid
a finger on an outright insult. It was plain that Monsenher Raimbaut was trying to provoke his antagonist to an actual passage at
arms, and it was equally obvious that the marquis had no intention of exposing himself to a physical encounter with a commoner.

Peire Vidal listened with growing consternation. Appalled by
each fresh revelation, and before the verdict was announced, he had
left the hall. The Lady Beatriz, contrary to her father's command,
had not attended the gathering. Obedience was not one of her
virtues. As he had feared, the tenson had disturbed the course of
his thoughts; his own sirvente became intractable and the stream
of music that was wont to pour unbidden through his mind ran
suddenly dry. Regretfully he laid his polished instrument away and
sought his pallet, the hardness of which was masked by silken
coverlets. But sleep was refused his eyelids. He tossed and turned
till dawn, seeing visions of an ever-changing form . . . the body
of Rambauda of Biolh, the head and hair of Adélasic des Baux;
but though he heard the elfin laugh of Beatriz, he could not see her
clearly in the dream. So, at the first green hint of dawn, he rose
and went to find his palfrey, thinking to wear these humors out
by hard riding. In the stables he came upon Raimbaut of Vacqueiras. By the mud on his boots and the sweat stains on his
breeches it was apparent that he had ridden far in the night. His
bronzed cheeks were haggard but his eyes glowed with dark fury.
He began to speak, without any preamble.

"They may take her away from me," he muttered, "but it will
do them little good. I will kill her and myself. Then we shall both
be consigned to purgatory till the end of time! There is a nest of
vipers here! There shall be an end to that! But before it comes the
cities of all Italy shall be raised against this cursed Montferrat; not
a stone left of this pit of iniquity! The fields shall be plowed with
spears and sown with skulls! Their policy—hah! I know enough
to make it crumble at a touch!"

"Your songs, Monsenher Raimbaut——" Peire Vidal was desperately seeking to comfort the madman.

"Songs!" he jeered. "We'll sing again when flames go up from this festering pile!" With that, he was gone, growling and babbling to himself.

Peire Vidal rode down into dewy fields where larks were beginning to circle and sing.

"I have it on very good and intimate authority," said Gaucelm Faidit, "that our estimable marquis of Montferrat intends to adopt you as his son, making you the second in the line of inheritance. I congratulate you on your good fortune!"

It was a month later and Peire Vidal had just returned from his mission of conciliation. He turned a startled countenance, then laughed. "To be a brother to the Lady Beatriz? You must have your jest, Gaucelm Faidit!"

"No jest at all," said the stout troubadour seriously. "He has spoken to the archbishop of Milan about it. You are to receive estates of some value. It's all fair enough. Pavia and Milan have become as cooing doves. Milan is being guided into the imperial fold. The empire in Italy is Montferrat. And it is all your doing! Truly, a large prosperous city is worth a few paltry acres and a castle, not to speak of the title of chevalier, possibly viscount. You can return to your Rainier on terms of equality. A fair prospect, my son!"

Peire Vidal let his bow slip across the viol strings. A phrase, gay and dancing, escaped from the instrument. "Are you ready to take ship from Genoa?" he asked.

"What! Are you going to banish me so soon?"

"I shall be going with you. Richard's fleet sails in a fortnight from Messina. He has sent word."

Gaucelm Faidit looked puzzled.

"What are you going to do about your adoption?"

"I am sailing from Genoa."

Gaucelm Faidit's face began to crinkle; he suddenly caught his friend in an elephantine embrace.

"What a nimcompoop and foolish noodle you are! Hah! Curse

that lascivious harridan if she has not kept my armor polished! Do we start tomorrow?"

"*You* start tomorrow with Guiraut de Borneil. I start today with ——I start today!" Peire Vidal was gazing reflectively at the ceiling.

"With whom?" asked his fat friend with a satyric leer.

"An amiable lady of Turin—Estefania de Berga is her name. I have promised her some entertainment for the night."

"I believe, Monsenher Lecher, that the great witch Venus has you in her keeping! They say the Lady Estefania de Berga is both fair in form and wise in love. I congratulate you!"

Chapter Thirteen

As the sails of the urser grew pregnant with an off-shore wind and the Genoese sailors broke into an ancient chantey, Peire Vidal's heart was smitten with the sharp hurt of leaving behind all the things he loved, especially the young laughter of the black-browed girl; and his viol gave forth a more plaintive sound as he sang:

> Many and grievous burdens are my share
> Of Love's inheritance. . . .

Spring was still blossoming in Italy, but the crusade would take no account of flowers in bloom or the songs of birds. He felt it was more than spring he was renouncing; rather, as though he were saying farewell to some fair season of his life. Yet there was consolation of a kind: the announcement of his departure had immediately effected a reconciliation of the lovers, and on his journey he had enjoyed the not unwelcome favors of the amiable Domna Estefania de Berga of Turin, a lady of fair proportions, for whom he made a very good song which greatly pleased her.

But not so pleased was King Richard when he received his troubadour at Messina. "So," he said, with his wintry smile, "you have been settling the affairs of cities! Monsenher, you had best keep your viol tuned to other themes. You have but played into the hands of the cursed imperialists who use this little marquis for their pawn. Had you asked me, I could have told you which way to fiddle in Italy, for I have my own interests there and a larger game than any Montferrat will play. Sirrah, there may some day be an empire of the Mediterranean, of which this Holy Roman figment will be a mere outlying province. But why enlighten you? You singers carry no more thoughts in your heads than a bit of tinsel reputation . . ." And so forth. Then suddenly—"Can you sing in Spanish?" Peire Vidal confessed that he knew only a little Catalan. "That is a pity. You should know more than the *langue d'Oc*. Raimbaut of Vacqueiras sings well in four tongues. But he is an outright fool. I offered him a good living if he would leave his princeling but he's tied to that hawk-nosed wench who has them all in leash. However, I must have an aubade in Spanish by the hour of nones tomorrow, when we weigh anchor with the tide. Will you search out Aimeric de Peguilha and send him to me, monsenher."

Peire Vidal's former audiart, now advanced to the rank of troubadour, occupied a sumptuous apartment in a palace overlooking the harbor. He boasted two Griffon servants and his apparel as well as his bearing bespoke prosperity. His quarters, richly furnished in the Greek manner, with much gilt and inlay, were lighted by an abundance of tall wax tapers and scented with musk as a lady's chamber.

"Peire Vidal—my friend!" he said. (He says friend like a courtier, thought Peire Vidal). "I hope your excursion has been pleasant and profitable. We here have been too busy for diversions." He stopped to give an order to a varlet concerning some silken cushions: "For the Princess Berengaria. You will get them from the steward at the treasure house; the king's, of course." It was evident he had become a person of importance. Peire Vidal delivered his message from the king.

"Ah! The aubade. I had forgotten. It will be ready. He always sends for me in a crisis," he confided. He stood frowning, plunged in thought. "An aubade for the princess. Tender, yet valorous. Not from a king but from a simple knight, a high-souled crusader, to his love. Richard to Berengaria, flower of Navarre. Pathos of part-

161

ing. They are not going in the same vessel, you know. They may not meet again until they reach the Holy Land. Meanwhile, tempests, danger! Death lurks upon the azure sea . . . but love, love——

> But Love that does not fear to die
> Will meet the challenge of the sky—

"For a beginning, 'twill do! Perhaps omit the reference to death. Some women are timid on water. Since it is an aubade, I must bring in the Watchman on the Tower——

> Watchman who pace your starry round
> Silence this day your trumpet's sound
> Lest it unlock our arms—

" 'Starry round' strikes the right note! Pardon, my friend, if I neglect you for a moment." He played a phrase upon his lute.

All this made no sense whatever to Peire Vidal.

"I thought," he said as inspiration temporarily failed the young troubadour, "that it was the French princess, Aloysia?"

"Oh, the Princess Aloysia is quite out of it. They settled that matter, the kings, after something of a rumpus. When our king's mother, Queen Eleanore, arrived here with the Damsel of Navarre, our Richard needed no second look to tell him she deserved to be queen of England. Those dark, fiery glances, and her quaint accent! But it was not so easy to void his nuptial contract. Diplomacy—there's none excels our Richard in that noble art! It was a complicated business, Richard being Philip's vassal. When Philip the Lamb learned of the Lion's intentions, he orders him either to go with him across the sea on the March passage—in which case he would be at liberty to marry Berengaria later—or else to keep his nuptial vows. Richard refused to do either. Then, the first week in March, he and King Tancred held a great love-feast, and the kings exchanged presents, Richard giving the Lombard the sword Excalibur that had belonged to King Arthur. And a few days later Tancred puts into his hands a letter bearing Philip's signature and saying, in effect, that Richard was preparing to break faith with

Tancred, and if he, Tancred, would attack the English, there would be help from the French. So, at their first meeting, our king shoved the letter in the Frenchman's face."

"Did Philip admit its authorship?"

"Not he! He said it was all an invention of Richard to escape his obligation to Aloysia. But the king of England had an answer to that!" Aimeric took his polished lute and the notes dropped from the strings like water from a jar:

> Lest it unlock our long embrace
> And veil the glory of your face.

"His answer?" asked Peire Vidal, feeling a great boredom at the intricate dealings of kings.

"That he could not marry Aloysia because his father, King Henry, had lain with her and had begotten a daughter by her; and that charge he stood ready to prove by many witnesses who were willing to take the judicial oath as to its truth and prove it by judicial ordeal, or combat."

Peire Vidal was silent a space, then he said, "It is somewhat strange that the old king should have possessed such potency! Moreover, since the last time when he was in France he was wholly given to defending himself in battles against Richard and Philip, he scarcely could have found opportunity to seduce the princess then. And the time before that she must have been no more than a child!"

"There are many mysteries of nature, my friend," said Aimeric de Peguilha complacently. "Why should we question what Philip was disposed to accept, particularly after he had seen our king's witnesses?"

"Who were they?"

"Chief amongst them was the great general, Merchaderius."

"That brigand and routier!"

"He has a strong right arm!"

"Doubtless! . . . So the king asperses the name of his father and defames the honor of his betrothed—in order to free himself from his oath!"

Aimeric de Peguilha stared coldly at his former master.

163

"It is well," he said, "that only I, who am your friend, have heard those words, Peire Vidal; for if they reached other ears you would be in great danger of being hung, drawn, and quartered!"

"It is a danger you will never run," said Peire Vidal turning toward the door. Aimeric de Peguilha had taken his lute again. He sang:

> For never in such amorous fashion
> Was honor glorified by passion!

Peire Vidal was glad indeed to seek the company of Gaucelm Faidit, whom he found drinking and dicing with that courteous gentleman, the Châtelain de Coucy, and the scholarly troubadour, Guiraut de Borneil.

The time of the spring passage to the Holy Land having arrived, the Wednesday before Good Friday, at the hour of nones, the great fleet sailed out of the harbor. The vessels were ordered out in squadrons, fan-shaped. In the first line were three large ursers, one of which contained the Queen Joanna, the Damsel of Navarre, and such courtiers and troubadours as would afford entertainment to the ladies on the long voyage to Acre. In the second line were thirteen naves, busses, and dromonds; in the third, fourteen ships; in the fourth, twenty; in the fifth, thirty; in the sixth, forty; in the seventh, sixty; and the last ship was the king's own galley, the esnecca regis, which was named the Trenchemer, or the Sea Cleaver.

Every vessel was hung with bright banners and gonfalons, and brimmed with crusaders in shining mail. As King Richard had been the first to enter Messina, so he was the last to leave. He wore a tunic of rose-colored samite and a mantle ornamented with small half-moons of solid silver set in rows, interspersed with shining metal discs that shone like golden florins. A scarlet cap covered his large blond head; his well-proved sword, with its golden hilt, was sheathed in a finely chased scabbard, edged in silver. He departed without music, for it was a solemn occasion. Less solemn, however, to the Lombards and Griffons clustered on the walls, who sighed over their losses, then returned to the routine of extracting reimbursements from the Jews and Moors among them.

Gaucelm Faidit, though he had been commanded to attend the queen and the princess, at the last moment escaped with his wanton to another ship, the king having expressly forbidden any but the queen's own ladies sailing in the royal vessel.

"Plague take them," growled the stout troubadour, "if they'll make me drown alone, without a cuff on the ear from my wench! If she sails in another tub, they will have raped her, from the captain down, before ever we touch Acre!"

Aimeric de Peguilha was everywhere busy on the queen's business. Guiraut de Borneil had no sooner set foot on shipboard than he turned a greenish hue and was seen no more above deck. To Peire Vidal, therefore, as the most eminent among the remaining troubadours, fell the duty of providing much of the music—a task by no means welcome when he had looked upon the hard, shallow features of Queen Joan. For the slender Spanish princess, however, he had only pity; she was so quiet and reserved, and endured all the discomforts of shipboard with such regal fortitude. He could envisage her yielding, immobile, to the histrionic embraces of her consort. Doubtless her very stillness fascinated the restless Lion.

Luckily for Peire Vidal as entertainer to the stony-faced queen, a furious tempest from the north came down upon them the second day out, scattering the lumbering fleet like leaves on a whirlpool and putting an end to all amusements. The oars were hastily shipped, the sails furled, and the bobbing vessels drifted at the wind's mercy. When they had ridden out this storm and it seemed that their voyage might run smoothly, there came a still more fearful wind out of the south and a pall of darkness hid each vessel from its sister ship. Then it was that the Gray Monks on board were in great demand, for all now felt assured that the wrath of God and of his angels had fallen upon them.

Before the wrack of the storm completely enfolded them, Peire Vidal saw with horror the other two ursers of their squadron caught in the grip of the sea, stripped of sails, and cracked apart like nuts. He thought he heard a great cry of anguish borne on the wind.

On the morning of the Feast of Cherubim the sun came up bright and warm over a placid sea; it shone upon a harbor, and on a fair large city, topped by strange towers and overhung by a towering citadel, with blue mountain ranges showing beyond. The crippled urser, flapping a pair of forlorn rags for sails and partly oared by the few blades not shattered, crept to the harbor's mouth and dropped anchor. The pale knights laid hands upon their swords and the weary yeomen grasped their pikes and flails, for none knew what land this might be. At first they had laughed and cheered, thinking they had reached Acre. But the ship's pilot, who had once put in at that port, said it was nothing like this: the plain of Acre was flat and desolate, whereas this country was one of great fertility, the nearby low hills verdant with vineyards and orchards.

A large boat left one of the city quays and darted swiftly through the anchorage toward the urser. As it drew alongside, a bearded officer in glittering mail gave a sharp command, the oars were suspended, and he hailed them brusquely in an unknown tongue. There was confusion on board. The white-faced troubadour, Guiraut de Borneil, essayed to answer the officer in Latin. He was understood, but received only curt and peremptory replies. At another command, the boat drew away and raced toward shore.

"He says," said Guiraut de Borneil, "that this is Limasol, the capital of the empire of Cyprus, the domain of the Emperor Isaac Comnenus; and that we may not enter the harbor until he has ascertained the will of his lord, the emperor. He's a very insolent rogue. When I told him that this ship belonged to King Richard of England, he pretended not to have heard of him." Knights, squires, and yeomen growled in their throats in good English fashion. "And he says that the English are too effeminate to grow beards; they wear only a little tuft on their upper lips!" By this time the whole urser was in an uproar. Some bold spirits declared for attacking the town at once, but upon consideration of their weakened state, more sober counsel prevailed. There was nothing to do but lie to and curse the Griffons roundly.

They waited two days under a fiery sun and two nights under a reddish moon for word from the emperor, but none came. They had thrown overboard much of their food and what was left was rancid and maggoty, and the little water in the casks had a foul smell. The queen and her ladies were ill; the knights, soldiers, and sailors were irritable with the heat; only the slender dark princess kept her still composure. On the third day, when they had just determined to go ashore at all costs, there was a hoarse cry from the lookout at the masthead, "The fleet!" and they all sank on their knees, uttering prayers of thanksgiving: The pitiable remnant of the fleet hove into view and dropped anchor. Within the hour the king had sent word to the emperor: he was to release any prisoners who had been castaways on his shore from the English fleet; he was to restore all goods washed up by the waters; he was to supply the fleet with ample provisions at nominal prices and provide decent quarters during repairs and overhauling of the vessels. The envoy returned with the report that he had been unable to gain admission to the imperial presence and that the officers of the castle had been singularly unresponsive to his demands. The king prepared to effect a landing on the day following.

At dawn the English beheld a curious sight. Overnight Isaac Comnenus, the emperor, had been busy. Between the city and the sea a barricade had been erected in a great irregular semi-circle, enclosing the harbor. It was composed of doors, window frames, shutters, barrels and casks, planks, steps, pieces of old ships, benches, shields and bucklers, discarded household furniture, and nondescript drift wood. Behind this bulwark the Griffon forces were arrayed, some on foot and some on horseback, some in gaudy armor, and some in flowing Arab robes, armed with lances, swords, scimitars, and other weapons that glittered in the soft light. When the English beheld this war-like spectacle they uttered a great roar of laughter and, in high good humor, cumbered with their mail and arms, tumbled down into their cockle-shell boats from the unwieldy ships which had been warped close into shore. The arbalestiers had been posted on the deck of every vessel and waited, with their machines wound tight, for the landing party to get away. At a signal the air became suddenly gray with flying bolts. Rank after rank, they aimed deliberately, fired, and re-wound their weapons, with precision and deadly effect. Hardly had the king leaped from the first boat into shallow water when the Griffons broke and fled.

The emperor was commanding his troops in person. Mounted on a magnificent chestnut Arab, wearing a robe bright with gold and embroidery, he galloped up and down, endeavoring to check the rout of his soldiers with the flat edge of his Damascus blade, but when he saw it was vain, he too took to flight. King Richard, out-stripping his followers, was running up the beach. He clambered over the rubbishy barricade and, looking for something to fight, found no one, only a raw-boned horse running loose with a sack for saddle and stirrups of cord. He ran after the animal, caught it, sprang upon its back, and dashed after Isaac the Emperor. But the emperor had no mind to joust with that madman and continued on his way. The English shortly invested and took the citadel and all of Limasol.

The next day they gained contact with the Griffon army, scat-tered it, and took much booty and prisoners. The emperor then came in and yielded, swearing fealty to the king and promising to go with him to the Holy Land with five hundred knights and a large troop of mounted turcoples, and to give twenty thousand marks of gold as surety and his daughter as a hostage. But the same day he repented of his bargain, and that night he fled again on his chestnut steed, who was named Fauvel, and there was no horse like him in all the East or West. When the king heard he had got away on Fauvel he made a grimace, saying, "We will have to let him go, for we have nothing to catch him with!"

Though they did not find the emperor, Guy of Lusignan, who had come from Jerusalem to aid the king, discovered the strong castle of Cerine which housed the emperor's daughter. The castle yielded, and the young princess came out alone, praying for mercy. The former proctor of the Holy Kingdom returned with her to Limasol, where Richard, having looked for some little time upon her beauty—she was scarcely more than a child—delivered her to his sister, Queen Joan.

The next day being the feast of Saints Nereus, Achilles, and Pancras, martyrs, Richard, king of England and duke of Aquitaine and of Normandy, and count of Anjou, married Berengaria, the daughter of the Sixth Sancho of Navarre. The nuptials were solem-nized with great pomp and ceremony in the castle at Limasol.

The Emperor Isaac Comnenus, in despair at his daughter's seiz-ure, yielded himself up and confirmed all his previous contract. And the government of Cyprus was given into the hands of Guy of Lusignan, which was the beginning of another dynasty of that island realm.

It was on this day that Peire Vidal first saw the child of the emperor. At once he felt great compassion for her, timid and bewildered among the loud-voiced host of English, the boisterous Normans, and the ogling lords from Jerusalem. He could not sing all day for thinking of her.

Chapter Fourteen

THE castle at Limasol was vast, labyrinthin, chill with the chilliness of walls immensely thick, and barbaric in splendor. The vanquished emperor shuffled about, his head bowed in his long grayish beard, attended by the suffragan of Limasol who carried a Greek cross of gold. The priest's dalmatic was studded with jewels and covered with embroidery in gold and silver, and he repeated endless prayers in his own tongue. The Normans sneered and crossed themselves when he passed them for he was a Griffon, and Griffons were image-worshipers, no better than infidels—worse, in fact, for they pretended to adore the Christ while practising infamous rites of black magic and demonology.

The child Xene, under the care of Queen Joan, was kept away from her father and from the view of the curious. The emperor's concubines had been distributed among whatever knights desired them. The Griffon ladies of the court were similarly dispersed, while to squires and yeomen fell the comely daughters of the city's merchants. Even the archers (though they found it difficult to keep them on threepence a day) were rewarded with the town's humbler wenches. But the troubadours, obedient to the precepts of their calling, refused all tenders of female booty.

That which seemed most sinister about the castle was its whispering silence; figures in mail, in cloaks, in mantles passed warily through hushed corridors, huddled in small groups, drew discreetly apart. Already there were cliques and factions, between barons and clergy, among Normans and English and the nobles from Jerusalem. But the invisible presiding spirit of intrigue was the Queen Joanna, with her narrowed eyes and lips always pursed as though tasting some malicious gossip. Only Richard the Lion's high-pitched voice echoed loudly where other sounds were muffled. Once Peire Vidal heard that voice raised in furious anger. "I tell you I am king in my own household as well as in my kingdom!" A low murmur answered. Again the king: "No! By Jesu! A thousand times no! She goes with me!" Silence. A single low word. A woman lifted the arras and passed the troubadour with quick, inaudible steps, like a cat. It was the erstwhile queen of Sicily, Joanna. She did not notice him, pressed against the wall.

Some days later Gaucelm Faidit paid a visit to Peire Vidal, who was gazing in melancholy dejection at his polished viol, long idle for want of inspiration. His corpulent friend wore an air of unwonted solemnity.

"You are unhappy, comrade," he said.

"Yes," said Peire Vidal, "for it seems to me that there is more evil done in the name of God than for any other reason."

"Progress, my friend, is manured with iniquities. The most vicious crimes may be the seeds of great good to mankind. The Emperor Manuel—in spite of what we Latins assert to the contrary, that all Griffons are devils!—was a great and good ruler of New Rome. His son, Alexius, was murdered by his cousin, Andronicus, a thorough rascal but a statesman of merit. But this excellent assassin lived to see Cyprus torn away from New Rome by this upstart general, Isaac, who made himself into an emperor. And shortly Andronicus was hung up and hacked to bits by his worthy successor, Isaac, well named the Angel."

"Strange!" said Peire Vidal. "All that was related to me by Adélasie des Baux. And she gave me this ring that had belonged to the Emperor Andronicus. And more curious, it had been sent to her from the Holy Land by that courteous monsenher, the Châtelain de Coucy, though not until this moment have I remembered that fact!"

Gaucelm examined the ring with great interest. The carnelian,

171

like a drop of fresh blood, was skilfully engraved with two griffons rampant, facing a trident.

"H'm," muttered Gaucelm Faidit. "If I were learned in emblems I would know the meaning. Perhaps, the two Comneni, Andronicus and Isaac, with the sea's sign between them. Well, from the loins of Isaac the Upstart has come a fair flower." He paused and then added gravely, "and God almost took her to His bosom!"

"What!" cried Peire Vidal, jumping up.

"Yesterday the Princess Xene was taken with a sudden illness. My good wanton, whom the queen made the girl's bower-woman, because none of the English jades would serve a Griffon, is somewhat versed in the art of medicine, which she learned while whoring at Monpeslier. Guilhelma gave her a heavy purge, opened her veins, and then administered a certain potion of great power to vitalize the heart when it has lost its motion. Tending her through the whole of the night, my wench brought the royal child back to the life she had nearly abandoned. Today she is weak but on the path of recovery—pray God that malady does not return!"

"What was the nature of it?" Peire Vidal found his voice trembling.

Gaucelm Faidit's lips formed a word but he did not utter it aloud: "Poison!"

"Jesu!" It seemed to Peire Vidal his own heart had stopped. "How do you know?"

"The fit came upon her just after she had finished eating some lentil soup. There was a little of it left. My wanton secreted the remainder in a phial and brought it to me. I gave it to an ape, and the poor beast was soon writhing in death pangs."

Then Peire Vidal again experienced the desire to kill. It seethed through his veins and through all his body, like boiling pitch. The muscles of his neck and arms were contracted by a spasm; his eyes became suddenly small and bloodshot.

"But," he croaked, "there is no reason for it!"

"Poisoning is not usually compatible with reason!"

"Who could have done this foul thing?" His friend was silent. Peire Vidal came and laid heavy hands on the other's shoulders. "Who? Tell me! You know something!"

"Nothing," mumbled the troubadour uneasily. "Less than nothing. I do not even hazard an opinion!"

Peire Vidal sat down on the floor and drew his knees up under his chin. Violence had ebbed from him, leaving him faint. His face was twisted in a scowl, not of anger, but of concentrated thought.

"It is jealousy," he said finally, "which is most poisonous—unless her father feared for her honor, and would rather see her dead. But I do not think that walking corpse is capable of such an act. . . . It is jealousy. . . . It is someone who hates her beauty and innocence; and her power to. . . ." He remembered the stormy sounds from that inner chamber; "to rouse the king to infatuation!"

"Stop!" whispered Gaucelm Faidit, looking about him. "You are treading dangerous ground!"

"No more dangerous than the life of the child!" He was again silent for a space. "Tell me, Gaucelm Faidit, of what did the Sicilian king, Joanna's husband, die?"

Gaucelm Faidit answered quickly, "William the Good died in the arms of the Church!"

"And of his wife!"

"Monsenher Vidal," said the fat troubadour with a grimace of alarm, "if you persist in such suppositions, I must leave you. I have no inclination to go the way of my ape; or worse, to endure the parting of my head from my body!"

"Harken to me, Gaucelm Faidit!" Peire Vidal spoke calmly now. "Whatever your inclinations, you must lend aid in saving this child from——" he choked—"from what may soon come to pass—her murder! If you do not go to the king and tell him of what has happened, I myself will go!"

"You are quite mad, my friend. The king! With an accusation against. . . . No! You might better denounce his mother! Poor knights do not cite royalty before the bar of justice!"

"Then, Gaucelm Faidit, I myself will take her from this loathesome hell-pit!"

Gaucelm Faidit showed no surprise; he merely grunted. "You understand that this princess is hostage for a kingdom?"

"What will she be, dead?"

173

"Not mistress of a king or of a witling troubadour!"

"I will marry her!"

The fat squire chortled. "A good Griffon you'd make—beard and all!" Then he drew a lugubrious visage. "I'd feel most uncomfortable, knowing you were in the torture chamber, my friend!"

"I am there now. I shall suffer torture beyond the rack and screw until she is away from that she-demon!"

Gaucelm Faidit scratched his head. "It is more than folly; it is madness." He paused, frowning. "It is worse than madness; it is the height of reason! Why shouldn't you escape the vengeance of the king, though his arm extends only from England to Arabia? Why not marry the princess and inherit the throne of Cyprus? There have been less gifted emperors than Peire Vidal. There will be others to come whose voices will be as chirping sparrows and whose brains might rattle in the skulls of rats! . . . But what if this little soft creature objects to your impetuous wooing?"

The troubadour's irony fell on deaf ears. Peire Vidal faced him with knit brows. "There is a bond between us, Gaucelm Faidit. When I gave my oath to you to follow the ways of knightliness I promised to defend the weak against the strong. I swore by the Blessed Virgin, upon my sword Durandal, I would succor the oppressed. The girl Xene is both weak and oppressed. . . . What would you have me do, Gaucelm Faidit; forget that I was made a knight at your hands?" He was pleading. There were tears in his eyes. Gaucelm Faidit coughed, fingering the white, straggly tuft on his chin.

"Well . . . well. If there is to be folly, let us have plenty of it; and if there is to be a hanging, two shall make good company. I will do what I can. But first I must consult with my wanton. She has more good sense than both of us. Do nothing until I return, but if you have any gold, keep it in your wallet; you will soon need it. And convert whatever goods of value you possess into coin. If you are offered booty, take it. For once it may be put to good use!"

For three days Peire Vidal saw nothing of Gaucelm Faidit. Then on the morning of the fourth day, at the hour of lauds, before any of the castle was astir, he was visited by his friend. The fat troubadour's face was troubled and at first Peire Vidal thought he had come to urge the abandonment of the project.

"It is arranged," he said, easing his bulk into a gilded chair. "It is a hazardous enterprise, but by the grace of Sant Julian you may come off with it."

Peire Vidal could have shouted with joy, but he held his peace. He noticed that the hands of the troubadour shook. It was plain Gaucelm Faidit had labored under mental duress, and that his strength was spent; he yawned.

"Ho-um! An act of mercy takes more exertion than seven rapes and robberies! My eyes have not known sleep for three nights. First: the damsel. She must be made to know her own danger at the hands of . . ." he lowered his voice to a whisper . . . "the king and his sister, the queen; and of danger of two sorts, against her body and her life; and of how a champion had come to rescue her and bear her away to safety. That delicate instruction was my wanton's work, and no easy matter, for the girl was terrified and would have fled straightway to her father, but Guilhelma let her know such a course might lead to the old man's death as well as her own. When she was pacified on that score, she feared to trust herself into a stranger's hands. So again my wench exerts persuasion; tells of your noble qualities, of your unquestioned rank and quality as a troubadour, and of your—hum!—personable bearing and elegance."

"Need that have been gone into?"

"Do you think, sirrah, that a princess wants to run away with a bumpkin? The first step accomplished, we proceed to the means. She agrees to fly, but how? At this point enters the superior intelligence of my wanton's master, myself. We must secure transportation and freedom from pursuit—not an easy matter, seeing that this is an island and all its ports are closely supervised and guarded. In brief, this is the plan: there must be a substitution. The king must not know of his deprivation until he reaches the Holy Land, else you would never cross the Mediterranean. And tomorrow is set for his departure. In the turmoil and confusion of that passage our design may meet with success. The emperor and his daughter will take ship——"

"How——" began Peire Vidal, but Gaucelm Faidit cut him short.

"What a day I had trying to match the build and features of

175

your Xene! But I found her, and like as a twin!—the choicest product of this city's brothels!" He groaned. "I am too old for such excursions . . . and how the lustful jades fingered me! It cost a pretty handful of sols to buy her freedom! I have not seen so much nakedness since I was twenty summers. Ah me, these old bones! I hope you do not by accident lay hands on this Jezebel instead of the little princess; it would do your health little good! We have her ready, and so the second step has been taken. The third will be a generous scattering of gold among certain varlets of the castle."

"What of our sea passage?"

"I have made discreet inquiries and find there is a small and shallow port a dozen leagues or so away along the coast, where only fishing smacks put in. One of these craft may be had for hire to take you to the isle of Candia, or as they call it, Crete. You are traveling as two young peasants to this port of Papho, which in olden times was a great city named Paphos. At Papho a certain former officer of the emperor will secure a boat for you. The rest is in the hands of God!"

"But what of yourself, my friend, and Guilhelma, when this imposture shall have been discovered?"

"We shall be half way to Genoa. Today I saw the king; complained of my old wounds; and how this cursed climate had sickened my wanton; offered my Saladin-tithe to be released from my crusader's oath. It was grumblingly accepted. You would think the taking of Acre depended on troubadours—as, no doubt, it does! At any rate, when the king sails for Acre, my wanton and I sail in the opposite direction. And I may say, I desert this holy cause with no compunction!"

As the event turned out, Peire Vidal's greatest grief was at parting from his sword Durandal and his polished viol. There was no means by which their return could be assured, so their owner left them, with heavy heart, in the keeping of a trusty squire from Provence, one of his own troop, with instructions to have them delivered to the Châtelain de Coucy after his departure.

It was the ring of the Emperor Andronicus saved the plan from failure.

The great fleet, once more assembled, and within the month refitted and overhauled, was ready to weigh anchor for the Holy

Land. The treasure ships were warped in toward shore and a vast quantity of rich booty was conveyed into their already laden holds while the bishops and archbishops stood by, offering benedictions and prayers for safe passage, and the Griffon priests, abhorred of all crusaders, hid themselves among the multitude, sullen in defeat. The menie of the king and of the queens was the last to embark. There was much scurrying to and fro to secure transport for the augmented household, concubines and slaves; so great was the confusion—what with the final tallying of precious goods and chattels —that it was dusk before the king's own galley and the queen's urser were loaded. The ships could do no more than gain the harbor's mouth and there await dawn for sailing.

Near the eastern postern gate of the castle, on a little crooked path leading into the hills and hidden from view of watch towers, a peasant sat upon a rock, his head sunken between his massive shoulders. In his rough skin cloak he looked half animal, bear-like; nearby, his tethered ass nibbled the sparse turf. Though he sat apparently patient and quiescent, Peire Vidal was in great torment of spirit, yet it was not the agony of a lover's suspense. A new song had come to him, and his fingers itched to try its music on the viol. A strange phrase tantalized his inward ear; he knew not if it were melody or no, only the instrument would tell him. And there was no viol. He was not thinking of the girl, or what would happen later, or whether there would be any love between them. All that belonged to fate or Sant Julian, patron of outcasts and troubadours, or to God.

The postern door creaked on rusty hinges. It opened outward sufficiently to allow a slim cloaked figure to emerge, then it closed again, with heavy finality. She stood swaying, as though from faintness or fright. He had got to his feet and stumbled clumsily toward her, a figure gigantic in the dusk. She gave a whimpering cry, reached for the door, and finding it shut, turned this way and that like a cornered doe. As he came closer, speaking reassuringly in Provençal, she slid suddenly along the castle wall and began to run, with little jerky steps, as one unaccustomed to common exertions; and he after her, perplexed and alarmed. He seized her as gently as possible and at once she became as water, sliding through his hands, inert, a dead weight. Yet she had not swooned; it was the resistance of ungovernable terror. Lifting her bodily, he carried her toward the ass, and continued to murmur what were meant to be soothing sounds. When he untied the tether and sat her on the under-sized beast, she slid off on the opposite side, and had he not clutched her cloak, would have fallen to the ground. Through all she had uttered not a sound. He started the animal moving but found it almost impossible to hold her on the pad that did duty for saddle and at the same time guide the small brute who had obstinate notions of his own. Never in his life had he felt so at a loss for what to do. So, through the deepening twilight they hitched along, he clutching and stumbling, cursing to himself his magnanimous folly in meddling with the affairs of Griffons and the Lion and the snake-eyed queen, while the girl drooped toward the creature's twitching ears, threatening at every step to slip from her perch.

Darkness descended on them like a fallen cloak. The stars glistened fiercely but the earth was black, the shepherd's trail indistinct, and this was a strange, dangerous country. They had reached the summit of a hill not over half a league from the city of Limasol when he knew they must then and there bed for the night if they were to save their necks. Down from the ass's soft back he drew her, limp as a rag, and set her among bushes that gave off a scent like aloes; then he tethered the ass, removing the pad and a sack of victuals. For pallet he made a heap of plucked leaves and branches, and threw over it his cloak, the hairy side down. There he laid her and tucked her in, with many misgivings as to her comfort, but thinking, this may be better for her soul than the silken sheets, set with jacinth, of Richard the Lion. And, entirely weary, he lay down close beside her, outside the cloak, and fell instantly asleep.

He was awakened by a tickling of his fingers, as of a mouse crawling over them. But it was other fingers than his, examining, creeping softly over his own. He opened his eyes to find that she had taken his hand and was holding it, staring the while at the ring of Andronicus. Then she raised her hand and removed from one of her fingers a ring that seemed identical with his. Holding the two rings close together, she laughed delightedly, as a child laughs, and looked into his face with complete confidence and

178

assurance. He grinned back at her, saying, "God bless you and give you health, Domna Xene!"

Whereat she got suddenly to her knees and taking a little silver cross from her breast, she held it up before her and began to pray in her own tongue; and the whitish dawn shining on her face made her look like one of the carven angels of the portals of Sant Trophime at Arles. Beyond and below them, the sapphire sea was thick with white sails unfurling and bellying before the wind that was to bear the great fleet to the Holy Land.

It was at Papho, or rather, on a hill overlooking that wretched little port, that the Witch of his visions again appeared to him. The journey had proved longer and more difficult than Gaucelm Faidit had foreseen. The slow pace of the ass and Peire Vidal's ignorance of the shepherd trails, to which they clung out of fear of pursuit, as well as the weakness of the princess under the fierce bright sun, consumed the hours of daylight till the sun rested his hard red face on the westering rim of the sea and long shadows trooped across the fertile vales.

Peire Vidal sang many melodies in a low voice. The daughter of the deposed emperor was silent, two delicate white arms braced against the shoulders of the padding beast. Seeing her sideways, in profile, he at times observed his prize with some curiosity: a being with none of the beauty or glamor of the women of Provence. Rather, like one of the tiny ivory figurines carved with exquisite skill by the Griffon craftsmen of Messina—so dainty and so useless! Yet as he studied her more closely he seemed to discern, in the almost straight line of brow to nose, in the cleanly cut curve of her lip and the firm rondure of her chin, a certain power, sharpened and pointed like a well made dagger of Damascus. She might droop, but she was no weakling. He wished she were more developed; her breasts scarcely swelled the tight-fitting garment she wore beneath her cloak. The gowns of Provençal ladies were loose and flowing, gathered low with a girdle, and their bosoms took the eye at once. This girl Xene wore a simple, sheath-like gown that looked uncomfortable and was outlandish and barbaric; he would see that she was properly instructed in the art of dressing.

Skirting the mountains, they came at length to an open space on a hill above the port of Papho, and the sun slid over the edge of the sea, drawing from it ascending veils of darkness. Peire Vidal was about to guide their animal downward when she cried, "Dieu! Dieu!" and pulled sharply at the rope bridle. She was pointing toward the brow of the hill. About the edge of this level expanse were marble ruins which, in the fading light, looked extensive; there were great square blocks, flights of steps, rows of columns with their architraves still intact. Xene was making signs upon her breast with rapid fingers, murmuring excitedly in her own tongue.

"Let us seek shelter below," he said in none-too-fluent French, which he was delighted to find she understood. "It is perhaps an ancient church of the Romans. We Provençals are really Roman."

"No!" she cried in her quaint dialect. "We do not go down to-night. This is a place of the Great Mystery. It belongs to my people, not yours!" This last was uttered with such imperious pride of race as he had never known in a woman, not even in Adélasie des Baux.

"I do not like the looks of it, and I have a cavity in my belly where food should lodge," he grumbled. In truth, Peire Vidal felt far from comfortable in this spot. It had an air of being frequented possibly by demons, at the least, by fairies or other unholy beings. Also, it were well to have this bride-to-be understand just who was master. He tugged stubbornly at the ass' halter, setting his face toward the harbor, but something in the willingness of the beast caused him to look back and he saw there was no rider. She had slipped off and was standing rigidly against the sky.

"Come!" he said brusquely. "We must lodge and feed, for to-morrow we sail to unknown parts."

"Go yourself!" was all she said and he had perforce to return, somewhat abashed. He made such provision against the inclemencies of the night as was possible, sullenly, for his limbs ached to lie on a good pallet and his stomach clamored to be filled. Into the humid blue twilight she vanished, leaving him wondering and uneasy.

In this silent place of white carved stone high above moldering Papho stars sprang into being with an almost audible suddenness. He wished Xene would reappear. She was comforting, if unaccountable; all Griffons were unaccountable—worshipers of images, always chanting, mumbling prayers; secretive, proud in subjection, delighting in richness of cloth, in gold and jewels and other barbaric trifles. They were too cleanly and perfumed to be quite honest.

There was a Power here. He sensed it in the tingling of his skin, felt it stirring at the roots of his hair. It was more potent and witchful than that of Venus. Though he had often faced death in battle without a tremor, his heart beat now with some feeling akin to fright. Finally he could stand it no longer and he began to run, in great bounds, searching for the child princess. He ran this way and that, peering, darting back, shouting, "Xene! Xene!" and so came to the summit of the mound. At this point was a square platform of marble, as high as his head, surmounted by three columns whose graceful shapes he could barely discern in the half-light of the stars. It might have been an altar built by a vanished race to a forgotten deity. Xene was on top of it, kneeling.

He was about to call out to her, to chide her for being an ignorant superstitious girl, when she dropped her cloak and stood up in the white robe that clung close to her and made her seem as straight and slender as a holy candle in the church of Sant Trophime. She raised her arms and was speaking; she was speaking to that invisible Presence whose influence permeated all of this region. He heard a word repeated several times, "Aphrodite! . . . Aphrodite!" It must be a Griffon sorceress, he thought; perhaps she is praying for a good outcome to her wedding night; she must be a good girl!

"Xene," he said softly, "come down!"

The princess slowly lowered her arms, then she came to the edge of the altar and without hesitation leaped into his arms. Peire Vidal was so astonished that he almost let her fall. He held her tightly; she smelled of some strange perfume that went to his head quickly, like strong wine, and her eyes glistened strangely in the starlight. He was dizzy, perhaps from hunger, and as she made no effort to walk, he carried her back toward the nibbling ass. He noticed that she wore a wreath of flowers in her hair and saw that they were poppies. He laid her down upon the shaggy peasant coat that stank of animal. Then, without knowing how it came about, he found himself pressing his lips to hers; it was as though she drew him in

181

to her; he could not have resisted, and all his strength flowed out of him and fastened itself upon her body. He had the sensation of falling, swirling in space; there was no more flesh, and there was nothing but flesh, and solid things melted and insubstantial thought took on material form; and he had a vision of a great sea with ships sailing across it, and then armed men running and leaping at a high wall, and the sun coming up and going down about the world that rested or floated like an egg on the fathomless liquid of the universe; and all this time his mouth never let go of hers, until at length he gave a great groan and sank down against her breast. Before God he was the husband of Xene, daughter of an emperor.

Without knowing when sleep came, he slept.

He saw the sea, calm and blue, and tracked with traceries of foam as after a great storm. And gliding on a foam-path came the witch who was sister to Venus, or Venus herself in other guise. She wore a wreath of poppies in her hair; myrtle clung about her feet and roses bloomed where she had passed; the air rained apple blossoms. Sparrows fluttered before her, swallows darted and doves circled and one great white swan paged her with arched and glistening neck, bill clacking as for food. She breathed forth incense and her naked beauty hurt the eyes. He noticed that as she came toward him, sinuously gliding, she bore in her right hand a circlet of shining gold, studded with jewels, and he was glad, for it seemed to be a crown intended for himself; but as she drew nearer he was smitten by unaccountable terror and would have fled if his legs had not been limp and powerless. She was smiling, her eyes glistened and shot strange fire into his veins, heating them in the way of heavy wine, and the beauty of her was unbearable. Then she raised the crown and laid it on his brow. It distilled instant poison that ate into his skull. He strove to tear it off, he was filled with horror, the sea was swirling round him like a blue platter, he was going mad, he cried aloud in mortal agony. . . .

Xene's arms were tight about his neck. She was kissing his throat. Sunlight touched her shoulder to warm cream and the morning sky flamed behind her head. She said, "Look!" He sat up, rubbing his eyes.

Below, in Papho, there was a stirring of life. The town was full of armed men. He could plainly see the sparkle of light on mail, the flash of steel weapons; armed men along the beach, pacing lanes, entering huts . . . the Lion must be loth to let slip his prey! He watched until at last, beyond the headlands, came the first of the great fleet, ursers, esneccas, galleys, naves—two hundred sail, in orderly formation; and last, the esnecca regis, draped with the banners of Plantagenet. The king's ship hove to outside the harbor. A boat filled with armed men put out from shore. Was the king in that boat or on board, grimly waiting? Peirc Vidal after one glance, did not stop to learn. The ass had strayed. They left it to its own devices. Up over the brow of the hill they scurried on foot, toward the range of lofty and forbidding mountains where lay unknown terrors, less terrible than the vengeance of Richard of England.

Chapter Fifteen

THE blessing of spring is that it breeds forgetfulness. It is thrice blessed in Provence where song is in the air and scents of various flowers perfume each wandering breath of heaven, and where the natural inclination of men is toward *joi*, gladness of heart, *joven*, young heartedness, *mesura*, a balance in all things, and *cortesia*, kindliness.

There were many things Peire Vidal desired to forget: the demon-haunted mountains of Cyprus, and the vast sad plain beyond; weeks of hunger and hardships when they two lived like wild creatures, hounded by the fear of Richard's men; and the miserable hamlet whence, on a black night, they made a perilous voyage to Canea on the isle of Candia or Crete; and the curious marriage ceremony performed by a bearded priest of the Greek church—a rite too heathenish to be reassuring to the troubadour. But there, at least, they were safe as long as the identity of Xene was kept secret, for the island was a province of New Rome and barred to the officers of Richard. With their gold they purchased suitable clothing and took passage in a Venetian galley for the city of the doges.

Peire Vidal, resplendent in a new suit and a surtout of silk trimmed with minever, on which Xene had stitched a red cross, gave himself out as a troubadour lately in the service of Philip

Augustus, who had been released by that king at Acre to return home to Languedoc. But with this vague account on his tongue he had not reckoned with the doge's officers. He spent an uncomfortable hour under the cross-fire of their examination and emerged with his wallet the lighter by twenty gold marks. Fortunately he was well versed in the private affairs of the French king and regaled his inquisitors with plausible indecencies of court life as well as an able exposition of the policies and antagonism of the two kings, a matter of absorbing interest to the shrewd traders of the Adriatic. Venice herself had eyes on the Holy Land. There followed weeks of dawdling in a palace while they waited permission to leave the city.

During all of this time they were under constant surveillance, and at length the attitude of the attendant officers made Peire Vidal suspect danger. Convinced that the emissaries of Richard had reached the city, he spread his gold right and left, secured a boat manned by a crew of villainous ruffians, and escaped in the dead of night. They were challenged and pursued, but his piratical oarsmen whipped the stagnant waters to foam as they bore away from their pursuers, into the blackness toward Italy. Then came a tedious voyage up the Po and a hazardous journey through Lombardy, skirting the cities, and so to Turin and the castle of the Lady Estefania de Berga, for here Peire Vidal trusted they would be safe.

In truth, he could not have found a more hospitable retreat. The lady of Turin was no great beauty but her heart was warm and spacious for those in need of succor. During the autumn and the whole of the winter following they lived quietly, in complete seclusion, in a high chamber of the castle; and to the servitors they were known simply as "the monsenher and his domna." Meanwhile the little princess was growing big with child, and in March her husband decided to venture toward Provence. Genoa to Narbonne; Narbonne to Belgueil by easy stages. Then home and safety and Jehan Porcelet grinning welcome, and varlets in neat livery bowing and scraping, and daffodils and narcissus blooms in the castle pleasance, and birds beginning to compose their albas and serenas to their mistress, spring.

Thankfulness and a great gladness filled the heart of Peire Vidal.

He was cheered, too, by the accounting of his property rendered by his bailiff, that erstwhile rogue, Porcelet—itemized with many deprecatory gestures and abject apologies for having overstepped the strict bounds of his authority.

"Our vintage this year was nothing short of miraculous, Monsenher Vidal. What with the shortage of wine from provisioning the crusade, it brought a good price. I sold the surplus, above our needs, to a Jew of Marseille, who paid me in Moorish coins minted by the bishop of Monpeslier—which is to say, money knows no religion. Our villeins are prospering on their land. I have made it a condition of their tenure that they must bring into fresh tillage each year for four years a quarter more than that of the year before, so that in four years we shall have more than doubled our yield. The moneys and dues of vassalage to our Good Count Raimon I met promptly at Candlemas, and was well entertained and furnished at Castle Bargarde by his lordship and his lady, though I grieved to find him in somewhat feeble health. If I may dare to say so, things will not go so well when the young Raimon comes into the inheritance. He lacks his father's noble qualities." And so forth, with all receipts and expenditures duly set down, to the last denier and obole. But when the business of the estate was finished, he still stood plucking nervously at the folds of his woolen tunic.

"You have something further to warn me about, Jehan Porcelet!"

"Pardon, my lord!" The man's face shone rubicund.

"Come, out with it! Do they say I have lost my skill at singing? You must get me a new viol at Toulouse, and I will show them!"

"No, monsenher, it is not that . . . but filthy tongues are clacking, monsenher . . . about your lady."

"Ah!"

"They say—it is going about, monsenher—curse their lying gossip and may the saints strike them dumb!—that you have brought a Greek slave from Cyprus, who was given to you by Richard the king! As if Castle Belgueil should ever have a mistress who was less than the daughter of a count!" Now that he had at last spoken, the bailiff looked relieved, yet waited eagerly his master's expected outburst of indignation. Instead, Peire Vidal only smiled blandly.

"But what they say is true, Jehan Porcelet."

"Master!" There was consternation in the factor's voice.

"It is true, so far as gossip is concerned."

"But sire, I do not understand――――" the man's bewilderment was comical. "Slave―and your wife, monsenher? Such things are―I beg of you, sire, not to permit your good repute to――"

"Jehan Porcelet, it is necessary, for reasons that I cannot explain, that the Lady Xene should have been a Greek slave. I myself have let it be rumored that she is of humble birth. And you shall substantiate my statement. However, within my castle, you will attend her as though she were of noble blood."

"As you command, my lord. Yet I would it were otherwise!"

Early in the month of April, when violets and primroses and joy flowers raised their happy faces to the gentle sun, there came to Belgueil a troubadour distinguished more for his gallantries than for his songs, though he was no midling singer. Gui d'Uissel and that famous wise lady, Maria of Ventadorn, had been lovers betimes; then he paid court to the Lady Gidas, niece of the Eighth Count Guilhem of Monpeslier. It was said that she offered herself either as wife or mistress, but when he chose to be her lover, she dismissed him and married a knight of Catalonia. Seeing how low was her estimation of human worth, Gui d'Uissel considered himself well rid of her. He was now on his way to Béziers, to try the perplexing charms of Azalais, countess of Burlatz and wife to Viscount Raimon Roger.

He had come to meet Peire Vidal and to satisfy his curiosity concerning the Greek slave, for he was one of those mortals who take an absorbing interest in the private affairs of others. There was no house in all Provence, or in Italy, Spain, or France, for that matter, of which the indiscretions of its members were not matter for his trumpeting tongue. If his life was not always safe where he had been entertained, he was usually made welcome by those not yet victims of his scandal-mongering.

He spent the night with his host and the Monk of Montauban, who had drifted back to Belgueil on the report of his friend's return, and there was a hearty sampling of the new vintage by the three of them. They missed the bibulous presence of Gaucelm Faidit, who had gone to the court of the king of Aragon, where, thought Peire Vidal, he was safe, out of reach of the Lion's paw. As the new wine quickened his tongue, Gui d'Uissel dispensed his store of intimate news.

Gaucelm Faidit, he averred, was more addicted to gaming than ever; he had lost heavily on the homeward voyage, and had even pawned his crusader's cloak.

"That is nothing," said the Monk. "The richest cities of France and England are in pawn for Christ's sake."

More gossip was retailed by his guest. He reported that Viscount Barrale of Marseille had put away his wife, Adélasie des Baux, for some unknown reason—though it might have been that his infant son resembled that upstart Folquet of Marseille more than himself (Peire Vidal spilled his wine); and she had flown back to her eagle's nest, Les Baux.

"You mean," said Peire Vidal, "they have ceased to live together?"

"Ceased?" Gui d'Uissel laughed. "They ceased long ago. She has been banished—kicked out of her lord's castle! As for Senher Folquet, he has become brother Fulk, a pious monk of the abbey of Le Thornonet, and nourishes his soul on breviaries!"

"Let us hope," said the Monk of Montauban, "that he serves God better than he did the Joyous Craft, for there was in his songs much matter but little meat."

Peire Vidal said nothing. But it was as though wormwood had been dropped in his wine. So Rainier had abandoned Na Vierna— shipped her off to the crags of Les Baux as though she were a disobedient serving wench! The thought sickened him.

"And now," said Gui d'Uissel when a second skin of wine had been opened, "let us hear of Messina and the Damsel of Navarre, and how the Lion got out of his contract with Philip the Lamb, and what he is going to do with the emperor's child."

Peire Vidal related the events of the crusade briefly and without fervor, for his mind was elsewhere. He skimmed lightly over the happenings at Cyprus which, he explained, were in the nature of an interlude and somewhat incredible. He himself had been taken with a fever, he said, and had begged to be released from his vow, a favor that was courteously granted by the king (strange, how he had mastered the art of plausible dissimulation!). But the other troubadour was persistent in his questioning concerning the matter of the emperor of Cyprus and his daughter. He had heard a rumor to the effect that Monsenher Vidal had secured a marvelously beautiful slave in Cyprus, whom he had taken to wife.

"True," said Peire Vidal carelessly. "I was lucky in the disposition of captives. Because of my slight service to the king at Messina I was given choice of the damsels of the emperor's household, and I selected a certain Thracian slave, a worthy and well-bred girl who had once attended the empress of New Rome. Her manners were so gentle and her intelligence so marked for her station that I decided to marry her, in order that she might become the mother of legitimate children. I have not been disappointed, for I have since learned that she comes of sound burgess stock—a family that had suffered the fortunes of war and endured captivity in New Rome. From there she was sold into Cyprus."

"I commend you for your common sense, Peire Vidal, and shall consider it a privilege to behold her charms."

"Monsenher d'Uissel, I fear that is impossible. My wife is approaching her confinement."

"Say no more, but allow me to congratulate you on your future offspring! We were speaking of the emperor's daughter, who has been taken to the Holy Land by Richard the Lion—for what purpose we need not speculate, I will tell you a remarkable fact about her."

"Let me fill your cup, monsenher! Proceed!"

"In few words, this princess is not the child of Isaac Comnenus!"

"Jehan Porcelet!" cried Peire Vidal suddenly.

"Yes, my lord!"

"Let us be served with dates and figs. And have we any spices?"

"Liquorice, sire, cinnamon, and nutmegs."

"Brew us a good hot spiced drink; and fetch with it sorb apples, brown medlars, pomegranates, and grains of paradise."

"Yes, my lord!"

"Pardon me, monsenher! You were saying something about the emperor's daughter?"

"She is not his daughter."

189

"What of it? An emperor may adopt any child for his own. Though I did not see her, I heard she was fair and noble in her demeanor."

"She might well be, seeing that she is the daughter of one who was emperor of New Rome!"

"You surprise me. What emperor?"

"The Emperor Andronicus Comnenus, by his wife, the Empress Theodora."

"You must be mistaken. Theodora and her two children were murdered."

"That was the tale, but only she and her son died. When she returned to New Rome, a soothsayer warned her of danger. She at once sent her little daughter, Xene, to her nephew, Isaac Comnenus, in Cyprus. She would have sent her son, too, but she feared he might be assassinated on the way, so she kept him with her. After her death Isaac adopted this Xene as his child."

"What proof have you of this curious supposition?"

"I have it on the best of authority, from the daughter of Eudoxia, empress of New Rome, who is the wife of Count Guilhem of Monpeslier to whose niece, the Lady Gidas, I paid court for some time. Further, the Greek name of Theodora was Xene. Personally, I am convinced that your king of England had learned of the circumstance of the Princess Xene's birth, and I do not hold it beyond his ambition to have planned eventually to marry her when he had disposed of the Damsel of Navarre. After all, he would make an able claimant to the throne of New Rome; and if he were no more than regent, his son would inherit the purple."

"It is all very interesting, monsenher, but relatively unimportant. Of greater moment is the fact that we have spiced hypocras and these seasonable condiments which are an excellent tonic for the blood in spring time!" Peire Vidal spoke with impassive courtesy. Under the table his hands were clenched.

"Why," said the Monk of Montauban, "do you say Richard would have planned this nefarious business? Is not the child still with him?"

"That is the strange part of it. It was given out in his court that he had sent Xene back to England, under the guardianship of the Châtelain de Coucy. But I know for a fact that the Châtelain was killed fighting at Acre. And I had it from a certain English-man, William Fitz Osbert, just returned wounded from the Holy Land, that the girl has vanished—whither, none knows!"

"Strange, indeed," said Peire Vidal, "that the king should lose his prize and with her the opportunity to become emperor of New Rome! Perhaps she has been poisoned. Such things happen. Well, it is no concern of ours. Will you try these sorb apples, monsenher? They are of our own harvesting, of our last season's crop, and my bailiff has found a remarkable method of storing them to keep, in our cold cellars. Then, if you will favor us with a sirvente?"

"Gladly, monsenhers!"

The nearness of his wife's confinement was no dissimulation. On the night following Gui d'Uissel's departure, while the vale of the Orbiel was clamorous with a sudden storm, Peire Vidal was awakened by groaning. He found Xene writhing on her silken pallet, her delicate fingers clutching her distended belly and her oval eyes dark with terror. She looked like a great white slug that had been mangled by a careless foot. Her face glistened with cold sweat, even her lustrous purple-black hair was dank. Peire Vidal, after one frightened glance, hurried to find Jehan Porcelet. He learned that there was no midwife nearer than Carcassonne; the serving wenches were all young and inexperienced. Jehan Porcelet leaped out into the dripping, roaring blackness, and returned soon with an aged crone, his master's sole surviving vassal. This feeble creature was deaf and almost blind but she brought with her a piece of hard wood, with certain magic properties, for the suffering princess to gnaw on when the pangs came; and she knew what steps to take to ward off fairies who hover about, seeking to snatch the new-born babe and change it for one of their own.

At dawn the child came, a lusty boy; already Peire Vidal had decided on his name—Andronicus. The grandam hobbled about, clucking incantations. Jehan Porcelet was all one broad grin. Peire Vidal went to the chapel of the castle and, kneeling before the little altar, prayed to the Blessed Mary, Mother of God, for he was a Christian; and to the great witch Venus, for he was a lover and troubadour; and to that unknown Aphrodite who had given him Xene in the island of Cyprus.

Three weeks later, when the world was a bower of flowers and the songs of birds scarcely ever ceased, he went with his bride and his son to the court of his lord, the Good Count Raimon, to have the child properly christened and that the count might stand as its godfather. He found the count, as his bailiff had said, in failing health. The great lord who had fought on many fields of battle and had long ruled with wisdom and justice, looked old and weary, as though he would willingly resign the jeweled mace of his authority to younger hands. On the pledge of secrecy and because he felt that his liege should know the truth, Peire Vidal related the whole tale of Xene and himself, repeated the account of her birth as he had it from Gui d'Uissel, and exhibited the two rings, identical save for the lettering.

Lord Raimon observed the child thoughtfully for a space, then he shook his head, sighing.

"I believe what you say is true, Monsenher Vidal," he said at length. "But it gives me no great satisfaction to know that you are the father of an emperor's grandson. New Rome, the last vestige of the Caesars . . . blood, blood! I hope that you will not be sucked into that whirlpool of human woe!"

"My lord, there is no danger. My ambition does not extend beyond Belgueil."

At that the Good Count Raimon seemed cheered, blessed the babe, and arranged for its christening.

"Also, there is the matter of your knighting. It was somewhat irregular, Peire Vidal. And since Richard of England, for your great services, has not seen fit to reward you, I myself will grant you arms."

Peire Vidal fell on his knees and kissed his lord's hand.

So, with due ceremony, and before the whole court of Toulouse, Peire Vidal, troubadour, received the accolade at the hands of his liege lord and was granted arms; azure, two viols saltire-wise, the dexter over the sinister, between four saltires argent. He had got his new viol and rendered for the assemblage a number of his latest songs which were received with generous applause, for all had heard of his exploits of the past year and they had ceased to consider him merely an inspired fool, though there were some who whispered that his final and greatest folly was in taking a Greek slave to wife. However, the young mother, the Lady Xene, bore herself with a composure and dignity that led them to marvel how she should so soon have acquired the deportment proper to a knight's domna.

The young Count Raimon, in particular, stared at her with such fixedness that had he been other than his lord's son and heir, Peire Vidal would have resented it. The ladies of the court, in their Provençal way, readily accepted the stranger as one of them; only the countess, being English, treated her with the stilted courtesy due inferiors.

So, after a fortnight's stay at Bargarde, they returned to Belgueil and there were merrily entertained by all their menie and villeins, who, under the direction of Jehan Porcelet, staged a mock tournament and other amusing festivities.

Shortly after, Peire Vidal received an urgent message from the Viscount Barrale, praying that he come soon to Marseille. The missive, coming from his Rainier, was so curious in its wording—"for there are matters of which I would speak privately with you"—that he was greatly troubled; but he could not make up his mind to undertake the journey, leaving his wife and child; and mostly, he was loth to see Barrale again. For he could not understand, and so could not yet forgive.

When, in the middle of the summer, the harvests of Belgueil promised an even better yield than that of the year previous and all things were prospering with him, Peire Vidal heard from the lips of Ugo Brunenc, a troubadour, of the death of Barrale of Marseille. He had died suddenly and unaccountably. Then Peire Vidal experienced the keen torment of regret, for Death now separated him from his Rainier and the secret he had plainly wished to confide.

Many months later, however, he got from a mendicant friar a curious version of the viscount's death: that Barrale, while stopping overnight at the Abbey of Le Thornonet, was stricken at meat in the refectory with a fatal seizure and died horribly before the startled monks.

"Le Thornonet . . . Le Thornonet . . . ?" murmured Peire Vidal, exploring his memory for the name. "Was it not there that the troubadour, Folquet of Marseille, came to expiate his sins by taking orders?"

"True," said the friar. "Brother Fulk has long been absolved of all fleshly errors and, by Divine Grace, has become most zealous in the labors of the Church. It was he, with the humility of the true Christian, who offered to wash the great lord's feet on his arrival, and when that was refused, he begged that he might be permitted to serve him lentil soup and thin red wine, the fare to which we are accustomed at Le Thornonet. It was while the viscount was finishing his second beaker of wine that the spasm came upon him. Surely a visitation of Heaven for refusing, with much scorn, the humble offices of my brother in Christ! Indeed, the holy abbot declared that at the passing of Barrale he heard the whinnying of a demon outside the door, waiting to snatch his lordship's unhallowed soul!"

"It was well, considering the presence of the demon, that this pious servant of God——" Peire Vidal choked——"was with his former patron when he died."

Chapter Sixteen

"C ONTENTMENT," says Peire Cardinal of the bitter tongue, "is one of the paths to obscurity."

Peire Vidal for the next two years was satisfied to remain at Belgueil though he received flattering offers to attend various courts. He was known far and wide as the troubadour who had let himself be attacked by savage dogs, for love's sweet sake; who had been favored by the Countess Adélasie des Baux and many other great ladies, and had chosen to wed a fabulously beautiful Greek slave; who had helped to take Messina, had saved the Lion's life in Italy, had chased the Emperor of Cyprus, had advised the Doge of Venice, had composed the quarrels of the cities of Italy, and had refused a dukedom at the hands of the great lord of Monferrat. His exploits and mastery of the Joyous Craft had become legendary—enhanced, no doubt, by Gaucelm Faidit with many additions and inventions of his own.

The troubadour-knight's continued retirement, however, gradually obscured his fame. Many were convinced that marriage had ended his singing, for it was well known that troubadours who took wives generally came to a bad end. They turned dull and phlegmatic; they ate too much, slept too well, babbled of their children, and spent uxorious days praising God for their blessings. Also, many new singers were coming into their own, clever fellows who played with words as a juggler tosses balls. The modern style was far other than the simple patterns of Arnaut de Maruelh and Peire Vidal. It was intricate, dextrous, packed with subtle meanings unfathomable to the vulgar mind.

Love, too, had changed. There were no longer earnest prayers to Blessed Mary for success, uttered by trembling aspirants; instead, an elegant gesture or a guarded phrase signalized merely another assignation. While the troubadours and courtiers and their ladies toyed with passion, the sluggish populace turned to religion, and the groping and rebellious spirit of the folk struggled painfully to understand the teachings of the Petrobusians, Catharins, Albigenses, Patarins, Henricians, Arnalists, and Poor Men of Lyons. Provence, stubborn in its opposition to Rome, seethed with heresy.

Peire Vidal, as time went by, found Xene no less unaccountable than when he first met her. She surrounded herself with images to which she prayed too often, and she hung charms and amulets everywhere about her chambers. She did nothing for herself, not even to the fastening of a single enameled brooch. The child was left entirely to the care of its nurse, a well-bred daughter of a worthy burgess of Carcassonne, who lived in terror of her mistress' low, imperious voice. She made a gulf between herself and her bower-women that they dared never overstep. To her husband she seemed utterly indifferent, save on those rare occasions when she was not so much loving as possessed by some potent daemon of love. He came to know the signs: the pupils of her eyes expanded until they were wells of fiery darkness; the slightest touch of her fingers then was intoxicating. It needed only one look for him to seize her in his arms and press her to him. And those nights were unfailing festivals of joy.

So he loved her, though she was at no pains to learn the soft Provençal tongue, cared little for his music, and less for the condition and affairs of Belgueil, to which he was by now ardently devoted. During these years his songs were composed for his own satisfaction and were sung in the seclusion of his chamber or in the open fields, watching the increase of his flocks and the growth of his vineyards. They were well fashioned songs. Yet there was lacking in them some vital element, some inner cadence that not even his great skill could supply. The truth was, he loved Belgueil, loved his horses, vines, the rich procreant glebe, loved the quaint small pattern of himself, Andronicus, and was genuinely fond of his lady; but he had ceased to be a lover.

The tranquil and untroubled course of his daily life was interrupted, however, when one day he received this message:

"If the Monsenher Vidal, of whom we have had tidings from Senher Raimon of Miravals, will care to undertake a journey to Biolh, he will be made welcome by Rambauda."

There it was. Her signature, fair and legible as a scribe's, firm as a man's. Undertake a journey: that left him free to decline, though the distance was short and the road good. Instantly, and with amazing vividness he had a vision of the darkling hold of the vessel in the harbor of Messina, and of their agreeable pastimes there, and of the cates and delicacies furnished by the amiable captain, and of his leaving her, wearing her delicately made shift which he had so bloodied. And at once the theme of a new song began to weave itself into his brain:

> *Non es savis ni gaire ben apres*
> *Cel que.s blasma d'Amor ni mal en ditz.* . . .

> He is not versed in love, nor very wise
> Who blasphemously speaks him ill;
> For Love bends all creation to his will,
> Making boors courteous; and tries
> Gently to give some joy to wretched wites
> Long cursing the emptiness of nights
> And their defeats; but failure has no stings
> In Love's proud eyes, who crowns their falterings.

He avoided Xene for he wished to be alone to struggle with the perverse imp of song, and to file his *vers* out, bit by bit, as one carves a wreath—flowers, stems, leaves, and fruit—from obdurate oak.

He approached the last stanza cautiously; cautiously yet firmly:

> This, then, I am resolved: to tarry

197

Near you, as long as life and fate allow
Such joys as burgeon from a solemn vow
Unknown to the voluptuary—
For he has only just begun to learn
Love's nobler aspect when his fancies turn
From frivolous intimacies, and carnal ways,
To find devotion as a theme for praise.

It promised boundless devotion; hinted at, but did not insist upon propriety; extolled *mesura,* the golden mean in life, balance in all things. He sang the whole piece, very pleased with his own music. He finished and laughed aloud. Then he was made aware that someone had been listening. He turned his head and saw the Lady Vidal, Princess Xene, daughter of an emperor. She seemed to have grown tall. He marked, with startled approval, her superb carriage. It was as though something very ancient, of inconceivable grandeur, infused her body with almost immortal dignity. Her words, however, were petty and spiteful.

"For what wanton," she asked, "do you make this pretty song?"

"For no wanton. A very noble lady. I am going to visit her soon, and I must bring a song to her."

"You do not find me a suitable subject for your singing?"

Peire Vidal was astonished and offended. No one had ever heard of singing to one's wife—a love song!

"Madomna——" he began. But he did not know how to explain. He started to say that it was unfortunate that the lady was a widow, because one usually made love to a wife—to someone else's wife. That was right and proper; but he suddenly realized that he would have to interpret all the Laws of Love to this beautiful barbarian, this unaccountable Griffon who prayed to images. It was impossible, especially as he saw that she took his faltering for some confession of guilt—though God knows of what he was guilty!

"Madomna," he said gently, as one speaks to a child, "I am going to see a fair and noble lady who is endowed with all the virtues that one could wish for. In this song I express nothing but my eternal fidelity and devotion to her because of the love she

198

has graciously accorded me. I would gladly make many songs for you, but you do not care greatly for music and——"

Quite unexpectedly, she dropped upon her knees, drew from her bosom an image, and holding it before her, began to pray in the Griffon tongue. This enraged him. He leaped at her and tore the idol from her hand and cast it on the floor.

"What are you doing?" he cried angrily. "Are you asking your magicians to put a spell upon me? I have done nothing wrong, and thought nothing evil. I am practising my craft as a troubadour and upholding the honor of love. You must not interfere with things of which you know nothing. This is Provence, not Cyprus or New Rome!"

For answer she burst into a passion of weeping. He was confused, and then alarmed; and in contrition, he took her in his arms and as he held her close to him, her oval eyes opened, showery with tears, yet dark and fiery too. He began to tremble and hastily undid the fastenings of her gown, fumbling clumsily with the strange Griffon garments she insisted on wearing. So then he held her naked and warm, kissed her breasts, her lips, her eyelids, and laid her on the silken couch.

That night, alone, he refashioned the last stanza, somewhat defiantly:

> This, then, I am resolved: to tarry
> Near you, madomna, as long as fate allows
> Pleasures that are borne of eager vows—
> Not of the mere voluptuary—
> But such as in the heart of him have risen,
> Who thanks his jailer for his pleasant prison,
> Happy to be there; and neither base nor vile,
> Meekly confined, as I, by your dear smile!

He made the preparations for his journey to Biolh as elaborately as his means and station now warranted. His menie had become extensive. His retinue was imposing in new livery. There were a company of men-at-arms, squires, officers of the castle, all mounted on spirited palfreys and roncins, while his own destrier was a splendid blooded Arab. One day the drawbridge was let down;

trumpets sounded; the banner of Belgueil was unfolded. The knight of Belgueil, without a parting embrace from his wife, was ready to set out on his courtly mission when there came a hard-riding messenger from Toulouse, bringing word of the death of the Good Count Raimon.

He did not go to Biolh. Though the news was not unexpected, the vassal of the great lord was stunned by it. He had made a number of journeys to Toulouse to pay his respects to his liege, but he reproached himself for not having made more. The aging count had always been so plainly glad to see him, so eager to hear his latest songs, and had so generously rewarded his singing: now an ivory casket of Byzantine workmanship to hold the Lady Xene's jewels; again, a bag of gold marks, tactfully tendered by the count's bailiff as he left Bargarde; and the last gift, an estate of some extent adjoining his own, had rounded out his fertile acres with crofts, meads, and woodlands, most pleasing to the thrifty eyes of Jehan Porcelet. This messenger of death brought with him a bequest to his knight of Belgueil from the lord of Toulouse; for the lady, an ivory comb with a saint carved on it, four wor-shipers and two angels; and for Peire Vidal, a sealed parchment. He opened it and read:

"To all Christian men, greeting! And be it known, that there appeared before me the knight of Belgueil, Peire Vidal, trouba-dour, the same being in my service, and made known to me cer-tain things regarding his lady, Xene, and by his evidence and my own conviction, his lady is, in fact, the daughter of the Emperor Andronicus Comnenus, who was the lord of New Rome, and basely murdered. Therefore, I declare, before God, that the Princess Xene is, by her right of inheritance, empress of New Rome, and that the child of her womb is the rightful heir to the throne, and I say this in full possession of my wits and affirm it on my honor and my precious soul. Witnessed at Toulouse this seventh day after Holy Children's Day, Anno Domini 1194, by the notary of Bargarde, Hugues of Les Puy, under the sign and seal of Raimon, Count of Toulouse and Marquis of Provence, his mark." At the bottom of the document the count had made a cross, shakily, as with aged fingers.

Peire Vidal stared at the missive, frowning. He paid the squire, folded up the parchment, and placed it in a small silver casket along with his investiture of knighthood. He said nothing to the Lady Xene about it. On that same day he placed his whole household in mourning. He had Jehan Porcelet remove from the walls all bright and gay cloths and arras; he hung the tower and parapets of Belgueil with black gonfalons, and had liveries of sable made for all his menie. He had the tails of all his horses, both of his own and those of his retinue, shorn to the bone, though Jehan Porcelet protested mightily against it. Lastly, he took his precious viol and had made for it a box of ebony wood, and having placed the polished instrument within it, he buried the box in his castle pleasance, under a cypress tree, at the grim hour of matins. Then he gave many great candles to the abbey near Carcassonne and paid for masses to be said for the soul of the Good Count Raimon.

Shortly he went to Toulouse to pay homage to the new count, the Sixth Raimon. A great festival was being held at Bargarde to celebrate the accession of the young marquis and the castle was gay with festivities, music, banners, and a vast throng of nobles, ladies of high degree, courtiers, troubadours, and lesser gentry, the vassals and well-wishers of the powerful young lord. Amid all this splendor and gayety the sable habit of the knight of Belgueil was remarked upon by all; it was intimated that Peire Vidal, fallen into eclipse, was now endeavoring to gain attention by fresh eccentricities, and they even went so far as to suggest—especially those who had not heard him sing—that his reputation was derived from his buffooneries. The mode was for fastidious niceties in manners. Punctilios and aptness in phrase-making were the order of the day. It was considered more civilized to turn an expression neatly than to give utterance to thought or to betray emotion. Any courtier who could tag a situation or abbreviate a personage to the space of a single breath was sure of popularity for the day, at least.

Among the newer generation of singers the most prominent was Aimeric de Peguilha, lately returned from the crusade where, he let it be known, he had enjoyed the intimacy of Richard the Lion, and had been the confidant of two queens. His courtly elegance, verging on the foppish but tinctured with a fine military bearing, as behooved an experienced crusader, endeared him at once

201

to the titled multitude, and he was everywhere in demand. It may have been for that reason that he had such scant courtesy for his former master in the Joyous Craft.

"Since you abandoned our holy enterprise," he said with studied indifference, "your name has fallen somewhat into disuse. It was ill advised. You lost a generous patron, even if you won a beautiful . . . Griffon. Are we to see the fair lady?"

"No," said Peire Vidal shortly, "she is not happy away from Belgueil."

For a brief moment the eyes of Aimeric de Peguilha narrowed, flashed a skeptical and almost contemptuous look as he said, "She must be a model of domesticity, since most ladies greatly desire to be seen and admired. But perhaps her former station has unaccustomed her to the company of the great." There was a dagger prick hidden in his words.

"It matters very little what her former station was, Aimeric de Peguilha, since her present station is that of Lady Vidal, wherein she is the equal of the son of a furrier of Toulouse, and also no less than the son of a draper of that city, who was once my audiart."

He went to find Gaucelm Faidit who, during the preceding three years, had declined greatly in fortune but not in his person. His shabby surtout, faded mantle, and cracked Cordovan boots measured his addiction to gaming, and his vast moldering carcass attested his fondness for the full tankard. It pained Peire Vidal to look upon his friend but his trouble of mind was more when he saw Guilhelma Monjo. Her once peerless breasts were become but flaccid bags of flesh; her hips were unwieldy with flesh; her hair, still long and thick, fell in frowsy braids, and her face was that of one whose price has diminished to a few sols a night. Together they mourned, two of them bibulously, the entombed greatness of the house of Toulouse.

"It is ever so," said Gaucelm Faidit, not troubling to wipe the red wine stains from his stubbly chin, "that mortals go up and down. As, for instance, myself and my wanton are for the moment under, as you might say, a brief cloud. In short, the new lord will have nothing for us but to decamp."

"You must come then to Belgueil, where there are ample provisions."

"No, my friend. Not Belgueil. Later, perhaps. We are faring to Spain where there is a good living to be had and much sport in one way or another." His blear eyes questioned Peire Vidal. "You and your lady are happy?"

"None could be happier!" said the troubadour quickly.

"That is very good. It is good to hear that someone is happy in these days. I fear there is a great darkness coming over Provence. The pope at Rome is beginning to stir. No matter, it happened in the ancient times to the Romans. Death and decay overtake us all, and why not a fair land such as this?" He drank deeply. Then he whispered, "Your . . . princess does not hanker for Cyprus or New Rome?"

"Oh no, she is quite content."

"It is well. I feared for you. I feared for you most, though, when I found he had blabbed to the king."

"He? Who?"

Gaucelm Faidit's head sank on his discolored bosom. He began to snore.

"What was he saying?" Peire Vidal demanded of the Monjo.

She came to him, slid onto his knee, and put her heavy arms about his neck. He could scarcely conceal his loathing. "Whom did he mean?" he repeated.

"He?" she said, pressing her heavily vermilioned lips to his throat. "That foul scorpion, Aimeric de Peguilha, he betrayed you to the king!"

Peire Vidal started up, pushing her off. "Guilhelma, I—God strike his craven soul!" His hand sought his dagger. "Kill him, Peire Vidal!" she hissed. "For he has turned the young Raimon against my dear lord! It is he who is driving us out! Slit his filthy gullet!" But suddenly, in the heat of his rage, he remembered the last time he had the impulse to kill an enemy: at Marseille, before Adélasie des Baux, when Folquet of Marseille came in to them. And he saw the calm eyes of the countess and heard her voice saying, evenly and steadily, "I give this kiss freely, and I accept Monsenher Vidal as my true and loyal knight, as he has always been!" And so his fingers relaxed their hold on the richly inlaid hilt of his weapon. Leaving a sack of bezants in the keeping

203

of the wanton, for which she thanked him with many fulsome kisses, he went to have audience with his liege.

He was kept waiting in the antechamber from the hour of sextes to nones, which he endured with stifled impatience for, after three days of Bargarde, he was anxious to return to Xene and Belgueil. He was glad now he had not gone to Biolh. . . . Xene's eyes would darken when she saw him. Her breast, that had filled out to the perfect mould of loveliness, would begin to quiver beneath her tight-fitting Greek bodice. She would place both her hands in his and draw him to her. . . .

"Monsenher Vidal, you are bidden into the presence of my lord, Count Raimon, marquis of Provence!" It was the chamberlain speaking. Like most of the young count's menie this fellow was haughty and supercilious.

In the great audience hall were several knights whose ceremonial attire shone against the walls like the bright plumage of birds woven in an arras. They stared with obvious amusement at the grotesque figure in black. Count Raimon, seated high on the great throne of oak carved with the arms of Toulouse, frowned. He spoke to an attendant; the officer said something in a low voice to the knights, and they withdrew. There was left standing at the right side of the lord of Provence only a clerical personage; probably the chaplain of the castle, thought Peire Vidal. His vestments, though they were of the lower order of the priesthood, were rich. His dalmatic of green silk was heavily embroidered with sacred emblems in silver thread; his stole was figured with the Cross and the Lamb, woven in seed pearls, and he wore a four-ridged beretta, indicating that he had taken degrees in divinity.

Peire Vidal approached and knelt before his lord. Count Raimon extended his finger tips, and the knight kissed them awkwardly, for he had never been accustomed to ceremony with the old count.

"Monsenher Vidal," said the young count, "it is rather curious that you come to our festivities clad in this somber garb."

"It is my humble way of honoring the memory of a great and good man, my lord."

The marquis stroked his small silken beard. His face bore the haughtiness of his English mother, but it was a feminine haughtiness, and his lips held the cruelty of a woman. Only his eyes and brow resembled those of the count his father, the first harder, the other narrower.

"Is it not something in the nature of presumption to extend mourning beyond the period accorded by the heir and all his kin?"

"I had no thought of presumption, but only of my grief. Your sire was deep in my love, my lord, and his going has taken some nobility and justice from the world."

"Indeed!" said the marquis acidly. "And do you think there is none left?"

Peire Vidal was silent with confusion. He had not expected that the interview would be awkward. With growing uneasiness he sensed that behind these speeches lay something of sinister import which he could not fathom.

The priest spoke.

"There is a time for all things, a season for grief and one for joy. It is arrogance against God to prolong one's sorrow beyond its natural term." Peire Vidal jerked his head toward the voice, bland and unctuous. It was the voice of Folquet of Marseille. The priest, as from an infinite height, a remote and elevated sphere, returned the startled gaze of the troubadour. "The Good Count Raimon," he went on, "was not exempt from mortal error. He died—" here his voice became stern and menacing—"in the Albigensian heresy. For that great sin his soul must meet its punishment." And after a moment he added. "As must all who covenant with Lucifer and Apollyon!"

"We are not here to discuss tenets of faith, Deacon Fulk!" said the count shortly. "Proceed with the business of the church, touching our vassal, the knight of Belgueil."

Now! It was coming, that deviltry hatched in the fertile brain of his whilom rival! Folquet seated himself with great deliberation, bent his brows judicially upon the troubadour, and said, "Do you profess the Holy Faith, Monsenher Vidal?"

A wave of angry resentment coursed up through the body of the troubadour and, reaching his face, twisted it into a grimace that was like a grin.

"Do you allow your vassal to be insulted by this priest who was better known as——"

"You will be good enough to answer the reverend deacon's

205

questions, monsenher—if you would follow your own interests!" The tone of the count's command was ominous.

"Very well, sire. I hold myself to be a Christian, and I have taken wounds in the service of Jesu Christus!"

The inquisitor continued:

"What is the Christian name of the woman whom you call your wife?"

"Her name is Xene, and she *is* my wife!"

"What were her birth and station?"

Peire Vidal looked quickly from one to the other. Trickery. Their eyes were stone. They waited, sure of their prey. He faced the count.

"My lord, the birth and station of the Lady Xene were well known to your father, and he counseled me not to reveal them. I hold myself subject to his advice."

"An obedient subject, indeed!" sneered the count.

"Where were the so-called rites of marriage performed?" The question came swift as the thrust of a poniard. Peire Vidal hesitated.

"They were performed at Canea on the island of Candia or Crete."

"You were married under the laws and by a priest of the Holy Church?"

"Yes! a priest of the Holy Church!" There was a loophole, for are not all churches holy to those who believe them so?

"The island of Candia is a province of New Rome. Its infamous temples that take the name of churches are administered by the sons of Belial, the Griffon magicians, calling themselves priests of God! They are ordained by the antipope, the patriarch of New Rome, the foul idolator and Antichrist of Romania! There *are* no servants of the Holy Church of Rome in that heathen island. In accepting the ministrations of one of these Cretan pagans you yourself have incurred the sin of apostasy. Your union with this woman of Cyprus, whatever her birth and station, since it is outside the bonds of holy matrimony——"

"Stop!" shouted Peire Vidal. "By the saints, I am not compelled to hear your lies, Folquet of Marseille!"

"You are," said the count coolly, "under a serious indictment that may lead to the confiscation of all your goods and chattels, monsenher! You had best give ear to the reverend deacon of Le Thornonet!"

Deacon Fulk seemed unperturbed by this outburst.

"Your union was illegal, profane, and unsanctified. As the vicar of Christ, I declare it void and dissolved. You have been living in a state of sin and harlotry; you have committed fornication on the body of an unregenerate Griffon and have begotten by her a bastard!"

Peire Vidal's face was contorted; the nails of his fingers, pressing into the palms of his hands, left red prints, like stigmata. He fell on his knees before the count.

"Sire," he stammered, "your good father was well acquainted with the circumstances of my marriage, and he never questioned its sacredness or validity!"

"My respected father overlooked many delinquencies in his subjects of which I am not disposed to absolve them. Do you, Peire Vidal, acknowledge the truth of this charge?"

"Yes! Yes! As you will have it; only tell me, what must I do? We will be married again before a priest of Rome. That is easily arranged."

"Not so easily!" said Deacon Fulk. "The Church must have ample evidence of your contrition, and to that end will impose penance for the grace and saving of your soul, and of the soul of the fallen woman with whom you have sinfully cohabited. But first she must be brought into the Christian fold and instructed in the blessed ways of God."

"Very well, reverend father. It shall be done!" said Peire Vidal willing now to promise anything so long as he might escape from this serpent's coil.

"For the better accomplishment of this worthy purpose," said the count, "it is our will and command that the Lady Xene be brought to Bargarde, where she may be placed under proper tutelage, under the jurisdiction of myself and the Church."

Peire Vidal felt himself growing dizzy. Leave Belgueil! Give up his flocks and vines to become a dependent of the count and a minor member of his lord's menie!

"Sire," he said, "I pray you that you do not remove us from our home which we both love!"

"You misunderstand," said the count coldly. "Only your lady will be brought here. You shall remain on your estate, subject to our disposition. We have no desire to impose any injustice upon you. If you display true penitence, it is possible that in time you may be legally united to this . . . mysterious woman."

"You intend—to separate us?"

"We propose to fulfill the edict of the Church!"

Trapped! He glared about him. At the doors were armed men. The word of Count Raimon imposed obedience, had power of life and death; his arm extended to the furthest borders of Provence. But beyond that were places of refuge, perhaps among savage and barbarous peoples. Then they would live as savages; live somehow, but free and safe! He must match force with cunning, ferocity with humbleness.

"Your command is my law, sire!"

He was already calculating how long it would take for them to reach Narbonne. Jehan Porcelet would arrange the details—money, disguises, the procuring of a coasting esnecca to bear them into exile . . .

The hard voice of the young count shattered his reflections.

"It is well that you have come to your senses, Vidal, for we have taken the necessary measures to insure that the woman Xene lead henceforth the life of a good Christian. Anticipating your compliance with our wishes, we have sent a message to her at Belgueil—in your name—to come at once to Bargarde." Peire Vidal's knees began to shake; he found it difficult to breathe. "She has left Belgueil under ample escort—in case there should have been any ill-advised opposition on the part of your bailiff or herself."

The great hall was turning around, the arras had caught points of fire, he was in a circle of fire and the flames leaped at him from all sides with serpents' tongues. He heard himself saying, "I . . . may see her when she arrives?"

"That is not possible," said Fulk. "She is to remain at a certain nunnery for a space until she will have mastered the rudiments of the Christian life."

"My child—" whispered the troubadour, "what of him?"

"The child is to be left with you, providing we are assured of its proper upbringing, for—" the count's words were honey-sweet —"we wish to temper justice with mercy."

The fire had reached his brain. He could hear it crackling and consuming. A voice spoke from the flames, harsh and automatic, "My lord, your will be done!"

"As for yourself, Monsenher Vidal," and each word was the flick of a scourge, "your penance shall be—" he paused—"banishment from Toulouse, until I give you leave to return!"

In the hall courtiers stood in files, whispering and pushing; their silken tunics rustled. As Peire Vidal stumbled through their midst, his head wagging, sunk between his heavy shoulders, one of them tittered, "Where is the bear-tamer? His beast is loose!"

He got on his black horse and rode away, across the great wooden bridge that spanned the Garonne, and it thundered under the hoofbeats. All about him there were flames and smoke, the stench of burning, cries and screams of those dying and being murdered. The Angel of Death, riding a great black stallion, was striking right and left. Daemons were flying through the darkened air like ravens, settling on the naked breasts of women and plucking out the eyes of children. The priests marched up and down the land, chanting *Gloria in excelsis*! The flames roared and walls fell crashing and the fields were churned to bloody mire and the cattle rotted, and famine and pestilence stalked abroad, marking the foreheads of their victims with a spot of red, and their tongues hung out and their bodies puffed up and exploded into slimy putrescence. Then the land was all quiet, bare and black and still. The walls were heaps of rubble where owls nested and foxes burrowed, and there was nowhere any singing but only universal silence. In this silence of the world God, the last troubadour, sang:

> "Whoever in the world would live,
> Must oft endure chagrin and pain. . . ."

Chapter Seventeen

OR six weeks the knight of Belgueil shut himself in a small tower chamber looking toward Toulouse. Here he sat the day long, staring vacantly through the narrow casement; and when an anxious servant, or more often Jehan Porcelet himself, brought him food, he hardly turned his head and spoke but few words. The bailiff, therefore, was secretly overjoyed when the Ninth Alfonso, King of Castile, called the Noble, sent an urgent invitation to Peire Vidal, seconded by the Viscount Raimon Roger, to come and sing at Béziers.

Peire Vidal, however, returned answer that he was overwhelmed by the interest of two such noble lords in his accomplishments, but that he was past singing. On receiving this communication, the king of Castile set out at once to fetch the troubadour to Béziers. His arrival, with a huge and fantastic Spanish retinue, caused something of a flurry at Belgueil. Jehan Porcelet, however, was unmoved by the advent of a mere king.

"He should have sent word beforehand. Tourneys and festivals and such cannot be run off at a moment's notice," he grumbled. "And what will their Spanish cooks be doing, upsetting our kitchens and wanting all sorts of outlandish victuals that aren't to be had for love or money?"

Nevertheless, they were served a refrection of warm, sweet, and savory dishes, ripe grapes, sweet figs and wine, the haunch of a fat sheep, well roasted, and wild fowl flavored with a sauce of ginger, grains of paradise, saffron and other spices. The king was well pleased, and after many potations offered to go to Count Raimon and demand the return of the Lady Vidal, and if the young lord refused, to bring an army and restore her by force to her husband; but Peire Vidal said that he would rather suffer anything in the world than be the cause of bringing bloodshed to Provence.

Thereupon the king had his chamberlain bring forth certain Spanish liquors of great delicacy and potency, whereof for that whole night they partook, until in the end they had become boon companions and Peire Vidal consented to accompany the king to Béziers, and, moreover, to exhume his precious viol.

On the journey Alfonso the Noble, as was frequently the custom, exchanged habits with the troubadour, and Peire Vidal wore the livery of a king of Castile.

At Béziers he found, among others, the Lady Rambauda of Biolh, who laid her hand in his and looked long at him, as one studies a tree to see how much it has grown.

"You have been living much to yourself, Monsenher Vidal," she said. "You bear the marks of loneliness."

"Yes, madomna."

"And what of the child of your marriage?"

"I have brought my son Andronicus with me."

"Would you care to have me . . ." she paused for a breath and continued, "take your child to Biolh until the mother returns to you?"

So quickly she arrived at one's needs!

"Yes, madomna, I—I wish that!"

At the insistence of the Viscount, Raimon Roger, and of Alazais, countess of Burlatz, he sang for the assembled court that night, choosing as his song the one he had made for Rambauda, *Non es savis ni gaire ben apres*. But when he came to the last stanza:

This, then, I am resolved: to tarry near you,

he remembered the last time he had held the wilful Xene in his arms, and broke down and wept without restraint. The Lady Rambauda came to him and drew him aside, saying, "Peire Vidal, you should not think of your wife now. She is, perhaps, not entirely unhappy. If you choose really to tarry near me, there is a house and a garden where you may remain undisturbed until you have somewhat recovered your peace of mind. You will be near your son, and if you wish to see me, I shall be there; and if not, it is no matter."

"Yes, madomna, I wish to be near you."

So he returned with Rambauda to Biolh, and she comforted him; and on the nights when he was distraught with anguish and unhappiness, she lay with him; and he found a sort of peace and clung to her, and in a slight measure was content. But it was only she who was truly the lover, obeying the Twenty-sixth Article of the *Laws of Love*: "Love can deny nothing to love."

As for the Ninth Alfonso, king of Castile, he went back to Palencia disconsolate, for he had discovered in the countess of Burlatz, Raimon Roger's wife, slight response to his wooing.

During the year that followed, Peire Vidal fashioned many good sirventes directed against injustice in the world. In an impassioned sirvente he vigorously defended the Albigenses, the occasion being the arrival in Provence of two Cistercian monks bearing papal authority to suppress all heresy. This last song was repeated at Bargarde by a jongleur who had heard Peire Vidal sing it at Biolh. There Deacon Fulk of Le Thornonet furiously anathemized the song and its author. It was warmly defended by the count's new secretary, himself a troubadour, Peire Cardinal, or Petrus Cardinalis as he was now known. Raimon of Toulouse, not indisposed to seek an excuse for breaking with the slightly officious deacon, with whose fulminations against his father he was growing bored, espoused the cause of Peire Cardinal. Deacon Fulk left Bargarde in a rage. The fat was in the fire; henceforth the young count was a warmer partisan of the Albigenses than ever his father had been; and from that circumstance befell many strange and terrible events. The sirvente was answered by the troubadour Izarn, a champion of Rome. The Albigenses sent hurriedly to seek aid of Bernard of Ventadorn, the son of a house-serf and the greatest troubadour of his day, who was known to be friendly to them; but the aged singer was forever silent at the Abbey of Dalon. When the eager messengers arrived, the monks were chanting a litany for the dead.

From one end to the other Provence rang with songs and counter-songs, but few of these were for the furthering of love. It seemed as though some great invisible hand were slowly stirring a gigantic cauldron wherein were mingled many potent and baneful ingredients; and the goddess Venus, whose ultimate refuge was at Les Baux, looked down upon the golden land and was dismayed.

Of all this ferment Peire Vidal, sequestered in his bower near the castle of Biolh, knew nothing. His long quiet days were given to the education of his small son, Andronicus, and to the gentle company of Rambauda of Biolh, who knew of his wants before he expressed them and whose presence was as natural and unassuming as the sun and air of Provence. Together they read many romances, of the knights Eteocles and Polynices at the siege of Thebes; of the witch Herodias who was scorned of John the Baptist; of how Sant Hermentaire slew the dragon of Griminum and Sainte Martha conquered the Tarasque by her holy power; but mostly, the marvelous story of the knights of the court of British Arthur, which they found, lately told by Chrétien de Troyes in his *Perceval le Gallois,* a French tale and highly diverting.

So the year passed, and toward the end of it, Count Raimon who had had the Princess Xene for his mistress all of that time, was moved, at the instance of his secretary, the troubadour Peire Cardinal of the bitter tongue, to give her up, and to seek a more tangible alliance in the hand of the English princess, Jeanne. Says Peire Cardinal, regarding the morals of princes: "They are not open to persuasion on ethical grounds unless it be greatly to their personal interest."

The Lady Vidal was returned, therefore, to Castle Belgueil under suitable escort, and with a message from Count Raimon to his vassal, the knight of Belgueil, that her Christian discipline was now completed and she was entirely weaned from intercourse with the diabolic powers of darkness in the Griffon apostasy. No sooner had she arrived at Belgueil than she commanded Jehan Porcelet to light all the gilded tapers before the various images, and for three days she passed from one holy niche to another, kneeling and repeating prayers in the Greek tongue to the saints of the hierarchy of New Rome.

When Peire Vidal, taking his son by the hand, said farewell to Rambauda of Biolh, she said: "God has been kind to me for letting me have you again."

Raimon Roger, Viscount of Béziers, had taken a great fancy to Peire Vidal and, knowing his distress of spirit, forgave the troubadour not making love to his wife, Alazais, countess of Burlatz, but she was less forgiving. When Peire Vidal explained to the viscount his marital predicament, that he had been wedded under the rites of the Greek faith, the viscount said, "That is easily mended. The saints are lenient toward those whose hearts are inclined to goodness. I will accompany you to Belgueil and there certify to your marriage, and if my estimable cousin of Toulouse takes any further steps against your interests, he shall have me to reckon with, even though he be my overlord." So he returned with Peire Vidal to Belgueil, bringing with him the venerable abbot of the church of Sant Nazaire, who was a kindly soul, filled with the love of God and of his fellow beings.

"It will not be necessary for the nuptials to be solemnized again," he said, "for I believe that the Greek priest, howbeit he may wander in error as regards the strict tenets of the faith, looks to God even as do we. But in order for you to execute your compact with your liege we will bless the marriage bed as though you were still the bridegroom and your lady the bride."

So, at nightfall, when bride and groom were placed in the same bed, the viscount of Béziers and the abbot of Sant Nazaire, filled with the zeal of the Holy Spirit, entered the bridal chamber bearing a vessel of holy water which they sprinkled on the pair. Then they passed completely around the bed, swinging their censers filled with precious spices, and called down upon those two the benediction of heaven and of all the saints of Provence. When they had performed their office with the greatest possible care and devotion, the abbot, still filled with the grace of the Spirit, raised his eyes and hands to heaven, and after blessing the newly wedded couple, said, "My dear son Peire Vidal, if it be true that a tradition of our ancestors gives us this right, then I bestow on thee, with clasped hands, the same favor of blessing which God the Father formerly gave to Abraham; and to thee, my daughter Xene, who come from a strange and far land, where the customs are not as ours, I give my blessing, even as though it were from the lips and hands of thine own father." At this Xene looked terribly frightened and shuddered, but the gentle priest took it that she was merely alarmed by the unfamiliar ritual of the true church and he bent down and kissed her tenderly on the forehead.

In that year the Emperor Isaac Angelus went a-hunting, and during his absence his brother Alexius seized New Rome and proclaimed himself emperor; the soldiers of the army, who despised the deposed emperor for his vices and whose pay had long been in arrears, hailed the new emperor with every sign of joy, while the polyglot populace, as usual, remained indifferent to a change of rulers. Then Isaac the Angel was blinded and immured in a lonely tower, where he remained eight dark and solitary years, until the door of his prison cell was opened by a troubadour from Provence.

Though the child Andronicus was not a second time christened, he got another god-father, Raimon Roger of Béziers. At the age of three Andronicus had a lovely face, his locks were gold, his skin white as the snow on the Cévennes, his eyes those of a young falcon, and his mouth sweet as the bloom of the brière. At four years old he was very precocious; he presented a pair of gloves, embroidered with gold, to the viscount, his god-father, saying, "I know how to mew the sparrow-hawk, and I can pipe and dance and sing!" At five years old he was able to play at chess, and to throw the dice.

The bailiff, Jehan Porcelet, also gave the lad certain instructions in good breeding: "Take no seat, but be ready to stand until you are bidden to sit down. Keep your hands and feet at rest. Do not claw your flesh or lean against a post in the presence of your lord. Make obeisance always when you answer, otherwise stand as still as a stone unless he speaks to you. When you are set at your dinner, keep your knife clean and sharp. Also be diligent not to dip your meat into the salt-cellar, or lick the dust out of your dish with

215

your tongue, or wipe your nose on the table cloth." During these courses of instruction the lad appeared to listen dutifully but in his eyes was a far-away look, as though he saw something invisible to his instructor. But when permitted to mount his father's huge charger, he was a picture of knighthood in miniature, wearing an expression of haughty benevolence and of secret power. Then he might indeed have been taken for the son, or at least, the grandson of an emperor.

For some time after the return of Xene to Belgueil Peire Vidal was aware of a change in her, but what it was, outside of an increased devotion to her images and amulets, he could not precisely fathom. She had brought back from Toulouse much jewelry and fine raiment which she wore both privately and publicly. To further indulge her fancy, for he was deeply desirous of pleasing her in everything, Peire Vidal purchased jewelry of Limoges, sumptuous silks of Mosul and Palermo, and from his store at Toulouse drew out priceless furs and rich stuffs, barter of Trebizond and Samarcand, fineries from the lands of Ind, of Prester John, and of Xengis Khan. Against the strong protests of Jehan Porcelet he also appareled his whole menie in rich liveries, suitable for the court of a prince. And he himself, when he went abroad, was clad like a king's son.

Though all this ostentation drained the resources of his estate, his fortunes had not greatly suffered, for the viscount of Béziers was generous in bounty and furnished him with other revenues and tithes in return for the songs that were the fruit of the singer's maturity in the Joyous Craft. But the Princess Xene no more came to him, her eyes engulfing him with the fire of the goddess of Papho, nor led him by the hand to her bed. So, after several halting essays at love-making, which she rebuffed by an assumption of frozen obedience, he kept to his own chamber and she to hers. However, he was somewhat compensated in his deprivation of her body by the greater attention she received from the lords and troubadours of Languedoc. These resorted frequently to Belgueil and were lavishly entertained. Gui of Cavaillon, a staunch partisan of the Sixth Raimon, came; and there came also Pons de Capduelh, and the gentlemanly Saint Circ, and the aging Baron Savaric de Mauleon of Châtillon-sur-Lêvre, who had loved the Countess Guillerma of Benauges and other famous ladies, and Ugo of La Bacalairia, and oftenest, Raimon of Miravals, Peire Vidal's neighbor. With this company of great singers to please and court his wife Peire Vidal was vastly gratified. Their courtships were an acknowledgment of the station of his lady, whom he now boldly addressed as Empress. And the monsenhers who attended the Lady Xene, at first from an amused compliance with her husband's vagary, but later from the half-belief in his preposterous claim, honored her with the title of princess.

Moreover, the assurance of the Lady Xene's being entertained by these courtiers gave Peire Vidal the opportunity he needed to exercise his gifts in other courts. He traveled widely, accompanied by an imposing retinue. And to all those distant places, to which betime he had been invited, he journeyed and sang; but the further he was from Provence, the greater the enthusiasm for his singing. In the golden land other and newer styles prevailed. Says Peire Cardinal: "Another age, another song." He was well received at the court of Duke Aimeric of Hungary, and was hailed in Castile and Aragon as the greatest of living makers of songs. It may be that these flatteries watered a vanity which was really prodigious but had been restrained by troubles and humiliations. It is certain that he came to believe that nothing—neither in singing, nor physical prowess, nor love—was beyond his attainment. And he then began to harbor a strange idea—the claim of little Andronicus to the throne of New Rome.

Chapter Eighteen

IN THE year when Andronicus, the son of Peire Vidal, was six
years of age, Fulk of Neuilly, a fanatical monk, once known for
his dissolute and drunken ways, began to preach a new crusade
throughout France. Dissensions and intrigue among the Christians
and the encroachment of paynim hordes had brought the Holy
Land into a sad plight. The Latin lords had lost most of the territories bought by Philip Augustus and Richard the Lion at the
expense of the blood of three hundred thousand of the best warriors of France, England, and Germany. Blood and treasure had
been poured into the Holy Land; there remained, on the road from
Jaffa to Jerusalem, only heaps of blanched bones, while in the
darkened courts of Christian barons the stealthy emissaries of
Khasis, chief of the Syrian Assassins, plied their furtive trade for
Christian gold.

Peire Vidal had been for some time at the court of the Second
Amfos, king of Aragon and count of Barcelona. At Barcelona the
young troubadour king entertained the wise, the witty, and the
learned at his court, and dispensed largesse to those of merit. Peire
Vidal loved the great flourishing Catalan city whose vast sea-trade
did not, as at Genoa, impede the progress of the arts and letters
among a people naturally inclined to more graceful ways of living.
But he loved more the gay company, and the freedom from bitter

controversy that was rending Provence apart and drying up the sources of song and laughter in the golden land. From Rome the great Pope Innocent had hurled anathema at the Albigenses and all their partisans, both high and low. Following the first two Cistercians, came two with greater powers, Guy and Regnier, and these were joined by Pietro of Castelnau, the most eager and zealous of the papal legates, with nine others, vested with powers of suspension and excommunication. They suspended the archbishop of Narbonne and the bishop of Béziers, and degraded the bishops of Toulouse and Vivera. At that the people muttered and the great lords set their faces against Rome and all its works.

All this turmoil sounded but distantly in the ears of the knight of Belgueil on the sunny shores of the Mediterranean, in the great castle high above the town, whence could be seen the commerce of all the lands plying in the harbor. He was happy, too, in the company of Gaucelm Faidit and of his devoted wanton, the Monjo, for under the liberal patronage of Amfos the pair had passed into the late summer of better times. The drab Guilhelma, now that she was no longer under the necessity of selling her scant charms to provide for her lord, had taken on a faint reflection of her old bloom. She kept herself neater and fastened her heavy braids with gilded clasps.

One lovely May day, when the sea glittered in blue flames about the red and orange sails of ursers and esneccas anchored in the port, the pot-bellied troubadour came to his friend, wearing a long face. He sank heavily into a carven Moorish seat and breathed a sigh that shook the creases of his fleshy jowls.

"Ah, Jesu Christus! The great pass from the earth, leaving a race of pygmies!"

"Who now has gone to paradise, Gaucelm Faidit?"

"It is Richard the Lion, but I think he is rather in limbo than paradise. He fell in the meadow called Rock Maumont, shot by an archer from the tower of the castle of Chaluz, in Limoges, where they fashion the finest of jewelry. My Monjo once had a brooch made in Limoges, but that was in the old days. We have descended to worse times since then."

"Having seen Richard, can you still believe him to have had any greatness?"

"Let us have a stoup of Spanish wine and then we will speak of greatness."

Peire Vidal poured flagons for his friend and himself, and they sat by the open casement, sucking in the briny air and the gummy fragrance of oleanders that bloomed profusely about the castle.

"Greatness," said Gaucelm Faidit, "lies not so much in quality of soul, which may be possessed by a beggar, but in power over the thoughts and imagination of men."

"Richard, if I knew him, Gaucelm Faidit, has caused the death of more men than any other of this age. He began by destroying his father. He robbed and burnt the Jews of England. He sold every office he could lay his hands on, and swindled the buyers. He ravished cities—in which, God help me, I abetted him!—and then he perjured himself and foreswore oaths and broke compacts. He was mean and deceitful, a liar, hypocrite, and rogue; and he led armies into the Holy Land to be destroyed. He was a usurer, and extorted gold from friends and foes alike. If they did not pay, he crushed them. He used the Assassins of Syria to dipose of Conrad of Montferrat and others, perhaps. In what does his greatness consist?"

Gaucelm Faidit sipped his wine reflectively.

"He was a great devil," he said at length, "and a brave man, and he made the English soldiers feared everywhere, and there was no one like him and never will be! For that reason I shall make a lament for his passing that will bring tears to the dark eyes of all our ladies of Barcelona and it will perpetuate his memory as the flower of knighthood and chivalry!"

Again they emptied their wine cups, and Gaucelm Faidit said, "The world goes up and down. Just now I think it is going down, for troubadours who do not thrive in love, thrive in the love of God."

"Of whom are you riddling?" asked Peire Vidal.

"A certain Brother Fulk, onetime known as Folquet of Marseille. He was lately abbot of Le Thornonet and proved so zealous in his conformity that he has been raised to the See of Toulouse."

"Folquet is Bishop Fulk!"

"Ay, and on his way to becoming archbishop. When that event occurs, Sant Julian preserve our land of Provence!"

There came into Peire Vidal's mind words spoken by Raimbaut of Vacqueiras at Béziers, long ago, concerning the aspic and Folquet of Marseille, but what it was about, he could not remember. However, he recalled the moment when Folquet ceased to be a troubadour.

"Gaucelm Faidit," he said, "it seems strange that I should have been the cause of Folquet's turning priest, and it was over the Countess Adélasie des Baux, and now, poor lady——!"

"Had you seen her lately before . . . ?"

"It was with her in my arms," said Peire Vidal, "that I learned what sorrow is."

He remembered that, too. Though he had never ceased making songs for her and had regularly despatched them to Les Baux by one jongleur and another, he did not himself go. At first it was because he could not bear to think of that refuge of Venus without his Rainier, the gracious host whose terse, sagacious comments and explosive laugh served as a foil to the invariable composure of the countess. And then, during the Christianizing of Xene, he was occupied with his brooding thoughts at Biolh; and after that he heard that Aimeric de Peguilha was paying court to Na Vierna, and had had the temerity to imagine he might step into the boots of the viscount—had not troubadours before him wed noble ladies? While Peire Vidal no longer had the desire to kill his former audiart, neither did he wish ever to see his face again.

So the seasons passed. It was in the year following his lady's return to Belgueil and when the deprivation of her body had set stirring vague desires of warm claspings and undenying response, that the message came from Les Baux:

"To Monsenher Vidal, knight, greetings and the blessings of God! As you are a troubadour and gentleman, come to Les Baux with all speed, for my lady, the Countess Adélasie des Baux, has the greatest need in the world of you. Do not refuse her, for the love of the Blessed Virgin. The saints keep you!"

It was signed Bertran d'Aurenga, chamberlain. Bertran d'Aurenga . . . he had been a squire; and once Peire Vidal, obsessed by the business of the boar and the well of Venus, had denied him a game of tennis. Well, he would not deny him this mission! For it could be nothing less than a mission to have evoked so urgent a plea. And as he thought of seeing her again, suddenly his heart beat with the quickness and fervor of youth.

"So slight a thread binds me to my domna, it is invisible to every eye but mine; yet chains of steel bind no more tightly!" sang Arnaut de Maruelh of his love for his lady, before he ceased to sing. Through every turn of love and fortune the image of Adélasie des Baux, now faint and again bright as rainbow mist, had followed Peire Vidal, subduing and restraining his fantastic fits, tempering his wild angers, and civilizing his passions. So that which people, and in particular the three who had loved him most, had taken to be his rare nature as a lover, was in truth the rarity of her nature mixed with his; wedded, but not in the flesh. The *hermaphroditus* of spirit.

"Each soul," affirms Peire Cardinal in a gentler mood, "is a composite of many souls; and the most gracious is that wherein many sweet human essences have lodged."

The journey, instantly undertaken, traced the identical route of his first expedition to Les Baux, but how different the circumstances! He took with him one trusty squire, known for his silence and discretion. It was winter, and all the roads save the ancient highways of the Romans, were dreadful to the passage of horsemen. The countryside looked bleak, for the season was unusually bitter. They saw wolves, the greasy smoke of huddled villages, black lowering castles, and then Nismes, and then the mighty flood of the Rhône, steely and thick with floating ice, where the crossing in a flimsy craft was hazardous. Snow lay in the country beyond, whirled down from the Alps, and the climb toward Les Baux was through a region of grotesque forms, clothed in a glaze of ice, like monumental effigies. But Les Baux itself, fanned by the warm sirocco, was dry and bare; gray everywhere, glittering, hard; the castle, molded from the mighty rock of which it was an indissoluble part, and the town at its base, too, part of the earth's gray ribs. Below, and southward, carpets of emerald, and remotely beyond, the great wide drifts and desolations of the outpouring of Father Rhône into the distant sea.

"Monsenher Vidal," said Bertran d'Aurenga on his arrival, "you will be good enough to come to my lady's chamber. God succor you for having made this journey!" He was coming bald, the one-time squire, and looked middle-aged and troubled. Sant Julian save us! thought Peire Vidal as he followed after him, has age overtaken him so soon? He himself had no consciousness of the oncoming of years. There was nothing he could do in that other year, that he could not do now, especially if it pertained to the *gai sciensa*. In fighting he was still able; in love, proficient; and in song, potent. Therefore, he was still young.

The chamberlain entered the sick-room, and returned. "Go in," he said solemnly. "My poor lady awaits you, monsenher."

Peire Vidal slipped off the lambskin cover of his viol, feeling a sudden strange uneasiness at the manner and words of the majordomo; then he pushed aside the arras. He was ready with the song he had composed on the way to Les Baux. Though he had not essayed a note of it, he knew the phrasing of it, down to the last measure and muted touch of the bow on the strings.

> *Be.m pac d'ivern e d'estiu*
> *E de fretz e de calors,*
> *Et am neus aitan com flors*
> *E pro mort mais qu'avol viu . . .*

I love drear winter's breath
No less than sultry hours,
And snow, even as the flowers;
Yea, I would welcome death
Without regret or ruth,
Though loving Love and Youth;
For there have come anew
Desires that renew
My thoughts of her whose grace
Lives in her form and face;
And I see how ice encloses
Joy and spring, and roses!

This sullen heart of mine,
Darkened and overcast
By severance, at last
Tastes the restoring wine

223

Of nearness, and revives
Delight in both our lives;
For your body, fair and sweet,
Contains both cold and heat—
Warm joy, and cool release
From cravings that never cease.
Sure, my love for you is more
Than Jacob for sweet Rachel bore.

He entered the chamber of the Countess Adélasie des Baux, and at first saw only three men; one, a priest, and one he took by his garb to be a physician, and the third was a lord richly clad, whom he recognized as Guillaume des Paux, her brother.

On a bed covered with red velvet, embroidered in gold and set with jacinths to induce sleep, and hung about with arras of red sendal, lay the countess; and her knight knew it was she by her hair spread out like a silken pillow of bronze gold all about her head. The chamber was so darkened he could not see her face, but he could see the whiteness of her arms lying at her side, and he saw the shape of her peerless body beneath the thin silken coverlet. He came nearer, trembling. The priest was repeating in a low monotonous voice, *"Kyrie eleison, Christe eleison, Kyrie eleison. . . ."*

The physician, with an air of profound mystery, was stirring some mixture over a small flame, that gave off a foul odor of herbs, drugs, and animal substances. Guillaume, prince of Orange, standing near the head of the bed, had the look of one who has often witnessed death, yet dreads it none the less. The priest ceased, waved his hands above the bed in the sign of the cross, and then the physician spoke in a thin, dry tone, like one delivering a lecture: "The infections and dark humors have permeated the whole body, and are taking possession of its last citadel, the heart. The elixir I have prepared, after the formula of the learned Nicolaus Prepositus, modified by my own knowledge and understanding, will be of little avail, I fear, unless we can further reduce the demands of nature on the patient's strength." He turned to the prince of Orange. "Sire, it is well known and expressly stated in the *Regimen Sanitatis Salerni,* that human hair is a sort of parasite, feeding on the body and independent of it. Indeed, we know this to be true by opening graves, where it is found that the beards of men and the hair of women have grown long after their flesh has moldered in corruption."

Peire Vidal began to shudder violently; he wanted to shout, to cry out; but he was powerless, entranced, and the doctor went on: "When we are in the flower of health this drain upon our vitality is of little consequence, though it is evident that the greatest warriors always have been those without beards. But at the time of the ebbing of life's forces any least additional tax upon our strength becomes of critical moment." Suddenly he spoke sternly and decisively. "You understand, sire, that I recommend shearing my lady's head!"

Guillaume des Baux said in a muffled voice, "You should know what is best, senher doctor. Will it save her life?"

"I cannot promise. That is in the hands of God."

"Very well. I would give my own blood if that would help." He drew a dagger from his belt, unsheathed it and handed it to the medical sage. The blade flashed in the dim light. Peire Vidal uttered a groan. "Ah, God! Stop, for the love of Christ!" He took a step forward.

"Stay where you are, troubadour! This is no time for a lover's foolishness!" In the lord's words was the menace of death. Peire Vidal halted, frozen. The bright blade in the doctor's hand was lifted above the pillow, the golden hoard was gathered up in one swift movement; Peire Vidal closed his eyes.

A moment later the doctor was drawing aside the arras that shaded the casements. A pallid wintry light flooded the chamber. The woman on the bed stirred slightly; her breath coming between her teeth made a whistling sound, and her eyes were closed. Peire Vidal looked upon Adélasie des Baux, and what he saw was an old woman. It was not merely that illness had destroyed the matchless smoothness of her neck and shoulders; the malady had ruthlessly torn off her mask of youth, had graven her face with scores of tiny and terrible lines, had worked its horrid will upon her lips, had dented and withered her cheeks. Age, since he had seen her last, had taken her suddenly.

The physician drew down the sheet, exposing her whole body,

225

and ran his nimble fingers over it, feeling and pressing here and there, as if seeking vainly to discover the source of the ailment that was sucking her life away. He looked gloomy and discouraged. "Sire and monsenher," he said, "we must leave her now to her father confessor, for we have done all that can be done."

Peire Vidal, out of his horror, marked with amazement the fair unfaded youthfulness of those marble limbs and the still-perfect rondures of her breasts. As if God allowed the feast of lovers to linger when the face had fallen into forlorn decay.

In the night, without having opened here eyes or uttered any sound, Azalais of Roca Martina died, and she was prepared for burial the following day. Her shorn head covered by a rich cap of woven gold, she lay in the midst of candles that shed a soft radiance upon her. Two priests chanted the litany for the dead while novitiates swung their censers, which gave off the rich fragrance of myrrh, balsam, and frankincense brought from Ophir and Ormuz. Among those who came to perform their last duty to their lady was the knight of Belgueil. He drew near to the gilded bier and gazed for the last time on the face that had haunted his dreams in all the years of his wanderings and despairs and triumphs. Then he marveled greatly, for a great miracle had taken place; the saints in heaven had been kind to her. After her death they restored her lost youth. Indeed, they had done more; she looked more tranquil and of fresher mold than at any time he had known her. It was the face of a young girl he saw.

The bright treasure of her hair was not buried with her. By order of her brother, Guillaume des Baux, prince of Orange, it was placed in a silver casket, together with her Book of Hours, and was secretly disposed of in one of the walls of her chamber; and none knew where, save the prince and a mason from Arles, one of the Comacine guild, who had to swear, by the honor and all the sacred canons of his craft, that he would never reveal its hiding place.

It was after this event that Peire Vidal took on the extravagance in behavior and the fantastic assumption of imperial splendor—even to wearing upon his livery the arms of the Emperor Andronicus, two griffons rampant—which brought him the reputation of being one smitten by lunacy. It seemed as though some invisible balance had been removed from his life.

There was one circumstance connected with the death of the countess, unknown to anyone. During those last hours he had watched beside her chamber door, a shadow immovable. It was some time between matins and lauds when he heard, within, a faint and yet terrifying sound. The priest came shuffling hurriedly out of her chamber. "Fetch my lord of Orange," he said. "She is dying!" But as Peire Vidal only stared at him stonily, the man of God hastened down the long hall, a black figure in a fluttering robe. Peire Vidal leaped inside. He ran to the bed and, without pausing, put his arms about her. She was still breathing, though ever so slightly, as if each breath might be her final sigh. Then, far down in the vale below, he heard the sound of a roaring, like the distant surf of the sea, and it drew nearer and gathered volume until it was as though great surges were breaking at the base of Les Baux. And at the sound of this approaching vast vague monster of sound he felt such terror as he had never experienced at any other time of his life. And his fright was mingled with a grief that seemed to shatter the very foundation of his brain. It was not grief for his lady dying, but for her ugliness. As the first hissing gust of the mistral burst through the casement and shook all the arras into a frenzy, once again, like a poltroon, he fled the presence of his lady.

Gaucelm Faidit spent some days composing his planh or lament for Richard the Lion, and when he sang it before the assembled court of Amfos of Aragon, there were few not moved to tears. Richard the king, so he sang, was a knight without peer; brave as Alexander; able as Caesar; noble as Brutus the Trojan; liberal in largesse, lofty in enterprise and purpose, generous to his friends, magnanimous to his foes, the quintessence of all chivalry. And such a figure as earth would not soon see again.

Amfos, who had greatly admired the crusading English king, rewarded the stout troubadour with a purse of gold bezants. Later, Gaucelm Faidit, in the ripe flush of his cups, confided to his friend the secret of his inspiration.

"I must tell you, Peire Vidal," he said, "there is a certain likeness between the arts of war and of singing,—they both depend for success on strategy. When I began my planh of the Lion I found I was in danger of suffering defeat, for my rebellious brain

227

could give me not so many instances of his virtues as of his vices. But one does not lament the passing of a villain. Then there came into my head a certain strategy, which was to think that I was really making a song for the great Saladin. So, with the Saracen in my mind—Sant Julian forgive me! I composed a song for Christian Richard. Every good quality lacking in the Lion I discovered in the sultan; the defects of the one were made up for by the other; and, believe me, I was so overcome by my own picturing of the glorious dead sultan that I shed tears for scurvy Dick!"

There were many contests and tensons among the troubadours of the court, who numbered among them singers from Lombardy, Burgundy, Aquitaine, and other lands, but there were no others from Provence except Gaucelm Faidit and Peire Vidal. The other singers, defenders of the orthodox Church, eyed Peire Vidal in particular with the green face of envy for his prowess; their envy, however, was mingled distrust of one tainted with heresy, for it was well known how he had sung for the Albigenses. Of this secret stirring against him the knight of Belgueil was wholly unaware. He was occupied with his own thoughts; as for the unfortunate heretics, his only interest in them was in their dogged resistance to that dogmatic authority emanating from Rome. This was his third year in Spain, divided between the courts of Amfos of Aragon and Alfonso of Castile. His son Andronicus would soon be eight, and he had seen him but twice in all that time. He even wondered at times about his lady, the precious Xene, and whether her lovers still pleased her.

There approached him one day a jongleur who made known that he was audiart to the very excellent troubadour, Monsenher the Marquis Lanza of the great city of Pisa in Italy; and that his master craved to engage in a tenson with the troubadour of Provence, if such might be arranged at his pleasure. Peire Vidal replied that he would be pleased to accept the honor; let only his master make all the necessary arrangements as to time, place, and form of the tenson. Such challenges could not in all gallantry be refused. Yet he was becoming curiously averse to appearing in public. The clatter of approving hands and tongues no longer thrilled him as before, and he would have preferred to sing at ease to a select few. The marquis he could recall only vaguely as a somewhat pompous figure, wearing clothes of great elegance, in a style outmoded.

In a day or two Peire Vidal learned that the occasion chosen for the tenson was no less than the birthday of the king. This anniversary would be celebrated with jousting and other festivities, concluding with a grand tornimen of song, of which the tenson was to be the final event. The arrangement was little to Peire Vidal's liking. It meant that the great hall would be crowded, not only with nobles and their ladies, but with officials of the city and burgesses; and the throng, coming hot and flustered from the lists, after much eating and drinking, would be noisy and inattentive, the air would be thick with human breath, and they would all expect to be entertained by a display of clever virtuosity rather than by simple merit.

"Our Emperor Vidal," sang the Marquis Lanza in a voice reedy and caustic, "is such a one as the world has never seen—without sense, talent, or understanding." Peire Vidal was startled. He had not foreseen a personal attack. The man must be mad. He glanced at the assemblage, sure that this sudden insult would meet with raised eyebrows, smiles of scorn; instead, the mass of faces peering from their finery looked strangely intent, almost savage. He did not know the whisper had gone about: "Vidal, the Albigensian; Vidal, follower of the antipope!" And Barcelona was not lenient toward heretics.

"Such a drunkard," sang the marquis bitingly, "never sat upon a throne; such a coward never bore lance or escutcheon; such a recreant never fastened on spurs; such a rascal never tried his hand at paltry rhymes!"

A hoarse whisper at his elbow: "Peire, my son, they are baiting you—Izarn of Rome and Fulk of Toulouse! and they send a raven to croak for them!" Gaucelm Faidit, his breath reeking of wine, chuckled. That genial sound steadied the troubadour's nerves. He feared nothing but his own wild rage.

"He is beneath contempt, but he doesn't throw stones," sang the marquis.

This last allusion was a play upon his own name, "Peire." It was a direct thrust, implying impotence. The audience tittered.

229

The marquis paused for his second verse. He had chosen a difficult form, in the then popular obscure style. Peire Vidal had to meet and answer it, phrase for phrase, keeping the melody and preserving the precise structure of the verse, so that the completed tenson would seem to have been the work of one mind, one bitter and poisonous mind. His own raced madly. The melody . . . the pattern . . . the rhyme system—a jumble of words! Then he began to sense the nature of it. Simple, after all; only dextrous. Music that was, in reality, inferior. He would master it, add a slight variation, improve upon the design, make it his own; he had it!

"Would that a sword might dent that bull-head of his," sang the marquis, "a dart of steel penetrate his stupid guts, and a pike gouge out his eyes; then we will give him wine, and do him honor by crowning him with an old scarlet bonnet without ribbons, and for a lance, a stout cudgel; so may he journey in all safety from here to France!"

The assemblage drew a long delighted breath. There were approving murmurs. The ladies fanned themselves, smiling maliciously; it was almost as good as watching the bull-fights. Peire Vidal saw that they were out for blood, and he was resolved to mince no words. Coolness of mind had come to him. He tuned his polished viol briefly, then sang:

"Marquis Lanza, poverty of mind, discomfitures, and bankrupt hopes have worked you into a frenzy, and you are like a blindman who befouls himself in the street, having lost all decency and understanding; and you have essayed strongholds and castles as often as an old woman squatting on a dunghill. Verily, if you were ever a free man, you are now enslaved!"

He then gave pause, and the multitude, taken by his deep strong voice and the harmony of his viol, were silent; if heretic, he was nevertheless a great singer. But Peire Vidal did not go on. There had come to him in a flash a sharply painful recollection: of Raimbaut of Vacqueiras engaged at Montferrat in a tenson with the Marquis Albert of Malespina, and how he had felt a deep abhorrence at this profanation of the Joyous Craft in the hurling of filthy epithets from one to the other. Here, too, there were young jongleurs present, eager to learn the rudiments of the great science from their elders. Should he fail them?

"Sire," he said, addressing the king, "may I be pardoned if I retire from this tenson, acknowledging my defeat."

Through the great hall ran a sound that was like the hiss of many serpents. The king frowned. Peire Vidal placed his viol in the hollow of his arm and drew a cover of purple velvet over it. Then, having bowed deeply to the king, he withdrew.

At dawn of the next day he set out for Provence and Belgueil, alone.

Chapter Nineteen

HE TOOK ship to Narbonne and thence journeyed to Béziers where he was warmly welcomed by the Viscount Raimon Roger, eager to have news of what was happening in the kingdoms of Spain. The viscount had a genuine interest in his contemporaries and also he evinced a mild enthusiasm for his wife's Spanish lover, Alfonso the Noble.

"Alfonso the Noble," reported Peire Vidal, "after the disaster of Alarcos, has had to maintain his arms against his Christian cousins, the kings of Leon and Navarre. Amfos of Aragon composes passable verses in Provençal, and for his gallant services at Cuenca has been relieved of his homage to Castile."

"Would to God," said the viscount, "that I might serve Toulouse in like fashion! Frankly, I do not care for my noble cousin." He bent his gaze upon the troubadour and Peire Vidal observed how obstinate and candid it was. "Not only because of his exactions," he added; "but his stature is considerably less than that of his father, the Good Count Raimon. Will you join this next crusade?"

"What crusade?"

"The one being preached by the Frankish monk who has the same name as our estimable bishop of Toulouse—Fulk, of Neuilly. Fulk of Toulouse, the one-time troubadour, salutes Fulk of Neuilly, the lunatic monk, as brother in the new crusade. Provence will soon be given into the hands of Fulks!"

"If I went on a crusade it would be in order to establish the kingdom of justice, over which my son Andronicus should rule as emperor," said Peire Vidal quietly.

They were drinking hippocras, a wine spiced with ginger, cinnamon, and grains of paradise, and pleasant to taste. The viscount held his flagon suspended while he studied the face of Peire Vidal.

"They say you are mad," he said at length; "and you surely have strange notions, monsenher. But I am not sure you are not saner than most of us. The world is so afflicted with madness it looks askance upon those who harvest a grain of sense from a world of fantasy. My supposition is, that you, or your son, have as good a claim to the throne of New Rome as the creature now occupying it—oh, do not suspect me of having pried into your affairs, monsenher! I am telling you this because I prefer to see you living rather than dead. And I know it for a fact, your life is not worth a denier in Provence!"

"Then I will remain here, for I value my self-respect at more than a denier. Who are my enemies?"

"Your greatest enemy is in New Rome, but your immediate enemy is now at Toulouse, and he directly represents the power of Rome itself. In short, my dear troubadour, having become implicated by accident in the politics of empires, you have become a thorn in the flesh of the two most absolute rulers of Christendom, the Greek emperor and the Roman pope. And they have come to agree upon one single point of doctrine—your elimination, as soon as possible!"

"What have I done to the pope?" asked Peire Vidal in bewilderment.

"You have upheld the Albigensian heresy."

"But that was only a matter of simple justice!"

"Justice is a frightful power. It disrupts kingdoms, destroys tyrants, wrecks established institutions, separates the closest of kin. It should never be tampered with—except by those in authority!" The calm irony of the viscount's words moved the troubadour, for he sensed behind them a cynical yet resolute will. "As one who has captured the imagination of the vulgar populace, the *questeaux*,

233

you are specially dangerous to the true faith in your championing of this accursed heresy."

"But I am a vassal of my lord of Toulouse, and he is openly for the Albigenses."

"True. He might protect you, if he had the inclination, and the courage; but you will pardon me, if I think that both are doubtful. For myself, I could not save you here in Provence, much as I should wish to do so, unless you remained in Béziers. You are welcome to make this your asylum."

"Thank you, my lord! But I will go to my estate. If my enemies want to find me, let them come to Belgueil."

"You display more hardihood than common sense, Monsenher Vidal. It is not you alone who will suffer."

He spoke so earnestly that Peire Vidal took thought of his words. It was true, others would suffer—the Lady Xene, and little Andronicus, and all the faithful members of his menie. The ways of punishment for offenders against power were sinister, and might be terrible. He had heard of the workings of the lately established inquisition. . . . He shuddered.

"What would you advise me to do, sire?" he asked humbly.

"Stay away from Belgueil. There are havens elsewhere."

"But my wife—my child?"

"They will be safer if you are not there. Your lady is known to have . . . accepted sound Christian doctrine under the tutelage of Fulk himself. Moreover—" he paused and let his eyes dwell with sardonic humor on his guest, "she is protected by the good name of her lover."

"Who is he?"

"Raimon of Miravals, the special friend of Abbot Fulk. An excellent singer, and without leanings toward heresy."

Peire Vidal sat deeply sunk in thought. He, who had everything, had nothing. Neither wife, son, nor home. "Must I then remain forever in exile?" he asked plaintively.

"I do not say that. I believe it will not be necessary. But for the present it will be best for the interests of yourself and those dearest to you. The time is coming soon when these matters will have to be settled. I fear for our golden land. We are disunited in all things except a common stubbornness toward Rome; and that is not a rod to lean upon. You never see two cities, or two lords, or even two peasants of Provence, who will agree to stand together for their mutual good! That is why we sing so well."

That is why we sing so well. There was a cryptic meaning in the sentence. Yes, he could still sing well. He would show his enemies how well! He would sing so well that they would not dare inflict upon him the fate of Marcabru, audiart of world-traveled Cercamon, called Panperdut by the nobles, the Lost Rag; they had murdered him because he rebuked their viciousness.

"Sire," he said, rising, "I thank you deeply for your good counsel. I am going to Italy to sing. And when I have sung in Italy— at Rome—I will go to New Rome, and sing for the emperor."

"Peire Vidal, now I know that you are indeed mad!"

He went to Italy. At that time there were few singers of any consequence in that troubled land, for bloodshed and rapine were the order of the day and the gentler arts, outside of Montferrat, had fallen into disuse. The party of the Ghibellines was fighting for the empire and the Guelph faction against it; and the Church was determined to subdue both; and they were equally resolved not to be subject to Rome. The free cities raised their strength against the nobles in their midst; and every great family held its allegiance one way or another, or changed it, or was divided among its own members. So there was little time and small occasion for any to master the deep and intricate science of song.

Peire Vidal sang everywhere, from city to city, before the great and the humble. He denounced injustice, tyranny, and grossness in love; and everywhere he was acclaimed for the excellence of his songs and because each party thought he might become its champion. When he arrived in Rome there was a great tumult going on between the shadowy senate, the citizens of the republic, and the soldiers of the pope; as all the houses were shut tight and barred, he chose a great open space, the Coliseo, in which to sing. Here, before grimy thousands—the fighting having ceased for that day, so eager were they to hear him—he did his best for the honor of the Joyous Craft. On the day following he was bidden to come and sing before His Holiness, Innocent the Third, at the palace of St. John Lateran.

235

The pope's residence was one of the few buildings of the city that looked to be newly made, and was almost as well furnished inside as the palace of Barrale at Marseille. When Peire Vidal had been announced, an attendant silently conducted him to a small library, stacked from floor to ceiling with quartos, folios, and huge tomes. The room had the smell of parchment and vellum, which was an intoxicating fragrance to Peire Vidal, who had possessed few books and loved more the sight of the print and the odor of learning than its accomplishment. Now that he had penetrated into the very fastness of his enemy, he was taken with dread; dread of the terrible old man, like the effigy of God at the Last Judgment sculptured on the front of St. Trophime, who dispensed blessings or hurled anathemas, and had power not only over souls but bodies as well. He thought to assuage his tremors by looking at the books about him.

It was plainly the study of a scholar; not only were the works of the Church Fathers to be seen but close beside them, boldly, stood the pagans—the *Metaphysics* of Aristotle, a rhetoric of Cicero, a grammar of Priscian, a medical treatise of Gallienus; even the poetry of Virgil the Necromancer, and the *Ars Armandi* of Master Ovid the Ancient. At sight of this last title Peire Vidal almost laughed aloud: the "Art of Loving" in the palace of the pope! Very likely this studious cubby-hole was unknown to His Holiness, and its liberal occupant, secretary or librarian, took care to keep his unholy learning out of sight of his ghostly superior, indulging his secret taste for amatory and cultivated literature in private.

On a small lectern near the window were several volumes that attracted the troubadour's attention by their rich new bindings, done in a fashion he had never seen before, with the vellum at the backs replaced by gold cords. One of these had an ornamented cover forming a diptych, both sides being gilt and silvered metal, with ivory carvings, figures in high relief, and inlaid with enamel of Limoges. He opened it and read the title: *De Contemptu Mundi, sive de Miseria Humanae Conditionis*. The author was one, Lothario Conti. The melancholy words impressed him—"Concerning the Low Estate of the World, being the Wretchedness of Human Existence." He turned the pages, delighting in the

236

beauty of the patient monkish lettering and the borders richly ornamented with scrolls of scarlet, azure, gold, and with foliage of ivory
work in the Greek style. But more than the artistry of these pages
was their contents. The liquid and sonorous Latin was the writing
of a craftsman of language; the somber reflections upon the
transitory nature of life were those of a philosopher—*Hic breve
vivitur.* . . .

He was reading aloud from the book when a step behind him
caused him to turn about. A priest had entered. He was a youngish
man, slightly older than Peire Vidal, and his simple vestment,
whose only ornament was a stole embroidered in silver crosses,
marked him as one of the minor clergy. But his finely cut, aristocratic features, the large intelligent eyes, and the nobly carved
brow gave him an air of singular distinction. Peire Vidal instantly
concluded that this was his study.

"You are Monsenher Vidal?" asked the priest, speaking in
flawless Provençal.

"Yes, Senher Father," said Peire Vidal with some embarrassment. "You will pardon me—I was engaged in reading to myself
from this remarkable work of an author whom I do not know, a
Lothario Conti."

The priest smiled. "I am Lothario Conti," he said.

This further embarrassed the troubadour. "Oh—Senher Father,"
he stammered, "allow me to say how much I appreciate this excellent treatise of yours. The originality of thought——"

"It is not wholly original, monsenher," said Lothario Conti, "for
it is merely an elaboration of the *De Contemptu Mundi* of Bernard of Morlaix, to whose writings I was devoted in my youth. If
it pleases you, I will see that you receive a copy of my book."

"Senher Father Conti! Nothing would please me more, for I
have no other books than the lexicons I brought from the collegium
of Monpeslier when I studied there. And now, if you will be so
good as to conduct me to the Holy Father——"

"Monsenher Vidal, you will have to go no further."

For a moment Peire Vidal did not understand. Then, realizing
that this was none other than his enemy, the pope, he was overcome by confusion. With a stifled exclamation, he sank upon his
knees, bowing his head. After a barely perceptible interval the

Pope Innocent bestowed his pontifical blessing upon the troubadour who had inveighed against him. Then he put the knight of Belgueil at ease by saying pleasantly, "Monsenher Vidal, I have heard more of you, seemingly, than you have of me." And taking a seat near the lectern, he indicated a carven chair close by for his visitor.

Peire Vidal waited for him to say that he had heard how the reprobate heretics had taken comfort in the troubadour's abandoned sirventes; instead, the pontiff said, "When you were composing the differences of Pavia and Milan, I was living, as a cardinal-deacon, a life of studious leisure, with no thought that I would soon have to assume the burdens—" he sighed, and his eyes grew somber— "of this office. I remember very well the impression your sirvente made upon me as it was repeated by the estimable troubadour Izarn who, I am glad to say, is now devoted to the service of the Church." In this last phrase there was a faint suggestion, the hint of an invitation. "The thought I had was, that your singing seemed to express the desire for justice in the world———"

"Yes," broke in the troubadour eagerly, "I desire that above all, Most Holy Father, even more perhaps than perfection in love!"

The pope smiled gravely, as though he were weighing the juxtaposition of two such diverse ideals. But he said with instant seriousness, "There is only one kingdom of justice on earth, and only one perfection in love."

"I do not know them," answered the troubadour with a tinge of stubbornness. He had heard those words uttered by persons of quite other complexion, though of the same garb, as this high priest, in whose whole bearing shone the greatness of a thoughtful man, determined on a difficult course.

"You confuse instruments with principles," said the pope, and added, more lightly; "but we are not here to discuss metaphysics. Italy is fortunate to have you. Would that you could, like Orpheus, tame the wild beasts of this distracted land by your singing! You find this city of ruined greatness, torn by civil strife. Yet it is less bloody here than elsewhere. Everywhere, ruthless ambition and selfish intrigue, accompanied by unspeakable savagery; the people crushed by their overlords, and lord against lord, and the hearth of no man safe—because there is no sense of unity. And without

238

unity, there can be no peace! *Miseria humanae conditionis!* . . .
So we have reason to be thankful for your singing that has brought
joy to the multitudes." He paused and looked inquiringly at the
troubadour, as though expecting some comment.

Peire Vidal looked at the floor. The palace was utterly quiet. No
sound of tumult penetrated its thick walls. Distantly could be
heard the chanting of young male voices. It was peaceful.

He raised his eyes and said bluntly, "I did not come to Italy
only to sing of joy. I came to find my enemy."

The pontiff's eyebrows made a delicate arch; in other garments
he would have made a personable cavalier except that his eyes,
which could be judicious, or stern and unbending, were those of
an able administrator. Peire Vidal wondered vaguely what was
concealed under the guise of scholar and recluse; whether earthly
passion had ever assailed him. If so, it was no longer visible.

"And who is that enemy?" the pontiff asked.

"I was told," said Peire Vidal, "that you were my enemy, Most
Holy Father." It sounded somewhat absurd, and he went on hurriedly, "That you desired my life!"

Pope Innocent seemed about to break into incredulous laughter,
but the impulse flashed and faded as he said gently, "You have
been misinformed, monsenher. I desire no man's life, least of all,
of one who furthers the finer arts of living through the practice
of the Joyous Craft." He rose. "Monsenher Vidal, I wish that
I might hold longer speech with you, for I still have the vice of
desiring cultivated company, but the affairs of the Church are
exigent. I will place you in the hands of our troubadour Izarn and
secure an audience for your voice within the hour."

The interview was over, and for the first time Peire Vidal realized that nothing had been said about the Albigenses. The pope
had not troubled even to go into the matter of his alleged enmity.
Izarn was hospitable and benevolent. He endeavored to find out
all that was happening in Provence, and he earnestly advised Peire
Vidal to ally himself with the authority of Rome—"for your soul's
sake, but mostly because it is ill considered to do otherwise. And
still less, to connive at senseless rebellion against established institutions." Peire Vidal returned cautious, non-committal answers.

But he sang excellently before the pope, several cardinals, and the officers of the palace, and was heartily, though sedately applauded.

He had in mind to go directly from Rome to New Rome and face the Greek emperor, but the time of the summer passage was already past; the next passage was not to be attempted until the coming March. Also, the hardships and dangers he had endured, the warfare and the filth of turbulent cities, and the strain of appearing before an alien people, had given him an overmastering desire to return to his homeland, troubled by fierce disputations, but at least reasonably free of blood-letting. He had word from Raimbaut of Vacqueiras that he would be most welcome at Montferrat, so thither he went, seeing on his way more misery and dead men than ever he wished to see again and being oftened hindered in his progress by roving bands of routiers in the service of Guelph or Ghibelline, of warring cities, or Teutonic adventurers bent on simple plunder. But his voice and viol were his passports; there was no rogue nor cut-throat too hardened not to melt under their influence. Outlaws offered him their services as a personal bodyguard through dangerous regions. Sour-visaged knights, speaking barbarous tongues, grunted their approval of his sirventes. Robbers tendered him booty and implored him to become their chief. Mailed brigands listened, and wept.

As he rode northward toward *bellissima* Chivasso, the image of the Fair Knight assumed ever fairer proportions. He saw her as she raised eyes of vair to his, over the chessboard; as she rode at a reckless gallop in the lists, a snarl of raven hair escaping from her coif of chain steel; as she lunged and parried in sword-play, her body lithe and nimble as a young squire's . . . and he saw her as she stood in the tinkling pool, letting the sinuous trickles of water trace liquid and shining paths along her cream-white limbs.

She was Joy and Youth; she was the fay of great enchantment, Love! He sang recklessly:

> *Per qu'eu no volh ricor*
> *Mas de joi e d'amor,*
> *Quar ben tenh a folor*
> *Qui trop vol requerir*
> *So don no pot jouzir . . .*

Wealth would bring little pride
Were joy in love denied,
And its sweet hours decried;
Fools only have obsessions
For excess of possessions.
Yet all their golden store
Is open to aggressions
By those that itch for more;
If I had not a penny,
I'd still be rich as any,
And richer far than many,
Loving my Bel Cavalier!

Leaves fell whispering and fluttering in the golden light while acrid smoke smells cumbered the air, and the stench of dead creatures drifted on the fitful wind. Flowers, fallen into seed-time decay, drooped submissive toward the wintry season. Peasants crouched or fled fearfully, with eyes of dull suspicion.

Que rosa de Pascor
Sembla de sa color
E lis de sa blancor . . .

Red roses of Pascor
Her redder lips deplore,
And lilies never wore
Her whiteness; God the Father
Went to a deal of bother
When, among other creatures,
He found that he would rather
Sculpture her perfect features.
The young ones and the hoary
Report the self-same story—
And madmen picture glory,
Loving my Bel Cavalier!

At Chivasso, where Bonifaz was holding his court, he found Raimbaut of Vacqueiras recovering from wounds of recent fighting, wherein he had borne a heavy part. As usual, the two of them were at swords' points, the troubadour declaiming hotly while his liege and patron harkened in ironical silence or cast in an acid phrase from time to time. Albert of Malespina, his tongue in his cheek, shot malignant glances at his enemy, the troubadour. And there, too, was Aimeric de Peguilha, handsomely attired and closely attentive to the Lady Beatriz; but when he saw Peire Vidal, he went softly from the hall and rode away. It may be that his conscience, or Gaucelm Faidit, had spoken to him.

La Bel Cavalier wore an overdress of ermine, for the air was cool. Peire Vidal was astounded to observe that she had cut her hair short, and it now hung in a fan of purple-sable down to her shoulders. Her gerfalcon nose and straight black brows and small red lips, the lower one larger and full of stubbornness, gave her a faery look. When she saw him enter, she did not smile or start to greet him, but looked at him fixedly, and he saw that she was no longer the damsel he had envisaged. It was almost ten years since first he had come to Chivasso. . . .

"Hah!" cried Raimbaut of Vacqueiras. "We have to wait through two crusades and fifty cataclysms to see you again, Peire Vidal!"

"One of those crusades taught me much," he said meaningly. "My lord marquis, I have found that the arts have not wholly perished in Italy, since you still live."

The lord's quick eyes beamed. "Honors and adventures have given you mastery of compliments I see, Monsenher Vidal. Will you try your skill with my daughter?"

As the Lady Beatriz gave him no sign of encouragement, he felt some embarrassment, but he said, "If Madomna Beatriz will permit me, I will put into music what I could only stammer in speech."

She nodded, without moving, and he, taking his polished viol from its covering, fingered it lovingly, then sang, *Per qu'eu no volh ricor*. His voice, deep and mellow from long and painstaking exercise, filled the hall with an air somewhat melancholy and richly sweet.

They received it in a silence more grateful to him than the vociferous applause of multitudes. She spoke: "You are forgiven your long absence, Peire Vidal, though it has made an empty space in a brief time of life. I wish your song were true; but it seems love wanes, afflictions never cease, and gentleness turns sour."

Raimbaut of Vacqueiras said, "It is good you have come to make love to her, for she has stopped listening to my singing."

Her large eyes flamed toward him, but she said nothing, and the marquis, tapping fitfully on the table, hemmed. "So! You will have to pardon all of us our domestic diversions, monsenher. In the romances the heroes die gloriously—and early. But in life it is our fate to outlive many desirable things. Your English king, for example, will have his infamies obscured by his noble end, which was the result of profound stupidity! I hear that Gaucelm Faidit did a very excellent planh for his death?"

"It was indeed a fine piece of craftsmanship, my lord," said Peire Vidal, remembering the artifice of its making, "and sincerely felt."

"While you were in Spain, planting the seeds of the Joyous Craft, our good Folquet has become a bishop girding at the Albigenses, who doubtless deserve it. Italy steams in anarchy. The pope thunders at all of us, including French Philip, because of his pretty mistress. What the world needs is a purpose, and leadership, else it turns rotten at the core!"

"Leadership will not come through the ravings of that other Fulk, of Neuilly," said Raimbaut of Vacqueiras contentiously. "Or Theobald of Champagne. Or Geoffrey of Villehardouin. Or Baldwin of Flanders. Or that oaf, Simon de Montfort! Or that——"

"Pardon," said the marquis acidly, "my interruption of your tirade, monsenher of Vacqueiras, but will you have a crusade of peasants?"

They were at it again. The Lady Beatriz, relenting of her hardness toward Peire Vidal, drew him from the hall. "They have been disputing over the crusade for weeks," she said.

"Will Raimbaut go?"

"He first swore he would not leave me; somewhat later he protested that it would kill him to leave me; after a time he said that our separation would be unendurable; then he declared that even *if* he went, it need only be for a short space, and he would not stay for the fighting. A bit later he told me that when the Holy Land is recovered, I shall come to him, or he will come back to me.

243

And yesterday he advised me that my husband, Enrico del Carreto is, after all, a man of distinction and honor, and would be kind to me if ever I should—Jesu Christus! *will* he go? How else can he be free of me? . . . Yes! He will surely go!"

They had reached her chamber. Her voice had in it such burning bitterness that Peire Vidal's heart sank. He had not expected to have to play the part of comforter. With her hand on the arras she turned suddenly upon him and said fiercely, "Tell me, Peire Vidal, do you love me, or is your song only another courtesy?"

"I love you, Madomna Beatriz." But he felt uncomfortable, wishing at that moment he had not come to Chivasso. She took his hand in hers and led him within. The room smelt of musk and balsam, of nard and frankincense. It made him dizzy, for he had been riding all day in the open air, and he wished that he might find rest and be at ease, without any thought or disquietude. But she was relentless. With nimble fingers she undid the golden fastenings of her gown, seeking no aid of him. Then she stood white and sleek before him, and coming to him, pressed her body against his, saying, "Take me, Peire Vidal, for I—I hate him! He has found a new mistress!"

"Who is she?" he asked uneasily, playing for time.

"Ambition. That is, wealth and power." And she added scornfully, "Booty! But he will deny that. He argues that he must go on this crusade for the love of Christ. Or from duty to my father. Ah well, we have enjoyed much love and now he is becoming bored. I do not blame him. Yet—" she flung her strong white arms about his neck—"for that reason there is no slight impediment to our loving!"

Peire Vidal would have drawn back, away from her; but she was insistent.

It had been long since he had looked upon the fair, fragrant, and delicious body of a woman.

Soon he returned to Belgueil, bearing for the first time a burden of guilt on his conscience. He had sinned against the Laws of Love, disregarding two of its articles: "No one can love, unless the soft persuasion of love itself compel him." There had been no soft persuasion. And: "Too easy possession renders love contemptible."

As he pondered his relations with the Bel Cavalier, his trouble of mind grew ever greater until he resolved at length to expiate his transgression by undertaking a pilgrimage. He would join the crusade, suffer the hardships of fighting in the Holy Land, and perhaps, leave his bones there to bleach on the blessed burning sands. When word came that the captaincy of the Christian host had been tendered to Bonifaz of Montferrat, Peire Vidal sensed the guiding hand of his destiny.

Chapter Twenty

THIS crusade, however, was unlike the expedition of the impetuous Lion in that it was no sudden avalanche of holy zeal; rather, the slow gathering of a mighty and puissant Christian host, bent on striking a last great blow in defence of the Holy Kingdom and the True Cross which, of late, had suffered considerable neglect. It was a project dear to the heart of the pope at Rome, intent on the unity of Christendom; again the cross of the crusaders was raised and sanctified, their debts suspended and their sins remitted while they served the Lord; again miracles in every land indicated the interest of heaven in the sacred adventure.

Stars were seen to fall from the sky, thick as hail; northern lights of unusual brilliancy flashed with flaming spokes like angels' wings from nadir to zenith; shepherds as they watched their flocks by night beheld a great glowing city in the air, with gates of bronze, battlements of silver, and towers of gold. A priest, as he walked with two companions in a wood, saw a huge sword carried along by the wind; and another priest, in broad daylight, witnessed a combat in the sky between two horsemen, one of which smote the other with a great cross, and thus became victor. Children were born twins, but fastened together and capable of speech, so auguring the union of schismatics with the Mother Church. Wolves appeared in great numbers and were slain and burnt as a warning to heretics.

Fulk of Neuilly affixed the cross to the shoulders of Bonifaz in the church of Our Lady of Soissons in the month of August. Early in the year following, the marquis went with an embassy to Rome to induce Innocent the Third to take up the cause of the young Alexis, the son of Isaac the Angel, whose throne had been usurped by the reigning Alexis; and the pontiff, having heard his plea and being favorably inclined in the matter, Bonifaz returned triumphantly to Montferrat. And it was agreed and covenanted that the great host of the crusaders should be assembled at Venice by St. John's Day, which was the day of Midsummer Eve, when fires were kindled in the streets and market places, and all the people held festival.

The doge, Enrico Dandolo, then eighty years of age and wholly blind, but not infirm in sagacity, had stipulated that the ships of Venice should carry the crusaders to Egypt, the agreed route in the enterprise, for the sum of eighty-five thousand silver marks. For the doge was of the opinion that the ways of the Lord could best be served by furthering the good estate of the republic of Venice.

Gui of Cavaillon, a former lover of the Lady Xene, and Gaucelm Faidit returned from Barcelona to take part in the crusade; the one, because he had not found the queen of Aragon amenable to his amorous persuasion, and the other, because he was utterly ruined in fortune through gaming, and he thought to better it by taking the cross. Though he could scarcely sit a horse, so vast had he become, nevertheless, his mellow and oleaginous visage beamed with anticipation of much dicing, carousing, pilfering, and a little mild whoring on the holy expedition.

All unexpectedly, the Lady Xene decided to accompany her husband, at least as far as Venice, and perhaps even to some city of the Holy Land still held by the Christians. More than that, she had resolved to take with them the boy Andronicus, who was now ten years of age. Peire Vidal agreed, since it seemed reasonable that she should wish to see again her native land and the crusade would offer an opportunity for safe convoy to the east. She had never before expressed a desire to make the journey, and that too was understandable, her foster father, the Emperor Isaac Comnenus, having been poisoned by his cup-bearer while a prisoner of Richard the Lion in the Holy Land.

Furthermore, the Griffon priest, Porphyros, by whose advice the Princess Xene was wholly guided, had assured her that certain spiritual omens indicated that the time was right for her undertaking the long and hazardous journey. She began forthwith to have all her precious charms, amulets, and talismans packed in chests and caskets. The sacred images and holy vessels were also made ready for transporting; and there were added bales of bedding, of rich cloths and stuffs, of raiment both for herself and for her bower-women; and there were, as well, a few coffers of spices, unguents, cosmetics, and jewels.

The knight of Belgueil had reckoned on taking with him a squire and ten men-at-arms. When his lady made known her intention, he saw that twice that number would be needed; and after all her belongings had been assembled, he perceived ruefully that not less than forty followers, and those well equipped and armed, would be required to safeguard his wife, her maidens, and their treasure, not to speak of the little Andronicus, though the latter expressed a determination to be his father's own squire. To please the lad, Peire Vidal consented, and had made for him by an armorer of Carcassonne a suit of chain mail, complete in all respects, with a green silk surtout to be worn over a hauberk of steel rings set edgeways, a bright sharp lance, light and strong, and a sword that was no mere plaything, for its blade had the temper of the best Damascus steel.

"If we are attacked," said the young squire, "I will kill all the heathen, and I will make them become good Christians like my lady mother!"

For the hiring and furnishing of his troop it became necessary, against the violent protest of Jehan Porcelet, to dispose of some of his property, and to place other portions of his estate in pledge. The store of furs was sold at Toulouse; the most of the vintage, harvests, and dues of his lands were hypothecated for the term of the crusade; and though, by a special rescript of the pope, crusaders who borrowed money were exempt from payment of interest, Peire Vidal came to an agreement with his lender that was fair and equitable, and made no mention of interest. Altogether he raised ten talents through various sources—a large sum and one that sorely depleted his capital, but he wished to be amply provided for in this great enterprise.

"Sire," said the bailiff sorrowfully as he witnessed the final preparations for the departure of his lord and the cohort, "we are stripped of our means, revenues, arms, and defenders. What now will protect Belgueil from assault and violence?"

"God," said Peire Vidal cheerfully, "and Sant Julian. Also, my friend, the pope has placed the lands and goods of the crusaders under the protection of the Holy See during their absence. You have nothing to fear. When I shall have shown what I can do on the field of battle, and providing the saints grant me a further term of life, I will go to New Rome and present the claim of my son Andronicus to the throne, and if it is allowed, I shall become the regent of the Greek empire. Then we shall see justice established among men, and a government based upon the wisdom and experience of the Joyous Craft."

The honest rogue stared sadly at his master; then he went away shaking his head, for he knew there was none madder in all the world, and he thought it a great pity that the best of all troubadours should have his brains addled by a crusading frenzy.

The start of the journey was made on Whitsunday which, as Easter fell early that year, would allow a full month to reach Venice—a sufficient space of time, providing all went well. They intended to go by boat from Narbonne to Genoa; thence to Tortona, and from there to the river Po where, by good luck, they might procure a barge or two to take them down as far as Ferrara. A road led from that city to Padua, and no doubt the kindly Venetians would provide conveyance over the lagoons to their city. Peire Vidal knew the route thoroughly for he had taken it before as a fugitive from the claws of the Lion, bearing away the king's cherished prize. He remembered how they had fled the city of doges in the sullen dark of night across the wide lagoons. Now he was returning in quite other wise, in the service of the leader of the Christian host, his friend who had once thought to make him his adopted son. And he bore in a tiny silver casket a parchment document, sealed and signed by the Fifth Count Raimon of Toulouse, that declared him to be the father of the heir to the throne of New Rome.

It struck him as curious: so much of his life had been spent, especially of late, in retracing his earlier steps. It was as though some large pattern or design of his life, like those skilful weavings of Poitiers and Limoges, were being endlessly repeated, but each time with a variation of the theme, now sad or again gay, but never as at first.

A morning of late May; a world of flowers and bird-songs, dedicated, it might seem, to *joi* and *joven*, gladness and youth. The company of soldiers looked hardy and gallant in their mailed hauberks; the banner of Belgueil was spread to the breeze that gave it dragon folds. The bright gowns of Lady Xene and her women; jingling of silver bells on the harness of palfreys and sumpter mules, and the proud snorting of the knight's own destrier; his son Andronicus, riding arrogantly with the squires and chanting in a high boyish voice a *lai* of his own composition, to which Gui of Cavaillon and Gaucelm Faidit listened with due solemnity; the shrill laughter of Guilhelma Monjo the wanton, who had sworn she would go with her lord—all these were greatly pleasing to the crusader, recalling the sirvente of Raimbaut of Vacqueiras:

"Galloping, trotting, leaping, riding, vigils, privations and fatigue will henceforth be my pastime. Armed with wood, iron, and steel, I shall endure heat, cold, frost; scattered meadows will be my dwelling place. Discords and severities must serve the place of love songs, and I shall maintain the weak against the strong."

As if to increase his sense of spiritual well-being, he seemed to detect in his lady's manner some trace of a feeling long dormant and that he thought had forever passed. Her oval eyes, fixed on a world within, of which he formed no part, shot an occasional glance of recognition toward him—"this is my husband, a man of no mean attainments, and of true Christian gallantry." At least so he read the look in them; though it may have been merely her great eagerness at returning to the land of jeweled mystery and rituals ancient as the flowing seas.

At Genoa, crowded to overflowing with the motley horde of crusaders, came the first setback to their plans. The Genoese, diligent to please their multitude of transient visitors, informed them that conditions of travel over the passes into central Italy were perilous in the extreme; the Ligurian mountains, so they said, were infested with ferocious bands of brigands and routiers, the backwash of internecine warfare; the valleys of the Tanaro, of the Bormida, and of the Lemma swarmed with outlaws of every description, waiting to fall upon and exterminate the unwary crusaders. It was not only unsafe; it was impossible to make the land journey to Venezia. But they need not be dismayed. Genoa, to aid the cause of Christ, stood ready to provide—at a reasonable figure—direct transportation to the Holy Land.

The crusaders were confused. Without leaders and generally lacking funds, they dreaded fighting their way through the Apennines to Venice. After all, they had enlisted in the service of the Chevalier Jesus, not to battle for their lives in Italy. A few of the hardier souls set out boldly to test the truth of the evil reports. The greater part embarked in Genoese craft for Syria.

Peire Vidal, with his precious freight, dared not risk the passes, for though neither he nor his fellow troubadours placed any credit in the Genoese tales of brigandage, the defection of the great body of crusaders would leave them with too small a convoy for such a hazardous undertaking. Yet Venice had been agreed upon as the point of departure. There the leaders would meet and determine the strategy of the campaign. To abandon that first objective would render this crusade liable to the same division and disintegration as had destroyed earlier efforts. But he quickly discovered that while the charges to go straight to Syria were not excessive, the cost of travel by boat to Venice was dear beyond all reason; in fact, the Genoese captains flatly refused to risk their vessels in the Adriatic which, they affirmed with many seafaring oaths, was over-ridden with pirates.

"Ha!" said Gaucelm Faidit, after they had vainly argued with the fourth shipmaster. "These Genoese and Pisans are more piratical than any other sailors in the world, but they will not venture toward Venice! The devil take me if I sail in any of their slippery bottoms! Blood of Christ, are we yielding our very souls for the Lord to have these rascals make jackanapes of us?"

He went off grumbling and returned an hour later, beaming,

with the tidings he had got of a fisherman that there was a town of Spezia down the coast, from whence a good road led over the mountains by way of the valley of the Magra; and there was a fortified place called Pontremoli that guarded the pass, and from there it was an easy stage to Parma, close by the river Po. This sounded fair enough, and the following day they set out for Spezia. But, as the learned Erigen somewhere remarks: "That which may be easily (*facile*) accomplished alone (*solus*), becomes a matter of infinite difficulty (*magno cum labore*) when attempted in the company of many others (*per multis*)." Had the knight of Belgueil been journeying only with his cronies, a squire, and a handful of servitors, they would have fared not so badly, but the great body of his entourage, the quantity of luggage and impedimenta, in particular, the ladies, both hindered rapid progress and made their nightly quartering a critical problem. Between Genoa and Spezia there were a few wretched fishing hamlets, an occasional walled town, without inns, and sullenly inclined toward strangers, but no friendly abbeys or hospices for chance travelers.

Fortunately, Peire Vidal had purchased at Genoa one diminutive pavilion, which was assigned to the use of the Lady Xene and her damsels, and with the beds they had brought, they did not suffer much beyond the bites of fierce insects and fear of the unknown dangers about them. The soldiers, vaunting their hardihood, slept on their cloaks of drugget, their heads pillowed on their helmets, and their captain likewise. But the other troubadours had providently furnished themselves with sacks of chaff, for, as Gaucelm Faidit affirmed, "The hardness of stones enters into the body and causes rocks to form in the guts." His own being of vast extent, his pallet was correspondingly ample.

The wanton, Guilhelma, though assumed to occupy the pavilion, was of a restless turn when evening came on. There were indications that she lay elsewhere than beside her lord or the damsels; but the captain of the troop had no mind to inquire into the strayings of his companions. Thus they fared tediously on to Spezia and finding a tavern there of a mean and filthy aspect but willing to accommodate them, they tarried a day to rest, then turned northward toward the looming Apennines and Parma beyond.

It was a fearsome journey, by a road that was no road at all but

252

only a rough track, cut by torrents and clinging perilously to cliffs over dread abysses, among barren and savage mountains. Passing the citadel of Pontremoli, that looked so grim they did not stop but skirted it, they were rewarded for their caution by a shower of darts. They had also to endure the heat of unshadowed days and chill of mountain nights, candled with glittering and relentless stars.

Only the boy Andronicus clapped his hands, laughed, sang, threw rocks into echoless depths, dashed up and down on his spirited little Breton palfrey, shook his sword at Pontremoli when the arrows flew, and otherwise conducted himself as the true son of a troubadour and grandson of an emperor. The bearded Greek priest, too, riding an ambling mule, bore himself with such cheerful fortitude that the others were heartened and felt they should do no less as true Christians. The troubadours sang endlessly. Thus they came down into the fertile valley of the river Parma and at length reached the city of that name, having been in the saddle a fortnight from Genoa, though it seemed twice that length of time.

The Monsignor Alessandro da Correggio, a friend of Gui of Cavaillon, received them courteously in his handsome palace, but his report of conditions along the route of their itinerary was disquieting.

"Monsignors, I beseech you not to go into the valley of the Po, or to seek passage down the river. Both from the information I have of those who lately ventured into that region, and by my own eyesight, I can tell you the road to purgatory is not more torturing. Your crusading army has come mostly over the pass of Monte Cenisio down through Lombardy. There are many thousands of them and they are at the mercy of the cupidity of the Lombards. What accommodations there are, these usurers hold at outrageous prices. The few boats long ago have been snapped up. The roads, through much travel and late rains, are quagmires. I assure you, monsignors, the plight of the Christian knights is a sorry one! Even if you cross the river and go on to Mantua, you will find things little better, for you will still be in the thick of the human tide.

"My advice is, that you go by a roundabout way, and strike the Po at the last crossing, near Ferrara. From here to Bologna you will be on one of the finest highways of the world, the Via Emilia, that was built by the Romans and is as good as it was in the days of the Chevalier Julius Caesar. It is no more than a three days' journey by easy stages, and you will get good quarters at Reggio and Modena. From Bologna to Ferrara the road is not so good as you approach the swamplands of the Po; still, it is passable and less abominable than the other way. You should be able to do that stretch in two days more. Altogether, ten days should see you in Venezia—with good luck."

The troubadours thanked him; sang for him; recounted for his great pleasure all the news of Provence and Spain: the affairs of lords, kings, and lovers, and he was gratified beyond measure. So they slept again naked between silken sheets, easing the aches and weariness of their bodies. When they set out the following day he gave them letters to the noble family of Garisendi; and to Peire Vidal he gave introductions to the rector scholarium of the Lombard university there, and another letter to the eminent jurist, Azo, who was lecturing on civil law under the faculty of philosophy.

"You will discover more zeal for learning at Bologna than in any place of Christendom, monsignor," he said. "No less than ten thousand students are entered in the faculties of the arts, and they are divided, according to their nationalities, into four or five universities, with their own government and their rights granted by the Emperor Barbarossa, who espoused their cause against the city."

"Monsignor," said Peire Vidal, "your highway should be named the Road of Learning, for that way go all those who desire to increase the extent of their knowledge. Were I not embarked upon this crusade, I would myself become a student again, in the late realization of how much the wisdom of the ancients and the learning of the doctors are concerned with the practice of wise living."

"Wise living," said the Monsignor da Correggio, "does not make a good song."

On the road to Bologna they fell in with several companies of students, distinguished as much by their high spirits as by their obvious scantiness of means. Peire Vidal, remembering the extreme wretchedness of his rebellious days at Monpeslier, and knowing too well the beggarly rewards in store for most of them, felt a great kindliness toward them and bestowed such largesse as he could afford, which they received happily and without servility. They implored the monsignors to sing for them, which the three friends did by turns, all the way to Reggio. There the troop halted for the night while the students, with many joyous cheers and good wishes for their entertainers, pushed on.

On the morning of the fourth day, with the sun glistening on the Apennines and the air scented with ripening grapes, they saw the high brick walls of Bologna, overtopped by countless spires and towers of amazing height, like a dream city rising from the fertile plain. But if their wonder at sight of this fair city was great, it was increased by the reception that awaited them. No sooner had they entered through the gate of Saint Donato than they were greeted by a delegation representing the corporations of the universities and student federations, headed by the rector scholarium in person, and were conducted, with a ceremoniousness befitting an emperor, to one of the palaces of learning, traversing streets lined with huzzahing citizens and students, strewn with flowers and gay with banners. Along the route of their triumphal march there were continuous shouts of "Viva, Pietro Vidale! Viva, Guido Cavallano! Viva, Gancelmo Faidito! Viva, crusaditori!" For the Bolognese had been informed by the itinerant students of the coming of their illustrious visitors, all of whom they knew by reputation.

That night, amid the flaring of myriad torches, the three sang before many thousands, who listened thirstily and cried out for more songs, though only a small part of them knew the meaning of the words.

That picture of innumerable eager, upturned faces, raptly listening, so many carved in the semblance of thoughtful speculation, quick with curiosity or sober with melancholy reflection, the earmarks of scholarship, remained with Peire Vidal when his company, having crossed the turbid flood of the Po, fell in with the doleful straggling army of the crusade. Struggling through the dust and sweaty tumult of that vast, disorderly, woebegone, and utterly weary host, Peire Vidal thought he had never witnessed large bodies of men who, at the inception of a great enterprise, seemed so broken in spirit. He found they had been misled, cozened by

255

preying innkeepers, delayed by snows in the Alps, drenched by storms and wetted by torrents on their descent, robbed by the Lombards, and waylaid by bands of routiers. The disciplined troops of the great lords, it is true, had come through in fine style. The soldiers of Baldwin of Flanders, of Hugo, Count of Saint Paul, of Geoffroi of Villehardouin, looked fresh and neat, for they had been well provided for, and had preempted the best of accommodations. But, on the whole, it was a disheartening spectacle.

Chapter Twenty-one

PEIRE VIDAL had remembered Venice as a seaport inferior to busy Genoa, substantial Marseille, vivid Barcelona, imperial Arles. But in ten years the city had greatly prospered. If any number of Byzantine caskets, studded with jewels, with silver and gold, with emerald and lapis lazuli, had been fashioned by a wizard into the forms of palaces and set down upon the sea, that would have been Venice. These palaces, set side by side along innumerable waterways in a bewildering maze, dazzled the weary crusaders by their splendor, as its haughty citizens amazed them by their show of wealth in costly robes and priceless ornaments.

The crusaders paid a handsome toll to be ferried from the mainland to Venezia. Here it seemed they could not move without digging into their wallets for more soldi. But they soon discovered that they were not to enjoy the pleasures of this fabulously wealthy city; a special camp had been allotted to them on the island of Santo Nicolo di Lido. Again they paid their ferrymen. The island of the Lido proved to be a sandy bar some three or four leagues in length but less than half a league wide, barren and desolate, watered by stagnant salty pools, its only verdure the rank coarse marsh grass, its sole dwellings the ruined walls of ancient Malamocco. Here were huddled the tents and pavilions of some thousand knights of the cross and sixty thousand foot-soldiers: French,

Bretons, Germans, Lombards, Burgundians, Spaniards, Gascons, English, and Provençals.

Across the intervening water glittered the jeweled Venezia; on the Lido the great host, restless and impatient, cursed the fierce sun of July, the gnats and savage flies, the lack of food and water. Then their allies of the island city sent over boats laden with victuals and wine. The crusaders found they could purchase a sistarius of corn for fifty soldi, a skin of wine for a hundred, a goat for five hundred. They grumbled, swore, and paid. The swift esneccas of the Venetians moved watchfully about the Lido, for the doge, Enrico Dandolo, had given orders that no one should ferry any of the foreigners out of the island. And the leaders of the crusade, those renowned counts and barons, went often to the city in the galley of the doge and returned with long faces; for it came to be known that of the sum covenanted as the price of transporting the army across the sea, there were still wanting thirty-four thousand marks. The doge was a man of his word.

The leaders despatched messengers in frantic haste to all the cities and ports, urging pilgrims to come to Venice. Gaucelm Faidit grinned when he learned of this.

"If Genoa is a sample, there will be none leaving for Venice from other places." He mopped his face and fanned away a cloud of midges. "But there is another good reason why we shall see no more simpletons trudging down the valley of the Po. Last week a party of Germans made their escape. They will spread word of our pleasant sojourn in this paradise of sand and grass. 'Twill stop any but Beelzebub himself who, I think, is already with us."

Peire Vidal and his troop had found quarters at the far end of the island, that was once Malamocco, where the Venetian fisherfolk long ago had made rude dwellings of sundried brick and had built forts against the hosts of Pippin the Short, father of Charlemagne. The Provençals occupied one of these ruined edifices and managed to make some show of comfort in their "castello," as Gui of Cavaillon facetiously named it. Besides the protection afforded by the crumbling walls, they were somewhat removed from the main body of the army and were thus spared the noise, stench, and disorder of that encampment. But certain knights and squires of Provence, upon discovering their retreat, moved into the neighborhood out of fellow feeling, and they were joined finally by two or three thousand Provençal foot soldiers, a light-hearted rabble given to dicing, singing, and other amusements.

The young squire Andronicus, out of all that crusading host, seemed the only one to be delighted with their situation. He moved like a proud and curious elf among the soldiers, answering their rough jests with swift retorts, examining their arms, listening eagerly to their boasting or bawdy tales, at times singing to them in his high, clear voice. And his mother, the Lady Xene, was entertained by the small court she had set up, in which she was sole queen, attended by several knights, and sung to by Gui of Cavaillon, Pons de Capduelh and by the trouvère, Quesnes de Béthune. The canon Béthune, a singer in the train of Count Baldwin of Flanders, was practised in French gallantry, for he had long courted Marie de France, Countess of Champagne, and was himself a native of Arras. The oval eyes of the princess once more took on a glamorous darkening, and she wore her jewels imperially within the moldering walls.

Andronicus, left to his own devices, had conceived a magnificent project, which he proceeded to put into effect. In the army of the crusade were a considerable number of youths of an age too green and tender for fighting, who, for the most part, performed menial tasks for squires and foot soldiers. Some few of these lads had more than a tincture of noble blood. Though they were all older than Andronicus, none was more gifted with the talent of leadership. He induced some two score of these young scamps to desert their labors and start a camp of their own, lying not far from the Provençals, on the seaward side of the Lido. Here, having demonstrated his superiority in feats of prowess and in fighting, Andronicus proclaimed himself their leader. He set them at once to constructing shelters out of camp rubbish and stuff filched from the soldiers, imposed a rigorous discipline, posted sentinels, and maintained military order. He also despatched foraging expeditions and he put them to such business as the making of bows and arrows, the first of which they fashioned out of willows salvaged along the swampy shore, and strung with thin thongs of leather. Darts they whittled from tough driftwood, giving them a pretty point. They made swords, shields, and lances, too. Then there were daily contests and tourneys, shooting at targets, races on foot and in the water, and on occasion blood flowed. The boys thrived and grew insolent toward the soldiers, who had named their camp the Frog Pond; but these latter were secretly entertained and often came to watch the boys at their play, though forbidden by stripling sentinels to pass beyond certain bounds.

Thus passed a week or two while the great camp, sullen in confinement, irked by the blistering heat, execrated the knavery of the islanders and fumed against the leaders who had got them into this infernal predicament. The jongleurs, and troubadours of the south, and the trouvères of the north were in great demand to entertain the idle foot-soldiers. Peire Vidal not only possessed a voice of great resonance, he had gained the power, in his tour of Italy, to adjust the tone of it so that he could be heard by a vast multitude in the open air. For that reason he delighted the soldiers mightily and had scarcely any rest day or night from singing; and he sang often of things long past, when the reason for it had been far otherwise. So, on one occasion he sang to them:

Plus que. l paubres que jatz el ric ostal . . .

"As the poor pensioner that lodges miserably within a noble mansion utters no plaint, despite his utter wretchedness, dreading to importune his patron; so I, stricken with melancholy, dare not voice my grievance. Yet who has better reason, seeing how my madomna, dearer than all else to me, chides my audacity? Ah, craven heart, fearful of her reproaches!

"Like one who, in the dawn-gilded mirror of a windowpane, envisages a fair country, when I picture her, such satisfaction fills me that all things base and dull desert my thoughts; but tender introspection is a rod one plucks for flagellation. Again I taste from my heart's chalice that stolen kiss, my passion's only souvenir. Ah, wretched, not to see one's dear beloved! Does she think exile is the surest bond?"

The soldiers, bearded and uncouth, sitting and sprawling, uttered their hoarse approval. It was all fine and elegant language, befitting a great singer, but the meaning was plain—to be deprived of a smart piece of flesh over a silly kiss. It had happened to many of them. Wenches were that way. They would be priggish and proper, holding you off and screeching if you so much as fingered them; and while you were away, some other varlet was climbing in the window!

Peire Vidal took his polished viol and with a great sweeping flourish broke into the Chanson of Roland. He sang it in French that all might understand. The sun over the Lido moved slowly westward, flamed above the Adriatic, slid down, lingered as an eye of fire, sank; and soon the bright stars quivered on the restless sea. The song ended. They gave a great shout and clattered their weapons.

Peire Vidal returned to his shelter across the gray sands where the ebbing tide had left upcast and drifting things; he was remembering the beauty of the Lady Adélasie des Baux.

"Ha, comrade, that brat of yours—what a bundle of boldness and deviltry!" Gaucelm Faidit slapped his broad knee in high good humor. "One 'ud think he was king of the Lido!"

"What has my little golden-haired angel been doing?" asked the Monjo, running her chubby fingers over her lord's bald pate. "Would he were large enough to go to bed with me!"

"He's large enough, you libidinous mopsy, but he's wise enough to know a mutton from a rank ewe! I declare, friend Peire, the lad's got the nature of a born ruler. I was over there to the Frog Pond to watch the tadpoles at their sports, and for a fact they are better ordered than our own camp. At the first barbican, which is an empty cask, I was halted by as fierce a pair of young scalliwags as ever drew dagger. I must wait permission of their captain-general, the Monsenher Andronicus, before I entered. Well, up comes the son, like the chief of the routiers, and greets me as ceremonious as a Saracen sultan. I am escorted through the encampment by an armed guard and shown the sights—fortress, pavilions, commissary, down to latrines—all in proper order, even to the dungeon where I find one prisoner.

"But that is not all. Let me tell you more of this little demon of yours. I had scarce left the camp when I heard a commotion and turned back. It seems, a half dozen young bloods, led by a squire of eighteen summers or so, had forced their way into the camp and started bantering the Frogs. Some words passed; then of a sudden out darts Captain Andronicus, whips his blade from its sheath,

261

and makes for the leader of the intruders. The fellow drew, too, and they went at it, hammer and tongs. But your son, Peire Vidal, has been well drilled in swordplay, and he's quick as a cat. He forced the other back, till his companions closed in to aid him."

"Sant Lazare!" breathed Guilhelma Monjo breathlessly. "They did him no harm?"

"Not they!" chuckled the stout troubadour. "For the Frogs came down upon them like a whirlwind and drove them from camp on the run!"

"God shield them all!" exclaimed the wanton. "I could kiss them every one!"

"I am glad he has shown his mettle," said the father, "for I should hate to think he was not so brave as myself."

Gaucelm Faidit eyed his friend quizzically.

"He has shown a like talent for getting into hot water," he said. "His opponent was the young Alexius, son of the Emperor Isaac Angelus, who is a claimant for the throne of New Rome, and the protégé of the captain of this crusade, my lord the Marquis Bonifaz of Montferrat."

"Ha!" exclaimed Gui of Cavaillon. "More trouble!"

"By no means," said Peire Vidal. "My son was somewhat hasty. He shall come to me at once, and when he has offered his version of the affair, I will see that regrets for this incident are tendered to Alexius, or better, to the marquis."

"The marquis is away raising funds to pay our thievish allies, and the camp is now under the marshalship of the French baron, Simon de Montfort, who is noted for his lack of humor."

"At any rate, Andronicus, since he has assumed responsibility for his camp, must face the consequences. It will be a good test of his discipline. And if he balks, I myself will dissolve his troop and keep him here with me."

At the summons of his father the young captain appeared immediately before the three troubadours, and not at all abashed, but very simply, he told his story.

"They came into our camp insolently, without asking leave, and began to jeer and scoff at us. And when I came to them and said that they had better go away, their leader asked, who I might be. I said my name was Andronicus Vidal. 'So,' he said, 'you are

262

the brat of the fool Vidal and his Greek slave. Your sire had done better to have stuck to his harp and his pig, and not give you the name of an emperor, even if he was a vile usurper and deserved to be hung up by the feet until he died.' I did not want to answer him because of my rage, but I said, 'My father gave me the name of Andronicus, my mother's father, and he does not play the harp, but the viol, and that better than any man living.'"

"You spoke truthfully," said Peire Vidal. "What reply did he make?"

"He said, 'Your mother was not even a Greek. She was a Saracen, and you are her bastard.' So then I could not think of anything but to draw upon him, but he would not stand and fight."

"H'm," said Gaucelm Faidit. "The High Council of Amity and Juridical Procedure will go into secret session over this matter. We will let you know our decision shortly, monsenher captain-general. You have stated your case well."

The youthful captain gave a military salute and turned on his heel.

"And, captain," called Gui of Cavaillon after him, "you had best put your camp in a state of siege. If you are attacked, send a runner to us and we will despatch assistance."

"I think," said the little general, "we shall be able to defend ourselves. The saints keep you, father!"

"And you, my son!"

The High Council, at its plenary session, voted unanimously that the cause of the Frog Pond was a just one, and that whatever befell, it would take such action as might be necessary to safeguard the principles of justice.

That afternoon Peire Vidal received a message, scrawled on a piece of parchment: "My esteemed father, do not, I beg, send any aid for we can take care of our honor and will die fighting or any way. Andronicus, captain-general of the Crusadatori." It seemed the lad had taken for his troop the name given his father's company by the amiable Bolognese.

The messenger returned with an official document, sealed, and tied with a silk ribbon. It read: "To the captain-general of the

263

Crusadatori, greetings! The High Council has passed judgment upon your case and affirms its justice. In the profession of warfare it is considered bad practice to die fighting unless there is no other honorable way. The army of Provence stands ready to aid you in your extremity. Signed, Gaucelm Faidit, commissioner."

That afternoon there took place the famous Battle of the Frog Pond, which was watched with the most intense interest by the Provençal partisans of the Frogs, clustered on every sandy eminence and on the ruined walls of Malamocco. The first sign of the impending conflict was the advance, from the direction of the main crusaders' camp, of a file of a round dozen foot-soldiers. When they came nearer it was seen that they wore the livery of De Montfort, and each one of them carried a stout cudgel in one hand and an unlighted brand in the other. They marched slowly, because of the heaviness of the sand, but with the deliberateness of a duty to be performed.

In the Frog Pond there were no signs of life. It might have been taken for a deserted stretch of beach, save for the curious tent-like objects here and there, over one of which floated a red gonfalon that rumor said had been the chemise of the camp-follower, Lysette. To reach the camp it was necessary for the little band of soldiers to pass through a narrow defile between two large sand dunes, covered at their tops by a rank growth of sea-grass. At this point occurred the signal disaster to the invaders that went down in the varied annals of the Lido as the Victory of the Frogs over the Toads. The ambush was sudden, and without warning save for a shrill concert of yells, "Au hazard, Crusadatori!" Even at the distance of the onlookers from the fray, there could be heard the snap of twenty bowsprings, as twenty sharp darts left the thumbs and forefingers of twenty experienced archers. From the soldiers of the great lord Simon de Montfort rose a bellow of surprise and rage. Eight of them had been hit in tender spots. One fellow, roaring curses, was trying to pluck a bolt from his nose; another was wiping blood from his cheek; a third was dancing without gayety, an arrow having lodged viciously in his unprotected rump. They were thrown into confusion. Several ran heedlessly on into the defile, only to meet another shower from unseen bowmen. The detachment, cursing by all the saints and demons, turned tail, fell in with their bewildered companions in arms, and the retreat became a rout.

The watchers on the heights, observing this brief and overwhelming debacle of the marshal's provost guard, cheered loud and long. Nothing could have given the Provençals greater joy than the vanquishment of Norman soldiers by fledglings, led by a child of their own race.

Within an hour Peire Vidal received a summons from Simon de Montfort to appear straightway before him. This time he did not take with him his viol, and though he was often stopped on the long torrid walk along the sands by soldiers begging him to give them a song, he shook his head and hurried on. The headquarters was a splendid pavilion draped with countless gonfalons bearing the arms and colors of Blois, Champagne, Flanders, Montferrat, and a host of other demesnes and seignories, and it was sumptuously furnished in every respect.

In a small chamber enclosed in arras he found four knights and a clerk. Two of the knights were playing chess, while a third stood looking on. The fourth knight, a man of scholarly bearing, was walking up and down, dictating to the clerk: ". . . the doge, Enrico Dandolo, when there had come to him Count Louis of Blois, Count Hugues de Saint Paul, the Marquis Boniface of Montferrat, and Geoffroi de Villehardouin, marshal of Champagne, made the proposal——"

"My lord marshal," said one of the chess-players without looking up, "why leave me out of your history?"

"Pardon, my dear Baldwin. Insert, 'Baldwin, count of Flanders.'"

Peire Vidal, who had remained unnoticed by the knights, glanced at Baldwin of Flanders. He was a young man, the youngest of the four, with a candid, ironic face.

"You may put me down for a rogue and brigand, I'll be underground when your readers are turning those pages over!" Baldwin, looking up from the board, noticed the visitor for the first time. "Monsenher," he said courteously, "we have been too busy with affairs of state for good manners. Have you business with any of us?"

"I was bidden to come here by the marshal of the camp, Lord Simon de Montfort."

"You are Peire Vidal, the troubadour?"

"Yes, my lord."

Geoffroi of Villehardouin, the historian, frowned; the Counts Louis and Hugues showed no interest; but Baldwin of Flanders rose and came to the troubadour.

"I have heard much good of you, monsenher, from my trouvère, Quesnes de Béthune, and long ago I was told of your voice by the Châtelain de Coucy, a good singer himself. Poor fellow, his bones are bleaching in the Holy Land, far from his beloved, the Lady of Fayel, for whom he made all of his songs—tender and delicate pieces they were, too."

"I saw him a great deal," said Peire Vidal, "but I never knew he sang."

"He sang for one person only. She made some very fine verses herself, I am told. So your son has been chasing the seasoned troops of De Montfort, eh? We have heard of the Battle of the Frogs." His eyes twinkled.

"A criminal offence! I'd have the young rascals flogged—or raised to squiredom!"

"My lord, you do ill to take this matter lightly," said the historian. "In the present state of our camp it's a serious reflection on discipline."

Baldwin said, "The only reflection on discipline is lack of it. For that condition we are accountable."

Count Louis of Blois now spoke: "It is truly no slight matter, but I believe that our marshal, Simon de Montfort, will be satisfied with a full apology from your son to himself and the Prince Alexius—providing that this troop of young routiers is disbanded at once. After all, they have duties elsewhere, polishing armor and what not."

Count Hugues de Saint Paul nodded his agreement. "That is a simple solution. Let your son publicly do homage to the prince, acknowledging his error, and all will be forgiven."

Peire Vidal ran his hand through his hair. "I fear, my lords, it is not as simple as all that. If the marshal delivers an official order for the dissolution of the lads' camp, it will be obeyed. If he de-

266

mands a personal apology, my son, or better, myself as his deputy, will tender it. But neither my son nor myself will do homage to this Prince Alexius or concede that the defence of honor against insolent aggression was other than just and reasonable."

This reply was received in dead silence. Only Baldwin of Flanders began to hum lightly—it was the first phrase of the crusading chant—*Baros Jezus, qu'en crotz fo mes*—Peire Vidal's own song. Count Baldwin broke off.

"You have put your case fairly, monsenher."

"We will take the matter under advisement," said Geoffroi of Villehardouin coldly; "and your remarkable statement will be reported to our lord marshal."

Baldwin of Flanders went with Peire Vidal to the door of the pavilion.

"My friend," he said, "you have stepped into a hornets' nest. Politics! Policy! I will do what I can. Privately, I advise you to forestall drastic action by persuading the scamps to abandon their encampment." He lowered his voice. "And on no account, should you or your son venture again within reach of gentle Simon. He is one of those who stand up for the Lord—and put their enemies to torture. Stay where you are until the thing blows over. We'll soon be under way, I hope, and fighting in Egypt, where these spiders will have less opportunity for spinning. Later, monsenher, we shall be hearing your voice, I trust!"

"Thank you, my lord. To you I say that I am sorry for all this, and my son is grieved, too; for what was the best of play has become an unpleasant business."

"Father, we will dismantle the camp." The young Andronicus stood up straight and spoke bravely, but there were tears in his eyes. "My soldiers have learned obedience to my command." There was pride in his voice. "Yet it is unjust to send them back to their places in the camp, if they will be punished."

"I do not think your followers will be punished, my son. Let them go one by one, without any fuss. The soldiers will see to it that they are not ill treated. I know it is hard, but it must be done."

"Yes, father. I thank you for your words. I wish I were old

enough to be a knight." His eyes, the color of vair, gave out tiny sparks of fire. "I would challenge Simon de Montfort to single combat."

Shortly, from the Frog Pond, rose smoke and flames. The Crusadatori were destroying their own work.

A few days later a squire reported casually that he had seen master Andronicus, shortly after daylight, footing it toward the main camp. Peire Vidal, accustomed to his son's lengthy absences, was not alarmed. It was a day when the heat was such that the metal of armor and weapons could not safely be handled. The Provençals, lovers of sunlight though they were, hugged the scant shade. The Lady Xene and her damsels, shutting their "court" against all gallant singers, drowsed in nymph nakedness under silken canopies. The glassy Adriatic scarcely turned one languid ripple on the glittering strand.

Toward evening Peire Vidal experienced a sense of uneasiness when there were no signs of the lad's returning. He traced him, by report, along the path leading straight to the great pavilion. There the trail ended. Peire Vidal was denied admission. He tried to discover the whereabouts of Baldwin of Flanders, but all he learned was that Baldwin, and the Counts Louis of Blois and Hugues de Saint Paul, with Geoffroi of Villehardouin, had been summoned to Venice to meet the marquis of Montferrat there for another conference with the doge. The marshal, Simon de Montfort, could not be seen by anyone. Peire Vidal returned in the humid and burning darkness to Malamocco; and his heart was dark with foreboding.

For three days he went to the pavilion, with the same result. The great lords were away. It was said that the marquis had despatched them on errands into Italy to raise more silver marks. It was not known when they might return. Indeed, no one knew anything, except that a soldier had sickened suddenly and died. The camp was stifled by heat, yet it stirred with a subdued, sullen restlessness. The provost guards, their weapons ready for instant use, were much in evidence. Knights stayed on duty, clad in full mail, their straight double-bladed swords at their hips.

On the fourth day the Provençals began to drift down toward

268

the main body of crusaders. They mingled with the foot soldiers of Champagne, of Brabant, of Lombardy and Burgundy and Flanders and Blois—with all but the Normans. It was a blistering day, yet the followers of the great war-lords were seen leaving their ragged tents. By dozens. By hundreds. By thousands.

Peire Vidal, who had not slept for three nights, that last night, close to dawn, fell into a heavy slumber, and when he awoke, the sun was well up. He pulled on his tunic hastily and ran down the beach. The whole encampment, save for the women's quarters, was deserted. As he approached the main camp he saw many empty tents but no soldiers. When he neared the headquarters pavilion, however, a great crowd of soldiers was milling about the emblazoned and magnificent tent. So great was the press he could not get within bowshot of the place. There was fighting going on up in front, or at least, a pandemonium of shouts and cries. And there was one shout that rang with peculiar ferocity above the rest, repeated by ten thousand voices, in a dozen different tongues: "Bring out the boy! Simon, bring out the boy!" Not: "my lord Simon" or "Simon de Montfort, my lord" but "Simon." It was a sound to strike terror to the heart of any lord who cherished his title—a sound never heard before on any of those dreary and disheartening expeditions known as crusades.

"Simon, bring out the boy! Bring out the boy, you Simon!"

The tumult died. Hush. A voice near the pavilion: "He's coming out!" A hubbub of voices: "He's coming out! Simon has freed him!"

A lane opened in the living wall. Faces that had been distorted with rage and rebellion were now eager and expectant. Down the center of the cleared space, accompanied by thunders of hoarse shouts, came Gui of Cavaillon, bearing on his back the lad Andronicus. Behind them trudged Gaucelm Faidit, mopping his brow. The face of Andronicus was pale and set. He looked neither to right nor left until he saw his father, then his tired eyes lightened as he slid from the troubadour's back, stood stiffly, or tried to stand, and was gathered into the great strong arms of his sire.

"I wanted to fight Alexius but they wouldn't let me. I said God might decide between us, but they only laughed. I said to Simon

269

de Montfort that he knew nothing of justice or honor. . . . They could not make me do anything I would not. . . ."

Simon de Montfort sat alone in his great pavilion. His face wore the sinister look of the priest who does no wrong and feels no pity.

He was brooding on the evilness of Provence. "Some day," he muttered, "I will scourge them all!" And he added, "In the name of the Lord!"

Chapter Twenty-two

THE measures Simon de Montfort had resolved upon to avoid a repetition of the recent disorders in the camp were stayed by providence. Pestilence broke out. It visited the noble as well as the base borne, both knight and foot soldier; and it inspired a fear greater than that of rack and thumbscrew. Men sickened, staggered, groaned, and died. Their fellows, with shrinking hearts, dug pits in the sand and buried them. Soon there were too many grisly barrows upon the Lido, and the living heaped up mounds of the dead and burned them. The island was darkened by a pall of charnel smoke and the sickly air bore an evil odor. And when they could bury and burn no more, they gave the dead to the sea, from whence, at the turning of the tide, they returned wanly and churned about Santo Nicolo di Lido, a pallid and spiritless host.

The graceless Provençals, in expectation of feeling the hand of the lord marshal laid upon them, had withdrawn to the furthest extremity of Malamocco, where, armed and isolated, they awaited what punishment might befall. By this rebellious separation they were spared the full effect of the plague, for when they got the first word of its outbreak, the troubadours forbade any man to cross toward the stricken camp. The wind, too, blew fresh from the sea on that side, driving away unwholesome vapors. A pavilion, at some distance from their quarters, was set aside for any who should fall sick, and almost hourly Peire Vidal, accompanied by a young student of medicine at Bologna, who had followed his train in the hope of glorious adventure, went amongst the soldiers examining into their state of health. By this and other means, and by cleanliness and watchfulness, and being sparing in their diet and drinking, there were not more than a score taken with the dread malady, but among them was Pons de Capduelh, the troubadour.

When Pons de Capduelh felt the first pangs, he said, "I have made my last song." He called for his lute and would have sung again, but the effort was beyond his strength, and as the fever mounted in his veins he begged his friends to sing for him. They were all there, Peire Vidal, Gaucelm Faidit, Gui of Cavaillon, and the Picard, Quesnes de Béthune. The Lady Xene, too, though they would have prevented her, had no thought but to remain by her one-time lover's side until he yielded his last breath. The Griffon priest, Porphyros, with silver cross and images, passed slowly about the tent, intoning an endless litany and swinging a censer which gave off the fragrance of burning incense. They sang for the dying man many gay and pleasant baladas, coblas, cansos, and sirventes; and the troubadour of Arras sang a fine crusading song,

Ah! love, how hard it is to leave you. . . .

So, as they sang bravely, the troubadour's eyes closed.

"It is very simple," said Gaucelm Faidit. "We do not have to pay this trifle of thirty-four thousand silver marks to our allies, the kindly Venetians, for conveyance to the Holy Land."

The plague had exhausted its fury. The last dead were buried. They could draw easier breath once more, drink wine of Chios brought by pirate esneccas, roast Dalmatian goats out of the same bottoms, and endure the sun of August, which seemed less fearful than that of July.

"And the doge's proposal?" Gui of Cavaillon's voice rose on the note of skepticism.

"That is simplicity in its most transparent guise, my lord baron!"

Gui of Cavaillon did not like to be called baron (though he had

272

actually come into his estate during his stay on the island of the Lido) for he had still to win his spurs. He had got to his baronetcy before arriving at knighthood, and Gaucelm Faidit missed no opportunity to twit him on his lordly degree.

"We were to go to Egypt," said Gaucelm Faidit, emptying his flagon with such ostentation that his wanton could not fail to notice. She hastened, with the dutifulness of an aging mistress, to fill it. "But we are not going to Egypt. It is an unhealthy spot, Egypt."

"Unhealthy!" growled Peire Vidal. "God's love—unhealthy!"

"Enrico Dandolo, the sage and doge of Venezia, says it is unhealthy, and who should know better, for has he not been the intimate of the sultan, Malek-Adel of Egypt?"

"What treachery is this?" snarled the baron troubadour.

"None at all," quoth the stout singer blandly. "We are not going to the land of Malek-Adel—because we are going on a little private crusade, in the interest of Dandolo and the Council of Five Hundred."

Peire Vidal leaped to his feet. "We have been betrayed! What is this crusade?"

"This crusade, my friend, furnishes a pretty illustration of the art of politics. To understand its present complexion we should have to study certain family connections. Take, for instance, the illustrious house of Montferrat——"

"The devil take *you*, Gaucelm Faidit! Tell us at once of the doge's perfidy!"

"Not so fast, baron. I spent several hours of my valuable time worming all this history out of our friend, Quesnes de Béthune, who gathered it by degrees from his patron, Count Baldwin of Flanders. To go back to Montferrat. A certain brave knight and gentleman, Guillaume Longespada, as he was called, father of Conrad and Bonifaz of Montferrat, married Sophia, the daughter of Frederick Barbarossa, the emperor, who is the sister of Philip of Swabia, head of the Waiblings, better known as the Ghibellines. This Philip married the daughter of Isaac Angelus, one-time emperor of New Rome, and since then blinded and imprisoned in the tower of Anema by the so-called Alexis the Third."

"Plague take your genealogies, Gaucelm Faidit!"

273

"As you know, the young Alexis, the son of Isaac Angelus, escaped from the tower of Anema. He betook himself at once to his brother-in-law, Philip of Swabia, and there met our marquis of Montferrat, about to start crusading. Bonifaz himself is the brother-in-law of the aunt of young Alexis. Ah! you see how simple it is! And Bonifaz, kindled by the wrongs of his *near* relative, goes to the pope at Rome to secure the papal blessing for the claim of young Alexis to the throne of New Rome, which is under the anti-pope and arch-enemy of Rome. Hence, the presence of young Alexis in our midst; and hence, the unlucky predicament of friend Vidal's son, who so ferociously attacked the nephew of the sister-in-law of the marquis of Montferrat."

"For the love of the saints, draw your tale to a conclusion, Gaucelm Faidit," complained the Monjo, "for all these marriages turn my stomach!"

"The tale, my beloved slut, is only half told. This crusade was led originally by the young earl of Champagne, Theobald, a noble and brave youth, and the nephew of Richard the Lion and of Philip Augustus. His unexpected sudden death was a serious blow to the hopes of his vassal, Count Baldwin of Flanders, who was forced to concede the leadership to Bonifaz. It was Baldwin's plan to go by way of Egypt. But we are not going that way. Instead, we are going by way of Zara, which we will first take and destroy."

"And what pagan city is that?" asked Peire Vidal.

"It is a Christian city, obedient to the pope at Rome, and belonging to our ally, King Aimeric of Hungary, who has contributed materially to this crusade!"

"Then why, in the name of Jesu, are we to attack Zara?"

"Because Zara is an eye-sore to the doge, Enrico Dandolo. It is a fine rich city, and the capital of Dalmatia. It seems that something over a hundred years ago one of the doges assumed the title of duke of Dalmatia; wherefore, you might say, Dalmatia belongs to the doge, and to Venice. But far from acknowledging the overlordship of Venice, Zara has set out to be her sea-rival. She must be taken and broken, and who can do it better than our army of crusaders shut up on the Lido?"

Peire Vidal was frowning. The face of Gui of Cavaillon was thunderblack.

"King Aimeric—Aimeric—why! I sang before Aimeric when he was duke!" Now Peire recalled the pleasure and the triumphs of that visit. "He is one of the most liberal and enlightened of Christian lords, a patron of the Joyous Craft and a scholar of parts. There is none more courteous, gentle, and generous in largesse. God forbid we should despoil him of his city to satisfy this fox of Venice!"

Gui of Cavaillon laughed harshly. "Your tale, Gaucelm Faidit, should be set to music as the Chanson du Diable. I begin to see the drift of it. We pillage Zara, and then plant the young Alexis on the throne of New Rome, and, if we have any time left, we treat with the Saracens!"

"No, no!" cried Peire Vidal, wrinkling his visage painfully in an effort to understand the full import of these revelations. "Such infamy is incredible! I can't believe my lord Bonifaz would bargain with the doge in the blood of crusaders! But if it is so, if he has sold out to that devil, by all the saints, let us have no share in it! Ay, and we can persuade others, too; you, my friends, and myself will make sirventes against their scurvy dickerings! We will sing them through the whole camp so every man may know the works of Belial in their leaders! We will get Quesnes de Béthune to join us, and Raimbaut of Vacqueiras——"

"Quesnes de Béthune," said Gaucelm Faidit, "will sing as he is told by Baldwin of Flanders, who is playing a waiting game. And as for our erstwhile comrade in the Joyous Craft, Raimbaut of Vacqueiras, he is too busy in the business of the marquis even to give us audience. I know, for I have tried it. This is very good wine they make in Chios," he added, wiping his lips. "Where are you, hussy? Will you let us go parched when there are full skins to be emptied? As regards your invitation to stir up rebellion in the camp, I may say that while I have no objection to being speared by Saracens, I have only a slight inclination to being stabbed or strangled by Christians! Were it even divulged to Simon de Montfort how I had related these things to you, I should never leave the Lido alive, nor will you, either, if you sing against the Zara expedition!"

"They would not dare touch us, who are not unknown by our singing!"

"As vassals of one of the great lords, we are granted what protection they can afford to give us; as troubadours, our protector is Sant Julian who, blessed though he be, is often somewhat forgetful. No, Peire Vidal, we shall do no singing of sirventes in the camp. We keep our mouths tight closed. We know nothing; we are surprised at nothing; we do nothing—until this cursed island is well behind us. Then, perchance, fortune may spare us further participation in the noble enterprise. Indeed, Monsenher Vidal, it is my solemn advice that you allow the rumor—which I have already set in motion—to become current, that you have been so humbled by your recent sad experience as to abandon singing altogether. The baron here, if he choose, may give out that he fears greatly the uncertainties of his inheritance may compel him to return, for the nonce, to Provence. Myself, I shall go about publicly groaning from old wounds received in other, and not so glorious crusades, which will be the prelude to my retirement from this one."

Though Peire Vidal and Gui of Cavaillon were men of spirit, they had to acknowledge the wisdom of Gaucelm Faidit's advice. After the recent happenings at the headquarters pavilion it was no time to tempt reprisals or to invite retribution that might involve the slaughter of their faithful Provençals as well as themselves.

Some days later Gaucelm Faidit brought word that the Cardinal Peter Capuano, the pope's legate, had arrived and had been snubbed by the Venetians for telling them that the crusaders were forbidden by Innocent the Third to attack any Christian cities or peoples. Little they cared for the anathemas or excommunications of the pope! And when the cardinal discovered that the crusaders could not by any means get to the Holy Land unless they accepted the doge's proposal, he, after great hesitancy and perturbation, said that it might be better for them to go to Zara rather than abandon the crusade altogether. Meanwhile, the army was kept in ignorance concerning the plan to take that city.

Then, on the day before Saint Mark's day, toward the end of August, Raimbaut of Vacqueiras came to pay his friends a visit. He was clad in full armor and looked very soldierly, not at all the reckless troubadour they had once known. He was courteous and affable, but wore the slightly distant look of a man of important affairs. He inquired after Gaucelm Faidit's old wounds and expressed concern over the troubadour's growing disability, the latter having groaned audibly several times. He congratulated Gui of Cavaillon on his baronetcy and trusted that home difficulties would not intrude at this critical juncture. He turned to Peire Vidal.

"Monsenher Vidal, it is curious how the paths of friends so often cross—Béziers, Montferrat, Venice———"

"The island of Nicolo di Lido," corrected Gaucelm Faidit.

"Tomorrow, my friends, it shall be Venice. You must join me on a pleasure expedition. It is the great feast day of the year, the day of blessed Sant Mark."

"Remembering Pons de Capduelh," said Gui of Cavaillon, "I would not call the saint exactly blessed."

"Our poor friend wears his laurels in heaven!" said Raimbaut of Vacqueiras. Then quickly, "Tomorrow at the hour of nones the barges of the doge will bring us to Venice for the carnival. A great and merry sight, I promise you!"

"They should be merry," observed Gaucelm Faidit, "now that they no longer have the stink of our dead in their nostrils!"

"It has all been very unfortunate," Raimbaut of Vacqueiras said, and as no one spoke, he added, with momentary but genuine emotion. "Horrible!" Then he pronounced formally, "You will be expected at the headquarters pavilion tomorrow." This was no invitation; it was a command. "My lord the marquis of Montferrat, of course, will acknowledge your attendance. And monsenhers, you may well believe that the marquis has done, and is doing all in his power to meet fairly and generously the difficulties that beset us. The saints be with you, monsenhers!"

"Sant Julian defend you, Raimbaut of Vacqueiras!" said Gaucelm Faidit, knowing well that the lover of the Fair Knight needed no longer to pray to the gentle patron of outcasts and troubadours.

When he had gone Gaucelm Faidit called violently for a full flagon from the Monjo. He took one deep draught and spat viciously.

277

"Thus do good men decay—toward glory!"

Peire Vidal had never beheld anything on earth so splendid, so dazzling in color as the interior of the great church of Saint Mark. The vast edifice was crowded with the members of the Council, the great lords and high officials of Venezia, the great lords and high officers of the crusaders; there were knights, squires, merchants, and important citizens. Armor glittered beneath silken surtouts, on which were sewn the cross—the scarlet of the French, the green of the Flemings, the white of the Normans and English, the black-on-white of the Germans, and the purple, a scant number, of the Provençals.

After a considerable space of time Peire Vidal was aware of a stirring in the multitude of the congregation. A chant of boys' voices rose somewhere in the distance: *In contemptu mundi.*

Hora novissima tempora pessima sunt vigilemus
Ecce minaciter imminet arbiter Ille supremus . . .

A figure in white was being led to a rich dais near the high altar, an old blind man with white hair to his shoulders. He was covered entirely by a white dalmatic, embroidered in silver thread, and a gold chain about his neck was clasped by a golden trident. This was the Doge Enrico Dandolo, duke of Dalmatia. His countenance was venerable and benign, the skin smooth and clear as that of a young man, and his features had none of the uncertainty of the blind.

He was speaking. The voice was low and uninflected, yet it could be plainly heard in the furthest corner of the place. "You are allied with the bravest men on earth." Thus he addressed the Venetians of his audience. "I am old, and weak, and infirm; as you see, I have need of rest; still, I know of no one more capable of taking command of your undertaking than I. If you wish that I should take the cross, and that my son should remain here to replace me, I will herewith take the cross, and will go with you and the pilgrims, to live or die according as God shall decree."

There was a profound hush; and by accident Peire Vidal

278

chanced to look across the assembly and saw the marquis of Montferrat. His face was a study in startled anger and consternation, as were those of the barons about him. But suddenly the Venetians burst into a wild clamor: "Come with us, for the love of Christ!"

Immediately a bishop in chasuble, stole, and miter came to the doge, took him by the hand and led him to the altar, where a cross large enough for all to see was affixed to his breast. The choir was chanting *in Excelsis Gloria*. A great many Venetians were shedding tears of joy and exultation. The crusaders sat glumly, overwhelmed by the realization that the Fox of the Adriatic was now their captain.

Peire Vidal recalled the ceremony of Richard the Lion's landing at Messina, and his departure from that port; it struck him that rapacity oftenest wore the guise of solemn pomp.

"God's blood!" chuckled Gaucelm Faidit on their return to Malamocco. "By the living saints, if that's not the sweetest jest in Christendom! There never was a pack of shrewd barons so shrewdly cozened! They and their politics—they have found one who throws better dice! And what a lot of proud hangdogs they were, to eat their vomit and like it! But did ye mark the visage of Count Baldwin? 'Twas the only one not thunderstruck. Mark me, he's playing his game, too. He was set against the Zara expedition but out-voted; now he'll go them one better and make them rue their poltroonery!" Gaucelm Faidit snatched the bliaut of his wanton, tossed it about his shoulders, composed his face to an expression of guilelessness, closed his eyes, and uttered in a singsong monotone: " 'I am old, and weak, and infirm; as you see, I have need of rest.' " And as his friends burst out laughing, he said, "He is as old as Solomon, as weak as Neptune, and as infirm as Mars!" The Monjo giggled and he turned on her, "Ay, you demirep, if that greybeard lays his claws on you, he'll get you a litter of lion cubs to suck!"

"May not I," said Guilhelma coyly, "sacrifice myself for your noble sakes? Since I am not like to beget even one kitten from you, my lord!"

Days passed, drooping in the lethargy of idleness. The pope's

279

legate had returned to Rome. The leaders of the crusade awaited uneasily what message Innocent might despatch to them.

It was mid-September. The army of the crusade had been on the Lido almost three months. Even the foot-soldiers were ready now for any deviltry, so it would get them away from that accursed spot. Again the troubadours were summoned to attend an assembly in Venice; and this time they went with their tongues in their cheeks. The meeting was held in the Campo di Marti, where the doge's pavilion had been set up; it was vermilion, embroidered in gold, and large enough to hold five hundred knights.

Before the conference Raimbaut of Vacqueiras, with an air of slight embarrassment, drew Peire Vidal aside.

"Peire Vidal," he said, "it caused me great dismay to learn that during our absence you had some difficulties with our marshal of the camp, Lord Simon de Montfort. It likewise grieved your friend, the marquis of Montferrat. We have been zealous in your behalf and desire to see you reinstated in the good graces of the leaders of this crusade, not only because you are, in a manner, attached to my lord Bonifaz, but mainly for your own sake. If any material benefits accrue to us, who are making the great sacrifice, it will be through harmony among ourselves." (God, thought Peire Vidal, he speaks the language of diplomacy!) "It is true, we are fighting for the love of God and Jesu Christus, but there is no reason why we should not be well rewarded. While we are establishing the Kingdom of Heaven on earth, there will be other kingdoms in the making. Now we are facing a crisis. Everything depends on this day's business, and how much fervor we put into our enterprise. It is not enough for us to show passive acceptance of certain hard conditions; we must be prepared to venture, with the enthusiasm that will assure success. My lord, Count Baldwin of Flanders, has suggested that you sing your great crusading song before us all, the one composed in honor of Richard the Lion." Without awaiting Peire Vidal's reply to this lengthy peroration, and taking his silence for consent, he added, "When I give you the sign, monsenher, it will be the moment for you to sing. We have provided a viol for you, and there will be many voices to take up your chant. I need hardly say that it is a most signal honor being granted you!"

"I appreciate the honor, Monsenher Raimbaut. I will do what I can."

It was well he had learned to control his emotions; to make the tongue, once bored through for its indiscretions, obedient to prudence. Lip-service: he could give them that, if it was the price of his escape. Do nothing, advised Gaucelm Faidit. Sing for them; stir them; and despise them! They were bound to go. It was all arranged; this was only the outward show; what matter if he, a minor puppet, were compelled momentarily to dance at their bidding? God would understand the rage and loathing in his heart, and would forgive him.

The doge, in full glittering chainmail, and a surtout of white silk, on which was sewn the gold Byzantine cross of Venice, presided. He said little. Others, the great barons, spoke of Zara and, with a show of indignation, revealed the iniquities of that city: It was arrogant, rapacious; it repudiated debts and treaties: it threatened the peaceful crossing of the crusaders (which was strange, Zara lying across the Adriatic!); in a word, it was an evil and unchristian city, that should be humbled. But the leaders of the crusade did not propose to force their followers to engage in anything wherein their hearts were not; they would put it to a vote: would they or would they not fulfill their oaths of knighthood, to right all wrong and to destroy wickedness, by going against the infamous city of Zara?

There was a moment's silence. Then in the vermilion tent of Doge Dandolo rose a man, with a white face, wearing a plain brownish tunicle, a priest's vestment. It was the abbot of Vaux, a Cistercian, who spoke out in a bold, clear voice: "In the name of the pope I forbid you to attack this city! It is a city of Christian men, and you are crusaders. You have another destination."

There was a sudden tumult. A band of Venetian officers, drawing their short, murderous estocs, rushed through the throng and closed in about the priest. Two Fleming knights drew their swords. The clang of steel on steel rang through the vast pavilion. The Flemings were stout and valiant; they held off the lunging bravos, drew the abbot away, and hustled him out of the tent. Raimbaut of Vacqueiras nudged Peire Vidal.

"Now!" he whispered tensely. "Sing, for your life!"

Peire Vidal took the strange viol, ran the bow across it; a hush fell. In those days music made all else cease. And when he played the spirited air of the crusading song they bent forward to listen, though there were only a few in that great assembly who understood the *langue d'Oc*. He sang:

> *A peu pauc de chantar no.m lais,*
> *Quar vei mort joven e valor*
> *E pretz, que non trob'on s' apais,*
> *Qu' us quecs l'empenh e.l gita por. . . .*

> Who's the fault if the voice fall mute,
> Seeing noble youth and valor end
> Humbled, and broken, and destitute—
> Hands that shake and knees that bend
> Servile before superior guile;
> Merit turned out to starve a while;
> Honor afraid to show its face,
> And wisdom strangled by power's shoe-lace!

A breath of approval swept the audience. Though they did not know the words, they could understand that it was a stirring song, sung with intense fervor by a practised troubadour. But a few knights and barons looked mystified. Among them were the historian-baron, Geoffroi of Villehardouin, Louis, count of Blois and Chartres, and Hugues, count of Saint Paul, all of whom were familiar with Provençal. It sounded to them curiously unlike a chant for a crusade; rather, a sirvente directed against—whom?
He sang:

> What's to boot, if all singing cease,
> The viol crack, and the bow be broken—
> Since the whole world is of a piece,
> Gain its motive, gold its token?
> Nowhere a spot on God's fair earth
> Made for a refuge to shelter true worth;
> Not a single face but lears or sulks
> According to how the booty bulks!

282

Someone was snarling in his ear: "What foolishness is this? Leave your prating and get on to the matter of the crusade!" It was the voice of Raimbaut of Vacqueiras. Bonifaz of Montferrat and other barons were beginning to glower. Those of the listeners who noted several angry faces began to be puzzled. What was the trouble with the song? It sounded like a very good one!

He sang:

> Why should any song be fashioned
> Fair and fine, or faithfully wrought,
> When no brave hearts grow impassioned
> And any man's honor can be bought?
> Save the world—

"No more! No more! This is no crusading song, but a scurvy piece!" It was Geoffroi of Villehardouin. He was standing and shouting, his face purple with rage. "Let be!" cried another voice. "He sings well!" There was instant confusion in the tent; some crying that the song should cease, and others urging Peire Vidal to continue; which he did, his mighty voice carrying above the pandemonium.

> 'Save the world!' they rant and howl;
> 'Yesterday wicked, today 'tis foul!'
> Ay, fouler still, when the hands of Venice
> Take the cross—in holy menace!

This time bedlam broke forth. A knight from Arles shouted, "Well sung, Peire Vidal! Let us have done with their infamies! We are no vassals of the doge!"

The Doge Enrico Dandolo had risen—a statue of white marble. He took one step forward. His blind eyes were as those of figures carven on tombs and his face was unmoved. The voice of the figure pierced the clamor as a sharp estoc driven to the hilt in a human body.

"Who is this man who has sung to us?" he inquired.

They cried, "Peire Vidal, of Provence!" And the doge, after a moment's silence, in which he seemed to be turning over within himself some distant recollection, said, "Is this that Peire Vidal who stole the Greek slave from Richard of England?"

"Yes!" cried Geoffroi of Villehardouin. "It is the same thief!"

"It is very strange," said the hard voice of the doge, "that you, as Christian men, permit a thief to stand up among you, who is still under sentence of death before the high court of England! And one who is notorious as the defender of heretics! It may not also be known to you that he proved to be a coward and renegade in the last crusade. But it is, I believe, common knowledge that he lately defied the authority of your camp marshal, the noble Lord Simon de Montfort." His voice suddenly took on the edge of Damascus steel. "As captain of the Christian army, I order the arrest of this man—thief, renegade, and rebel—who has dared most vilely and maliciously to impugn the motives of the crusaders, and most flagrantly has vilified and belittled our sacred enterprise!"

When the officers of the republic of Venezia moved toward Peire Vidal, there were no blades raised in his defence. He submitted without protest for he knew he had done a foolish thing. It was discourteous to have caused the Marquis Bonifaz annoyance when he had been so generous in largesse. He had really meant to sing *Baros Jesus* but when he took his viol in hand, there came into his mind quite other words, words that poured violently from his lips, without premeditation, as though his good or evil genius were speaking through him. Harsh, crude lines, unworthy of even a journeyman singer! It was unfortunate, also, for a song should be chiseled and hammered into shape, then polished, practised, reworked, and delivered out of the coolness of the brain, even though its matter might be fervid enough.

His captors were far from gentle as they hailed him along by devious ways and flung him at length into the dark chamber of a tower. He did not chide them for he was absorbed in considering the great potency of words . . . .

284

Chapter Twenty-three

THE devil take you, Peire Vidal!" said Gaucelm Faidit, puffing audibly after having climbed one hundred and thirteen stone steps to the tower prison of his friend. "I am three silver ducats and a gold florin out of pocket, just to get sight of you, and you do not fall on your knees and give thanks to God!"

"It is very good of you to visit me, Gaucelm Faidit," said Peire Vidal, rising, unkempt and spectral, from his musty straw. "How are my son and my lady?"

"Well enough; and your young jackanapes would have persuaded us to rescue you. That would be a commendable enterprise, had we boats or any encouragement from our fellow crusaders. But there is not so much as a stick of driftwood left to get us off the Lido; and the noble barons show every inclination to let you rot here. You are really a great problem to your well-wishers, my friend! Raimbaut of Vacqueiras accuses you of base ingratitude, and even hints that you turned the Fair Knight against him. As to your present status, they are in a quandary. Geoffroi of Villehardouin and Simon de Montfort would have you delivered to the tender mercies of the Secret Ten; but Baldwin of Flanders declares that the Council has no jurisdiction. You were arrested by the Fox, acting as the captain of the crusaders, not as doge of Venice. But the crusaders are loth to have ought to do with your trial for the very good reason that every foot-soldier knows your infamous sirvente by heart, and the mood of the soldiery is anything but submissive. For that and other reasons our leaders are anxious to get away as quickly as possible. They dare not return you to camp, nor give you up officially to Venice. Wherefore, as usual, they will place their trust in providence and hope that you will be properly disposed of."

At this moment the Venetian guard entered and sat down comfortably, just within the door. Gaucelm Faidit made a wry face, groaned, and searching in his wallet, produced a silver ducat which he held out to the soldier, as one tempts a surly dog with a tidbit.

"Here, my jolly lad," he said in uncouth Italian, "is your gratuity. Now take yourself off so that we can plan how to get this great troubadour out of your lousy den!" When the fellow had accepted the bribe, tried it with his teeth, and retired, Gaucelm Faidit said, "We are—I mean, *they* are leaving tomorrow when the tide is full. A good part of the army and most of the equipment are already on board. Gui of Cavaillon and myself have got our passports to leave Venice—signed by the doge—and we decamp tomorrow for Provence—may their hulks all sink before ever they reach Zara!"

"But what of my son and my wife, and my faithful troop?"

"Ah! You ask such difficult questions; but we have a plan. . . ."

The Venetian guard entered casually, accompanied by another. They squatted on their haunches and began to cast dice.

"What!" cried Gaucelm Faidit. "Are you knaves already dicing for his garments?" He went over and gave one of them a kick that sent him sprawling. "Out, you dogs!" He flung a silver florin on the floor. "I believe you are Lombards, you itch so for lucre!" The second guard snatched the money and the first tumbled out after him. "At least, a certain great baron, who is well disposed toward you, has a plan."

"The marquis——?"

"Bonifaz of Montferrat," said Gaucelm Faidit dryly, "has washed his hands of you. He says you were always unruly and—" the troubadour grinned—"led his innocent daughter astray! No,

286

there is no help from that quarter. But you have a secret friend, and he will see that you and your lady and son get safely out of this imbroglio—how, I cannot say. I believe your deliverance is at hand, but I have been warned that it will be absolutely impossible for you to leave Venice with us. Every boat to the mainland is examined; and you are a prisoner of state. It is easy enough to get to this cursed city of islands but devilish hard to get away without their passports."

The captain of the tower, in the smart livery of the republic, made his appearance, and after bowing civilly said, "The time is up, monsignor. Will the monsignor trobador desire a roast pullet and a cup of wine for his dinner?"

"Ha!" whispered Gaucelm Faidit. "You see, you have a friend at court!" He took Peire Vidal's hand and held it long. His voice, when he spoke, was husky. "I—we have had many partings, my friend, and it is no telling when the last one comes. Ho-um. Time goes past us and leaves us little the better. We have heard many good songs together. When I made you a knight, Peire Vidal, in that old rookery, I knew not how well you would live up to those vows, simple though they were. You have not done so ill. Your last song would have been better, could you have put more time to it, but no matter; it struck at the root of things. In a world of lackeys it is good to hear one solid voice raised. They will risk their skins for glory but durst not utter a peep against rank infamy! Sant Julian keep you, my friend!"

"Go to Belgueil, Gaucelm Faidit, and wait for me. I shall return —some time. My factor, Porcelet, will be glad to have you there, and I, I want you to be there!"

"Perhaps. These old bones will find a roost somewhere. But first I must see a few more fair faces and hear other gallant tornimens." He spoke to the gaoler. "Monsignor captain, you have the honor to guard the greatest troubadour in Christendom. Remember that! And see that he gets two roast pullets and a skin of wine!"

The fleet was sailing. Peire Vidal could see it from the tiny window, actually no more than a narrow slit, of his high tower. The sea was so covered with vessels that no water showed between them and sails of many colors were spread to the very verge of the horizon. Every ship was hung thick with banners and gonfalons and girdled at the bulwarks by a solid belt of shields, like a necklace of polished steel. The doge's urser, however, stood out from all the rest. Its sails were vermilion; it flew the Lion flag of the republic; and the banks of oars in triple tier lashed the waters with inhuman precision. On the castles at the cross-trees of the ships were perched heralds with silver trumpets and priests in white robes, and as the great ship, decked like an emperor's, swept down athwart the others, the priests burst into the solemn chant, *Veni, Creator Spiritus*, and the trumpets blared a silver chorus.

Looking through the window, Peire Vidal observed a spider's web, whose owner was busy repairing rents caused by errant moths. The insect went about its task methodically, working from the outermost circles toward the center and stopping at each intersection of a radial strand to glue the delicate thread drawn from its body, in ever narrowing circles. Suddenly, from a corner of the wall, darted a larger spider, having long legs and a hairy body. The builder ceased his operations and at once attacked the intruder. There was a brief scuffle and the web-weaver was pitched from his home. The other, clambering awkwardly about the web and tearing it ruthlessly, set about catching his prey. He leaped at a white moth, clutched and held its fluttering wings, rolled it over and trussed it tightly, and began leisurely to devour the helpless victim.

So absorbed was the troubadour in this miniature drama he did not notice the eventual disappearance of the fleet. He looked up finally. A red light flooded his chamber. The sun rested on the sea, a crimson bubble. Far to the east the last sails hovered on the earth's rim; they looked like flecks of blood.

Hours passed, with the blank tediousness of unused time. He felt more lonely and deserted than on that occasion when he had worn the wolfskin in the Black Mountains; then he had been hurrying to pay a curious homage to Loba of Puegnautier, wearing the guise of Loba the Wolf, his thoughts far from wolf-like; now he was utterly alone, confined in an alien city, very splendid, but hard, mysteriously cruel in its zeal for commerce. For the cruelty of conquerors is as nothing to the irreproachable ferocity of the world's traders; they bind their victims in silken meshes and devour them at their leisure. The conqueror has a certain gusto in his savagery; he spills blood carelessly in the pursuit of grandiose honor. The man of commerce is a dainty feeder; he battens on ruined hopes, on wounded spirits, he gnaws the marrow of dead souls. At some hour of the night—he had no means of reckoning time—he heard the grating of the iron door at the foot of the tower as it swung upon its hinges. Voices murmured, then steps were audible on the stone stairway, and a tremulous flicker of torchlight approached the arched stone doorway. Two figures were outlined against the uncertain light, the warden and a knight; or at least he seemed to be a knight, for Peire Vidal glimpsed his armor and silver spurs, and beneath a dark cloak, the green cross of the Flemings.

"Come forth, Monsignor Vidal," said the captain of the tower, shading his eyes and peering into the shadows of the chamber.

"Here I am," said Peire Vidal. He rose and brushed the moldy straw from his clothing, feeling his beard, for he had been three weeks in the dungeon. "Not so clean but in excellent good health," he added with a touch of levity.

"Monsenher Vidal," said the knight hurriedly, "I will ask you to come with me and to make no sound."

They descended the stair in silence, the troubadour's legs none too steady from want of exercise. It was black outside, and water gurgled in the darkness. Down he went, following whispered directions, and felt his way into a boat, which began immediately to slip through the water under the soundless propulsion of unseen oarsmen. Ghostlike and gray, all their glamorous colors of one tinge, the close-set palaces of the city became one endless and monotonous succession of round Byzantine arches, with fortified towers at regular intervals. Save for an occasional streak of light at some upper window and the faint shrilling of timbrels and tabor, they saw nothing, heard nothing of the citizens of Venezia. It was a well regulated city; the more so, thought Peire Vidal, since they were thrice challenged by vigilant guards. Each time the knight produced a passport which was closely scrutinized under the flare of a torch. Whatever its contents, it seemed to be satisfactory, for they passed safely at length from the bounds of the city and out into the soft, starry swell of the harbor, heading toward the island of Santo Nicolo di Lido.

"Monsenher Vidal," said the knight, speaking naturally for the first time, "I must apologize for my brusqueness. But this is all very risky business. Now, thanks be to the saints, we are comparatively safe."

"Shall I see my son and my lady soon?" asked Peire Vidal, his voice trembling.

"Yes, monsenher," said the knight slowly, "they will be on the ship waiting for you."

"Praise Sant Julian!"

"I must inform you, however," said the knight reluctantly, "that only they and the Greek priest will accompany you. In order to effect your release, which was accomplished by my liege, whose identity I may not reveal, it was necessary to deliver all your goods and possessions to the Council of Ten; your company of Provençal soldiers have been assigned to the captain of the Christian army as his personal bodyguard. In short, monsenher, while your passage on the vessel we are now approaching has been paid for, you must count all else as lost."

After a space during which Peire Vidal had been thinking of Jehan Porcelet and how deeply the estates of Belgueil had been pledged, he said, "I am content, so that I may see my own blood again. I thank you, chevalier, for your goodness and courage in delivering me, and I will offer prayers for your liege, whose name I may be permitted to guess. Tell him, from me, that if ever I may be of like service, or of any service at all, he may command me!"

At the moment of boarding the strange dark vessel, which at once hoisted sail, it occurred to him that he had no least idea as to his destination. But that and all other matters were of no consequence when his son Andronicus leaped into his arms, and the Lady Xene cried fervently, "Praise God, the All-Father, you are here!"

The Venetians had been thorough in collecting the ransom. They had left neither himself nor his lady anything but the clothes they were wearing. All the considerable treasure of household goods and gear, jewels and fine raiment—even his viol—had been taken. Luckily, he had brought along the borrowed instrument, of which his captors had not thought to deprive him. The Lady Xene had managed to secrete in her gown a small bundle of precious relics and a single string of pearls; and Andronicus, with great pride and pardonable vainglory, produced the silver casket containing the document signed by Count Raimon of Toulouse.

"Father," said the lad, "I did not know what was in it, but I knew you treasured this silver box so I told the Venetian soldiers that it had a charm in it that would keep anyone from death by drowning. They laid hands on it at once and would have borne it off, and I pretended to let them, but I said, 'You must be sure to say the right words when you open the box or the plague will light on you. It was this way the plague came to the Lido, a thief stole it and opened it, thinking to find jewels, but he was taken with the plague and died horribly.' So they cast it down with terrible oaths."

"Why did you first tell them it was a charm against drowning?"

"So that they would want it and take hold of it. Then, when they were afraid of it, they would throw it down, and they would not think I was trying to keep something of value."

Peire Vidal put his arms about his son and gave him a kiss, to which the lad submitted with manly reluctance; and the father thought, he has greater wisdom than I.

Their quarters in the vessel were cramped and uncomfortable, and the hard faces of the crew were far from reassuring. The captain, especially, might have been brother to Beelzebub. They spoke Italian of a sort, but what dialect Peire Vidal did not know, and no information was vouchsafed concerning the ownership, trade, or port of hailing of the vessel. The sailors went more heavily armed than was usual on a trader, and the troubadour noticed on the deck several machines similar to balistas, which he suspected were employed for throwing Greek fire.

The Lady Xene, lacking her bower-women, tended herself as if she had been a woman of the lower order, all her life used to nothing else than hardship. She even washed and mended her husband's jerkin of camlet, his sleeveless linsey surtout, and his mantle of black cendal, which had suffered from rough handling and prison wear. For the first time since he had known her she seemed gentle, sad, and frightened. Once he caught her weeping and tried to comfort her for the loss of her many pretty and costly things.

"Oh no, no," she said; "they were baubles . . . but little Alys . . . and the fair Blanchette, and Douce, and Faidide—they were brutal, those soldiers!—and Alys and Douce had been virgins—wicked! wicked!"

He had forborne to inquire concerning the fate of her maidens. What his own followers would suffer in the way of discipline he could readily guess, but they were men. Damsels of Provence, tender and light-hearted, to be fingered, stripped, beaten, ravished, and thrown into the brothels of Venice! Solemnly he laid a curse upon that white-haired ancient spider, the doge, and he called down the vengeance of God upon the gilded whore of the Adriatic, Venezia.

The captain of the vessel, he learned, went by the name of Matteo El Grosso. He was a Pisan and so were all the crew; and that, apparently, was all there was to be known. They sailed southerly, coasting at a distance from a shore that may have been Dalmatia, then easterly, for many days, and with no show of speed. Peire Vidal had never seen so cleanly a lot of mariners nor so immaculate a ship. Matteo El Grosso was always at them, setting them to scrub, scrape, and polish, and they obeyed his orders with utmost zeal, though he never swore at them. There were regular calls to prayer on shipboard. The sailors were forever kneeling while the captain mumbled rapidly a curious jargon that he took to be the sacred Latin offices. Peire Vidal made offer of the priest Porphyros for this purpose but the captain gruffly declared that the Greek wizard would only lay a spell upon them, and that the Griffon must have the evil eye for they had had no luck at all on the voyage.

"What luck," asked Peire Vidal wondering, "would you expect at so great distance from ports, unless it be favoring winds?"

Instead of answering, the captain stroked his bristly black beard with ferocious intentness. "You are a Frenchman, eh?" he inquired unexpectedly.

"No, messer captain, I am a troubadour of Provence."

The swarthy and malignant visage of the captain melted to something like benevolence.

"Ha! And I took you all along for a villainous low Frank! Yes, signor, I thought you were no more than one of those scented rascals such as pandered to their King Philip Augustus on his last plundering expedition to the Holy Land! A plague on all these crusades and crusaders! They think wearing a cross gives them leave to steal and pillage! There is not one of them has any good in him, saving Baldwin of Flanders! It is they and the Venetian dogs who are ruining our honorable business with their swindlings and treacheries! Well, signor trobador, it is indeed an honor and a pleasure to have you with us, and I trust you are in good voice, for my lads have a great fondness for singing, though I keep them from the profane and lewd chanteys of the sea. I beg you, sir, to entertain them; only, let us have no love songs, for I have trouble enough with them on these long voyages without arousing their amorousness."

Peire Vidal promised that as soon as he should have refurbished some of his sirventes he would sing for them. From then on he and his small ménage were treated with the greatest consideration. They dined with the captain, and if the food was not exceptional, it was better than they had had most of the time on the Lido. Porphyros, however, because of his reputed evil eye, was not asked to dine with them.

This saintly man, whose silence, piety, and fortitude had begun to make an impression on Peire Vidal, came near to suffering martyrdom on the voyage. They had been becalmed on a glassy sea for three days. The sails hung flaccid; the oarsmen labored diligently at the long sweeps; and the mariners, scrubbing the vessel and praying, cast apprehensive looks at the bearded Griffon as he passed amongst them. The sun on the third day sank spiritlessly in a gray bank of cloud which lay along the horizon like a distant mountainous shore, seeming so solid that for a space Peire Vidal took it for land. But the dun-colored bank rose with visible rapidity from the green sea until it enveloped half the sky. Though there was no wind as yet, the captain, Matteo El Grosso, began to shout like a madman. The oarsmen drew in their blades and tied them to the oarlocks. Sailors leaped aloft; the lateen sails came

293

clattering down and were lashed to the deck, and the ship rode still and ghostlike, under bare poles, awaiting the portentous on-slaught of the storm. Darkness and the tempest came together. The troubadour, his wife, son, and the priest, shut in a little cubicle aft, felt the vessel rise and heel over. From then on it seemed that nothing built by human hands could withstand the combined force of wind and sea. But he had been through two such storms in the cumbersome ursers of Richard the Lion, and this craft, he felt assured, was more seaworthy.

Still, the night was one of terror. Even the young Andronicus quailed at the appalling clamor of wind and waters as the stout galley took their buffeting, rising on its very beam-ends and drop-ping away as though about to make its last plunge. At daybreak the gale increased in violence. Then it was that Matteo El Grosso came to them with a grim face. He had to shout to make himself heard.

"Bring out the Griffon enchanter!" he cried hoarsely. "He has unloosed the demons and turned the wrath of God against us!"

"What do you want of him?" yelled Peire Vidal. "He is a harmless man!"

"He is a wizard and evil sorcerer! He will be our doom! He must be sacrificed to still the waters!"

"What! Are you afraid of your own element, messer captain?"

"I tell you, my men are mutinous! They will kill you all if you do not give him up!"

"Come, messer captain, I will sing to the sea and tame it!"

"You are a great fool, signor trobador!"

Peire Vidal, having kissed his wife and son, went forward with the captain. They had to fight their way, holding to each other, across the deck, foaming with angry waters.

"Lash me to the mast!" bellowed the troubadour.

The captain did so, and the troubadour raised his voice and began to sing. The wash swirled about his feet and flying spray almost choked him. Nevertheless he sang a stirring sirvente; and as that had little effect on the tempest, he sang other songs, songs of love, danger, sorrow; some with pathos, and others with anger and indignation, or with contempt for baseness and servility. After a time two sailors, clinging to ropes, crept to him and unlashed

294

him, saying that they had all taken heart, and it was no use a man drowning before his time or spoiling his voice to make them ashamed of their cowardice. In a few hours the violence of the storm subsided; the sun came through the wrack, glistering on scudding waves, and far on the vessel's port there showed a great urser, with a broken mast, helpless and wallowing in the seas.

"Ha!" cried the captain. "Our luck has changed! And now, messer trobador, you will need to rest. So go to your cabin and shut yourself in, and do none of you come forth, for we have our own work to attend to; and tell your Griffon priest he may thank you for his life."

Peire Vidal sank down on his pallet of straw and fell into deep sleep. The heavy door was closed and bolted from without; and they scarce could hear, through the heavy planking, what strange tumult and singular activities transpired on deck. It was perhaps well, seeing that the business of these mariners was far from reassuring.

"I want," said the young Andronicus at dinner of the day following, "to be a pirate."

"So," said the captain, raising his black bushy eyebrows, "you want to be a pirate!" He looked so fierce that one might have thought the simple statement was highly presumptuous. "And why, young sir, do you desire to follow the profession of piracy?"

"Because they are clean and obey orders willingly, yet they are free men and do not have to cringe before any lords except their captain, and he is a king of the sea."

"Well answered, young sir! But what think you of their taking booty?"

"All people, except poor and humble ones, and troubadours, take what does not belong to them. Venice, and the crusaders, and Richard the Lion, and Alexander the Greek, and many other famous ones. But they do not like pirates because they cannot control or manage them. Is that not so, father?"

Peire Vidal hesitated. He saw that his son, by his own observation, had formed a low opinion of certain things held in high esteem. He wished to encourage the lad's independence of judgment, but after all, piracy!

"It is true," he said, "that much fame and perhaps all government is based on the unjust seizure of the goods or possessions of others. And all cities and states have grown great by feeding on the lesser ones. Peire Cardinal has said, 'If a poor man steal a shroud, he goes to the gallows; but if a rich one steal a house and all in it, he goes straightway to the emperor's court.' That seems to be the law of life. Perhaps piracy is in disfavor because it builds no monuments from its gains and founds no dynasties."

"Ha!" exclaimed the captain. "You speak truly, signor trobador! But I cannot countenance the stealing of certain things— love, for instance. Let me tell you, signor trobador, how a horrible villain wooed and seduced my lawful wife. He induced her to follow him and I have never seen her since. At that time I was captain of a Pisan merchant vessel. He was the owner of a fleet. It happened while I was on a long voyage to England." Matteo El Grosso choked. The veins on his forehead showed purple, and his beard was agitated. He controlled himself and went on, "When I returned and learned what had happened, I took my ship from that port, secured a crew of cut-throats, and became a pirate. I have warred since then on all merchants. And God has permitted me to punish many of them for their rogueries! Was I not right in seeking vengeance for such wickedness?"

"Who am I to judge of rightness?" said Peire Vidal. "You did what seemed fitting and proper to you, and I suppose that was right for you. Yet I have always held love to be entirely free, and as not belonging to any person except by permission."

"Pardon me, messer trobador," said the pirate captain thoughtfully, "if I say that that idea seems to me very strange and profane. Marriage, as we know, is a sacred sacrament. What stability can we find in life if love may be bandied about, from one to the other? Goods, on the other hand, are material possessions whose ownership is an accident. That merchant prince who stole my wife had inherited his wealth from his sire, and he got it by fleecing a hundred victims. Thanks to the saints, the adulterous villain lost most of his chattels to a shrewder rogue. And so it goes. But marriage is indissoluble before God and man. Whoso transgresses its holy bonds sins before heaven."

"Ah, yes," said the Lady Xene, "to love unlawfully is indeed a sin, but it is a pleasant one, and usually is expiated to the full!"

"It is no sin whatever," said Peire Vidal stubbornly, "but a natural right of all people. Priests and nobles have made it a sin in order to preserve the sanctity of church rituals and the convenience of inheritance."

"I see, signor trobador," said the captain, "we shall never agree on what is right or wrong. Nevertheless I trust we shall remain friends!"

"You honor me, sir," said Peire Vidal.

Young Andronicus raised his head. "I want to be a pirate," he repeated.

For the first time, the Lady Xene, with an almost maidenly timidity, besought her lord to sing to her. This request put the troubadour in a momentary quandary, for there was no mention in the *Laws of Love* of a husband singing to his wife; indeed, there were implications to the contrary. The whole object and purpose of the *gai saber* was to achieve that which was difficult; more, the Court of Love of the Lady Constance at Castle Bargarde had specifically ruled that there could be no true love between married people because mere propinquity and legal sanction made access to the precincts of love so casual an event that it could have slight significance. But the princess looked so pale, fragile, and forlorn, seated on her pallet of straw in the dingy cabin, that Peire Vidal's heart was touched. After all, had he ever actually enjoyed the love of this unaccountable being whom, for all these years, he scarcely knew? He had won her without wooing her. His possession of her body was an accident of war, not the accomplishment of desirous intention. In the early days when she had yielded to him, or rather, had drawn him to her, it was as though she were drawing something of herself, under the potent influence of some invisible vast power, into herself. He was merely the instrument. No, he had never won her love! He might, therefore, be permitted to sing to her without violating the rigid canons of illicit love. Indeed, as he looked at her, thinking of her not as his wife but as a possible mistress, he noticed with some surprise that she was still very fair, possessing the beauty of perfectly formed

297

limbs, of dainty and delicately molded breasts, and with the mystery of strangeness.

So he took his viol in his hands, caressed its polished surface, touched the bow gently to the strings, and after a little deliberation sang:

> *Anc no mori per amor ni per al,*
> *Mas ma vida pot be valer morir . . .*

> Neither love nor any malady conspires
> To end my days; yet all unscathed, I see
> My life in the likeness of mortality,
> Since the dear object of my sole desires
> Kills them with cold aloofness; so we face
> A sort of death as old age comes apace:
> And though this waste of my own youth I hold
> Sinful, her loss is worse a hundredfold.

There were other verses but of too intimate a character to be recorded here. As he sang, the eyes of the Princess Xene seemed to grow larger and darker. A little tender half-smile formed fleetingly on her lips like a ripple on still water; and her breasts under her tight-fitting Greek gown swelled and subsided with increasing agitation. The salt waves could be heard swashing and sucking in the wake of the ship, and overhead the pirates were chanting in hearty though unintelligible unison.

That night Peire Vidal dreamed again of the witch-goddess. She rose, it seemed, from the curled waves, and about her fair white limbs were herds of fleecy clouds. But strangely, this being seemed composed of two—the great golden Venus of Arles and the dark-eyed, awesome and dreaded Aphrodite of Cyprus, boding ill to men, yet the giver of the greatest gifts. She, or they, stood poised upon the obedient waters; the expression of the composite face was distant and inscrutable; if anything, sad. He woke. The Lady Xene, who had given herself, after a long space of absence, to his embrace and to the violence of his passion, lay sleeping; so still, so hardly breathing, that for one frightened moment Peire Vidal thought that he lay beside a white corpse. But, as though his staring had penetrated her slumber, she opened her eyes, and looked at him with such intensity and fixity of love as he had never seen on any woman's face before.

"Signor trobador," said the pirate captain with an air of mournful solicitude, "it grieves me to tell you that I must disembark you and your estimable family at a port far from your home. I had hoped that if trade were good, I might venture to return to the western Mediterranean, to Sicily or Spain where you could get ship for Provence. But that ungodly tempest has driven us so far out of our course that the only near ports are those of the islands of Cyprus and Candia. Unfortunately, the authorities in those places harbor ill will toward the members of our profession. However, by accompanying us to New Rome you will be assured the finest sight in the whole world."

"New Rome," said Peire Vidal eagerly, "is the object of my present quest!"

"Good!" said the captain. "It seems that providence has attended us on our voyage, even though profit has not. If you are going to remain in that great city, I will take you to the house of my brother-in-law, Buonardo Spazio. Although he is a merchant, he is a man of honor and good taste, and he is the leader of the Pisans there, who have the largest colony of foreigners in the city. It is through my brother-in-law that I dispose of my cargoes. You will be able to secure all necessary credit for the refurbishing of your apparel and whatever other needs you have through him, for his ships and caravans carry his name from Barcelona to the kingdom of Prester John."

"As for credit," sighed Peire Vidal, "my estates are pledged to the hilt, and I lost much treasure to Venice."

"That alone will suffice for your surety, as Buonardo Spazio hates Venice more than the Fiend himself. Besides, you are a brave man and sing well. In any case, I shall be glad to commend you to him, and that will be enough to insure ample hospitality. At his house you will find many curious sorts of persons, including heathen. He himself is indifferent to the true faith, being somewhat of a philosopher, and that is the only fault I have to find with him."

"No doubt," said Peire Vidal, "your brother-in-law may be of great service to us."

"We have passed the port of Abydos," said Matteo El Grosso, scrutinizing the faint coast-line to the east, "and we are entering Saint George's channel, which is frequented by more shipping than all the rest of Christendom combined."

They began to hail vessels of all kinds, ursers, esneccas, galleys, naves, and imperial transports. To Peire Vidal it was pleasing and marvelous to behold this beauty of sail and of craft under oars. They made such speed going up the channel that by the evening of the second day they came to Saint Etienne, an abbey three leagues from New Rome. And then they saw clear before them the capital of the empire. When Peire Vidal beheld the lofty towers and walls by which the city was surrounded, and the countless high domes of churches, of which there were so many that no man could have believed it if he had not seen them with his own eyes, and when he saw the length and size of the town— that city which was mistress of all others—he felt his flesh creep from sheer awe and a certain terror, knowing he was coming penniless and with no backing other than his own conviction, to claim the throne of the Greeks for his son.

One of the pirate crew had been detailed by the captain, busy with navigating, to point out the principal sights to his passenger.

"There are three sets of walls," said the mariner, "and no one of them may be scaled by any human being. The newest are those of the Emperor Manuel. Behind them is the palace of the emperors which they use more than the palace of Bucoleon on the Marmora, and they say there is nothing in the world like it for splendor. It is called the palace of Blachern. Next to it is the Fanar quarter where the rich Greeks have their palaces. Between each wall is a moat, deep enough to drown an army; and each wall toward the city is higher than the last. On the other side of the Golden Horn lies the Galata suburb where the merchants live, and the Pera, where is the Pisan quarter. That strange building is a Saracen mosque. 'Tis a queer thing to see them worshiping next the Christians, but they have always had the emperor's protection. The Pisans are the defenders of the city, and the Waiblings from the north are the emperor's bodyguard. These Waiblings are of the same race as the Flemings, and hard fighters. That nest of tall buildings is the great law courts. On that high hill you can see the church of the Divine Peace, Hagia Sophia, called the Great Church, and close to it is the temple they call the Divine Wisdom of the Incarnate Word—which makes no sense to any but the Greeks. There is greater wealth in New Rome than in all the kingdoms of earth together and—" the sailor lowered his voice— "if a man wants pleasure, there's more kinds of it to be had than the angels ever dream of!"

Peire Vidal took his viol and began to sing. The priest Porphyros was gazing in mystical rapture upon the city of many Holies. The young Andronicus, wild with excitement, was clambering and gibbering in the rigging like an ape, causing great concern to the pirates, who had grown to love him and did not want to see him break his neck. His mother, the Princess Xene, gazed upon the vast populous city of her own people with the look of one who sees a vision fulfilled.

The pirates seemed pleased at the prospect of better food, of carousings, and of relished delights in quarters where the women of Lesbos, of Cyprus, and of lands beyond the deserts awaited their coming with all the mysterious rituals known to those versed in the art of love.

Chapter Twenty-four

THE difficulties of the chance traveler entering the empire, such as securing an imperial passport, Peire Vidal escaped in the company of Matteo El Grosso, who seemed to be well known to the port authorities and in the official register bore the title of "Pisan merchant." It was the first indication to the troubadour of a broad tolerance in regard to men's business, opinions, race, and religion, the like of which was unknown even in the golden land. His first impressions of the city were of vast crowds that never hurried and seemed to have nothing but endless leisure for strolling, gossiping, or any sort of dallying in the great squares and thronged marts; peoples of every race and language: tall fair men of the north, dark-skinned richly dressed personages from Persia, Ind, Cathay; haughty Saracens, Spaniards, Genoese, Pisans, merchants and soldiers; a detachment of the Varangian guard marched past, wearing the livery of the empire. . . . "And there," said Matteo El Grosso, leaning from the litter he had engaged, "goes the stride of Rome! They haven't forgotten the trick of the armies of the Caesars! For ages Rome has taken the barbarians and made good soldiers of them. It makes my heart jump, signor trobador!"

Peire Vidal was impressed most by the city's spaciousness and the splendor of its architecture; and he realized now, that all the seeming grandeur of Venice was but a cheap and tawdry imitation of this great original. "Everything that Rome and Greece were, is here, signor trobador, untouched! Old Rome—why, that's a dunghill covering some fine ruins, but this town has never been taken—not in something like a thousand years!"

"If only the emperor could match his capital in greatness!" said the troubadour.

"The emperor? He's a cuttlefish—stuffed and gilded! My brother-in-law is worth three emperors! Yes! Buonardo Spazio's a queer one. He's a bachelor and doesn't even keep any concubines!"

He looked a queer one, too: a small portly man with a large, bald, knobby head, a closely trimmed gray beard, protruding as though pressed outward from within, and the whole face expressing a kind of patient curiosity and speculation. He was dressed in the conventional Greek costume, a close-fitting under-garment reaching to the feet, over which a dalmatic was worn, meeting in front in two narrow bands of gold chalons, encrusted with jewels; had he worn crozier and miter, he would have passed for a bishop. In fact, Peire Vidal never learned to distinguish between laity and clergy in New Rome. Accustomed to the flowing dress of the west, to his eyes the tightly sewn eastern garb seemed awkward and uncomfortable.

"The name, monsignor?" asked Buonardo Spazio, rising with cupped ear—for he was quite deaf—from a great carved and gilded chair.

"Pietro Vidal!" said Matteo El Grosso loudly. "A singer, trobador, from Provence. He was robbed by the Venetians, brother —scoundrels that they are!"

"So!" said the merchant, holding out his hand. "We have all been robbed by them at one time or another." A reddish gleam flickered in his eyes. He looked at the troubadour with such intentness that Peire Vidal felt impelled to explain, "It was because of a song I made against the doge."

"Good!" said the merchant, smiling grimly. "I would you had made a whole canticle against that fox!" He continued to stare at his visitor; then, "Pardon, Monsignor Vidal! Be seated. I am rude. But first tell me, are you really that Peire Vidal who was with Richard the Lion in Cyprus?"

303

Peire Vidal betrayed astonishment. "Indeed, it was I and no other, Signor Spazio."

"The ways of providence are indeed mysterious! For you to be brought here by my respected brother-in-law—extraordinary!"

"Not more so than how I came by him!" roared the El Grosso. "I, my dear Buonardo, in the very jaws of Venice! I took away a candle from Saint Mark to prove it! Also, I emptied a fat urser passing the Lido, as you shall see when I unload my chests for you."

"You were always singularly careless of your neck, Matteo!"

"The saints have my neck in their keeping. When they think it has been whole long enough, they will break it for me. But to continue; slipping past the harbor guards, I landed and on my way to mass whom did I see but the count of Flanders!"

"A good man," said the merchant reflectively, "in bad company."

"At once he signals me with a wink, and as I come out, there meets me one of Baldwin's lackeys who whispers that his master earnestly desires I should accept certain unknown persons as passengers, who had fallen under the displeasure of the doge. 'Tell your master,' says I, 'for the love I bear him, and my hate of Venice, I'll load my hold with all it will carry!' And that is how I came to know Signor Pietro, who can sing in all weather, I assure you!"

The merchant turned to Peire Vidal. He looked curiously solemn. "Is your son Andronicus with you?"

What a man this is, thought Peire Vidal, who seems to know everything!

"Yes, Signor Spazio, he and my wife, the Lady Xene, are still on board ship."

"Brother Matteo," said the merchant briskly, "you are sailing tonight!"

"What!" roared the captain. "You can't mean that, brother Buonardo! Why, if I do not let my crew have their fling ashore, they'll mutiny!"

"If they do, you are no captain!" The merchant's tone was firm and imperative. "I will see that they are satisfied. My factor will send a bag of silver to the ship; let them spend it in Abydos. None of them must leave the ship under any condition. My own men will unload whatever you have for me. And, brother, let there be no single word uttered, now or at any time, in regard to our friend here, Peire Vidal and his family. I will send a closed litter for the wife and son. Of course my house will be your residence."

"Thank you, sir," said the troubadour, "but there is also a Greek priest, my wife's personal chaplain."

"H'm," said the merchant gravely, "that complicates matters. He must come to my house. Is he to be trusted?"

"He has honesty and bravery. Otherwise I know little about him, for he speaks only Greek."

"On second thought, Matteo, I will return with you and we can do our accounting on board your vessel. There are important affairs to be discussed."

"As you will, brother," said the captain with what Peire Vidal thought was surprising docility. "Signor trobador, I trust we shall meet again when we may share a little light wine together!"

"I hope so," replied the troubadour, quite mystified. "And thank you for your great kindness, messer captain!"

"While I am gone, Monsignor Vidal," said the merchant, "you may enjoy whatever reading you care to do in my library. You will find a collection of Provençal songs and several chansons of the northern singers as well as many other good books of the ancients. And may I ask you, in the meantime, to choose a name for yourself." Seeing Peire Vidal's bewilderment, he added, "It will be necessary, as I shall soon explain, for you to remain as my guest under an assumed name. Let me see—your accent betrays you as a southerner even when you speak French. Have you by chance ever studied any of the learned professions?"

"I studied a little law and I have had a smattering of medicine at the University of Monpeslier, though not much of either has remained in my head."

"Good! You are a doctor of medicine from—from Avignon. You have come to New Rome to perfect yourself in your professional studies. That will be your excuse for going about the city to see some of its wonders. Keep your given name so that you may not be taken unawares. Peire . . . it should have a sententious sound . . . Bartholomew! Or, in your public guise, Petrus Bar-

305

tholomeus. Excellent! I bid you farewell, Signor Petrus Bartholomeus!"

He whisked himself off, spryly for so stoutish a man, and Peire Vidal was left to wonder at the strangeness of human affairs and at the queerness of his extraordinary host.

The world to which Petrus Bartholomeus was introduced differed so greatly from all he had ever before known that his life at the house of Buonardo Spazio had for some time the quality of a dream. This house was in reality a palace of noble proportions, exquisite in its multiform detail. Here he perceived with amazement that people could affect sunlight in their dwellings. At New Rome, especially in the palaces of the suburbs, its citizens spent the greater part of their days in spacious sunlit courts, musical with the sound of falling waters, verdant with aloe, tamarisk, pomegranate, and strange fruits and herbs, alive with small apes, paroquets, doves, peacocks; spots devoted to the leisurely enjoyment of conversation and the drowsy monotonous music of curious instruments, played by dark-skinned desert folk. But what he most admired was the intricate delicate patterns, the carvings and arabesques, the abundance of sculptural detail visible in every doorway, window, and wall. The round-arched Byzantine windows that seemed so novel in Venice were here the very poetry of stone and marble, no two alike, yet all in harmony. As for the merchant's library, the whole collection of Pope Innocent would have been lost in one corner of it. Yet Buonardo Spazio was far from being a learned man.

"What I have got from books," he told Peire Vidal, "I have dug out for myself. I was as unlettered as any sailor's son; could write my name and no more. When I suffered exile through the unfortunate affair of my sister and her husband—which was aggravated by the impetuosity of my brother-in-law—I decided to seek an asylum at New Rome. By being somewhat bolder than other merchants in exploring distant trade routes I have had considerable success. And by submitting to the dictates of prudent policy I have managed to maintain a certain influence in a city where all things are unstable. At length I found I had leisure, but no good way to employ it, and by degrees I turned to the cultivation of the slight mental powers I possessed. Laboriously and painfully I taught myself to read my own language, but I found little of importance had been written in the vulgar Italian tongue, and set myself to master the ancient Latin. Monsignor, there are books in the libraries of New Rome that have long been lost to us western barbarians! I resolved to seek the clue to human wisdom still further afield, as I had done in the way of commerce, with my ships and caravans. Then, fortunately, I discovered a scholar who consented to be my teacher and adviser—the Grand Logothete, Nicetas, a great sage, and a good old man. Through him the doors of the golden past have been unlocked, and though I have only had a glimpse of the treasures within, they are beyond anything you can conceive, monsignor! By the way, has your son learned any language other than the Provençal?"

"He speaks the popular Greek fluently, for he has been tutored by Porphyros."

"Good!"

He uttered the word with the same finality that Peire Vidal had noticed the day of his arrival; as though some large desgin were in his mind. Yet he had not as yet revealed either his intentions or the source of his information concerning the events of the troubadour's life.

The house of the merchant in the Pera district was the meeting place of two groups of men, of which one assembled during the day time in the spacious court to drink amber and greenish liquors and a thin yellow liquid flavored with essence of roses. The guests of daylight hours included a Persian poet, an Arab mathematician, several Greek philosophers and dialecticians, a prince from far-off Ind, and a strange, almond-eyed individual who was said to be a traveler from Cathay. The latter wore flowing robes of bright yellow silk and his skin was the color of old parchment. He applied an outlandish instrument to his mouth and blew clouds of smoke through his nostrils, to the intense astonishment of the young Andronicus. Their talk was of high matters: poetry, philosophy, music, the soul, the art of love. They treated Peire Vidal with respect, and since no one of them was versed in medicine, he found that he could answer almost any question by referring vaguely to a "flux" or the "dark humors of the spleen" or to the works of the learned Gallienus or other hypothetical authority in that science. He was known to them only as Petrus Bartholomeus.

The other group came by night, in closed litters, without even torches. They met in one of the chambers of the palace, drank little if anything, and argued hotly. They were nearly all Pisans, though there were among them several Greeks; all were youthful, one in the livery of a minor imperial officer, a couple with a clerkly look, probably officials, and a priest of the lower order. Peire Vidal met them only once. It was an unusual introduction. He entered on the arm of Buonardo Spazio. A dozen men rose ceremoniously.

"This, my friends, is Peire Vidal, the father of Andronicus!"

They eyed him searchingly, bowing with a certain deference. Peire Vidal felt slightly embarrassed before these strangers; as his host made no mention of their names, he was about to add, "The heir to the throne of New Rome," but he remembered his tongue and said, instead "Monsignors, I am honored by your courtesy. It is not necessary for me to commend myself to you, since my noble host, Buonardo Spazio, has done that for me." He said it with all the dignity and graciousness he could command, and he noticed their instant, though scarcely perceptible approval.

That was all. As he left the room, they resumed their seats.

At times another visitor appeared, whom Buonardo Spazio was not so well pleased to see, though he received him with his customary genial courtesy. This was Theodore Lascaris, the son-in-law of the Emperor Alexis. He came in a magnificent imperial litter, plated with gold and curtained with the finest cendal. He was attended by a bodyguard of Waiblings or Warings, huge flaxen-haired, bearded warriors, bearing shining battle-axes, which the Flemings called bills. "Those fellows," the merchant told Peire Vidal, "have something of a history. In Germany they are called Waiblingen, and in Italy, Ghibellines. Those who have remained at home are vassals of Philip of Swabia, who claims the throne of New Rome through his wife, the daughter of Isaac Angelus. Philip heads the imperial party in Italy, and would wear the eastern crown also, thinking of himself, belike, as a modern Caesar of the whole world—but he has far to go before he enjoys that honor!"

"Philip—but he is a friend of the marquis of Montferrat, who is promoting the claims of the young Alexis!"

"Ha!" exclaimed the merchant sardonically. "'Tis all one with those political freebooters! The young Alexis is only their catspaw —an excuse to get their claws into New Rome—the Fiend take them! They and the doge will stop at nothing. You were indeed lucky to come off with a whole skin from Venice, considering the stakes they are playing for—and the inheritance of your son!"

So Buonardo Spazio was acquainted with the claim of Andronicus! The merchant eyed his guest quizzically.

"I do not want to seem inquisitive, my dear Monsignor Vidal, but may I ask whether you brought with you the certification of the birth and heritage of Andronicus, issued by Count Raimon of Toulouse—the elder Raimon, called the Good?"

The troubadour gasped. So far as he knew, that document had never been witnessed by any living soul, save the count, himself, and a notary—unless . . . yes, there was a strong possibility that the count's secretary, Peire Cardinal, he of the bitter tongue, was privy to the secret.

"I have it with me, Signor Spazio, in a small casket which I guard."

"If you will pardon me the liberty of suggesting it, I beg you to entrust its keeping to me." He saw Peire Vidal's doubtful expression and added, "As you are entrusting your life, Monsignor. Let me tell you now, that if it were known to the imperial household that you and your family were residing in New Rome, you would need twice the strength of the Varangian guards to keep you and them from a most sudden and unfortunate demise!" He paused, and added significantly, "Our present ruler has a fondness for extracting the eyes of those with whom he disagrees; and that is only one of his mildest diversions."

"I will give you the casket Signor Spazio. Have you, by chance, ever heard of the troubadour, Peire Cardinal?"

"His verses and maxims are well known to me," said the merchant casually, "and I have a copy of his interesting brochure in verse, *On the Ideal State*—the work of a cynical philosopher and a poet of no small gifts. Now you will have to be on your guard, for the emperor's son-in-law is about to announce himself.

He is utterly stupid, but a magpie for prying. Remember your native Avignon, Petrus Bartholomeus!"

The scented and glittering dandy who entered looked far from dangerous. His curled beard fell in silky billows to his breast. His dalmatic was covered with jewels mounted in chalons of gold, and an orarion, or stole, richly jeweled and embroidered, hung before and behind over his left shoulder and reached to the ground. His tightly fitted sakkos also trailed about his feet, necessitating the taking of short, mincing steps. A stranger creature Peire Vidal had never seen, and stranger was his manner of speaking French. He pronounced the words with a lisp and an air of condescension, as though he disdained the use of a such a barbarous tongue.

"We have heard, Signor Bartholomeus," he said, "of your arrival from the city of Avithnon. We had always understood that only the unworthy breed of troubathours were to be found in Provence. Is there indeed such a thing as learning among you?"

"Learning, noble sir," said Peire Vidal, restraining his annoyance, "is not developed to the degree that it is here, and it is true that our profession of song is highly esteemed among our lords of Provence, who hold that the human voice can be put to no better use than to make good music."

"Ah," said the noble, caressing his beard, "and such music is sweet in the ears of the lords' wives, no doubt! Is it true that Proventhal women conthider adultery a virtue?"

Peire Vidal pressed his teeth viciously against his tongue. "Our customs, noble sir, do not differ greatly from those of other lands, but we strive to give dignity and elevation to love by acknowledging its vagrant nature and by enshrining it publicly in song."

"I would, Signor Petrus Bartholomeus, that you could prescribe an elixir for the greater potency and prolongation of passion."

"Many philters have been compounded to that end, noble sir, but it has been found that while the temporary excitation can be stimulated and an earlier summation of physical responses can be achieved, there is a resultant subsidence of flux, and a general decadence of the humoral vigor, resulting in the formation of dark humors. As the learned Gallienus has so well enunciated——"

"Never mind," cried the prince petulantly, "if it can't be done, there's an end of it!" And he went on to recount the latest happenings at court, a narrative of great length and tediousness which left his Provençal listener with the impression that the affairs of an empire, when seen at close range, are as the prattle of children, only more malicious and destructive. As Peire Cardinal says in his brief treatise: "The art of government is chiefly concerned with the daily well-being of its beneficiaries."

Quite otherwise was Peire Vidal's interview with Nicetas, the Grand Logothete. His white beard hung to his middle, about which was a plain woven girdle knotted over a white sakkos, without dalmatic, maniple, or orarion, and his face wore the look of a benign and scholarly priest. He was, Peire Vidal judged, close to the age of the doge, but no two ancients could have been more unlike, the one of steely temper and subtle, devious ways; the other bearing the indefinable aura of great books studiously perused. Speech between the logothete and his visitors was made difficult by the fact that outside of Greek, ancient and modern, he knew only Latin, speaking it too fluently for the troubadour's unattuned ears; but what was lacking in direct communication was made up for in understanding, the patriarch soon perceiving that he had to do with a man of taste and discernment.

Buonardo Spazio was especially desirous for Peire Vidal to view some of the works of art, of which the city was one vast treasure-house, not to be seen briefly or in a single tour, as with the casual traveler. Unexpectedly, the logothete volunteered to accompany them on a round of the city. In the merchant's closed litter they passed through the Fanar and Droungarios and the quarters where were situated certain churches, libraries, and other public buildings housing the treasures of the past, and as their guide named the works to Buonardo Spazio, the latter translated them to Peire Vidal. In the Panhagia of the Blachernae Palace they saw the Bellerophon and Pegasus, a divine horseman and his wondrous steed in marble that quivered with life. Behind the high altar of Hagia Sophia, the Great Church, stood a mammoth statue of the Virgin, cast in bronze. She wore a crown set with precious stones and rayed with an aureole of pure gold. "A later addition," said the merchant. "The venerable Nicetas thinks it was originally a pagan goddess, converted to the true faith by Christian artisans!" Before the law courts towered a colossal Hercules. "The sculptor

Lysippus of Sicyon made it as his crowning achievement. It is the greatest picture of strength in the world—a vision by man, of a giant's power!" The Juno of Samos by the same artist, her colors undimmed by the ages, shone in all her glory in a dim recess of the inner courts. "The pagans understood the meaning of nobility," said the merchant. "But there is one statue in New Rome greater than this goddess. First, though, the bronze horses of the hippodrome."

As no races were being run that day, they had an ample opportunity to examine the extraordinary group from every angle. "Those who come here have little interest in ancient works of art. Were the city to fall tomorrow, they would lay their last wagers on the blues or greens!"

In the temple of the Divine Wisdom of the Incarnate Word they found a statue of such marvelous and vital beauty that Peire Vidal exclaimed, "What god created this vision of woman?"

Buonardo Spazio conferred with Nicetas, then he said, "It is given out to be the statue of a saint, but the logothete has evidence that it represents Helen of Troy, and was executed by the sculptor Scopas, or by one of his followers. It is indeed a joy to the beholder and a pleasure to the eyes. It is, I take it, after the war, and she reflects upon her conquests and ruins, feeling an exultation in the power of her beauty to cause death. It is her revenge for the death that will take her from the world."

"Is this, then, the finest of the statues?"

"You shall judge for yourself, monsignor."

They passed to one of the seven heights of the city where stood a small but exquisitely proportioned temple. Its high door was barred but the Grand Logothete made himself known to the caretaker, who opened the iron grille and allowed them to enter.

"According to our friend," said the merchant, "this was built by Constantine the Great as a place of private worship. He prayed with the Christians in the church below, but here he did reverence to the gods of his ancestors. From Athens he brought one statue to adorn the place. It is Aphrodite, done in marble by Praxiteles."

For a moment or two Peire Vidal could see little save a majestic form, of ivory tint, but for some reason his heart beat almost to suffocation. Then he saw that it was indeed the figure of his dream:

mysterious, she stood as though poised upon obedient waters; the expression of the face was distant and inscrutable; if anything, sad, as though foreseeing the extinction of faith in her divine power, potent over men for good and evil. He gazed long and long, oblivious to all things else. That ancient world, at which, in the pool of Nismes, he had stared, ignorant and indifferent; that he had glimpsed vaguely in the library of Pope Innocent, now, under the tutelage of Buonardo Spazio, born the son of a ship's captain, began to reveal itself in all its antique splendor. He wished he knew Greek, to offer up a prayer.

Chapter Twenty-five

P<small>EIRE</small> V<small>IDAL</small> did not learn Greek, save for a few simple expressions in the popular dialect, but the young Andronicus pursued the study of that language, both old and new, with great diligence. The priest Porphyros continued to tutor him in the modern tongue, while the Grand Logothete, after he had seen the lad and had observed his quickness of wit and aptitude for learning, offered to instruct him in the ancient Attic, that he might in time master some of the works of those authors whose names, once so resplendent, were now known only to a few choice souls and to the learned bibliophiles of New Rome. It was fortunate for the lad's course of study under the logothete that the old man dwelt close to the Pera quarter, for Buonardo Spazio was insistent that he should not under any circumstance traverse the city itself; and even for the short distance he had to go, Andronicus was always accompanied by three stout men-at-arms of the merchant's menie. He was also urgent against Peire Vidal sallying forth alone. The troubadour, without questioning the merchant's reasons, complied with his request. That these precautions were not without justification soon became apparent.

To the Lady Xene and his son he had given such a glowing account of the pieces of sculpture he had seen that Andronicus was devoured with eagerness to look at one of them—the Hercules.

He begged his father and Buonardo Spazio to take him to the law courts, but the merchant at this time was overwhelmed by the demands of his trade, since several of his caravans were on the point of departure. While Buonardo Spazio was absent on his affairs and the logothete occupied with the important festival day of San Stephano, about to be celebrated, Peire Vidal thought it a suitable opportunity to satisfy his son's curiosity. He ordered out the merchant's closed litter, therefore, and with the usual small guard of household retainers, proceeded toward the law courts. As they passed through the gate of the strong walls surrounding the Spazio estate, a hideous beggar squatting near it held out a claw for alms. Peire Vidal tossed the creature a coin. A moment later Andronicus, who had been staring back at the repulsive being, cried, "Why! father, I thought he had no legs, and he got up and ran away!" The troubadour laughed. "My son," he said, "it is righteous to bestow alms; we should never wonder at any miracles that follow!"

Andronicus crowed with excitement at all the sights. The Hercules, however, was somewhat of a disappointment to his expectation of seeing a giant large as a church. He did admit that the fellow in marble looked strong enough to overthrow several ordinary men.

"Who is this Hercules, father? Is he living near here?"

"He was an ancient, long dead. He could carry a bullock on his back, and other such things, they say. He lived in the time of Alexander the Greek, who conquered twelve kingdoms in twelve years, and at his death divided his empire into twelve parts; and each of the princes became a great emperor. That is all I know about Hercules."

The law courts were closed that day so they could not view the Juno of Samos, a lucky circumstance, for Peire Vidal, thus was able to escape further questioning by his eager-minded and persistent son. They were making slow progress homeward through a narrow and tortuous street, lined with wine shops and the stalls of the poorer quarter, and the princeling was singing to amuse himself, when the litter came to an abrupt halt. A crowd had gathered in front of them, and there was a tumult of wrangling and oaths in vulgar Greek. Their outrider had disappeared ahead, and the two in the rear had permitted a considerable throng of ragged mendicants to press between themselves and the litter. These filthy alms-seekers suddenly swarmed about the litter like hungry flies, extending bony fingers with menacing arrogance.

"Go on!" cried Peire Vidal to the bearers. "Don't let them stop you!"

The men shouldered their way through the clamorous mob. Then the troubadour, feeling an instinctive apprehension, was witness to a horrid deed. There was a quick movement among the disputants in front. Steel flashed; the litter's forward bearer twisted sideways, dropped the pole, and fell across it. The litter crashed to the ground at that corner. At the same instant a group of beggars flung themselves savagely upon its occupants. But Peire Vidal at the same moment had an inkling as to the nature of the attack. He was unarmed, but he leaped from the litter and struck out with all his might at the grimy bodies and ferocious faces. They drew back, so unexpected was his lunging defence, and he was given a brief space of time to meet them as they closed in again. The shaft of the litter, crashing to the cobbles, had split. He reached down, broke it off close to the frame, and with this sharp stave lunged at the crowd. He smashed hands holding daggers, clouted a pair of ruffians over the head, turned the point into the cheek of a third with bloody effect, and shortly cleared the horde from about the wrecked vehicle. Meanwhile the riders, hearing the sound of the conflict, spurred their horses straight into the crowd. As the retainers struck right and left with their naked blades, the rabble yelled, broke, and fled. While they were lifting up the dead bearer a provost guard of Warings bore down upon them. To the lieutenant in command Peire Vidal had to give a complete account of the whole affair; then the litter was repaired and the officer, still not fully satisfied that they were peacefully inclined, rode back with them to the merchant's palace.

The city of New Rome was, on the whole, well policed.

"You have perhaps heard of the sect of Syrian Assassins," said the merchant, "who acknowledge the chieftainship of Khasis?"

"Yes," said Peire Vidal; "I have been told they were employed to dispose of Conrad of Montferrat . . . by a certain king."

"They are for hire," said the merchant grimly. "They do not always use steel. The deposed emperor, Isaac Comnenus, for instance, while a prisoner of King Richard, was poisoned by his own cup-bearer." He paused. "You are now being honored by their attentions."

After that Peire Vidal remained mostly within the walls of the estate and the young scholar had his lessons interrupted. The Grand Logothete, however, found many pretexts for visiting his friend, and the study of the ancient language did not wholly cease. Peire Vidal, in return, unfolded to Nicetas, to whom his identity and past history were known, the mysteries and excellences of the Joyous Craft. He described and sang for the aged scholar the canso, sirvente, vers, planh, balada, cobla, retroensa, and other forms, and he explained the tenson and tornimen.

"These remarkable songs," said Nicetas, "resemble in some respects the Persian ghazéles and the Arabian cassides, but in Provence they achieve a perfection unknown in any other land, ancient or modern. It must be that the charm and intelligence of your women call them forth. The art of love among us has so long been reduced to formula that its conventions are more rigid than the laws of the empire. Only among the hetairai is some degree of originality permissible."

"I had gathered as much from my wife, the Lady Xene," said Peire Vidal.

"Your lady," said the logothete, "is a paragon among women. She has the bearing of an empress and the spirited graces of your Provençal ladies. There is none in New Rome who approaches her, I assure you."

Peire Vidal was tempted to ascribe the Princess Xene's cultivation to his own tending, but remembering the court of Toulouse he said, "Her education has been in able hands."

In the learned and traveled coterie of Buonardo Spazio's house she maintained the poise of a great lady; at the same time she betrayed a responsiveness to their sallies and an interest in their world of ideas quite foreign to their eastern conception of womanhood. At first they were puzzled and even disapproving, but by degrees she seduced the attention of the meditative Persian poet, of the grave and inscrutable Cathayan, and even of the taciturn

317

Arab, and they accorded her the rare honor of admission to the circle of their conversation.

Peire Vidal, watching her with some astonishment, was delighted. But he took an even deeper pleasure in her company. Together they fed the peacocks and doves, and the swans sailing like graceful galleys on the merchant's miniature lake; together they plucked and ate pomegranates, dates, and strange sweet fruits whose names they did not know; and gathered sunbright poppies and the scarlet hibiscus blossoms. Or Peire Vidal read to her from the precious manuscripts of Buonardo Spazio the tale of Lancelot du Lac, written by Arnaud Daniel, and full of miracles and adventures; the tale of Perceval le Gallois and of the Chevalier au Lion, composed by Chrestien de Troyes; and the stories of wizard Merlin, and of Tristan and Yseult, a poem of great beauty and sadness.

"Andronicus," said Buonardo Spazio to Peire Vidal one day as they sat in the palace pleasance, "gives promise of fulfilling the expectations we have had of him." As the troubadour looked inquiringly at his host, the merchant continued, "He is a born leader. Look how he manages his fellows!"

The lad at the moment was engaged in directing the strategy of half a dozen playmates of his own age in the penning-up of a flock of nimble white goats which had escaped from their enclosure. With pardonable pride his father observed how readily the band of youngsters obeyed their small captain and the despatch with which the maneuvers were executed.

"Indeed," said Buonardo Spazio, watching the play with relish, "the remarkable art of ruling often is not greatly different from that of the herdsman!" He looked strangely at Peire Vidal, and added, "Come with me to my library, monsignor, and you shall hear my confession over flagons of my Syrian vintage."

"You may have wondered, Monsignor Vidal," he began as they sipped the golden wine, "at my acquaintance with the details of your private life. New Rome offers many opportunities for conspiracy and intrigue. Its throne has usually descended through usurpation or murder. We Pisans are moved entirely by self-interest. The present emperor does not please us. He has been courting Genoa. It happens, moreover, that a considerable body of his citizens are also wearied of his costly ménage and his habit of blinding and torturing his enemies or rivals. He is, altogether, a contemptible figure, and he is rapidly bankrupting this already impoverished empire of Romania. Therefore we have plotted to displace him. There is another party favoring the restoration of the deposed Isaac Angelus. Our objection to this scheme is that the unfortunate victim of Alexis is all but feeble minded. As an emperor he neglected the trading interests of New Rome, with which we are primarily concerned. His son, the young Alexis, you have met. He has his wits, it is true, but little else to commend him. We turned, then, to another heir, or presumptive heir.

"It has long been rumored that one of the children of the murdered emperor, Andronicus, had escaped the assassins. We set about discovering the possible whereabouts of that child, aided by my good friend, the Grand Logothete Nicetas. It happened that your notorious exploit at Cyprus became one of the legends of the Mediterranean. You were supposed to have ravished a Greek slave from the very arms of the amorous British monarch. Your subsequent flight to Venice was likewise well known, for our spies there reported that the doge himself had seen fit to undertake the restoration of Richard the Lion's prize. At the same time we discovered that the daughter of the unlucky self-styled emperor of Cyprus had vanished. This daughter, according to the very precise information of the logothete, was none other than the Princess Xene, daughter of the Emperor Andronicus. It was not difficult to arrive at the conclusion, especially as the doge was not likely to have concerned himself over so minor an object as a Greek slave. Then we heard that the troubadour, Peire Vidal, was going about pretending to have sired the heir to the throne of New Rome. This rumor, I may say, penetrated to the Blachernae itself and caused no slight stir in that quarter. The emperor, I believe, was so far perturbed as to despatch a band of Assassins in the direction of Provence. That they failed of their purpose is evident. For an inoffensive person, my friend, you have acquired a remarkably large number of powerful enemies—the pope, the doge, and the emperor of New Rome! My confidential agent at Toulouse, having positively identified your son Andronicus as the

319

grandson of the Emperor Andronicus, had you under constant surveillance."

He rose suddenly.

"Thank you for your patience in listening, monsignor! We, the conspirators, are satisfied that you are worthy to be the father of the future emperor; and I am convinced that the young Andronicus gives promise of courage and independence, much needed in New Rome."

Peire Vidal looked at his host, at the rotund, energetic figure in its absurd Greek garb.

"God has sent you, Monsignor Spazio," he said, "to strengthen my confidence in the destiny of my son and myself."

The merchant chuckled.

"Without exactly questioning the divine element, monsignor, I suggest that you wait until events have justified your trust in God in this matter."

The troubadour had reached New Rome toward the end of October. The days, weeks, months slipped past in bright serenity in the sheltered gardens of the merchant. They heard that the crusaders had captured and pillaged stately Zara and, having given most of its disobedient citizens to the sword, were encamped there for the winter. But there was no winter on the Golden Horn. When the sun shed less warmth, they sat within, on silken cushions, in chambers amply lit by sunny windows overlooking the busy harbor, the many-towered city glowing like a great jewel of myriad facets, and there they conversed and heard Peire Vidal's songs many times over.

Toward the patriarchal Nicetas the troubadour felt a growing affection. The logothete had the wisdom drawn from great books, modified by a multitude of contacts with all sorts and conditions of men, and he was, moreover, an important figure in New Rome. On the occasions when young Andronicus had a lesson, and if there were no other guests, the old man remained a while, and they usually fell to talking of what manner of government is best for human beings, and which is the most equitable mode of governing, and what can be done with the poor human material offered for that purpose.

"Venice," said Nicetas, "is well governed under a tyranny of commerce. Its god is profit, and its ideals those of acquisition. Venice is young, energetic, and utterly unscrupulous. I greatly fear for New Rome. The empire of Romania, tottering anachronism that it is! is stripped of its fleets. It has often been shaken and pieces shredded from it, but the city itself has never been violated. It believes in its invulnerability, like a man who has never suffered illness."

"True!" said Peire Vidal eagerly. "But the weakness of the empire could be made the greatest strength of the city. If the empire of Romania were dissolved, the city of New Rome would remain, stronger than ever. It is a matchless port, a channel of trade between east and west, north and south. If the people here are indifferent to their government, they will not object to being well governed. In time they may learn to govern themselves. Oh, New Rome is vast and tolerant! It should be a haven for all the talented outcasts of earth, and for all those who suffer under oppression, and have no where to lay their heads! Let them exhume the treasures buried in the libraries and palaces, in the churches and museums, to become the seeds of fresh thoughts in the minds of the western barbarians! The city is a great midden heap of learning, rotting now, but capable of fertilizing the whole world! From one book, one statute of the ancients may come countless works of unknown, unborn young men!"

Peire Vidal had risen. He was walking up and down, waving his huge arms like flails. His face was flushed and his eyes shone with unnatural brilliance. The merchant wore a peculiarly sardonic expression.

"Monsignor Vidal, father of the Prince Andronicus," he said, shifting his portly figure to a more comfortable pillow, "I shall endeavor to render your Provençal fervor into equally fiery Greek; and as a conclusion to your exodrium I shall add that the empire may soon experience that dispersal that you advocate. Venice and the crusaders have decided to take the city of New Rome."

Peire Vidal stopped. His arms sank to his side. Outside in the sunladen court all was breathlessly still save for the chittering of spurting water. Then a bird sang, with a sweet, tremulous cadence.

"They have razed Zara, there is not a stone left standing, and they are on their way to New Rome," said the merchant. "They have sworn to uphold the just claims of the lawful heir to the throne."

The Grand Logothete stroked his silvery beard thoughtfully. "What does the pope say to this?"

"My agents report that he sent messengers to them while they were still at Zara, warning them not to attack New Rome on pain of excommunication. He also removed the cardinal, Peter Capuano, as legate with the crusaders. His message was not communicated to the army, which seems to have been growing restless. There was considerable fighting between the crusaders and the Venetians after the capture of Zara; that is, among the commonalty, who appear to be under the impression that the barons kept the loot for themselves. Twelve of the leaders of the Christian host, with all their followers, seceded from the rest, withdrew to a neighboring valley, and established a parliament of their own. It was not until the barons had come to them and solemnly vowed to take them at once to Syria that the seceding leaders repented. The barons had agreed to this with many pious oaths, though they had no intention of sailing to Syria. This was early in April. They are now at Corfu fitting out their ships for the expected battle with the imperial fleet."

"We have no fleet," sighed the logothete.

"More correctly," said Buonardo Spazio, "we have no crews, for the emperor has diverted their pay to his own coffers, to support his eunuchs, comedians, actors, buffoons, jugglers, musicians, and mistresses. The vessels are without naval stores or engines of war since our admiral, the worthy Michael Struphnos, has appropriated to his own uses all the supplies for the fleet. But we have an army, such as it, and we have walls that no barbarians have ever scaled."

"How could the barons break their oaths? Have they no scruples whatsoever?" exclaimed Peire Vidal.

"They have scruples—or had, until Boniface and Baldwin received a tender of one hundred thousand Venetian marks each. Now they are scrupulously bound to do what they can for the young Alexis, and he, in return, has agreed, when restored to his crown, to pay the upkeep of the whole Venetian fleet for a year,

322

and to supply ten thousand men for service in the Holy Land, and pay another two hundred thousand marks. He is a generous, nay, lavish young man with the imperial treasury!"

"Does the emperor know about all this?" asked the logothete.

"Alexis is too busy at court to be disturbed by unpleasant rumors. He, or the eunuchs, are planning a great water fête. I understand that it will be an imposing spectacle—a thousand nymphs to be drawn from the harems to disport themselves on the caïques in the Golden Horn. The courtiers are promised a rare treat, and the gilded youth of the city will perform as fauns and satyrs—somewhat pagan, it would seem. A festival in honor of Saint Aphrodite, illustrating the pure, naked souls of Christians on their way to paradise! I fear a good many will soon be on their way elsewhere. Our good friend and estimable eunuch, however, the prefect of the city, is quietly making his own preparations for defence, aided by the commanders of the Pisan and Varangian guards. The senate will meet as usual, and after listening to windy speeches on the greatness of the empire, will pass a resolution censoring those who spread alarming reports. The populace, reassured by the indifference of the senators, will go to the hippodrome, as usual, to witness the races and lose their small savings. The astrologers will be consulted, and they will issue vague but hopeful prognostications. The jugglers will have invented a number of new tricks. The ladies of the Blachern will dispense new and delightful perfumes. And we Pisans and the Warings will bear the burden of defending the city. It has always been that way."

"When should it be announced to the people that their true emperor, Andronicus Vidal, is among them?" inquired Nicetas quietly.

"We will do so when there is no longer an emperor on the throne!" said the merchant.

Peire Vidal paled. "There cannot be—must not be—assassination!" he stammered.

"There will be no need for that," stated the merchant grimly.

Chapter Twenty-six

THE month passed in dreamlike quietude. There was no perceptible change in the city. Nightingales sang in the shadowy gardens of Buonardo Spazio, while Peire Vidal sat with the Lady Xene beside a fountain whitened by moonlight. The city of seven hills and five hundred churches showed its innumerable torchlights like fireflies in the night. Below them, in the Petrion quarter, fronting on the Golden Horn, where clustered a great dark mass of churches and monasteries, the priests were intoning a Greek liturgy. The Princess Xene made a sign and whispered a prayer. From a higher level of the Pera and Galata hill, in the Jewish quarter, came the strange monotonous chanting of many voices. Only the mosque of the Saracens was dark and silent, and would be until dawn. The white marble columns, everywhere dotting the city and reminding beholders of the ancient dead, marked the moonlit squares with alabaster shafts. The ancient and the modern world, past and present, living and dead, mingled and were one. From across the Golden Horn the massive circle of its triple walls could be plainly seen, and the vast towers that rose at short intervals. Nearest them, on the Galata side, was the immense Galata tower or castle, guarding the chain of mighty links that closed the Horn at the approach of an enemy. Beyond, at the head of the Golden Horn, a fine stone bridge spanned the waterway. The spacious villas of the nobles and rich merchants fell away on all sides, each a little sequestered retreat from cares and trade.

Old Rome was dead. Its corpse lay still unburied beside the Tiber. Here was all of Rome, all of Greece; and the son of Peire Vidal, troubadour, was heir to it! He touched his viol musingly and the strings responded to the bow's caress.

> *Be m'agrada la covinens sazos*
> *E m'agrada la cortes temps d'estiu*
> *E m'agradon l'auzel, quan chanton piu. . . .*

Dear to me is the clement season
And dear to me the summer's gentle ways,
When the small ecstatic songsters raise
Their "piu" and "pweet" in lyrical unreason;
And dear to me are flowers of all kinds;
But dearer, the intercourse of noble minds;
Most dear, community of understanding
With her who has my heart, without demanding.

Happy am I, madomna, pondering
Your excellence, happy to me made
Your willing vassal, happily unafraid
To call a truce to feckless wandering
And fear no softening of my lusty blood
In soft subservience to your womanhood,
For happily my vagrant fancies press
Like homing birds about your comeliness.

God keep you, sweet, and may He preserve you
In the fair mold you have! May He confound
The fingering of time, and the subtle wound
Of jealousy. Humbly I serve you;
Therefore, God keep me and make me strong
Against any who might do you wrong.
God give our mating relish, come what come—
And God confound me if I bring you tedium!

"Come," she said, "let us go to our bed."

That night he dreamed of the sage Nicetas. The aged man was slowly turning the pages of a great book. "Men," said the logothete, "are ever impatient with life. They seek to assuage their uneasiness and despair by inviting death. In the days of the ancients they feared happiness; the gods were jealous. The Christians also fear happiness. In Provence you almost discovered it. But all things pass, like ships on the sea. Look!"

Peire Vidal looked and saw the figure of Aphrodite, standing with averted countenance. Behind her rose the column of prophyry near the hippodrome. It was taller than the tallest tower of New Rome. As he looked it began to smolder. He was horrified to observe that the statue of the goddess was without a head. . . .

"As ships on the sea," murmured the Grand Logothete. He also was turning to marble, and the marble was slowly crumbling. But the lips still murmured monotonously, "As ships on the sea, ships on the sea, ships on the. . . ."

"Look!" cried the young Andronicus, leaping on the couch of his father and mother. "There are many ships on the sea!" Peire Vidal sprang up, and hastened to the window; he saw that the whole of the Marmora, beyond the column of Theodosius, was covered with sails; ursers, esneccas, naves, transports; banners and gonfalons fluttering and showing a thousand colors in the dawn; glistering of armor; rhythmical beating of banked oars. They could even distinguish faintly the sounds of neighing horses and the chant, *Veni Creator Spiritus*.

Andronicus was wild with excitement. "It's the crusaders, father!" he shouted. "I shall see my friends again! Hugues and Gui and the rest!" He had forgotten that he had once disciplined Hugues, the son of Lysette, at the Frog Pond.

Peire Vidal turned from the sight of the host to look at his wife. The beauty of her delicately molded limbs, and the sleep still lingering in the violet shadows of her oval eyes moved him so greatly that he gathered her into his huge arms and held her there, tightly pressed against his hairy naked chest. Andronicus was capering madly about the room.

Someone was pounding on the door.

326

"Peire Vidal!" cried the voice of Buonardo Spazio. Andronicus leaped to the great wooden door and opened it. The rubicund face of the merchant peered anxiously in. "Pardon, monsignor and my lady, but you must be moving. I shall have to send you into the city."

"What for, Monsignor Spazio?" asked the troubadour. "What is the haste?"

"Because, my friend," said the merchant, "the Pera and Galata are without defence against your Christian friends!"

"Will you resign me to the hospitality of the emperor?"

"The emperor will be too occupied to think of you. You must hurry, for they will soon be closing the bridge and locking up the harbor with the Galata chain. I shall remain here. Perhaps the Count Baldwin will afford me protection because of a great service I once did him. He is not likely, however, to give you much attention—pardon me, signor! But you will be much safer lodging with the captain of the Pisan auxiliaries. And you will have an excellent opportunity to witness the military tactics of the crusaders from the palace of the Porphyrogenitus, near the Blachern."

They made what haste they could but the sun was well up before they reached the Galata quarter, which they found all a-stir with lively commotion. The populace, however, seemed aroused to expectancy rather than alarm. Accompanied by a small guard of the merchant's menie, they made their way out of the suburbs, past the great Galata citadel, and on into the country beyond, by a road that followed the Golden Horn until it reached the stone bridge, a mile to the north and west—the sole crossing to New Rome. The only sign of military activity to be seen was the lowering of a massive chain across the Golden Horn, from the Galata castle to the city wall, and even this enraged the imperial eunuchs, who had marked out a passage for pleasure boats at that spot.

At the bridgehead they were halted peremptorily by a guard of Warings, armed with glittering battle-axes. A considerable crowd had gathered here, mostly rich Jews and their families, and all were clamoring volubly for permission to cross. The guards were obdurate. They said little, but brandished their weapons when the refugees approached too near. The merchant's retainers understood not a single word of the barbarous northern tongue, nor did Peire Vidal. However, one of the Pisans finally produced a pass, and the imperial lieutenant, with a doubtful and skeptical mien, examined it. The document was all in due order; permission was given the doctor, Petrus Bartholomeus, his wife, and son, and the priest Porphyros to enter the city of New Rome, and there attend the needs of the Captain Piozzi of the Pisan guard and his men, at the palace of the Porphyrogenitus in the Blachernae quarter. Signed by Theodore Lascaris, commander of the Scholarii Legion. The Greek lieutenant studied the signature, at length accepted it as authentic, and bowed in deference to the name of the emperor's near of kin. Spazio's Pisan retainers turned back. Peire Vidal, the Lady Xene, and the Prince Andronicus passed over the bridge, and they were assigned a member of the lieutenant's detachment to accompany them to the gate of Saint Romanos where, after some parleying, they were admitted.

If the quarters across the Golden Horn were only somewhat disturbed by the approach of an alien army, the city showed no trace whatever of alarm, and even scant interest. Some sight-seers among the nobility were going down in their litters to view the fleet from the Geranion, an old palace that offered a good view of the Marmora. They were in holiday mood, for the water pageant was to take place in the afternoon. But the populace were idling as usual in the bazaars, watching cock-fights, gossiping, laying wagers on their favorite color to run at the hippodrome. A procession of communicants, wearing white tunics and carrying gilded tapers, were following a priest in a richly embroidered dalmatic toward the church of Saints Sergius and Bacchus. Scholars in purple gowns loitered about the entrance to the Orphanotrophaeum, loth to enter, for it was a mild, pleasant day. Small boys rolled colored hoops among the legs of passersby. Doves circled about or rested, cooing softly, on the rim of the great dome of Hagia Sophia.

The presence of the priest Porphyros allayed any distrust on the part of officers and soldiers, while his kindly and winning manner made him a valuable interpreter. During the long litter ride he explained in halting French many points of interest and named antique monuments that had escaped the attention of Buonardo Spazio. Also, he secured several Greek servants for their menie at

328

the palace. "The Pisans," he said, "are good people, very good, but bad servants."

"Is the city as strong as it looks?" asked Peire Vidal.

"It is strong beyond comprehension. Everywhere there are vast cisterns of pure water, both closed and subterranean. The walls, properly defended, cannot be forced. Many armies have tried, greater than the crusaders.' There is only one weakness—indifference."

"Is the emperor as contemptible as hearsay would have it?"

"To wear the mantle of greatness is hard for even the best of men; power magnifies human infirmities by removing comparison with others. Yet the desire to choose the best way often causes grief and suffering. The divine will is inscrutible in that respect."

It was the first time Peire Vidal had ever held serious converse with his chaplain. It surprised him that he had scarcely taken notice of a person of such intelligence in his household. To his further surprise, the Captain Piozzi, who seemed young to hold a post of great responsibility, received him with marked deference. The priest and the captain appeared to be well acquainted. It was evening by the time they were settled in their new lodgings, apartments of considerable if faded magnificence. The young Andronicus fell asleep at once on a couch where many a prince and princess of the imperial line had doubtless slept—some, perhaps for the last time. . . .

A fortnight after their first appearance on the Marmora the crusaders attacked. Every move of the invaders showed the greatest deliberation, the counsel of utmost sagacity. The first day the fleet sailed directly under the sea-walls of the city, swung in a vast arc, and came to anchor opposite Chalcedon. When the army had disembarked, foraging expeditions were despatched throughout the adjacent countryside. From the high towers of the Porphyrogenitus the watchers could see smoke rising lazily from burning villas, and they caught the distant glint of steel in meadows where the early harvest stood ready for the reapers. On the third day the fleet sailed up the Bosporus to ancient Chrysopolis, now known as Scodra, and anchored. Here the army encamped for nine days, burning and plundering. On the tenth day, so the Pisan captain

329

reported, the emperor of New Rome sent Nicolas Roux, a Lombard, to treat with the Venetians and Lombards and others of the host, saying in substance, that since they were both Christian peoples, he would be glad to supply whatever provisions the crusaders stood in need of, and would give them safe conduct through the imperial domains to the Holy Land.

The trouvère-canon, Quesnes de Béthune, replied for the crusaders that the so-called emperor need not trouble to give them permission to enter Romania, or to make offers, since he did not rightfully possess his title to the empire; but if he would peaceably yield up the crown to his nephew, the young Alexis, they would try to persuade the latter to pardon him, though he was an usurper, and might even grant a pension.

"Our trouvère," said Peire Vidal when he heard of this reply, "has become the mouthpiece of Enrico Dandolo." And he judged that all the subsequent tactics emanated from the brain of the octogenarian who was "old, and weak, and infirm; and had need of rest."

The messenger had scarcely returned when the fleet got under way. Again the ships, laden with men in steel, with blaring trumpets and fluttering banners, sailed close to the walls of the city, so close that its disdainful citizens might have spat upon them had they chosen. The great urser of the doge took the lead. About its gilded prow were grouped certain knights all in the brightest of armor, with the gonfalons of many famous houses hanging above them and over all, the Lion of Saint Mark. As the vessels reached a point close to the column of Theodosius, they drew apart, and there was revealed a youth clad in armor so burnished it looked to be of gold. A loud voice from the ship hailed the people clustered thick on the walls with: "Here is your rightful lord!" The knights, crusaders, and all the host set up a great huzza, but the Greeks, laughing heartily, cried down at them, "We know nothing about him! Who is he?" And they made many gestures in a ribald and indelicate fashion, indicating their derision.

Peire Vidal, no longer fearing to go about the city, had brought his son to see the naval pageant. The young Andronicus, perched in the midst of chattering Byzantines, gazed upon the ships with large and thoughtful eyes. Then he spied the gilded youth, Alexis.

"Why!" he cried suddenly. "That is the knave who put the lashes to my back and twisted my arms in the headquarters tent on the Lido! The people do not like him, and neither do I!" and he shook his fist at the mailed figure on the doge's urser. It was the first time he had ever spoken of what occurred in the marshal's headquarters. Peire Vidal bit his lips wolfishly.

The next day at dawn the ships approached the opposite shore of the Golden Horn. They drew in close to the Tophana quarter; great gangplanks were thrown across; the bulwarks opened, and mounted knights rode across to the land, without opposition. File after file, horse and foot-soldiers disembarked, passed through the Pera and Galata quarters in orderly array, and deployed in the Jewish quarter above. The Pisans in the Porphyrogenitus eyed the hillside anxiously, for their wives, friends, and near of kin were at the mercy of the host. But there were no signs of pillage or of burning buildings.

"We have told them over there," said the captain, "to show no resistance and to treat the crusaders as their friends. We can only offer prayers and hope there will be no trouble."

"Why," asked the troubadour, "have you made no move to oppose them?"

"My friend, the experience of a thousand years has taught New Rome that it is safe within its walls. Here there is assurance; outside there is uncertainty. Besieging armies have always worn themselves out and gone away, defeated by their own impotence. . . . Look! the fools!"

The heavy drawbridge of the Galata citadel was being lowered. Hardly had it settled into place when a troop of mounted knights in the imperial livery galloped across and clattered up toward the Pera. Behind them trotted the Waring foot-soldiers, who, cumbered with arms, began to slacken their pace as they advanced up the steep slope. There was a movement among the crusaders. A glittering phalanx of knights wearing the cross swept over the crest of the Pera hill in a cloud of dust. At the same moment another squadron was to be seen winding swiftly down through the Galata quarter.

331

"Ah! saints preserve us! They are going to flank them!" cried the captain.

A third column of Flemish foot-soldiers was worming its way down the slope of the Jewish quarter straight toward the Golden Horn. None of these movements was visible to the Romanians, still arduously climbing.

"Saint Bacchus! Both flanks!" groaned the captain. "Idiots! To let themselves be drawn out of their walls! Stupid! They will all be lost, for the Galata guard will raise the drawbridge when they see the crusaders!"

The vanguard of imperial troops were now engaged with the first of the crusaders. It was hand-to-hand fighting. The crusaders were slowly giving way, but with a circling movement that only led the Greeks deeper into the maze of streets in the Galata quarter. The second squadron had reached the shore and was turning toward the citadel when they encountered the rear of the imperial soldiers, the Varangian guard, who were no match for mounted knights in full armor; and though they battled desperately, were ruthlessly cut down. Having disposed of the foot, the squadron turned up the hill, now in the rear of the Greek horsemen. The two columns of crusaders had caught the imperial force between the pincers of its tongs and they ground it, hopelessly outnumbered, to pieces. Dust hid the ending of the sortie.

The Flemish foot-soldiers, arriving from the other direction, and finding little opposition at the lowered drawbridge of the Galata Tower, fought their way across it. Peire Vidal and the Captain could see bodies being flung over the parapet into the Golden Horn. The engagement had lasted less than half an hour. The captain was sweating profusely. His eyes were bloodshot.

"My—my brother . . ." he stammered, "is—*was* in the tower! . . . A good fellow——" He choked.

The crusaders were already busy hacking at the links of the great chain that closed the Golden Horn. After a short space it fell with a splash of green water and white foam. In a steely stream the invaders were pouring into the Galata quarter and others were massed about the citadel.

"I must go to the walls," said the captain, who had somewhat recovered his soldierly bearing. "If you wish to see the fighting, there is plenty of armor about. They will not know you, Monsignor Vidal! Go to the Blachern. It gives the best view of the waterfront. Wait! I'll give you a pass." He hastily scribbled on a piece of parchment and signed the document with a flourish. "There is a good blade in the cabinet yonder. Keep your helmet on out of doors. Those Norman bolts have a long range."

He went away, girding on his sword. There had been moisture in his eyes.

From the imperial palace of the Blachernae the troubadour witnessed the destruction of the imperial fleet. The war galleys of the Venetians overwhelmed the anchored vessels of the emperor as swiftly, and with as little effort, as a gerfalcon its winged prey. The imperial sailors, fighting bravely and hopelessly, were doomed from the start, for all the water-gates were closed against their retreat. The Latin host remained four days in the Galata in order to rebuild the stone bridge at the head of the Golden Horn, which had been destroyed. The crusaders drew the timbers down, hewed them to fit, and flung them across the channel under the continuous fire of mangonels and other mighty engines of war and of showers of bolts from the city walls. By night they worked under torchlight. Then, when the bridge was completed, the army crossed and took up a position at Gyrolemna, facing the walls of Heraclius where they joined the new walls of Manuel. It was apparent that the attack was to be concentrated upon the Blachernae Palace and the quarter about it, the fleet operating from the Golden Horn, and the army on the land side. This was the one spot in all the city's defences where cooperation between the two military branches was possible. The troubadour could not but admire the strategy of the leaders—rather, of the scheming Fox who, he felt sure, was the directing mind behind this incredible energy of destruction.

Peire Vidal went freely about the imperial palace, wearing simply the livery of the Pisan lieutenant, the most effective of disguises, for no one paid attention to soldiers, with whom the vast establishment was crowded. Once he saw the emperor, in his cups, and at the moment occupied with emptying his stomach. His eunuchs let him retch, and when he could no more, they helped him away, wambling on his legs and protesting incoherently.

333

The crusaders at that moment were launching their final onslaught. On the landward side the Flemings, covered by a flying curtain of Norman bolts—in the style of Richard the Lion—sought to effect a foothold with scaling ladders on the walls of Manuel. But the outer moat, filled with water, held up their progress, though they threw temporary bridges across it, and the sheer walls rose high above the longest ladders. The attackers suffered, too, from a downpour of hot lead and boiling pitch, and from the great stones dropped upon them. The water of the moat thickened with bodies. The crusaders had built a great truye, or "sow", and brought it to bear against the gate Polyandrion. The machine was two stories in height and advanced on crude wheels; it held more than a hundred men, who operated its massive battering ram. The width of the fosse, however, diminished the power of the ram's blows, and though the gate shook under them, it held firm.

While the land forces of the crusaders were attacking, the fleet on the Golden Horn went into action. Under the fierce beating of the oars, the huge ursers bore down upon the walls protecting the Blachernae quarter. Each ship was armed with a mangonel, which was loaded and fired with remarkable precision and accuracy. These were answered by the imperial engineers, but with poorer marksmanship. The Norman archers and crossbowmen kept up a rain of bolts as the war vessels worked their way in. When these reached shallow water, their stems were moored to the narrow strip of shore between the channel and the walls, and anchors were thrown from the sterns. The cross-trees of the ursers were high enough to be on a level with the walls; and now the watchers observed an amazing thing: from every cross-tree a gangway, wide enough to allow three men to advance abreast and protected by coverings of stout leather, was dropped onto the walls.

Quesnes de Béthune, chanting his battle-song and carrying the gonfalon of Flanders, was the first to achieve the ramparts of New Rome. He was followed by a horde of Flemings who got a foothold but no more, for the Warings, using similar weapons and speaking the same tongue, resisted every inch of their distant kinsmen's advance.

The doge's urser, plainly visible with the Lion banner of Venice flying from its masthead, at length found anchorage, and Dandolo himself, bare-headed, his white locks flying, was seen at its prow. The old man broke loose from his squires, clambered over the bulwark, and dropped down upon the shelf of beach under the walls. He stumbled and almost fell, picked himself up and felt blindly for the base of the wall. A great shout went up from the ships nearby, and knights and foot soldiers began to tumble over the sides of the ships, bearing scaling ladders. The priests on board sang fervently. Norman arbalastiers took up the chant as they wound and fired their machines. The soldiers and knights joined them. Above the clamor and din of battle the song rose, deep and hoarse:

> *Veni Creator Spiritus*
> *Mentes tuorum visita*
> *Imple superna gratia*
> *Quae tu creasti pectora*

The ladies at the palace windows were thrilled. The western barbarians were such fine soldiers! It was a pity so many would be uselessly slain!

> *Qui diceri Paraclitus*
> *Altissimi donum Dei*
> *Fons vivius, ignis, caritas*
> *Et spiritalis unctio*

The scaling ladders were up. As the knights mounted them many were pushed over backward and a torrent of mailed bodies cascaded into the waters of the Golden Horn.

> *Accende lumen sensibus*
> *Infunde amorem cordibus*
> *Infirma nostri corporis*
> *Virtute firmans perpeti*

The Warings, feeling the impact of the irresistible force from below, were giving way. As the front rank fell back, it became entangled with the rear ranks. There was some confusion; an

335

order given by a Pisan officer was misunderstood; there was danger of the disorder turning into a rout.

> Hostem repellas longius
> Pacemque dones protinus
> Ductore sic te paevio
> Vitemus omne noxium

The Pisans, thrown in to support the Warings, had to dodge the swinging blows of the great double-edged battle-axes of their allies. They themselves fought in close formation, using lances and guisarmes, which made concentrated defence impossible.

> Per te sciamus da Patrem
> Noscamus atque Filium
> Teque utriusque Spiritum
> Credamus omni tempore

The crusaders had seized a tower. Before the survivors could warn those in their rear, the next tower had passed into the enemy's hands; there were no survivors.

> Deo Patri sit gloria
> Et Filio qui a mortius
> Surrexit ac Paraclito
> In saeculorum saecula!

In rapid succession tower after tower along the sea-wall fell, until eight, ten, fifteen, twenty-five towers out of the ninety-six were lost. The rush of the attackers carried them into the Blachernae quarter, even into a corner of the imperial palace. The Venetians fired the neighboring buildings. Smoke thickened above them; the stench of things burning filled the air. The eunuchs were hysterical. The ladies fled, shrieking, from the palace windows whence they had been idly watching the progress of the battle.

With growing restlessness Peire Vidal had watched the course of the fighting. He felt helpless and troubled. The crusaders were his own people, from far across the sea, embarked mistakenly on this unfortunate expedition. Here he was an alien; an alien, but with a personal interest in the welfare of the city. Here, too, were his friends, the merchant Spazio, the captain Piozzi, the priest Porphyros, the sage Nicetas, all that company of gentle and learned men with whom these many months he had held enlightened converse. When he saw the doge leap ashore, he realized that New Rome was in grave danger. That which had lasted a thousand years was threatened with extinction. He paced from corridor to corridor, clad in his Pisan armor and with his great double-edged sword sheathed in its scabbard, carrying on a muttered dialogue with himself.

"You are a sort of coward, to skulk about when there is fighting. . . ."

"Well, what would you have me do—fight my own blood? Perhaps my very own Provençals?"

"Sant Julian witness what a turn-tail you are!"

"The saints know I have shown courage before!"

"What will you do if they take the city and find you sneaking about?"

"The city is in the hands of God!"

"It may soon be in the hands of Dandolo and Simon de Montfort!"

"By God, I know not what to do!"

He was on the point of returning to the Porphyrogenitus to assure his family of protection when he was aroused from his state of uncertainty by the clattering of mailed feet. The tumult approached. A little band of Pisans entered, bloody and desperate, flying in utter panic. One of them groaned and collapsed, sprawling grotesquely. His comrades, without looking back, pressed on. A sudden flood of anger welled up in the troubadour's heart; a rage so blind that he knew nothing of what he did next. He drew his sword and sprang at the men, beating them with the flat of it and shouting in Italian; "Advance!"

Astonished at the sight of a Pisan officer, the soldiers hesitated, then they turned and followed Peire Vidal as he plunged into the dark corridor. There other Pisans and a few Warings, believing that reinforcements had arrived, joined the little force, and by the

337

time they reached the walls there was a considerable company of them.

The rush of crusaders, carrying them beyond the line of towers, left their flank exposed where the outworks of the palace joined the city's walls. At this point the Pisans and Warings broke through, fighting with the furious exasperation of despair. They drove the invaders back to the last tower captured, but the Latins, better disciplined than their adversaries, closed the tower gates against a further advance. Though the Latins still held the line of towers, they had been stopped. The battle subsided, the crusaders caught outside the towers being readily disposed of. In time the Captain Piozzi appeared, bringing up a battalion of reserves. He walked with difficulty, for he had been wounded in the leg. A bolt had also pierced his ear, leaving a bloody gash.

"God shield you!" he said, clasping Peire Vidal's hand warmly. "You have saved this part of the city! Our captain-general, Lascaris, has been slow in getting under way. But you will see a sight, signor!" He drew the troubadour to one of the embrasures of the battlement, from whence they had a clear view of the Cosmidion district outside the walls of Heraclius.

The great gate of Saint Romanos had opened and the drawbridge fell with creaking and clanking of machinery. The legions of Romania, pacing evenly and solidly in endless ranks of horsemen, passed over the bridge and deployed upon the plain beyond, where the crusaders, frustrated in their land attack, had withdrawn to Gyrolemna.

"Those are the Dalmatians in the embroidered liveries. To their right, the Macedonians of the great heteria. You can see the kind of swords they use, very deadly; silver belts, gilded shields, and gilded battle-axes. Much gilding, but they are good warriors!"

There was a steady roll of thunderous hoofbeats crossing the bridge. The armored legions, dividing into companies, with beautiful precision opened out wider and wider, in a dazzling array of colors, like an immense peacock.

"There's the legion called Candidati, a very select one, too, as you can judge by their uniforms! And the Scholarii Legion, of Lascaris himself—all nobles. The Scythians and Warings are cover-

338

ing their flanks. This will give your Frankish barbarians something to think about!"

Indeed, the crusaders obviously were alarmed. They had drawn together, with their center faced about. Their archers were gathered in a dense mass, but there was no shooting as the strong columns of the imperial forces deliberately took up positions along the line of walls. It was evident, too, that the holders of the towers were impressed by this demonstration, for the forces of their comrades in the plain below were no match for the army of Alexis, fresh and unbreathed. Within an hour or so, under cover of approaching darkness, the Latin soldiers were withdrawn from the walls. There was no further fighting. The crusaders clambered back into their ships. The Romanian legions, after several feints and much skilful maneuvering, withdrew to the gate of Saint Romanos. The crusaders followed them cautiously, but made no attempt to force the gate. New Rome was intact, save for the section that was still smoldering.

Peire Vidal returned in time to calm his excited son and to see him to bed. He had to sing the long chanson of *Girartz de Rossilho* before the young prince finally closed his eyes.

Chapter Twenty-seven

Y OU will please come at once to the Blachern Palace. Respectfully, Piozzi."

The messenger, a Pisan sergeant, waited while Peire Vidal
hurriedly clothed himself. The Lady Xene sat up in bed, watching him dress, with eyes that were wells of strange darkness. Her
white body was rigid, alabaster in tint, and of the modeling of
Lysippus.

As he kissed her farewell she said, "It has come." She laid both
her delicate patrician hands on his broad heavy shoulders and,
drawing him down, stared searchingly into his face. At length, as
though satisfied, she said, "You are great, my husband. Everything in the world is less than that." Her kiss, long and tender,
was the seal of her confidence in him. He took his sword in hand.
A brown stain showed upon its edge. He wondered vaguely if he
had killed anyone that afternoon. . . .

The hour of matins was being tolled throughout the city and
from its five hundred churches came the sound of chanting, the
liturgy of Saint Basil. This solemn intoning grew louder as they
passed down into the Blachernae quarter where the great church
of Saint Mary of Blachernae dominated the housetops. The streets
were filled with troops, and in the short distance from the Porphyrogenitus to the imperial palace the little escort was challenged

three times. Companies of Pisan guards were standing under arms along all the approaches to the palace, and sentries were posted thick upon the walls. The burnt section still glowed dully, like a great live coal. A peculiarly unpleasant stench hung upon the heavy air of the mid-July night—burning the dead. . . . There were no signs of royalty or even of nobility throughout the vast chambers of the palace; only soldiers, sleeping on the floors, talking in low tones, or passing, by squads, down echoing corridors. The city of New Rome had been shaken out of its lethargy; it was now fully armed and ready. Before a bronze door ten cubits high, and richly decorated with sacred and legendary figures the sergeant halted. He spoke to the sentry and Peire Vidal was admitted.

It had probably been a council room, for the emblems of the empire—the crescent, the eagle, and the white lion—were everywhere in evidence, carved on the furniture and embroidered on the hangings. And everywhere, too, were icons, but there was no incense burning before any of them. By the light of torches Peire Vidal saw plainly a number of familiar faces, the Captain Piozzi, some of the visitors at the house of Buonardo Spazio, and, to his surprise, his chaplain, Porphyros, and the emperor's brother-in-law, Theodore Lascaris. The glittering uniform of the latter was in singular contrast to the simple chasuble of rough fustian worn by the priest. At his entrance they all rose and bowed respectfully. Without preliminaries the captain spoke.

"Monsignor Vidal, you know most of us. We have summoned you in order to tell you that New Rome is now without an emperor."

"My exalted brother-in-law, Alexis," said Theodore Lascaris dryly, "has departed the city, with ten thousand pieces of gold and his favorite hetaira, abandoning his wife, Euphrosyne, his legitimate children, his numerous bastards, and the city to their respective fates. New Rome is now in the hands of the Council." There was no affectation in the man's speech; still the dandy, he was more the soldier.

The Captain Piozzi was fingering a document. The members of the Council leaned forward, tense and expectant.

"By the Emergency Council," said the captain, "I have been

341

empowered, in the event of the defection of the emperor, to proclaim Andronicus Vidal emperor of New Rome. . . ." The room swam before the eyes of the troubadour. He placed his hand on the back of a chair to steady himself. ". . . and to declare you, Peire Vidal, regent, acting in conjunction with the Permanent Council; and with its advice administering the government, the affairs, and the functions of the empire of Romania, in the best interests of all its people, through the favor of God and the holy saints!"

Peire Vidal could not speak. His tongue ached but he could not speak. The priest Porphyros said in a gentle and kindly voice, "It is not necessary, monsignor, to thank us. Thank God, who gave you the Princess Xene and made your son the legitimate heir to the throne."

"I do thank God!" said Peire Vidal fervently.

"The ceremony of investiture will be simple, and it will take place at once. We have no time to lose. There is Isaac Angelus, the former emperor—still a captive." Something about the tone of the captain-general's voice made Peire Vidal raise his head sharply. "The city is in a ferment," continued Theodore Lascaris. "The people, wearied at last of the emperor's vices and blaming him for the city's peril, have been threatening to rise and restore the deposed emperor. Alexis has been not only stupid, he has shown himself a craven. His flight, which is unknown to any but ourselves, has left the way open to a genuine restoration—if we act with resolution and promptness. By good fortune we control the Pisan auxiliaries, and the secret party of Andronicus has a large following among the lower clergy, the students, and the younger officers of the imperial army. The remainder of the forces, especially the patrician legions, will be disarmed if they offer resistance. Naturally, we desire to avoid all unnecessary bloodshed. That, however, can be easily affected."

"How?" asked Peire Vidal. His mind was beginning to fumble with some problem. No one answered at once. He looked from face to face. There was a certain common grimness in their expression that made him ask, unwillingly, "You will, of course, continue to protect the deposed emperor?"

342

Then the Captain Piozzi said, "Sentence of death, in the interest of the empire, has been passed upon Isaac Angelus."

"He merits such an end," said Theodore Lascaris quickly. "For it was he who exposed the Emperor Andronicus Comnenus to death by horrible torture. This and the other crimes of his reign have been carefully considered by the Council." He paused, then added solemnly, "The verdict was death. But you are not a party to this decision and need share none of the responsibility for our action. So far as you have any knowledge, the criminal has already paid the penalty of his transgressions—by starvation and neglect. We have arranged that the body shall be discovered by the leader of the so-called legitimist party, Alexis Ducas, the Protovestiarios, known as Mourtzouphlos. You need not concern yourself further, monsignor, about this little matter." He rose, as though intimating that the sitting of the Council was at an end. "We will attend your son, the emperor-elect, within half an hour."

"Monsignors of the Council," said Peire Vidal haltingly, "I must ask you to wait a moment while I consider . . . what is about to be done." Thoughts, terrible and swift, were hurtling through his brain. He dared not stop to examine them. The members of the Council, with an air of surprise, seated themselves. The captain-general's fingers tapped impatiently upon the table.

"The destiny of the empire, monsignor, hangs on moments!"

His brain was filled with fearful images. It seemed to him, in that brief instant, that all the ghosts of murdered emperors, of those blinded and deposed, were crowding into the council chamber. Would that the merchant Spazio and the philosopher Nicetas were here to advise him! But walls, water, enemies divided him from their counsel.

"Monsignors of the Council, it seems to me that we may devise some alternative to assassination."

"The alternative," said Theodore Lascaris curtly, "is civil war. And seeing the strength and boldness of our enemies, we can hardly afford to engage in an internal conflict. The legitimist party is strong among the ignorant, who are moved by compassion, and among the aristocrats, who are inspired by greed. The latter prefer a weak and indulgent ruler to one who might deprive them of any

343

of their pleasures or privileges. Moreover, you, the father of our choice, are a Latin. Mourtzouphlos and his party hate the Latins. They say the westerners are all barbarians."

It was curious to hear this member of the royal family describe the weakness of his own class. Strange man, this military fop! He went on: "If we spare Isaac Angelus we play into the hands of the crusaders. They will continue to fight for the righteous purpose of freeing him from imprisonment. If we let him go free—which is unthinkable—he is a living menace to any government we set up; and we may not be able to set up a government while he lives. In order to spare this miserable wretch, this feeble remnant of a man, would you have the blood of ten thousand slain citizens on your head?"

They awaited his answer. His thoughts raced: "The alternative is civil war. The blood of ten thousand—perhaps a hundred thousand citizens. The life of an old blind man, of an evil old man. The child Andronicus, innocent and brave, becomes emperor after a simple judicial murder. A deserved execution. It is the deliberate verdict of upright and conscientious men. A sentence passed by common consent, not a killing from motives of hate or ambition. No one guilty. All guilty. But in the law that is a daily occurrence. Blood spilled must be satisfied with blood. Judges condemn. These are judges. I am a judge. I send a squad of soldiers to strangle this old imposter with a piece of rope or stifle him with a cloth. Wait! Why send others? If you believe this to be the only right and true procedure, do it yourself! Do not inflict the responsibility upon others. If the choice is yours, let the execution be yours! Throttle him yourself! He is old and blind, as blind as the Fox of Venice, he will offer no resistance; take his scrawny neck between your huge fists, press upon the windpipe—and presto, the deed is done! Hail to the emperor! Hail, Emperor Vidal! . . . Ah, God, a truce to thinking!"

The members of the Council were growing restless; courtesy scarcely veiled their impatience. Why, in the name of the saints, was this troubadour hesitating? Did he, perhaps, hope to be emperor himself?

" 'Emperor Vidal. . . . If wisdom could make you emperor, I would crown you now, Peire Vidal. . . .' In her tower chamber

344

Adélasie des Baux placed the ring of the Comneni upon his finger. That ring had brought him to this room. That ring had given him a son whom he loved above all things on earth. That ring had given him torment and delight beyond all belief. . . . 'Blood, blood. I hope you will not be sucked into that whirlpool of human woe!' What would the Good Count Raimon do in a case like this? Yet, in spite of his warning, he had certified, unsolicited, to the heritage of the child. . . . A strange thing, life, with its solicitations and withdrawals, its demands and refusals. 'Who would touch life, tastes poison,' says Peire Cardinal of the bitter tongue. And he says further, in his poetic treatise *On the Ideal State:* 'Crimes of policy differ from ordinary ones in that they reflect foresight and vision, if successful; if not, history condemns them.' But when is the taking of a life not a crime? When is it just . . . Justice, the city of justice . . . ah, God, I am going mad!"

Sweat started on his forehead. His eyes bulged from their sockets.

" 'It has come. . . . You are great. . . . Everything in the world is less than that.' "

Suddenly the tension was relieved. His forehead ceased to throb. His pulse returned to its normal beat.

"Monsignors of the Council," he said evenly, "I cannot permit my son to become emperor at the present time. The rest is in your hands."

It was finality, and they knew it. Theodore Lascaris said instantly, "Then we must send at once and release the Emperor Isaac Angelus! We place ourselves at the head of the legitimist party and invite the young Alexis to share the throne with his father. The crusaders may proceed to the Holy Land. Captain Piozzi, the Council charges you with the safety of the emperor of Romania!"

They paid no further heed to Peire Vidal.

"Captain Piozzi," he said hesitantly, "may I be permitted to accompany you in freeing the emperor?"

"You shall open the dungeon gate with your own hands, monsignor," said the captain, "but you are the greatest fool living!"

Thus it happened that the knight of Belgueil went with the Pisan guard, first to the tower of Anema, and when they found the captive was not there, to the gloomy dungeons of the Diplo-

345

kionion; and there they found him, crouching in a corner, in his filth and rags, a creature that had no light in its empty eyesockets and clawed feebly at the slimy walls when the torches' smoke blew in his nostrils. They hailed him forth and proclaimed him emperor of Romania at the sad wan hour of lauds when all the vast restless city was sleeping fitfully, fearful of the morrow.

When Peire Vidal returned, his wife was still sitting up, rigid, in the bed of state. He tossed his sword into a corner. It fell with a hollow clang of steel on stone. He came and looked down upon her. She shivered slightly.

"You are not the mother of an emperor!" he said harshly.

Slowly and timidly one alabaster arm rose toward him, the fingers cupped to take his.

"But I am still your wife, Peire Vidal."

He dropped upon both knees, burying his head in the smooth soft hollow where the unborn babe Andronicus had been. He was shaking with sobs. Her fingers ceaselessly caressed his massive head.

"Let us return to Belgueil where we were often happy," said the Lady Xene. It was a fortnight later.

Peire Vidal looked at his wife. Her cheeks seemed whiter than usual, with the pallor that comes of confinement in chambers scantily lit, for the castle was very ancient, built in times when barbarian hordes threatened the empire.

"I know that this palace, madonna, is not a good place to dwell in. There are no pleasances, and the walls are damp. But it will not be for long. The crusaders have promised to leave at Michaelmas, then we can return to the Pera and the sunny gardens of Monsignor Spazio."

She looked at him strangely, with veiled anxiety.

"I am afraid here, Peire Vidal."

He was startled. It was the first time she had ever confessed to fear. He wondered if perchance she might be pregnant again. That would not be a misfortune. If they returned to Provence it would be pleasant to have a child tumbling about Belgueil. The young Andronicus had become so much of a sturdy squire, for his twelve years, that he would no longer be coddled. He had insisted upon

346

going alone to the Hagia Sophia to see the investiture of Alexis and Isaac as joint emperors of Romania; alone, for his father refused to witness the ceremony. He did not care to watch the satisfaction of Bonifaz and Dandolo and the crusaders at the successful consummation of their plans.

Actually, those distinguished leaders were far from happy at the unexpected outcome of the siege. When Constantine, minister of finance, sent word across the Golden Horn that Isaac Angelus was released from his long imprisonment and was prepared to accept all the conditions and ratify all the promises of his son to the crusaders, the doge, after a moment of hesitation, answered that they would have to see how Greeks would keep promises.

Buonardo Spazio had spied Andronicus in the crowd at the church and returned with the lad to the Porphyrogenitus. "Though there is no Alexis the Third on the throne, I would not let this young scapegrace run about the streets by himself," he said to Peire Vidal in private. "A gentleman named Khasis is too well known to our Venetian friends. Ah, what a generous soul is that old man, Enrico Dandolo! Would you believe how easy he has made it for the Greeks—simply, that young Alexis binds himself to put the empire of Romania under obedience to the Roman pope; to donate two hundred thousand silver marks to the army of the crusaders and provisions for a year; to supply ten thousand infantry, and cavalry in the proportion they, the crusaders, shall designate and keep them at his expense for a year in Egypt or the Holy Land; and to maintain in the Holy Land, during his life, five hundred knights with their squires and appurtenances! Why, 'tis a pittance when you think of the trouble the crusaders have been put to, elevating Alexis to the throne! As for the damage the invaders have inflicted on New Rome, the devastation of the region all about it, and the occupation and plundering of the Pera and Galata—wherein I have suffered with the rest, in spite of the Count Baldwin—they are writing all that off as an indemnity for the crusaders who have been unfortunate enough to lose their lives! They are true Christians, my friend, and do everything from a sense of righteousness!"

The merchant's irony had a venomous ring. His eyes looked small and bloodshot. He went on, "They have turned my estates

347

into stables. Not an article of value they haven't stolen or destroyed. The damsels of my household have been given to the uses of the common soldiers. They have seized my ships, my warehouses; my cargoes have been distributed, and my books of accounts placed in the strong boxes of the doge—may the Fiend take him! I went to my friend, the Count Baldwin of Flanders, and reminded him of the moneys I had advanced him, without interest, at a critical time in his career. He was occupied, and when he saw me—he was very busy. He was excessively sorry, overcome with mortification at the conduct of his allies, but what could he do about it—he, a poor simple soldier of the ranks? He did nothing. Our venerable friend Nicetas has lost much—more than I, for they have burnt the notes and records he was preserving for a great history of these times and of past times, and they are busy shipping back his precious library of rare books to Venice. There is nothing they overlook. So I say—keep your son off the streets!"

That had been two weeks ago. And now, the Lady Xene was afraid.

"Yes," said Peire Vidal slowly, "it would be best to return to Belgueil." The sunny and spacious gardens of Buonardo Spazio, he felt sure, would never again be their refuge. He had refrained from telling her that because, in truth, he had no idea how they would manage to return to Provence. Still, he would make the effort. He had reassured her about the condition of the city, how there were bound to be disorders when a dynasty fell, and so forth. But he would not allow her or his son to leave the palace. There were no Pisan guards about any longer. He slept with his sword within reach, Andronicus on a pallet at their feet.

Buonardo Spazio had never reproached him for his decision at the meeting of the Council. "You acted as you thought best, and who can say what is really best? Only God. I myself did not foresee the unexpected flight of the emperor. I had thought it would come later, for I knew he was a coward. If we had had time we could have rendered the party of Isaac, especially Mourtzouphlos and Constantine, ineffective by showing how Venice and Rome, enemies of Romania, would gain control through the accession of the young Alexis. But now the legitimists are busy weaning

348

Alexis from the influence of Bonifaz and Dandolo. They are preparing to unite all the Greeks against all aliens, and so they are the popular party. As for Alexis, he is a feather, blown on whatever wind may come. There is no red blood in all the imperial family, save in Theodore Lascaris, who has shown himself to be something of a man, and in the wife of Isaac, the Empress Margaret. And that is because she is the sister of King Aimeric of Hungary."

Peire Vidal had gone over in his mind all the persons to whom he might apply for aid in escaping from the city. Bonifaz—once, but not now; nor Raimbaut of Vacqueiras, who had passed him in the Blachern quarter without salutation or sign of recognition. Quesnes de Béthune? Unlikely, after that mêlée on the walls! Baldwin? The count's present temper was evident. There remained Theodore Lascaris and—the Empress Margaret, sister of that king who, as duke, had invited him to Hungary to teach his unlettered subjects the mysteries of *el gai saber*. He had, it is true, been entertained by Duke Aimeric with the greatest kindness, and had been generously rewarded. There was a possibility that Margaret might respond to his appeal.

He went, therefore, to the quarters of the captain-general of the imperial army. And when the dandy heard his simple request—an imperial passport to take him and his family from New Rome—he was not too busy to give sympathetic attention to the troubadour's plea.

"It will be very difficult, Monsignor Vidal," he said, frowning thoughtfully, "for all the vessels in port are either Venetian or under Venetian control. However, there is a Genoese merchantman leaving soon for Italy with a lading of refugees who were burnt out in the Galata quarter. We have given her clearance but are still awaiting the official imperial sanction. In your case, because of the Venetian espionage system, it would be needful to secure a passport signed by the emperor himself. The doge is a vindictive old man," he added grimly, "and he will not let you out of his clutches if he can help it."

"I once knew the brother of the empress, King Aimeric."

"Good! Then we will go to her at once, for whatever she says, the emperor does."

349

The audience with the empress proved to be more fruitful than either of them had expected. She was dressed simply: a kindly matron, aged by years of anxiety, and anxious still over the health of that wretched figment of empire, her husband; long white braids that once had been silky yellow, the toast of all Hungary! But she remembered Peire Vidal, the troubadour, even remembered the song, "When the wind rides over seas from Provence." Would he consent to sing it for her?

He sang, and her eyes filled with tears. "That is the way I feel about Hungary. I long to see again the Carpathians and the green fields of the Little Alföld. Or breathe again the wind called *délibáb*, that brings the image they call Fata Morgana. But I do not think that will be possible. Is the monsignor a troubadour with the crusaders?" she asked Theodore Lascaris, with some embarrassment.

"No, gracious lady," said the captain-general, "he is a friend of the good merchant, Buonardo Spazio. It was Peire Vidal who opened the door of the dungeon that held your husband, the emperor."

Unexpectedly, she fell upon her knees and kissed his hand. She pressed it to her withered lips, saying, "Oh, you must be very good, monsignor! God will protect you and yours, I am sure, for that deed!"

Peire Vidal, not knowing what to do or say, bent and kissed her on the forehead. "He, or the great goddess Venus gave me the will to free your husband," he said.

At the mention of Venus she rose, crossing herself. "You still remain with us as court singer, will you not, Monsignor Vidal? I would you could teach the Greeks to sing. They can only chant! And I pray that you will consent to be my son's teacher in the graceful arts of the west. It would greatly illumine the court and the empire if east and west could be brought together and joined in one harmony of love and song. Alexis, I am sure, can profit from your instruction."

Theodore Lascaris, making an ironical grimace, observed, "The monsignor, my empress, is very desirous of returning to his native land which he has not seen in over a year. It is very difficult to secure a passport———"

350

"You shall have one at once, my dear Peire Vidal, though I wish it were otherwise. Perhaps you will return to us in happier times?" She held out her hand, patrician under its wrinkles. "When we shall have extended justice and love to all parts of Romania!" She felt in her gown and drew out a small purse of cloth of gold. "There are only a few silver coins in it, monsignor, but they are yours. And with them, the love I bear you for your great charity and goodness!"

He left the audience hall, glad now that Isaac the Angel was alive. In the purse was a handful of ducats. They bore the lion of Venice and the image of the doge. He threw them into the street, tucking the purse into his bosom. And with the imperial passport, bearing the signature, scarcely legible, of Isaac, he returned triumphantly to the palace of Porphyrogenitus.

Chapter Twenty-eight

AND I shall have my own horse to ride!" shouted Andronicus, dancing about the gloomy chamber. "Jehan Porcelet will see that I have a new and larger saddle. And I am strong enough to hold a full-size lance, am I not, father? How long will it take us to get home? Will the hawthorne and eglantine be in bloom then?" Without waiting for answer he chattered on, "The primrose is a sweet flower and so is the jasmine, but I like the joy flower best. I have not forgotten one of them! We can go a-hawking, and I think you will let me ride on the boar-hunt for I have fought in the crusade. They will not believe half of the things I shall tell them, and what a city this is—the greatest in all the world! Yet I think it is pleasanter at Carcassonne and Béziers, where the flower girls speak our own tongue. The girls of Provence are much prettier than any here. They can laugh and dance better, too. Will you get me a viol in Toulouse, father, for I must learn to make good sirventes. Father, will you get me a new viol when we come home?"

Peire Vidal, wearing his faded surtout that the Lady Xene had refurbished as best she could for the journey, was staring from the narrow slit of a window that looked toward the east, giving a view of the whole city, its hills and valleys, churches, palaces, marts of trade, and ancient great structures whose uses he did not know. Further still, the outlines of the hippodrome, of the old palace of the Geranion; then the blue waters of the Bosporus, where they met the deeper green-blue of the Marmora. It was all bright, quiescent, basking drowsily under the fierce heat of an August sun. Yet Peire Vidal continued to stare, unmindful of his son's eager questioning.

"Father, why don't you answer me about the viol? I will pay for it, myself!"

"We must be going," said the troubadour briefly. Hastily he began to gather together their few belongings, now reduced to the compass of a little wooden chest, made of cedar of Lebanon, and of Saracen workmanship. "You must wear a veil as the Greek high-born women do," he said.

The Lady Xene, trembling, searched for a piece of material and found an old wimple. "Yes, yes, let us hurry," she said nervously.

"Is it a closed litter?" asked Andronicus eagerly.

"It is a closed litter."

"But, father, I want to see things as we go through the city. It has been such a long while since we have gone anywhere."

"Not today, my son. We shall see the city much better from the deck of the ship. The air at this time of year is very unhealthy. Come, why are you dawdling?"

They scurried down through the palace, inhabited of late by strange Greeks, persons they did not know and did not care to know. Still, they had been allowed to keep their apartment, for no one dispossessed them. No one bothered about them. The three of them, with Peire Vidal lugging the box and the viol he had preserved, and no one else—not even the priest Porphyros who had disappeared after the meeting of the Council—made their way down the stone stairs and through the interminable galleries and corridors until they reached the street where the litter was standing.

"Father, what is burning? Do you see that great cloud of smoke? It is like a serpent, father!"

They climbed into the litter. The litter-carriers, gabbling volubly, set off down the hill. They bounced and jolted, sometimes, as the curtains flapped open, catching sight of people running.

353

They were all running down toward the harbor. After a long time, for it was a great distance, the litter was halted. The curtain was jerked open. A soldier in the uniform of the Pisan guard thrust his head in.

"You cannot go further," he said gruffly in Italian.

"I have a passport to go on a ship that is sailing," said Peire Vidal, presenting the document. The soldier examined it, held it upside down, grunted. "What is the name?" he asked.

"Peire Vidal. You see, it is signed by the emperor himself, and countersigned by the captain-general, Lascaris. Pray, let us go on! We have little time to lose."

"Peire Vidal!" the man whistled. "Listen, my friend, I have heard of you. You are a friend of our captain Piozzi. Well, you are good fellow. But you can't go on. There is riot and bloodshed. The city is burning."

"I must get to the harbor! The ship is sailing, I tell you!"

"Listen, friend Vidal. You are a good fellow. Well, if you go down there they will kill you. I mean the Greeks. Those dogs of crusaders, Flemings and Venetians, they came over about the hour of sextes, when everyone was taking their mid-day nap, they came over looking for what they could find. They got down in the Saracen quarter and began to lay their dirty hands on everything —goods, girls, everything! Then they started in on the mosque. They were looting it when the Greeks in the neighborhood got wind of the affair and came to help out the infidels. And then there was a set-to! Blood ran like water. And so the swine from Venice touched off the city in several places. It's burning all the way between the Great Church and the sea, and with a wind from the Bosporus behind it, there's no telling where 'twill end. And the blood of the Greeks is up. They're driving all the Latins out of the city. It's hell let loose, I'm telling you! Your life wouldn't be worth an obole down there, and, the harbor is cut off by the fire. You couldn't get around that. No, friend Vidal, you will have to right-about-face. I'm sorry, signor!" Seeing the stricken faces of the litter's occupants, he said kindly, "Where have you been staying?"

"At the Porphyrogenitus," said Peire Vidal in a choked voice.

"You had best not go back there. The Greeks are in an awful

354

rage. Believe me, signor, no ship will be sailing today. The Venetian fleet is patrolling the harbor. Everything's upset. But don't go back to that palace, for they'll get you, sure! Listen, my friend, you had better turn down this way to the house of the logothete, Nicetas."

He guided them through a maze of crooked little streets of the Phanar quarter, lying between the fifth hill, that held the cistern of Arcadius, and the Blachern quarter. This, the Greek quarter, was in a tumultuous state of excitement but the presence of the soldier spared them any unpleasantness. They passed by one mob engaged in mauling a merchant and rifling his shop. "Genoese," said the soldier. "He had no business trying to trade in this part. The Greeks are going crazy, and you could hardly blame them!"

The aged savant greeted them cordially.

"These are poor lodgings, my friends, but you are welcome to all I have." Peire Vidal had mastered enough of the vulgar Greek to understand his words, and returned thanks in the scant phrases he knew. It was a small house of two stories, attached originally to the neighboring establishment, the monastery of Saint Babylas. From the few and simple furnishings the troubadour judged that the logothete had used it only as a place of occasional resort when he was staying in the city; now it was the old man's sole retreat, his other mansion in the Petrion having been appropriated by the crusader historian, Villehardouin, who appreciated its conveniences.

They settled into a new and less pleasant existence. After two days and nights of anxiety, during which the sun was wholly obscured and the night sky lit by a fantastic glare as though from a volcano, they learned that the fire had died down, leaving a strip half a league wide from the Golden Horn to the Marmora; what had once been palaces, monuments of antiquity, dwellings, churches, and places of business were now cinders, blackened beams, crumbling stones. The Greeks in their fury had driven all Latins from the city and these, Genoese and Pisans mostly, to the number of some fifteen thousand, had fled to the Pera and the doubtful protection of the crusaders. Peire Vidal and his family dared not show themselves out of doors, nor did they during the months that followed. Once Andronicus, disobeying his father's command, ventured into the street. They rescued him, bruised and

355

bleeding, from an enraged swarm of young Greeks. He wept, not for his hurts, but from anger at being called a "Latin pig."

One of their fellow lodgers was a Pisan clerk, Jacopo, a minor figure in the activities of the Council. From the complexion and cast of his features, and the fact that he wore the national dress, he passed for a Greek, and so was enabled to go in and out without arousing suspicion on the part of their neighbors. Peire Vidal was glad to have him there, for it gave him someone to talk to and the young man brought them all the news of happenings in the city. No sooner had the Greeks driven the aliens from New Rome, he reported, than they made a futile attempt to burn the Venetian fleet by setting adrift fire-boats, laden with Greek fire, in the direction of the galleys moored in the harbors of the Golden Horn. But the wily sailors of Venice pushed them off with long boat hooks and only one vessel took fire; it was a Genoese merchantman, about to sail.

"It was a terrible sight, Monsignor Vidal, to see those unfortunate passengers leaping overboard, their garments all afire, into the Golden Horn, and they all drowned, for neither Greeks nor crusaders would give them any succor."

"The blessed saints," said Peire Vidal fervently, "preserved me, for we had our passage engaged on that ship!"

They heard that Bonifaz, marquis of Montferrat, in order to separate the young emperor from the influence of the popular party, had taken him off on some expedition in pursuit of the fleeing Alexis, once known as the Third. He did not return until the second week of November, having been unable to catch the erstwhile emperor. Then the young Alexis, relaxing after the ardors of the campaign, set out to enjoy the special perquisites of his high office. The actors, mimes, acrobats, dancing girls, and eunuchs trooped into the Blachernae palace once more; the veiled ladies resumed their mysterious occupations; the gaming tables were crowded with crusaders, and the sportive monarch allowed his fellow-players, often the palace guards, to exchange their woolen caps for the imperial diadem. But the populace, learning that their new ruler had renounced the Greek faith and had embraced the easier tenets of Latin Rome, began to mutter among themselves. Buonardo Spazio, driven into hiding, sometimes came by night in a covered litter to the house of the logothete. He had aged greatly and his face showed haggard lines, but his small eyes burned with a continuous reddish glare of hatred. His once rich and immaculate dress looked shabby. His voice trembled with fury whenever he spoke.

"The most exalted ruler of the East is getting somewhat uneasy," he said one night, with an air of bitter satisfaction. "He has gone to the Pera secretly to persuade the crusaders to remain until next Easter—as though they needed persuading! He told them that if they left, the Greeks would kill him. He is right. So he has promised to bear all their expenses and to pay the Venetians their freight for a year. Prodigal emperor! As for his father, that relic has given himself into the hands of astrologers and necromancers, who have assured him that he will be the most superlative emperor of all history; will regain his eyesight; and will be cured of his gout. Miracles without end! The magicians, to insure the success of their spells, have had transported from the hippodrome to the Blachern the statue of the Caladonian boar, one of the masterpieces of antiquity. So you see, my friend, the ancient faith in the gods has not wholly perished! Indeed, only yesterday a mob broke up the great bronze statue of Minerva, because she appeared to be beckoning the Latins toward New Rome. The people, too, believe in their old gods! Only the crusaders believe in nothing. Except loot. To tell the truth, though, the Franks are in a bad way. The common run of soldiers are slightly weary of all this dickering, from which they profit so little. They are getting restless, but Bonifaz and Dandolo, at the risk of losing their own prestige, dare not quit the city. They have imposed the most rigid discipline, but the army is in an ugly mood!"

Jacopo, the clerk, brought his sister Beatrice to live with them. She was a child two years younger than Andronicus, dark-eyed and vivacious. Her coming was a blessing, for the young squire, penned within the walls of the little dwelling, had grown pale and sluggish. In her sprightly company his zest for games and story-telling returned. There was laughter again where melancholy silence had prevailed. But the Lady Xene wilted like a flower deprived of sun and air and moisture. She grew thin, denying herself to feed the others; her eyes had a strained look, as though

357

she were waiting only to hear of some fresh misfortune. Their little store of money and valuables dwindled steadily. Peire Vidal, through Jacopo, sold the last of their jewels, except the rings of Andronicus. Then they were compelled to live upon the bounty of the logothete and what Jacopo, an unscrupulous forager, brought home to them after mysterious expeditions. Nicetas, though he still held his office, had been unable to collect his modest stipend from the new government. He, too, pawned his belongings.

In January the despairing Greeks made another attempt to burn the fleet. It succeeded no better than the first, and the great city of Constantine was daily drifting toward chaos. Toward the end of the month Jacopo returned from a foray in search of food, bringing exciting tidings. "The senate and college of pontiffs have been meeting all day in the Hagia Sophia to choose a new emperor. A great crowd was milling about the church, shouting for them to depose Alexis and Isaac, and so they began to propose various names from the nobility, but no one wants to be emperor now!" He shouted with laughter. "You should have seen how, with a show of humility, they all declined the honor! The fact is, I wouldn't want that office myself!"

"No," said Buonardo Spazio, who had come on one of his rare visits, "no one wants to carry the crusaders on his back! Did they elect anyone?"

"A fellow, Nicolas Kanabos, was finally chosen, though he kept protesting that he would have none of it. They rammed the imperial purple down his throat, however, and they are going to crown him tomorrow."

"They will not," said the merchant. "There is one factor they have not reckoned on. Those shadows of the greatness of Rome have wasted their votes!"

"Who is that?" asked Jacopo.

"You will know tomorrow, young man," said the merchant with his grim, secretive smile.

In the morning they learned that Mourtzouphlos was emperor of Romania. Alexis was under arrest. Isaac was dead. Alexis, when Nicolas Kanabos was named emperor by the assembled dignitaries, had invited Bonifaz to fill the Blachern Palace with crusaders and to take possession of the city. But before this project could be executed the treason was made known to the Protovestiarios, Alexis Ducas, known as Mourtzouphlos, who acted with energy and swiftness. The Varangian guard was withdrawn from the palace on a forged order. Mourtzouphlos, using the right of entrance to the palace accorded him by his office, entered and secured Alexis. He seized the imperial insignia, assumed the vermilion buskins, emblems of the empire of Constantine, and was saluted as emperor by the officers of the army of New Rome. Isaac, when he heard of his son's arrest, put his hand on his heart and fell dead.

A few days later Alexis was dead. The manner of his demise could not be determined. And no one cared to ascertain the facts. For some time the crusaders were actually unaware that their cherished figurehead was no longer among the living. The Emperor Mourtzouphlos straightway levied a large assessment upon the nobles, paid no heed to their anguished outcries, and sent the "contribution" to the crusaders—with a certain sardonic humor, "in the name of your devoted friend, Alexis." And a little later the leaders of the crusade discovered that the deposed emperors were deceased, without benefit of Latin clergy.

"Ha!" cried the merchant, bursting in on the logothete's household. "My friends, the magnificent farce of empire and crusade is still being played! The pious gentlemen of the Pera are mightily indignant at the turn of events. Why, they say this Mourtzouphlos is no more than a usurper and murderer! He has committed a 'horrible treason'! And they have taken it upon themselves to be the 'defenders of the right'! They are determined that the throne shall be restored—but to whom? To Alexis the Third? They drove him out! They can't very well bring him back! And there's none left in the immediate line—or so they say. Wherefore they are looking over all the cousins, second-cousins, cousins-germane, and what-not. Well! Philip of Swabia is related by marriage to the blood of Isaac, and so, for that matter, is Bonifaz, your excellent marquis of Montferrat. Bonifaz, the brother-of-the-husband-of-the-aunt of the late Alexis is now regarded as a candidate for the imperial throne! However, there is a fly in the ointment. Our cautious doge has no mind to see Bonifaz wearing the diadem. There are many political skeins entangled there. So there has been a slight chilling of the warm esteem with which those two noblemen regard each other. Also, a mission has arrived from the Holy Land, imploring the crusaders to come to the aid of the Latins there, for they are hard beset by the infidels. But even if Bonifaz greatly desires it, he cannot retire from New Rome with his army without the permission and transportation of Venice. He will have to pay the doge, or fight him. Moreover, he's lost face among his own followers for allowing the old Fox of the Adriatic to out-maneuver him in leading the crusade. It's a pretty dilemma, and my heart bleeds for him!" In truth, the murderous expression of the merchant somewhat belied his words.

That winter was bitter cold on the Golden Horn. The "Thracian Wind" blew all of two months, bearing icy blasts from the country of the savage Russians. Chilling frosts blackened the exotic shrubbery of the imperial gardens. The city woke on several occasions to find the glittering domes and columns and housetops sheeted with white. Its citizens, under the stern and tireless dictatorship of the new emperor, labored furiously at heightening the walls and improving the defences; and they had good reason, for it became known in March that the parliament of the crusaders had met, had agreed to the capture of the city, and had arranged for an equitable division of the spoils. The emperor was to be chosen by a commission of six Venetians and six crusaders. It was all done legally, and set down in writing, signed and sealed by the representatives of the Christian host, and blessed by the bishops of the Latin Church.

"No people," says Peire Cardinal in his verse treatise on government, "is great; but history asks no more than that, in times of crisis, they preserve the semblance of greatness."

The citizens of New Rome, having recovered from their frenzy of hatred and despair, went about their affairs calmly; the shops even did a little business, mostly in barter, for there was no money to buy even the poorest trinkets, and the food was strictly rationed. The main difference was that the litters of the nobility and the wealthy had disappeared from the streets, nor were there in evidence any of the brilliantly attired officers of the Dalmatian Legion, of the Scholarii, or of the Candidati. These exclusive organizations had been disbanded. Everywhere were visible the ensigns of the Romanian cohorts, the simple uniforms and bands of the Deuteron Legion, the Triton, Pempton, Hebdomon, and others that had seen service in lands far beyond the sea, and had each a tradition going back into the remote days of Constantine. And from the eyes of soldiers and citizens alike shone the pride and consciousness of being Greeks. Even the Saracens tried to look Greek. By a supreme convulsive effort the Romanians, long indifferent and diverse, had become one ancient race again, defying the western barbarians outside the walls, Franks, Flemings, Lombards, Burgundians, Germans, Normans, islanders of Venice, to whom the culture of a thousand years was less than one *Kyrie eleison*.

Chapter Twenty-nine

O N the first day of April there was celebrated the feast-day
of Saint Macrina, a virgin of pious memory. The occasion
was one of especial solemnity, for it was apparent from the
activities in the camp of the crusaders in the Pera that they were
completing their preparations for the attack. The ceremony was
held at the church of the Pantocrator, situated on the hill of the
Holy Apostles at no great distance from the Blachern quarter, and
Peire Vidal, on the advice of Nicetas, decided to go with Jacopo
and the two children to witness the spectacle.

Andronicus and Beatrice were in ecstasy at the prospect of
release from their dark quarters. Indeed, they could hardly be
called children any longer, for Beatrice had grown to be a demure
young lady and Andronicus was as stalwart a squire of thirteen
as you might lay eyes on. So the suits of all were cleaned and
freshened as well as might be, the Lady Xene brushed her lord's
surtout, fringed on the edges where the threads had raveled out,
and they set out in the clean bright air of the new month, filled
with a happiness that no foreboding on the part of the elders could
dispel. Jacopo's jests made them all laugh. Peire Vidal sang little
snatches of doggerel verse to old Provençal airs. Andronicus, wearing his sword, which he had polished until it glittered, strutted
like a peacock. Beatrice cast glances sideways at good-looking

Greek youths they passed. The streets were filled with boys and girls, the girls in white robes, wearing imitation poppies in their hair and carrying sprigs of myrtle, the boys holding willow-wands. The hill of the Holy Apostles was white with the multitude of children. Securing a vantage point near the top of the hill, they watched the endless procession of participants, the white-robed nuns of the Ayasma of the Sleep of Saint Mary, the monks of Saint Nicolas, the priests of the churches of Pantocrator, of Saint John of the Studium, of Saint George of the Cypress in Psamathia. Jacopo named them off, saying, "The Greeks wake with a prayer, work with a prayer, eat with a prayer, sleep with one. As for me, let me have a virgin, fresh and wholesome, who has prayed for a lover! And I can tell you, friend Vidal, this day does not end in such holiness as it begins, let the priests do what they will. Many a maid here will sleep with something besides a coverlet between her knees before the night is done!" He began to look about him, with an opportunist eye.

The ceremony was a lengthy one, concluding with the intoning of a liturgy by the priests and nuns at the Maiden's Column, which was then heaped high with poppies, myrtle, and willow-wands until it was almost buried in the mass of green and yellow. The children had grown restless, for they were beginning to be hungry, and Peire Vidal was on the point of turning homeward when someone touched him on the elbow, saying in Provençal, "Master!" He turned, startled beyond words to see a ragged wite who looked to be a beggar and stood grinning uneasily.

"It is Hugues, master. Hugues of Trencavel on the Aude. One of your own company, master!"

"Sant Marti keep us! And what are you doing here, Hugues?"

"Looking for you these three days, my master—and now I have found you, bless Sant Dalmatz!"

"Go on, Jacopo," said Peire Vidal to the clerk. "Take them home and I will soon follow."

When the children had gone with Jacopo, Peire Vidal said, "Let us go apart and talk, Hugues." They went down the hill into the nearby valley and found a spot beneath the aqueduct of Valens, screened from observation, where they could sit comfortably in the sun with their backs to the vast wall of masonry.

363

"How did you get into the city, Hugues?"

"Once a day they open the gate called Charisius, in the valley of the river Lycus, to let in hucksters with provisions. There are no crusaders on the land side now. Well, I was a huckster. I bought ten oboles worth of lentils, garlic, and stinking fish, and came in. I stank so they did not bother to examine me. And whenever they looked at me I swore by Constantine, who is one of their saints, I think. In I came, and here I have been, eating garlic and lentils, and looking for you!"

"How did you know I was in the city?"

"We in the Pera had heard that there was a madman—pardon, master!—who fought with the Pisans on the walls, called Vidal. We did not fight on the walls, master, for we are in the service of the doge—may Satan eat his bones!—who kept us guarding his treasure boxes while he went off to lead the fighting, the old bastard! Then, when the Pisans and Genoese were all driven out of the city, we asked of each and everyone if they knew of a Peire Vidal, and none knew save one old fellow whose son was in the Pisan guard. He said there was indeed a Pietro Vidale, who had turned the palace guard in the nick of time on the day of the fighting—a terrible man he declared, as bloodthirsty as a bull! So we knew it was you!"

The soldier took out a piece of dry fish, and with a wry face nibbled at it.

"Why have you risked your neck to see me, Hugues? Do you know that if they catch you, you will be hung as a Latin spy?"

"Not so bad," said Hugues, "as going back to that devil, Dandolo! But I did not come to see you, captain, much as I like your face!" The old Provençal impudence, thought Peire Vidal. "Our company are very sick of this business, master, and especially because there is no singing. Not a peep nor a warble; nothing but the orisons of our cursed priests night and day, and drill, drill, drill!"

"Have you no singers left?"

"The song-birds are roosting in other trees. This Canon Béthune mixes only with the generals and bishops now. Raimbaut of Vacqueiras, who used to make good songs, is a member of the supreme council of the parliament, and deep in their devilish politics and plottings. Others of them have been killed or went home after the Zara hellishness—a nasty piece of work, that! Blood and rape and burning, that was all there was to it, but it turned my stomach. We had no quarrel with them. The doge has been leading us all by the nose. Now we are on the edge of starving, but he's well heeled, you can wager! But, master, we are sick at heart and we need to hear a good song. My company sent me to find you and bring you to the Pera to sing for us!"

"Friend Hugues, do you know it is impossible for anyone to leave the city? And besides, I would be no safer in the Pera than you are here. Don't forget, I fought the crusaders on the walls!"

The man's face fell. He rose at once. "Well, it's as you choose, master. You know what can be done. Still, we are hungering for song."

"Hungering for song." The fellow had risked his life to find a song! He had spent ten oboles out of his scanty pay. He was going back, if he could get back, disappointed in his captain. Peire Vidal rose and shook his great shoulders.

"Wait! We will first try what can be done. I know someone who might help me to get to the Pera."

Theodore Lascaris was by no means so ready to grant this strange request. The dandy of the court wore the simple uniform of an officer of the Hebdomon Cohort. He eyed the Provençal soldier sternly.

"So you got into the city without a pass, eh? We'll have to correct that! How do I know you're not a spy?"

"He was one of my own men, general," said Peire Vidal.

"In the pay of the doge, monsignor! Money corrupts the best of us." Suddenly the captain-general asked, "When will your army attack?"

"You know as much as we, general," said the soldier.

"I'm not so sure. Suppose I send you to Mourtzouphlos and let him get some information out of you." His tone was deadly. Hugues did not flinch.

"General, you can use the rack and thumb-screws. I didn't come here to get or give any information. I came here to bring our captain over to sing for us. As for anything more—the devil take you!"

After a moment of contemplation the general said, "You Provençals are a stubborn lot! Listen, Monsignor Vidal, I hold my present rank on very doubtful tenure. Mourtzouphlos doesn't trust me because I'm an aristocrat, and because he knows I hate him. If I let you both out of the city I'm in some slight danger myself. Still, I will do it. At least, I shall try. I can't see any harm in your singing in the Pera, if you want to take that chance. Tonight at the hour of matins be at the water-gate Xylocircus, near the Balata quarter. That is part of the burnt section and it is patrolled by the Hebdomon Cohort, my own troops. This pass takes you through the lines, and I shall leave word with the guard at the gate to have a caïque ready for you. I shall explain to the captain of the gate that we have secured important information from this Provençal, and that you are on a secret mission to the disaffected element of the crusading army. You must return promptly on the hour of lauds. If anything goes wrong, I shall not know you and I shall declare that the pass was forged. So make no mistake! Good luck to your singing!" He was smiling sardonically as they left him, uttering their thanks.

Peire Vidal did not take Hugues to the house of the logothete; he showed him where it stood and told him to return before midnight. That evening he entertained the two children with their favorite tales, of Flore and Blancheflor; the tale of the Twelve Great Emperors; and the tale of the Seven Champions of Christendom. He sang for the Lady Xene a new serena—"Winter with dour and sullen mien,"—a song that made her eyes grow dark and velvety with adoration; and then, the children having gone to bed, he lied to her. He was going, he said, to sing for the general, Theodore Lascaris, and some of his officer friends; and with that, he began busily to hunt for his helmet and hauberk.

"This night," he heard her say in a voice that she tried not to let tremble, "I wish you would remain with me, Peire Vidal. When you are away I am lonely and terrified. I cannot sleep when you are not at my side."

"My lady, the Emperor Mourtzouphlos has made this city as safe as—as Béziers! I have told them I would come, madomna. You would not have them think I am afraid to go about?"

"No—but I am afraid!" She ran to him, clung to him. He

366

pushed her gently off and, standing erect in his mail, declaimed the lines of Raimbaut of Vacqueiras:

> I stood in arms like a Brabançon
> With helmet, hauberk, and thick gambeson!

"The knight of Belgueil chides his lady for her timidity. You shall sleep without me, princess! Ah, soundly, soundly!" He pinched her cheek, buckled on his sword, and laid the precious viol in its case. "When I return we shall know the meaning of love once more, madomna. . . ." Her lips brushed across his cheeks, found his, remained long there, as though seeking to shake his resolution. But he was adamant in gayety. "Pray to Sant Julian to put me in good voice, madomna!"

"Saint Therapos keep you, Peire Vidal!"

He bent and kissed the curls of young Andronicus, now yellowish brown, glossy as the feathers of a bird. The boy stirred slightly in his sleep, muttering, "Let them all come—!" and struck out blindly with his little fist.

"He is not afraid!" said the father proudly.

When he left her she was standing by the lad's pallet, fair and frail, murmuring a prayer in Greek. He descended the stair (they had the upper story to themselves), and found Jacopo putting on his best finery. Beatrice was watching him, bright-eyed, from her pallet. From behind a tattered arras candlelight showed in the chamber of Nicetas, where the old man was pouring over his few remaining records. From time to time could be heard the scratching of a reed pen on parchment.

"What! you, too, friend Vidal?"

"I, what?"

"A sally for love, eh? This is the night of Venus, you know!"

"I am going out to sing for friends," said Peire Vidal.

"Ha! 'Twill do to tell!" The young man, laughing, drew a silk sticharion over his head. "No ducats in the wallet, but fire in the heart!" He adjusted his girdle of woven silk and thrust into it a misericorde—the dagger used to despatch knights when they are down. "Taking no chances, Peire Vidal, on the jealousy of these Greeks. This little instrument has seen a lot of fighting and has

367

probably put many a crusader to his last sleep. My father used to collect such oddities. The misericorde is a useful tool for close work. Now, sweet sister, lie down and go to sleep. A night like this is not for young virgins to think about."

The three of them, Peire Vidal and Jacopo and Hugues, walked down through a city given to festival. The wineshops were open and thronged with patrons. In the public squares before the churches where huge bonfires had been lit, youths and maidens were dancing hand in hand. No veils were worn this night, and the white robes of the damsels fluttered with an abandon quite foreign to the worship of blessed Saint Macrina. Within the chapels the monks and priests raised their voices in fervent chants, save for those who crept out to watch furtively the abominations which had been reported. It was said that some of the nuns of the Ayasma of the Sleep of Saint Mary were missing from their customary devotions. Where the revelry was maddest Jacopo left them and they went on, unchallenged, into the Balata quarter, through empty spaces of cinders and blackened ruins, and to the water-gate Xylocircus. Here the captain of the Hebdomon Cohort, having inspected their passes, wished them luck and showed them a caïque, manned by imperial sailors, almost the sole remnant of the great imperial navy.

"You had best head for the Tophana quarter," he said. "The Venetians are thick as flies on the Golden Horn. Steer straight out into the Bosporus; the tide will be with you. If they catch you—overboard! 'Twill be better than to fall into their hands. At lauds the gate will be opened again. If you are not here, so much the worse for you! May the black scourge take the Latins! Saint Nicolas bless your mission!"

In a few moments the dark waters, rolling in, wind-driven, from the Marmora, were tossing the light craft as it bore away toward Scodra, on the opposite shore of the Bosporus. Soon they veered and headed back toward the dark slopes of the Pera and beached the vessel at the exact spot where the crusaders had disembarked nine months before. Here the invaders had razed a number of buildings, and the open space formed a rough amphitheater, framed in by the ancient warehouses of the quarter, the oldest on that side of the Golden Horn.

368

"Master," said Hugues, "it will not do for you to venture further. I will go up into the camp and tell my comrades. They can sneak away without the sergeants noticing, and in no time you will have listeners."

Peire Vidal began to tune his viol, the damp air having affected the strings, and hummed as he did so snatches of the songs he had made during his many years of wandering, thinking at the same time now of one or the other of the fair women for whom they had been composed. "Lark and nightingale I choose. . . ." Adélasie des Baux. Again for her: "Not of delights, but of my heart's bereaving. . . ." And for his faery love, La Bel Cavalier: "For wealth I have no craving without the joy of loving. . . ." And it startled him suddenly into thinking that it was because of her he had come on this crusade, to expiate the sin of not loving her when he had taken her. He wondered when that sin would be forgiven him, or if it had already passed from the minds of the witch Venus, and the Blessed Virgin, and Sant Julian, patron of outcasts, and singers. Perhaps they had pardoned him when he defied the doge in "Who's the fault if the voice falls mute?" Or perhaps they were on the side of the doge, won over by Saint Mark. Finally, after long years, he had sung for Madomna Xene, aboard the pirate ship: "Neither love nor any malady conspires," and tonight he sang for her again, a new song, made in the shadow of the army of death. . . . And other songs, of vague desire, ecstasies, or poignant grief, the pattern of the years he had lived.

Lights were beginning to twinkle among the shadows of the Tophana quarter. They bobbed from side to side, steadily growing brighter. It was the foot-soldiers of the Latin army, carrying torches. Angular shadows leaped in and out as the stragglers approached. There were more coming down the hill from the Pera; thin streams of torchlight were pouring over the edge of the Pera, dribbling down toward the harbor. Soon the procession of torches became a river of light, accompanied by the clinking of mail, the clattering of heavy boots, and the murmuring of deep voices; light boiling over the crest of the Pera, light rippling and swaying downward into the darkness of Tophana. . . . The foot-soldiers of the crusade were coming down to hear Peire Vidal sing!

"Where are you going?" shouted a sergeant on the hill. "Back to your quarters!"

"The devil take you! We are going to hear some singing!"

"Turn, you varlets! You sons of Belial!" cried a mailed knight, sleepily aroused.

"Turn yourself! We are going to hear a song or two!"

"It is past the hour of matins! Return to your quarters and pray!" shrilled a priest, shaking his silver cross at them.

"Pray to the devil he does not catch you and boil you, you pig-brain!"

They were laughing and waving their torches. They thronged the open space, clambered on the rubbish, roosted on the heaps of horse-dung, crawled up and sat on the housetops, perched on the wooden piles, hung perilously in the niches of rotting walls; bearded, gross, dirty, obscene, ruthless; knaves, villeins, rascals, thieves, lechers, the scum and drift of great demeisnes, the varlets of mighty barons, the hinds of the field, pressed into military service; Franks, Bretons, Germans, Lombards, Burgundians, Gascons, Normans, Flemings, Spaniards, Provençals—common soldiers of the crusade—with no love of Christ, serving their masters for three pence a day.

The torches shone on thousands. The great mass of them stank; they shuffled, grumbled, scratched themselves, chuckled, turned their heads and bodies this way and that; and then they were still. Only the sputtering of the torches could be heard. They were as still as the black night with its stars.

In that breathless stillness a thin sweet sound took form; no louder than a bird-song, all heard it. The bow caressed the viol. Then Peire Vidal sang.

His songs were of many kinds: alba, ballada, cobla, retroensa, pastorela, canson redonda, comte, roman, salut, and escondich; a plaintive planh, and many a stirring sirvente, barbed with satire. They would scarce let him stop for breath, crying in a dozen tongues: "More! More, Peire Vidal!" He sang mostly in Provençal, but he also knew a few French, Italian, and Spanish songs that he had picked up in the course of his journeyings. So more than two hours passed, and at length one of his boatmen nudged him, saying, "We must go now. It is getting on toward lauds and

370

they'll close the gate." Then he sang his last song, the serena he
had made for the Lady Xene.

> *Pos vezem que l'iverns s'irais*
> *E part se del tems amoros . . .*

Winter with dour and sullen mien
Still keeps the blessed time away
When birds in orchard bowers are seen
Singing and pert in amorous play;
But nothing in these somber days
Shall stay me from my heart's desire—
To love, and to make songs and lays.

Proud am I now; proud have I been;
If pride is sin, then must I pay
The penalty for what I win
Of love, for I was made that way;
Yet pride attaining to a place
Of eminence and rich attire
Oftener bends to something base.

A fool is he who scans the scene
And witnesses, without dismay,
Worship of what is low and mean
And for the profit of the day—
A fool, who turns a reverent gaze
To what all sycophants aspire—
Prestige—and scorns the simpler praise!

The world is filled with fools, I wean,
Whether of fine or coarser clay;
And soon comes Death, hungry and lean,
To herd the flock of fools alway.
Power crumbles; good or ill, it stays
No longer than a burning pyre,
Then falls to ashes, and decays.

Yet, though the hours and days careen
Madly toward chaos, and the ray
Of youthful love no more is seen
Lighting our years, still must I say
Its light will shine in other ways;
And in other lovers, finer fire
Will give them bright, unsullied days.

Again they were quiet, while those who understood the words explained to the others the meaning of the song. Pride in power; high as it mounts, so low it falls. Love passes; new loves come; songs remain. The Provençals came forward from the throng, among them his own men, and pressed near to him, trying to kiss his hands, and calling him master and captain. He put the viol in its case and turned toward the boat. The keel slithered over the gravel beach and the dark Bosporus licked it gingerly. Then a hoarse voice from among them cried suddenly, "Emperor!"

They knew his story. They knew the tale of the boar; of Loba of Cabaretz; of the taking of Messina. They had seen him and listened to him on the Lido; they knew by heart his sirvente on the doge. They knew that their leaders would have abandoned him to his fate. They knew, also, that he had fought against them on the walls of New Rome. They knew what it was to be a fool— they had all been fools, were fools now to be following Bonifaz and Dandolo.

"Emperor! Emperor! Emperor Vidal!"

There was no mockery in their cries, but a strange thwarted passion of devotion. Ay, they would rather a thousand times see this fool from the Aude upon the throne of New Rome than all the wise and potent lords of Christendom! Why not? Had he not shown himself the wiser when he refused to join in the taking of Zara?

"Emperor Vidal! Emperor Vidal!"

As the boat bore softly into the black waters the shout swelled to a mighty thunderous bellow. It echoed among the stone walls of Tophana; surged up and was carried on the wind across the Pera; and it greatly troubled the uneasy rest of the lords of the crusade, bishops, and abbots, princes and barons, counts and knights.

The stars shivered with unearthly brilliance. Tiny flecks of light hung on the crests of the oily swell, vanished and reappeared. The Greek sailors sang in a low voice an ancient air come down from the days of Constantine. Peire Vidal was silent, thinking, how sweet, soon to hold Xene in his arms!

At length they were admitted at the gate Xylocircus just as the bells were ringing for lauds. In command was a stranger captain wearing the band of the Deuteron Cohort. He gave a curt command and a squad of guards placed themselves about Peire Vidal.

"You are under arrest," he said to the troubadour, "by order of the Emperor Mourtzouphlos!"

Chapter Thirty

PEIRE VIDAL knew the prison, for he had been there before. From a dungeon of this same fortress, the Diplokionion, he had set free that shadow, Isaac Angelus, and to a similar dungeon he was himself returned. His gaoler was a Scythian who spoke Greek. He observed the prison routine, spoke few words, and paid no attention to his prisoner. For the next day or so Peire Vidal, thinking of his wife and son, was in great anguish of mind.

One day he said to the gaoler, "You are married?"

"If I am, what of it?" answered the Scythian and, setting down the platter of bread and lentils, he went away.

The next day Peire Vidal, though with some difficulty because of his manacles, played on his viol, of which luckily he had not been deprived. The gaoler stayed to listen. "What of it?" he said at length. "If I am married?"

"I am married to a Greek girl whose name is Xene," said the troubadour, "and my son, Andronicus, is just past thirteen years of age."

"You have given him a great name—Andronicus," he pondered.

"I named him after the emperor, Andronicus Comnenus."

"That is strange. My father was at the killing of the Emperor Andronicus. They tortured him cruelly for two days, until he could stand no more of it and died. He was a good emperor. My

374

father fought under Andronicus when he was a general. He was a good general." The man went away, wrinkling his brows.

"They will not let your wife and son come to see you," he said the next day. "You are a political prisoner."

"My wife does not know where I am. She was expecting me to come home."

"That is too bad. Where does she stay?"

"At the house of the logothete, Nicetas."

"He is no longer logothete. He also is in prison."

In the afternoon he returned to the cell, although usually he came only once a day.

"We have sent word to your wife where you are," he said. "She is well taken care of. The clerk, Jacopo, an Italian, is looking after the house. You need not be troubled."

Peire Vidal offered him a coin, but he waved it off. "No, you will need all you have got. Though you may not be able to use it after all, for you will probably die. Still, we shall see. The Latins are getting ready to attack the city. I don't think they can do much, but they are devils. Our emperor Mourtzouphlos is a good general, but he won't get away with being emperor for long. The aristocrats are blocking him every way. And the people don't care who is emperor so long as they are not bothered. These Greeks are a poor lot of fighters. It is the Scythians who are fighters. You will like this fish." He put down a platter of dried fish and stood wrinkling his brows. "I tell you this, the people have cared for none of these emperors since Andronicus Comnenus. It may be he did evil; we all do. But he was a just man. If there was any of his blood and kind here the people would want him to be emperor." Then he went ponderously away.

At dawn Peire Vidal was awakened by a persistent thudding sound, accompanied by a continuous rattling and intermittent crashing. He recognized the machines that were causing the commotion. The thudding came from missiles hurled by ballistae. These were fired pointblank at walls and towers. The crashes were the heavy stones, cast by the mangonels, which whirled in a high trajectory over the ramparts and fell on the roofs of buildings beyond. The rattling was the hail of quarrels, bolts, and metal projectiles flung by the huge espringales mounted on wheels.

375

Then came the answering volleys of the defenders. These he distinguished, by the grinding of the winches as the steel springs were wound tight and the subsequent shriek of the released coils of steel as the projectiles left the machines. Through a tiny aperture in the cell, above shoulder height, he could see the dun gray sky in the direction of the Golden Horn lit by fiery streaks, like falling stars; the Romanians were throwing Greek fire. From the direction of the sounds he judged the crusaders were attacking east of the Blachern quarter, all along the walls facing the Golden Horn. Evidently they had given up hope of success on the land side of the city. The tumult continued throughout the day, dying away at times, only to be renewed with greater vehemence. Toward afternoon a new sound was added to the distant pandemonium—a deep booming that came at regular intervals. "The battering rams going into action, probably against the watergates." The Venetians had brought up a ram to face every gate on the Golden Horn, and in spite of the difficulty of operating these machines from on board ship, were pounding away at the entrances to New Rome, while the men at the rams worked under cover of a barrage of crossbow bolts.

At twilight a sudden hush fell over the city. Bells and chanting from five hundred churches ushered in vespers. The prisoner wondered whether the Latins had secured a foothold on the walls or if they now held part of the city. He also wondered vaguely why he and Nicetas had been arrested. Would he be accused of being a Latin spy, of attempting to open treacherous communication with the foe? That, at least, could easily be disproved, unless he were tried in the summary fashion of war-time. He felt distressed about Nicetas, for apparently his presence in the logothete's house had brought trouble to the old man. Perhaps, had he resolutely ordered the death of that corrupt fragment, Isaac, the city would have been spared this further carnival of death. "If the lover of justice and mercy desires to exercise those virtues," says Peire Cardinal in his poetic treatise *On the Ideal State*, "he is welcome to the hermit's cell."

The attack fell on a Friday and the two days following were ones of uninterrupted calm. The Scythian went about his few duties as usual, reporting the whole onslaught in a single sentence:

376

"They came at us hard, but we beat them off!" Later he said, "The Latins have drawn back into the Pera, like wolves when you kill a few of them; but they will be back. They are just licking their wounds!" On Sunday night, when the bells were ringing in the hour of complines, the gaoler came into the cell carrying the key that unlocked Peire Vidal's manacles and foot-chains. Behind him in the corridor the shadows of a file of soldiers loomed grotesquely.

"Gentleman-singer," he said as he fumbled at the chains, "you have seen men die in battle. It is harder to be in a room where they are about to condemn you. Is there anything I can do for you?"

"Yes," said Peire Vidal, feeling suddenly sick at his stomach, "my little instrument here. If I do not return, I want my son to have it. And you will send a message to my wife Xene that I had no fear, and looked like a brave man."

"She shall know all about it," said the man. He did not look at Peire Vidal, who had turned a pasty color and was rubbing his hands across his lips. "Put this in your mouth, my friend," said the gaoler, pressing a small shrunken object into the troubadour's clammy palm. Peire Vidal put it in his mouth and bit into it, tasting the tartness of a dried lime. His legs felt so uncertain that he was glad when the gaoler took his arm to lead him to the door. A lieutenant wearing the band of the Deuteron Cohort gave a curt command. Peire Vidal's heavy limbs moved reluctantly as the squad set out on the brief march to the imperial palace. Troops everywhere. Greek cohorts in their simple uniforms, but no foreign mercenaries. Quiet, watchful, determined, proud of their birth, no longer indifferent. The city quiet and waiting, silhouetted in a thousand shapes of domes, spires, columns, on its seven hills, chanting the *Kyrios eleison* in its five hundred churches. A crescent moon, attended by one star incredibly bright—the ancient symbols of the city itself—hung above the infinite forest of roofs.

The council chamber was filled with officers of the cohorts, stern young men whose plain dress hardly distinguished them from the ranks. The room was hung with the vermilion of Romania, and the banners showed the imperial emblems, the white lion of Byzantium and the eagle of Rome. A larger banner covered

377

the whole wall behind the imperial throne, upon which sat Alexis Ducas, known as the Emperor Mourtzouphlos. Nothing but the vermilion buskins and the diadem marked him out from the other officers; nothing, save the immobile countenance carved in stern, adamantine lines; such a face, perhaps, had the Senator Marcianus, who drove back Attila and became emperor; or Belisarius and Nares, in the time of Justinian; or the rebel, Leo the Isaurian, who stopped the Saracens, or others lesser known—Romanian generals and emperors of fortitude in times of disaster. Rome on the Tiber had suffered death and had not yet attained transfiguration; Rome on the Bosporus had never yet been conquered.

The accused, of which there were about a dozen, sat together on a single long bench below and to the left of the throne. All but two or three Peire Vidal recognized as members of the Council: Nicetas in his white dalmatic; the Pisan merchant, Buonardo Spazio, unkempt now and ill-clad, looking as though he had been manhandled by the guards; and the ardent young Greeks of the council, sons of merchants and minor officials; and, at the end of the line, in the unadorned sticharion of a private citizen, immaculately neat, the dandy, Theodore Lascaris. As Peire Vidal took his place among them, the latter shot one quick ironic smile in his direction; it was curiously heartening, and the troubadour felt better. He felt less as though he were about to vomit.

At the left of the throne, below it, was a small cluster of men whose legal bearing indicated that they were from the imperial courts of law, the younger and more zealous practitioners of that great institution. In their midst stood the priest Porphyros, and Peire Vidal, in a flash of understanding, recognized their betrayer and accuser.

The emperor, without formalities or preliminaries, rose and said, "You men have been accused and judged guilty of conspiracy against the empire of Romania. You have been accused and judged guilty of an attempt against the life of its emperor, myself. You have been accused and judged guilty of treacherously inviting the Latins to take possession of the city of New Rome. The evidence is all in my hands. The sentence is, death!"

At the sound of this word several of the accused men stiffened; a young Greek drew in his breath sharply; but neither Nicetas nor

378

Buonardo Spazio gave a sign, and Theodore Lascaris continued to smile. The emperor went on gravely, "We have neither the time nor patience to enter into the proceedings of a trial. The city and the empire are in extreme danger. You have conspired to raise up amongst us a false emperor, the son of a Latin who is nothing more than a common singer. This man is with you. I do not desire to be wholly unjust. I do not know whether he is merely your tool and victim, or whether he induced you to commit the crimes I have mentioned. If he is an innocent instrument of your outrageous ambitions, he will be delivered into the keeping of the Latins, to be judged as they see fit; if he is a ring-leader in your conspiracy, of course he must die with you. Because I am still uncertain in my own mind in regard to this matter, I desire to hear what you have to say, and I will then make my decision according to my best judgment, may God and all the archangels bear witness!"

The council chamber at the conclusion of the indictment remained so quiet that the dying chant from the church of the Ayasma of Saint Mary in Blachernae could be distinctly heard.

Then Theodore Lascaris rose and spoke. "Emperor," he said, "our candidate for the throne, Peire Vidal's son, Andronicus, was denied the right to that office by his father. I ask the priest, Porphyros, who was present at the meeting when the decision was made, to affirm the truth of my statement."

The emperor turned his head. "Porphyros, stand forth!" The lawyers drew away, leaving him alone. "Make the sign of the Holy Cross and affirm or deny what was just asserted by the former captain-general, Lascaris!" The emperor's deepset eyes bored into those of the priest.

Porphyros, with trembling hands, made the sign. "It is true," he stammered, "but they have not ceased to think of him as the true emperor!"

"We are not concerned with their thoughts," said the emperor harshly.

"Pardon, my emperor!" It was a lawyer. He elbowed his way to the front. "In the official testimony it is stated that this man, Vidal, was acclaimed emperor as late as the evening on which he

379

was taken into custody, and by the crusaders themselves!" The officers of the court stirred.

"Where did this occur?"

"In the Tophana quarter, below the Pera, between the hours of matins and lauds. The information was given to us by our courier and agent, Manuel the Thracian."

"By what means did this Vidal secure permission to leave the city and cross to the camp of the crusaders?"

"I gave that permission, emperor!" said Theodore Lascaris promptly, and before he could be interrupted, he went on, "I gave him a pass to the captain of the gate Xylocircus, who was of my own cohort. I gave him permission because he desired to go and sing for the soldiers of his own race, who had sent a messenger into the city for that purpose. Monsignor Vidal came to me in the company of this man, a common soldier of the retinue of the doge, and I said that it would be dangerous both for himself and for me, but that I could see no harm in his singing for the soldiers of the Pera. Songs never betrayed a cause—as praying has done!" He stared contemptuously at Porphyros. The informer kept his gaze fixed on a vermilion banner draped from the ceiling.

"If it is as you say," said the emperor knitting his thick eyebrows, "he went to sing for them, why did they hail him emperor?"

"As to that——" began Theodore Lascaris.

"Because they love him!" It came from Buonardo Spazio, riven out of him, almost like a groan. "They love him, and they do not love their masters!"

Again that stillness, broken by the emperor.

"But why," he persisted grimly, "did they dare to name him emperor?"

The merchant jerked himself up on his stout unsteady legs. His flabby face was very red, his voice shook with the hysteria of anger. "Ask him!" he shrilled, pointing a finger at the priest. "Ask him why, for twelve years, ten years—I don't know—he was chaplain to the troubadour, Peire Vidal—why he was the tutor of his son, Andronicus—why he joined with us willingly in the proposal to defend the rights of the grandson of Andronicus Comnenus——"

380

"So," said the steely voice of the emperor, "you admit that this Peire Vidal did lay pretensions to the throne as long ago as ten or twelve years; that he is, indeed, no scapegoat, but the instigator of this series of crimes against the empire!"

The merchant sank down, rubbing his hand across his forehead, as one who is dazed by a blow. Nicetas had risen. He was sustained by a young Greek on either side. His voice could scarcely be heard, the voice of an old and broken man.

"Emperor, you have said you desired to dispense justice. You have called on God and the blessed archangels to be your witnesses. You have refused us a legal trial because of the imminent danger of the city. In all these things you have exercised your right, and we grant that the sentence you have pronounced is also your right to give. But as men who stand in the face of death we have the right to be heard. If our voices are not heard now, they shall be heard in heaven, before that Judge of us all." He paused. The emperor made no motion to stop him. "You are an able general. You have saved the city of New Rome. I believe you will save the empire. But the truth must be made known. This man whom you have called a false claimant for his son, is the father of the grandson of Andronicus Comnenus. As the Grand Logothete I examined the evidence and was convinced. There is a document which confirms my belief. It is in the possession of Buonardo Spazio." His voice died in a whisper.

"Let us see that document."

The emperor might been asking for a report from one of his officers. The merchant plucked at his dalmatic. His fingers fumbled clumsily, then he drew from his breast a roll of parchment, yellowing, crumbling at the edges. He gave it to an officer, and it was passed to the emperor who broke the seal, glanced at the deposition, and handed it to a lawyer. "It is in the Provençal tongue, emperor," said the lawyer. "I cannot understand it." After some delay, an interpreter was found who could read the *langue d'Oc*.

"To all Christian men, greeting! And be it known, that there appeared before me the knight of Belgueil, Peire Vidal, troubadour . . ." The scribe stumbled over some of the words and his voice was monotonous. ". . . and therefore, I declare, before

God, that the Princess Xene is, by her right of inheritance, empress of New Rome, and that the child of her womb, Andronicus Vidal, is the rightful heir to the throne . . . under the sign and seal of Raimon, count of Toulouse and marquis of Provence."

"Give me the document!"

The interpreter handed the roll of parchment to the emperor, who took it, tearing it across, then turned it about and tore it again and, dropping the pieces on the floor of the dais, placed his vermilion buskin upon them.

"There have been pretenders with better witnesses than a count and marquis," said the emperor. "Is there any reason why this Vidal and his son should not die together?"

The logothete was still standing. "Yes, general," he said. Peire Vidal noticed with a start that he addressed the emperor as general—strange old man! "There is a reason. When Monsignor Vidal refused the crown to his son, the deposed emperor, Isaac Angelus, was in danger of his life. It was Peire Vidal who secured his release from the dungeon in the Diplokionion."

"He set loose a murderer to become emperor again!" Mourtzouphlos snarled. It was the first time he had shown the slightest emotion.

"That murderer, general, had caused the death by torture of the grandsire of Peire Vidal's son. Yet Peire Vidal gave him his liberty! The son of Isaac Angelus, the young Alexis, had cruelly misused Andronicus, the son of Peire Vidal, yet Peire Vidal allowed him to share the throne with his father! When you were an officer of the bodyguard of Andronicus Comnenus and shared his campaigns with him, I believe you pledged your loyalty and devotion to him and to his cause. I know that you tried to kill yourself upon learning of his death——"

"Stop!" cried the emperor furiously. "I will hear no more of this!" He raised his hand, as though about to give an order to the guards, then slowly lowered it. "What further evidence have you that Andronicus is of the blood of the Comneni?" he asked slowly.

Peire Vidal stood up. He took from his finger the ring that had been given to him by Adélasie des Baux, and held it up. "This is the ring of Andronicus Comneus. It was given to me. But my wife, the Princess Xene, has a similar one, given her by her father, the emperor."

"The best evidence, general," said the logothete, "is to be found in the Princess Xene and in her son. She wears the very features and is of the build of her mother, the Empress Theodora, known to us as Xene; and her son, Andronicus, is the image of his grandsire. More than that, general—" his voice was persuasive yet inexorable—"more than that, all the details of the early life of the Princess Xene, and the circumstance of her secret removal to Cyprus as a child are well known to the renegade priest, Porphyros! God forgive him for his change of heart and treachery!"

"Is this true?" asked the emperor. Porphyros was still staring at the imperial banner overhead. He lowered his eyes unwillingly to the level of Mourtzouphlos. He was shuddering, one hand plucking convulsively at his orarion. Suddenly he drew something bright from its folds and plunged it into his breast. There was a stir among the lawyers, several nearest him grabbing at his arms. Porphyros stood balancing uneasily for a moment, then crumpled into a white heap among the legs of the advocates. They pulled him back, out of sight of the emperor.

The emperor sat down and Nicetas and Peire Vidal resumed their places on the bench. There was audible only the shuffling of feet as court attendants carried out the body of the informer. Mourtzouphlos turned his impassive gaze toward Theodore Lascaris.

The face of Mourtzouphlos, which up to that moment had remained immobile as one of the bronze busts of the early emperors, now, like a mighty frozen river breaking its glacial calm, expressed an agitation that twisted the hard line of his lips and contorted the steady brows of the soldier into a glare, as of malicious ferocity. The truth was, however, that the former general of Andronicus Comnenus was suddenly smitten by a vision of his master's death under torture; and he recalled, unwillingly, his oath of fealty to the imperial line:

"To the Most High Emperor of Romania, and to all his kith and kin, insofar as they obey the constituted laws, and to all his heirs and assigns, as they touch the perpetual well-being of the Empire, I, Alexis Ducas, pledge my blood and my life, my strength and my soul to fulfill my duty, as soldier and servant of the Empire, so help me Almighty God and all the Saints of Heaven!"

Before him—he knew it in his heart, on the word of the venerable logothete—stood the Latin father of the heir to the Greek throne, the young Andronicus. And as the general stared fiercely at the troubadour whose power—whatever it was—was something different from his own, and yet potent in its way, hatred of an alien race was mingled with respect for the living man before him, who had come across the great sea seeking justice, and had risked his life for a song.

A swift decision was registered on the dictator's iron countenance.

"Officers of the legions and cohorts of the empire," he said, "I am now of the conviction that the youth known as Andronicus Vidal has true and valid claims to the throne of Romania." He paused, his heavy eyebrows lowered in one single black furry line. "When I assumed the diadem and imperial buskins I did so for the good of the empire. If I resign them, it will only be for what I think is the good of the empire. Draw your swords—all of you —and swear, by saints Bacchus and Sergius and by the Holy Mary of Blachernae, that you, too, will follow only the good of the empire!"

A hundred blades flashed in the air and turned in the quick imperial salute, the salute of the Pretorians, dissolved by Constantine, but whose military customs still survived.

"We swear!" they cried in unison.

"I propose," continued the emperor, "to salute the grandson of Andronicus Comnenus as emperor of Romania, to assume the office of regent of the empire during the years of his minority, and to yield the government of it to him at the proper time. But there are conditions." His face grew harder and sterner. "This prince, Andronicus, must be raised as a Greek among Greeks. He must know nothing but the Greek way of life, speak nothing but our language, conform absolutely to our faith, and above all, forget his Latin heritage!" His voice took on the passion of the fanatic. "He must come to hate the Latins and all their works, their false doctrines and their barbarous manners, and he must forever keep them from soiling the lands of the empire with their swinish presence! He shall be known as Andronicus Constantine the First!"

Again he paused, fixing his eyes on Peire Vidal. "As for you, sir, you are permitted to remain within the borders of the empire on one condition—that you become a true Greek. You must give up your son entirely to the disposition of my counselors and myself, to train him as we see fit. You will receive a post befitting your position as father of the future emperor, but you will be known as Peter Constantine. That profession of song which you have honored with your achievements is not for the father of an emperor. If you still choose to follow it, you may do so—in perpetual exile from Romania!"

Peire Vidal's heart leaped into his throat. He a Greek—Peter Constantine! Petty court official. Committed to the customs of this strange land; to its multitudinous ceremonies of church and state; to its life of intricate convention, to its rigidity of thought and custom. Or . . . eternal separation. Never again to hold Andronicus against his breast. Never again to lie close to the sweet body of his wife. To be silent and dumb, or to be alone, in exile.

He glanced at his comrades on the bench. They did not look at him, for they knew their fate was in his answer.

"Do you accept these conditions?"

"I accept them, in their entirety!"

The guard of honor, composed of officers of the cohorts, accompanied Peire Vidal and Theodore Lascaris on their short journey in an imperial litter to the house of the logothete. The two friends were silent; it seemed there was nothing to be said. They were to bring the Princess Xene and her son back to the Blachern palace for the ceremony of salutation. As they neared the house Theodore Lascaris broke the silence with, "When it is over we must despatch Manuel the Thracian to the Pera, to spread the news among the soldiers. If I guess right, there will not be a man-at-arms among them who will cross the Golden Horn to fight against us, and a goodly number of the knights will follow their example. They are on the verge of open revolt now. I wish to God they'd force the doge and his scoundrels to take to the ships! . . . You are not happy, Monsignor Vidal?"

"No," said the troubadour.

"That is to be expected. Elevation is not without grief."

When they reached the house in the humble little street, two of the officers entered with them. As they opened the door softly, they heard no sound. "They are sleeping," said Peire Vidal. A single candle was burning in the lower chamber, almost guttered out. The pallets of Jacopo and his sister were empty. "If they are asleep, I will wake them. They are probably all together upstairs." Peire Vidal began softly to mount the stairway. They heard his steps overhead, and then silence came, a strange pervasive silence.

Then there was a cry or shout. It seemed to come from below them.

"What is that?" said one of the officers.

Again the cry.

"It is someone in a chamber underneath," said the other officer. "But there seems to be no stairway." He began looking about the room. "Here is a trapdoor." He bent down, the ring of the door clicked; its hinge rasped as he threw it back. A face, startled and bloodstained, raised up out of the dark hole. It was Jacopo.

"Oh!" he cried. "Bless the saints that you have come!" He clambered out, then stooped over and pulled the child Beatrice up out of the darkness. There were traces of tears on her cheeks. They stood blinking at the torches. "Sirs, you have come at the right time. Within an hour there was——" He glanced quickly about the room. "I do not know what they have taken, for we have little enough. A band of robbers, sirs! They forced their way in. When the first one knocked, I thought it was a beggar. Then the others pushed in. They hit me on the head." He felt his forehead, where a cut showed, clotted with blood. "Disarmed me, and thrust us both into that little black hole. We could scarce breathe! I fear they may have frightened the signora and her son above. I had better go up and see."

"I will go with you," said Theodore Lascaris, whose face had gone white. He whispered to one of the officers and the latter went to the door. "Go with this soldier, my child," he said gently to Beatrice. The other officer took her by the hand and led her into the little chamber of the logothete, screened off by the arras. Then Theodore Lascaris and his fellow officer mounted the stairs.

By the feeble light of a taper they saw Peire Vidal standing in the center of the room. His huge bearish head was sunk between

386

his massive shoulders and his face wore a vacant expression. At his feet lay the young Andronicus, sprawled out, face down, as though sleeping, a child's sleep. One hand held his naked sword, that light and slender blade of steel, and his fingers were still gripped tightly about the pommel. His tunic showed a great splotch of dark red. The red had spread out in a thickening pool, and the boy's silky hair touched one edge of it. A dagger, the misericorde of Jacopo, lay close by.

Across the pallet lay a white bundle, limp arms, a single dark strand of hair. She had been strangled.

The room was in violent disorder. There had been a struggle.

Theodore Lascaris saw a small bright object in a corner. He went over and picked it up. It was a gold ducat, bearing the image of the doge, Enrico Dandolo.

"Khasis is well paid," he muttered.

They laid them side by side on the bed of the emperors of Romania in the Blachern palace. Mourtzouphlos came and took the diadem from his own head and placed it on the silken pillow embroidered with the eagle of Rome. He removed the imperial buskins and placed them at the feet of the Emperor Andronicus Constantine the First. Then all present knelt, while the priest, swinging his censer, murmured, *"Kyrios eleison . . . Kyrios eleison. . . ."*

Mourtzouphlos, when the liturgy was ended, took up the diadem and the buskins again, but his face seemed to have lost some of its resoluteness.

In the darkness before dawn, for it was close to the hour of lauds and the moon had gone down, the little cortège made its way down through the silent streets of the city, hearing and returning the challenges of sentries. As it passed the column of Venus the bells from the five hundred churches tolled the hour of prayer. Soon they reached the cemetery of the Byzantines, where many emperors had been laid with great pomp. There was no pomp now. It was necessary to hurry, for they had received word that the crusaders would attack at dawn.

Chapter Thirty-one

THE crusaders' attack on Friday having failed, principally because of the heightening of the walls by the Romanians, the foot-soldiers began to exhibit alarming symptoms of disaffection. It was necessary for the knights themselves to lead the assault, and when the long day's battle ended with the defences still intact, the soldiers returned to the Pera to grumble and sulk. Unluckily, the following day was spent on short rations, the foraging parties from the back country having arrived with but a meager supply. Men-at-arms everywhere left their encampment in bands, roamed through the Galata and Tophana quarters, and finding little food, broke into the wine shops. By evening they were all in a merry mood, roaring out ribald snatches to holy tunes, and tumbling the draggled jezebels of the camp about till even the hardiest drabs were fain to cry mercy. By midnight the Pera had become a bedlam of carousing.

The next day being the Sabbath, the priests drove the women from the camp before the soldiers had recovered from their stupor and set about the purification of the Pera and the restoration of its morale. All day they preached and exhorted; bishops and abbots labored fervently in the vineyard, crying out that Mourtzouphlos was none other than Judas returned to plague the faithful and deliver them to the Evil One. The men of the cloth testified that the idolatrous Greeks worshiped anti-Christ and consorted with devils; they were gluttons and epicures; they reveled in incontinence and debauchery; they invoked Belial, Sammael, Zamiel, and lesser demons to aid them in defeating the heavenly host; and they were children of Abaddon and Apollyon, holding intercourse with the Powers of Darkness. The final argument was that God would deliver the city into the hands of the Latins because the Greeks had asserted that the Holy Ghost proceeded from the Father only, and because they celebrated the mass with leavened bread.

By the end of the day the soldiers, exhausted by their late debauch and by the ceaseless praying, preaching, and chanting, were in a contrite frame of mind. Then the priests retired, having bestowed their benediction, and the lay orators, knights and barons, took up their work. They spoke briefly and to the point: New Rome must be taken or else they would all starve; and when it was taken, the soldiers would share the booty.

So at dawn of the next day they went into battle with right good will, lean of belly and thirsting for blood, as wolves that come down out of the Thracian fastnesses, scenting the flocks in the sheepfolds.

Enrico Dandolo ordered a change of tactics. On the first day of battle each transport had been assigned to a separate tower of the walls along the Golden Horn, but the limited number of soldiers thus made effective had proved insufficient to obtain a foothold. The doge shortened the line of battle, lashed his transports together in pairs, and held the ursers, carrying mounted knights, in reserve. The gangways at the crosstrees also had been raised higher to meet the level of the ramparts. A north wind and strong tide aided the crusaders. The ships, Pilgrim and Parvis, freighted with armed men and showering the defenders with crossbolts, bore in toward a tower opposite the monastery of Pantepoptis in the Phanar quarter, where the Emperor Mourtzouphlos had established his headquarters. The wide gangways dropped to the parapets with a crash of wood and metal, and the Flemings, brandishing their bright-edged bills, rushed across. Here, for a time, the advance was held up by the Varangian guard, headed by a madman.

He wore nondescript armor and wielded a huge double-bitted battle-axe, a weapon that he swung with the ease of a reaper swinging a scythe. So great was this man's strength and so irresistible the force of his blows, he clove through hauberks and gambesons, lopped off arms and removed heads, like the very image of Death itself. At the same time he kept up a sort of brutish, inhuman bellowing, as terrifying as the destruction he caused. The fire of the arbalestiers was finally concentrated at this point and a well-aimed bolt took him a glancing blow in the forehead. By a dispensation, such as often attends those crazed by God, he tumbled from the parapet, falling on its inner side among a heap of dead men-at-arms, and the rush of the attackers passed him by.

In quick succession four towers were captured and three of the water-gates were battered in. The ursers in the offing drove in under lashing oars, the bulwarks opened, and knights on horseback charged across lowered gangplanks. Meanwhile the crusaders were scaling the walls and pouring over them in an increasing stream of men and steel. A division of knights made its way through the quarter toward the emperor's tent, overbearing the light-armed cohorts by their sheer weight of horse and armor. Mourtzouphlos, who had shown greater uncertainty of mind than at any time before, tried vainly to rally his guards but they, experiencing the crushing impact of cavalry for the first time, gave way and fled. He was carried with them as far as the palace of Porphyrogenitus.

The crusaders fired the quarter to the east, along the water front. Soon all was in flames from the monastery of Everyetis to the Droungarios quarter and, as the historian Villehardouin relates with satisfaction, "In three days there were burned more buildings than in all of the three greatest cities of France." Then, since it was late, the crusaders called a halt for that day, Bonifaz, Marquis of Montferrat, occupying the vermilion tent of the emperor. He at once sought out Margaret, the widow of Isaac Angelus, and offered her his protection.

The next day the city was draped in the cerecloth of its conflagration. Mourtzouphlos had fled. The crusaders found no opposition save for the desperate rear-guard action of the Hebdomon Cohort, commanded by Theodore Lascaris. They fought to save the remnant of the army and the host of refugees pouring out through the Golden Gate near the Marmora. As the crusaders passed through the city, women, old men, and children, and those who hoped to preserve some of their goods, made the sign of the cross. They hailed Bonifaz with the name of "king" for they had seen him in the company of the young Alexis and believed that he desired to rule them. He led his division to the palace of the Bucoleon, long the imperial residence, and there, after a courtship necessarily brief, took in marriage the aging widow, Margaret, once empress.

Of what took place in the city of New Rome under its funereal baldachin of smoke one chronicler declares: "Never since the world was created was there so much booty gained in one city. Each man took the house which pleased him, and there were enough for all. Those who were poor found themselves suddenly rich. There was captured an immense supply of gold and silver, of plate and precious stones, of satins and of silk and of furs and of every kind of wealth ever found upon earth. The lust of the army spared neither maiden nor the virgin dedicated to God." The nuns of the Ayasma of the Sleep of Saint Mary were violated before the altar of that church; and so were those of the Ayasma of Saint Mary in Blachernae; and of the Ayasma of Saint Therapos; the daughters of the Greeks and their children were violated in their homes and on the streets. The crusaders jerked the robes of the Greek priests from their backs and piled these rich vestments on their horses, and they cut off priestly beards with swords dedicated to Christ. A knight bore on the end of his lance something small, white, dangling; that morning it had sucked its mother's breasts. "Slaughter was without end and without measure," says Nicetas in his account of those three days.

There was much treasure of various sorts in the churches, in part precious and sacred objects, and in part ancient works of art. Icons were torn from the screens and broken. Chalices were stripped of their precious stones and used for wine flagons. Altar cloths and screens of cloth of gold, richly embroidered and bejeweled, were hacked to pieces or borne away in bundles on the backs of yelling varlets. The altars of Hagia Sophia were broken up to get precious metals and jewels and stuffs of which they were made. The vandals had to take horses and mules into these churches, for human hands could not hold all they helped themselves to. On the patriarchal dais of the Hagia Sophia a prostitute

391

danced and sang ribald songs for the soldiery, and in the emperor's chair a naked slut fornicated with a foot-sergeant.

Many of the statues and works of art were of bronze and some were ornamented with gold and silver. These they melted down in the furnaces they had set going. They melted the great statue of Juno; and that of Paris and Venus, a piece of rare workmanship; the Hercules of Lysippus; the figures of Romulus and Remus and the Wolf, brought long ago from Rome; and the huge statue of the Virgin, whose eyes were jewels and whose robe was of silver and gold. And they melted down the bronze statue of Helen of Troy that had pleased the eyes of men for many ages. The statues of marble were broken up, for they savored of paganism and idolatry. And thus they broke to pieces the statue of Aphrodite. The four great bronze horses, which the Emperor Theodosius had brought from Chios and had set up in the hippodrome, went to adorn the church of Saint Mark at Venice; and many of the writings of the ancients and the records and tomes of the law courts and libraries went with them (though many, too, were burned lest they contaminate the true believers); for the Venetians desired to improve themselves in respect to culture and civilization.

The distribution of the spoils, collected in three of the largest churches, was on a fair and equitable basis. The Venetians, after they had been paid the balance of what was due them, and the crusaders, each took half. Two foot-sergeants were allowed, in the soldiers' moiety, as much as one horse-sergeant, and two horse-sergeants as much as one knight. To the lords and barons went the territories and domains and provinces and islands of the empire of Romania.

At length the leaders of the crusade wearied of lawlessness, and they hung one knight for refusing to put his private plunder in with the public store.

Though Bonifaz, Marquis of Montferrat, known as the Giant, was conceded by all to have the most imperial presence among the candidates and though his claim through Margaret to the throne of Romania was acknowledged, he did not receive the vote of the electors. They decided, after a long and heated session, that Baldwin, count of Flanders, an amiable and ingratiating young man of good connections, would be more likely to secure absolution from Innocent the Third for the error of the crusading army in taking a Christian city on the way to the Holy Land. Baldwin, therefore, became the first Latin emperor of New Rome. Bonifaz, following a trade with the doge, got the kingdom of Thessalonica and so received a crown, howbeit a minor one, for his efforts.

Raimbaut of Vacqueiras became a baron. Quesnes de Béthune was rewarded with a principality and high offices in the empire, and other troubadours were recompensed according to their merits.

On the third day refugees were still pouring through the Golden Gate, past its seven great flanking towers of marble, into the open country beyond. It was a dismal throng. These were mostly the very poor who had lingered in their wretched dwellings until fire and sword drove them forth; having little, they were the more attached to their slender possessions, and they carried on their backs some crude piece of household furniture or some useless bit of cheap finery as well as all their icons, though these last had been impotent to save them from calamity.

From the multitude there came a monotonous chanting, *"Kyrios eleison . . . Kyrios eleison . . ."* mingled with sobbing and lamentation, and an occasional shriek as some hysterical woman cast herself upon the road and beat her forehead, remembering her husband or her child. In the endless procession was a small group of eight or nine persons, clad like the rest in the shabbiest garments and wearing rough skins thrown about them. Their faces were smeared with filth and hidden by folds of dark cloth. In the center of this group walked several women, and on the outside tramped the men, all looking neither to right nor left, as though fearful of spying eyes. They had reason to be afraid, for they were of the family of Nicetas, Buonardo Spazio, and another Pisan merchant. Many of their compatriots at that very moment were being tortured to reveal hidden treasures that may or may not have existed. Jacopo and his sister and the madman, Peire Vidal, were of this company.

A band of mounted men-at-arms, following a knight and his

two squires, had gone on a plundering foray to the church of the Holy Apostles but finding it already occupied by the bishop of Beauvais and his men, who were engaged in rifling it of holy relics, they continued in the direction of the Golden Gate, hoping to pluck something of value from the fleeing host; the spectacle of the tattered emigrants, however, was hardly encouraging to their hopes and, disgruntled, they were about to wheel and gallop off when the knight spied among them the child Beatrice. Hearing the clatter of hoofbeats, she had looked up, startled, and the knight saw that in spite of the stains on her cheek she was young and fair. He stared, grinning. Then with an oath he spurred his destrier into their midst and, bending out of his stirrups, seized her about the waist with one mail-clad arm and dragged her across his saddle. Even as she shrieked he had reined his charger back on its haunches and was forcing the animal through the dense throng.

Jacopo leaped and caught the bridle. A squire whipped his blade out and thrust it straight and true into the young man's breast. Jacopo's face was suddenly contorted in a hideous grimace, but the dead hands kept their grip. The great horse reared and plunged; Beatrice slipped from the knight's hand and fell beneath the churning hoofs. One of the company drew her out from under the charger, but she never again opened her eyes.

Then a curious thing happened, for the madman, like some untamed beast, launched through the air, laid his huge arms about the knight, and dragged him from the saddle before the squires could come to his succor. The destrier, suddenly released, uttered a loud snort and plunged against the horses of the squires, entangling them in its harness. The knight lay on the ground, the hands of the madman about his throat. They were hands like those of a great ape, and the shoulders bent above him were knotted in bands of sinew steely in strength. These hands were wont to guide the bow of that delicate instrument, the viol, but they had also been used to wielding a sword. They were capable hands. They tightened about the knight's gorget. When the men-at-arms pulled him off, the knight lay still.

The squires had extricated themselves. They looked at their lord, and one of them said, "You will be hanged, drawn, and

394

quartered for this!" But Peire Vidal said nothing, and his expression was vacant.

"He is a madman!" cried another. "The madman—Peire Vidal!"

"Peire Vidal," said a man-at-arms, peering into the troubadour's face. "Ay, it is Peire Vidal, who makes songs. And he is indeed mad! God protects madmen. We must not touch him, comrades!"

They bundled the body of the knight on the charger and led it away.

The procession continued. Two of the men carried Jacopo. Peire Vidal bore in his arms what had been the child Beatrice. They went slowly through the Golden Gate toward Silivria.

Chapter Thirty-two

THE city of Arles, beloved of emperors, was celebrating the *fête de l'âne,* the Feast of Fools. Though this annual festival had been banned by a decretal of Innocent the Third for its misprision of sacred things, and though it gave no end of trouble to the authorities in the way of licence and riot, it was too deeply grafted in the custom of the populace to be wholly dispensed with. The bishop of Arles, therefore, closed his eyes to the strange activities of the lesser clergy on the first day of April. On this day the vicious and malodorous citizens of the great walled Arena, once devoted to the worship of Venus, swarmed from their dens and burrows and overran the city while the respectable burghers and their families stayed within doors. The shopkeepers closed and barred their places of business, and the provost guard remained watchfully posted in all the streets adjacent to the ceremonies.

A high moment of the festival was the investiture of the *dominus festi,* who at Arles was known as the Pope-Fool. The cardinals of the Papi-Fol had been chosen from among the most sportive of the vicars of St. Trophime, and these in turn had announced their choice of pope of misrule. At the convent of Saint-Césaire, by permission of the amiable abbess who had, as was her wont, bestowed largesse and provided roast capons and other delicacies for the revelers, the Maîtrise des Fous—or, as one would say, the

Queen of Fools—had been installed, and there she received the candidate for the satanic papacy, who came riding on an ass, gaily trapped, and accompanied with bells and music. Together they returned to the church of St. Trophime, where a scaffold had been erected near the portico, and this was all hung with myrtle, paper poppies, and the black-and-white banners of the Papi-Fol, emblazoned with grinning skulls.

The candidate was led to the foot of the scaffold and induced, though with seeming reluctance, to mount its rickety steps. Upon the top of the platform was a mock throne, draped in cerecloth, and here he took his place, while a mock cardinal ascended, dressed in black and with the figure of a skeleton painted on his vestment; he carried a great pair of shears, a pail of water, and a sharp razor blade. The candidate's head was then bared, and he was shaven clean to the skull, so that every knob and protuberance shone clearly to the delighted spectators. When the shaving had been completed to the satisfaction of the cardinal, the latter raised the pail of dirty water and overturned it suddenly upon the white skull of the candidate, crying loudly, "O fool, in the name of Beelzebub, and of all vile and unholy things, and by the grace of the Powers of Darkness, Belial, Sammael, and Apollyon, I baptize thee—Tityrus, Papi-Fol!"

And the multitude cried aloud, "Tityrus! Papi-Fol!"

Then the other cardinals mounted the platform, and as they vested him in full pontifical garments and symbols they sang:

> Haec est clara dies, clararum clara dierum,
> haec est festa dies, festarum festa dierum,
> nobile nobilium rutilans diadema dierum!

Then two or three voices in high falsetto:

> Salve festa dies, toto venerabilis aevo,
> qua Deus est ortus virginis ex utero!

Having vested him in cope, miter, pectoral cross, gloves, and crozier of sorts, the preceptor stultorum, or Master of Fools, gabbled, "Pax Domini sit semper vobiscum semper sit Domini pax

397

Domini sit semper vobiscum sit Domini pax" until he was out of breath. The cardinals who, meanwhile, had been gesticulating lasciviously from the platform, now began to sing:

> *Gregis pastor Tityrus,*
> *asinorum dominus,*
> *noster est episcopus*

The vast stinking multitude took up the chorus:

> *Eia, eia, eia,*
> *vocant nos ad gaudia*
> *Tityri cibaria!*

And again the cardinals, alternating with the chorus:

> *Ad honorem Tityri,*
> *festum colant baculi*
> *satrapae et asini*

> *Applaudamus Tityro*
> *cum melodis organo,*
> *cum chordis et tympano*

> *Veneremur Tityrum,*
> *qui nos propter baculum*
> *invitat ad epulum. . . .*

Thereupon the Pope-Fool, accompanied by the Queen of Fools, was escorted down from the scaffold and once more set upon the ass, but this time riding with his face to its tail; and the cavalcade and multitude, with music and dumb show, and prancing and capering, and singing of bawdy snatches, and such abominable inventions as pleased their fancy, went in a procession through the city of Arles, beloved of emperors; the whole of this part of the performance representing, in atrocious travesty, the Flight into Egypt.

398

Among the onlookers at the Feast of Fools was a group of gentry on horseback, whose presence gave no little concern to the manful captain of the provost's guard. Though he was a soldier not lacking in courage on the field of battle, this officer had a dread of civil riot that amounted to terror. And he well knew that the temper of the rabble from the Arena was not complaisant towards gentles on the day the *questeaux* ruled the city. He had, therefore, flung a cordon of his trusty pikemen about the well-dressed company just before the head of the procession reached the square. It was well he did so, for the rout that burst into view had been mightily refreshed at the taverns, and were in a dangerously frolicsome mood.

"It is a lewd spectacle and should not be permitted, but it has been traditional for a thousand years or more, and we dare not interfere with the ways of the people. You can give them a dozen kings in succession, but the saints protect you if you touch their holidays!" It was the canon, Poncius de Barcia of Arles, addressing his guests, visitors to the city.

"It is better, perhaps, my dear canon," said the knight of St. Gilles, "that they follow their customs, even though they be somewhat robustious, than that they entertain such vile heresies as the Albigensians preach!"

"True," said the canon, "and I believe the heretics will soon learn to their discomfiture that Rome is not to be defied."

The Papi-Fol and the Maîtrise des Fous were nearing the place where the visitors, leaning forward from their horses, were endeavoring to get a better view above the shoulders of the stalwart guardsmen. The procession advanced slowly, for its members were weaving from side to side in an uncouth dance, tossing faggots before the ambling beasts and singing,

Eia, eia, eia,
vocant nos ad gaudia
Tityri cibaria!

"Who is this Tityr whom they celebrate?" inquired the marquis of Sorgues, Antoine Beaujeu.

"It is the name they have given their Papi-Fol for the day. They always choose fanciful appellations. His real name is Peire Vidal, and he is a jongleur of the Arena."

"Not Peire Vidal the troubadour!" exclaimed the marquis.

"No longer a troubadour, monsenher. He has been deprived, rightfully, of his honors and dignities, and now he is a jongleur and consorts with the lowest in the Arena. As you see, he is also half-witted."

Indeed, as the Papi-Fol Tityrus passed through the crowd on his ass, he turned his head from side to side, mechanically as though it were fixed to a pole, and a grin spread from cheek to cheek; such a grin as small boys make when they place their fingers in the corners of their mouths and draw them apart. He looked the fool in every way.

"I cannot believe it!" said Antoine Beaujeu. "I knew that man many long years ago; we went on a journey together, from Béziers to Nismes. He was then a jongleur, but of a gay and inquisitive mind, though he was at the time recovering from a wound in the tongue he had got at Castle Bargarde. Some act of jealousy, and quite unjustified!"

"Ha!" said the knight of St. Gilles with acerbity, "no doubt he professes his innocence, but I know better, for I was at Bargarde at the time. It is common knowledge that the fellow was always a loose-lived and a dissolute knave, and that he got his goods from the wives he seduced!" Indeed, the dolorous knight of St. Gilles had spent much of his life wondering precisely at what time his wife, Yolanz, had been seduced by Peire Vidal.

"Of that I am not informed," said the canon politely. "When I knew him he was a melancholy young man, crossed in love, for he had been exiled from Les Baux because of a piece of indiscretion. It was then he inherited a fortune from his father. But it was not loose living lost him his fortune. He went on the holy crusade to New Rome, that nest of infamies—turned renegade, deserted his comrades, and adopted the cursed faith of the Greeks. He fought against his former comrades in arms and was unlucky enough to murder a Christian knight. For a time he disappeared, and it is said he lived with the Saracens in the desert, on locusts and honey. Then he found his way back to Provence. For his many misdeeds he would have been hanged for a murderer and burnt for his apostasy but the intercession of Pedro, king of Aragon, saved his life. The young king appealed to Archbishop Fulk in person, offering with good reason, the man's obvious witlessness, for his whole life has testified to his madness. The good archbishop at length consented to accept the estates of the troubadour in lieu of more serious penalties, and Fulk since then has made the castle of Belgueil his residence. Having neither property nor honor, the troubadour was reduced to the station from which he sprang, but his days of singing are past, and he is no more than a poor sort of mime and mountebank. Peire the king offered Peire the jongleur an asylum in Spain, but the fool would have none of it. He drifted finally to the Arena, where he is maintained by the employment of the creature riding at his side—the most notorious whore of all Arles!"

The chief figures of the procession were now passing before the gentle spectators, among whom was a lady seated upon a palfrey richly caparisoned. She had been listening with a curious expression to the words of the canon. Her companion was a knight in semi-armor. They spoke Italian.

"Who," asked the lady of the canon, Poncius de Barcia, "is the woman on the ass?"

"They call her Beatriz des Arène," he said, "and there is a tale that she is of noble Italian blood—I shall not mention the family—and that when her father and lover were both killed in a great battle in the East, where they possessed wide domains, her husband, an Italian lord, came and secured her in her castle, and took her by force, and that she escaped from him. But she cannot be the lady they say, for that one has been dead these two years. The family of her husband built a tomb for her. And what woman of a noble house would come to Provence to search for a jongleur and a witless mooncalf to boot?"

The Lady Estefania de Berga did not answer. Her gaze was fixed with strange intensity on the Papi-Fol.

"Who indeed!" said the knight of St. Gilles sourly, pushing back his helm. "It's devilish hot for the first of April. Sant Dalmatz, how the rabble stink!"

From lusty throats came the verses of the song, each new one bawdier than the last, while grimy thousands chanted:

Eia, eia, eia,
vocant nos ad gaudia
Tityri cibaria!

The miter which the Papi-Fol wore was of metal, crudely made, so that it dropped down to his ears and was only sustained by them. The effect was ridiculous, giving him much the aspect of his patient ass. On the top of the miter they had stuck an old scarlet bonnet without ribbons, and the pectoral cross he bore was a stout cudgel, with a crosspiece of iron tied to it. It was a heavy implement and because of the heat of the day he was fain to let it sag, but the multitude cried out continually for him to bear it up like a good Pope-Fool, there being a superstition to the effect that if the cross were allowed to drop on this day it would bring bad luck upon the Arena for the year to come. So the Papi-Fol raised the cross from time to time as high as he could, grinning at his cardinals and his followers.

Eia, eia, eia,
vocant nos ad gaudia
Tityri cibaria!

The refrain rose to a vast bestial chorus as the revelers poured through the square, reeling and dancing, fingering the wenches, who gave them blowsy kisses, opening wide their gowns of cheap cisclaton to bare their breasts. And the Maîtrise des Fous, to win their favor for her lord, emulated them in their wantonness, leering prettily upon them, her lips a red gash beneath her falcon nose and straight black brows. Sometimes she held up the naked mannikin she bore in her arms, and made a show of fondling it, which caused them all to scream with laughter.

"Papi-Fol's bastard!" they cried. "The son of Tityr and Beatriz des Arène! He'll live to be emperor! Bastard-emperor, Lord of the Arena!"

Just behind the two asses came two enormous figures, those of a saint and of a witch. The one was a representation of Saint Julian, patron of outcasts and singers, a jolly red countenance with wine-bibber's nose, who held a sort of viol in his limp hands as he turned around and about, blessing woodenly his faithful. Beside the saint swayed Witch Venus, a naked image, of which it were best to give no picture seeing that the drawings and scratchings of men in all times have lewdly conceived her. Such she was, but she turned neither to right nor to left, her great face set proudly and lustfully straight before her as she loomed above the crowd.

The gentle lady on horseback drew sharply at the bridle-rein. She nosed her palfrey through between two guardsmen, who turned their heads, muttering beneath their breath.

"Peire Vidal!" she cried.

Eia, eia, eia,
vocant nos ad gaudia—

"Peire Vidal!"

Her voice shrilled above the universal clamor. He turned his head toward the sound and stared fixedly, still grinning. Plunging golden spurs into her palfrey's side, she drove the animal headlong through the crowd. With a shout of alarm her attendant knight flew after her; and after him, his squires; and after all of them, the provost's guard—a flying wedge that drove straight to the side of the ass bearing the Papi-Fol.

The Lady Estefania de Berga seized him by the arms crying, "Peire Vidal! Come away!"

As he stared at her, his mouth open wide, the Maîtrise des Fous, with a strident oath, lashed the two asses. They started forward; the Lady Estefania held onto him with both her hands, and he slid off the ass; slid off and fell on his face, dropping the cross. Beatriz des Arène screeched—such a horrible sound as only an enraged virago can utter, and, cursing with red-lipped fury, she clutched his garments. The squires, seeing their lady determined to bear this Pope-Fool away, laid hold of him. The rabble, becoming aware that their elected Papi-Fol was being abducted, were in no wise willing to abandon him to the accursed gentles. They flung themselves into the mêlée, clutching his legs and feet, all the while hurling imprecations at the interlopers. So the Papi-Fol was torn this way and that between the two forces, as a carrion is torn between vultures. The breathless and exasperated

403

guardsmen lowered their weapons; the vast multitude closed in menacingly. But the provost had been prepared for such an emergency. On every housetop about the square files of arbalestiers had been posted, and now, at a signal, the sharp-pointed bolts began to shower into the square, laying men and women down helter-skelter. A company of horse-guards in mail debouched from a side street and charged with lances in rest. The crowd broke and fled, leaving figures on the paving stones, that wriggled and squirmed or lay languidly sprawled. Three of the guardsmen were still struggling with the Maîtrise des Fous, whose outcries were those of a soul being given to the flames of purgatory.

The miter had been pressed down by a blow, and as it was pulled off, a bloody circle was left girdling the white skull of the Papi-Fol.

Once again Peire Vidal was "monsenher." Again he wore rich garments, and ate of delicate food, and slept naked between silken sheets, set with jacinths to induce slumber. But he was restless at Turin and did not sleep, so the gentle-hearted Lady Estefania de Berga (who long ago had so briefly loved the troubadour when he left Montferrat, after his first visit, to join Richard) took him to the estate of her lover, the noble Count Blacatz, protector of troubadours. This was at Aups, not far from Marseille, but here also he seemed not at ease; so the three of them went to Malta, whose Count Henri loved good songs. Here he was well provided for in every way, and he appeared to be contented; yet, though he saw and understood everything, he remembered nothing, neither his name nor his art. If someone spoke to him, he would say, "I, Tityr, am here." By degrees he ceased to grin, and even came to smile, though not at jests; rather, at some jape whispered into his ear by the Unseen Ones.

By degrees he learned to make songs: simple, and in a few words, and he could sing them well, for though he had forgotten, his voice remembered. He learned to play upon the lute, but he could never manage the viol.

Chapter Thirty-three

FULK, Archbishop of Toulouse, to His Holiness, Pope Innocent:

"Most Holy Father, in other epistles (for whose lamentable import as they may have troubled your worshipful spirit I beseech pardon) I have related the grievous condition of the Holy Church of Rome in the exercise of its sacred functions in the dioceses of Provence. The growth and spread of the abhorrent and hideous Albigensian heresy throughout this region is not unknown to Your Holiness, as is the history of your mighty efforts, during the past twenty years, to check the inroads of the dread apostasy. Of late it seemed that the zealous ministrations of the vicars of Christ, and in particular, of your excellent and most deserving legate, Peter of Castelnau, in disciplining the Count Raimon of Toulouse, had met with considerable success in turning a stubborn people from diabolical pursuits and false prophets. It is my sad duty to inform Your Holiness that all these persuasions, inducements, and earnest exhortations have been brought to naught through the recent relapse of Count Raimon and of his followers into the schismatic tenets of anti-Christ. Furthermore, many of the kingdoms of Spain, as well as demeisnes contiguous to Provence in France and Italy, reveal the evidence of secret corruption by harboring and entertaining the ministers of Darkness. In all this, I must add, the wily troubadours—though they are scarcely above paganism themselves—have played a conspicuous part by defending the Albigensians in their songs, and by flouting the priests and offices of Rome in scurrilous sirventes. This they do, not out of conviction in heresy (which they hold as of little moment), but from studied insolence toward all external government other than their own base desires.

"Of the evils and outrageous practices among these singers, especially such lewd institutions as the Courts of Love, I have no need to tell Your Holiness. But humbly I inquire of Your Holiness, what it behooves the Church to have labored a thousand years in these fair vineyards, if we are to witness an outright reversion to paganism in the worship of the foul witch, Venus, with whom, by some dreadful and perverted sophistry, they have linked the name of the Blessed Virgin? Knowing the greatness and gentleness of mind of Your Holiness, I hesitate to urge upon you measures of severity beyond those you have seen fit to promulgate; but permit me, Most Holy Father, to instance the results of exercising clemency. The troubadour, Peire Vidal, who, as you know, was once notorious as a defender of the Albigensians, was convicted of certain crimes against common law and the canons of the Church, for which he merited the sentence of death, which thereupon was imposed. This sentence, because of the solicitations of the king of Aragon, was suspended. I, and others of the ecclesiastical court, were persuaded that the said Vidal, disgraced and dishonored before the world, would live to expiate his sins as an outcast; and so, for a brief space, he did. But having been chosen, during the abominable Feast of Fools, as lord of misrule at Arles, he was delivered by certain misguided persons of noble station, the deliverance being accompanied by riot and bloodshed, and now once more he enjoys the esteem and privileges of a knight, on the island of Malta. And his example has inspired other singers again to take up the cause of the Albigensians, to the great peril of the established Church of Christ."

Pope Innocent the Third, his hand shaking slightly, laid the parchment on the lectern. His face was graven with deep lines, lines chiseled in his fine aristocratic features by ceaseless struggles with lords, barons, kings, in a chaotic world. One by one, he had subdued them, or rendered them impotent, bringing them to acknowledge the conception of world-unity in the Church. But he had suffered defeats, too; one of these was the taking of New Rome against his explicit injunction, and the subsequent failure to rescue the Holy Land from infidel domination. And another was the persistence of heresy in Provence.

He turned to Izarn the troubadour.

"It is true. They must not tempt me too far. What was the news you wished to impart, my dear friend?"

Izarn, who, during the reading of the lengthy epistle had worn an expression of strange dismay, seemed loth to speak.

"Most Holy Father," he said at length, "they sent me to tell you, though I scarce have the heart to do it. Oh, Jesu Christus——!"

"Speak, Izarn!"

"Most Holy Father, word has just reached us that your legate, Peter of Castelnau—oh saints in Heaven——!"

"Dead?" the pope's voice trembled; he had loved this austere priest.

"Murdered! In a tavern on the Rhône, near St. Gilles, by a retainer of Count Raimon!"

There was a long silence. Young male voices could be heard distantly chanting. Then the pope, Innocent the Third: "So! . . . God has spoken!"

He groaned.

At length the Church hurled its thunderbolt:

"Since, according to the canonical sanctions of the Holy Fathers, faith must not be kept with him who keeps not faith with God, such must be removed from the communion of the faithful. All who are bound by oath to said Count Raimon of Toulouse, by any fealty, federation, or treaty, ye shall declare absolved by apostolic authority; and it is allowed any

407

catholic saving the right of the suzerain, not only to persecute the same but to occupy and hold his land, since it is fitting that the hands of all should be against him whose hands are against all."

The pope then commanded that a crusade be undertaken for the total extermination of the heretics of Provence; and for whoso should take part in this crusade all indulgences and pardons should be granted; whoso should undertake to fight for Christ against those that dreaded no vice and believed in mystery would be held to be a saint and hero; his family and goods would be under the special protection of the pope; and he need not pay his debts. During the time of the crusade, the crusader, whatever he did, could do no wrong. And this declaration was carried through all Christendom, even to the empire and kingdoms of the Latins in the East that had been Romania.

Baldwin, however, that amiable young man, was no longer emperor, for in the year following his accession he had been taken prisoner by rebel Greeks and Bulgars, and died in captivity at the hands of the Bulgar king. In the same year died Enrico Dandolo, doge of Venice, at the ripe age of ninety-seven, and he was interred with signal pomp and ceremony, having made Venice an island empire and the richest city of the Christian world. And not long after, Bonifaz, king of Thessalonica, and Raimbaut, a prince of the realm, fell fighting in the bloody disaster of Satalia.

Learning that a crusade was forming in the West, Christian knights of the eastern lands hurried home in great numbers. The Holy Land was almost emptied of its ardent defenders since they could get the same indulgences in Provence, and it was a pleasanter place to do battle in; there were neither deserts nor Saracens here, but rich fiefs, bountiful harvests, fair fruits, and fairer women. The priests preached the crusade far and wide, enduring the rigors of the season cheerfully as they exhorted the faithful to take the field against the Albigenses. Multitudes so urged sacrificed themselves to the cause, took leave of their wives and mistresses, forgave their creditors their sin of usury, and enrolled under the banners of the bishops.

At the court of Count Henri of Malta they heard of what was happening in Provence and tried to keep the knowledge of it from Peire Vidal, but he heard of it through the chatter of serving men, and though they set a watch upon him, he escaped by some means; and, by a miracle that only Saint Julian could account for, made his way to the mainland and, blindly and stupidly, calling himself Tityr the jongleur, got to Narbonne and thence to Béziers.

The hosts of the crusade descended the Rhône by Lyons, Valence, Montelimart, and Avignon. At Avignon Simon de Montfort, the captain-general, ordered the consuls to destroy the château of Sorgues, since it was a fief of Toulouse. And the consuls, aided by the dreaded White Companies, did so. To the flames they gave Antoine Beaujeu, his wife, his children, and all his household, sparing not one; and the priests with the crusaders, singing the *Veni Creator,* watched them burn with infinite joy, or in the words of their own chronicler, *cum ingenti gaudio.*

But before the crusaders reached Valence, Count Raimon of Toulouse, overcome at length by terror of their numbers, yielded to his archbishop, Fulk. He consigned to the apostolic notary seven of his principal castles and, a naked penitent, with a cord about his neck, knelt at the portals of St. Gilles, was conducted past the tomb of Peter of Castelnau, received discipline from the archbishop within the church, professed himself a true believer in the Catholic faith, and was then permitted to take the cross and to guide the army against his nephew, Raimon Roger, viscount of Béziers, who had shut himself up in the strong city of Carcassonne. The count went to Valence and led the crusaders to Monpeslier, where the three great hosts met together.

As the crusaders passed from the Rhône, following the ancient Roman road into Provence, by which, ages past, the great armies and beasts from Spain and Africa had advanced toward Rome, they left a mark upon the country. It was mid-June and before them the golden land blossomed in yellow roses, buttercups, eglantine, flowers of the thorny acacia, purple clouds of thyme, and tufts of lavender, wild rosemary, and the joy-flower, flor de gaug. The fields were spread with carpets of grain coming into ear; the flocks showed the increase of mating; the birds still sang. Behind them, as they passed, no flowers bloomed and no birds sang. The fields were wastes; villages were heaps of smoldering rubbish; proud castles, rubble.

And as the host moved on leisurely, taking a month to reach Béziers, that little city, shut within its walls, waited for succor to come from its viscount, Raimon Roger, or from the other puissant nobles of Provence. But all these were closed up within their own walls, for it was always the way of Provençals to act alone.

At length the citizens of Béziers, watching from the walls with their faces turned always toward Monpeslier to the northeast, saw all the sky on that side gray with a strange haze that dimmed the golden sun. Day by day this shadow grew darker and more ominous, blotting out, as it advanced, the gay and cheerful light of day. By night, peering from their hilltop citadel above the gentle river Orbe, they saw, at first remotely, the glimmering of many fires close to the earth, and these flames grew brighter and more numerous on each succeeding night. They strained their eyes to the west, searching the distant hills for the sheen of metal, for the bright flickering of banners of their overlord, the Count Raimon whom they trusted to save them.

The setting of each sun now was crimson behind its veils of sullen smoke. Then, of a dun morning, they saw the vanguard of the host entering the valley, knights in white, flashing in chain mail, bearing white gonfalons emblazoned in a scarlet cross. These they knew for the White Companies, and so they grimly manned their engines of war and posted their arbalestiers.

Tityr the jongleur had got lodging with Guilhem the cobbler. He had come to the shop of Guilhem clad in a mantle of coarse drugget, footsore and weary, begging a crust of bread, and the cobbler took him in and gave him a clean straw pallet. And Tityr became the cobbler's apprentice.

On the second day after his arrival a man came into the shop holding a pair of great boots of Cordovan leather. He set them down, saying, "Cobbler, these are good boots, and they were given me by the greatest troubadour in all the world, so see you do not botch them in the mending. And I must have them at once!"

"Take your time, master," said Guilhem, smiting a small nail into a sole with one tap. "The soldiers must be patched before the citizen. A nail in the heel might lose us the city, when these White Companies get here!"

"Hark you!" said the man. "I am worth a whole company of soldiers, for I am setting out tonight to ride to Carcassonne, to fetch back our lord Raimon Roger, with his fighting men."

"Why do they send a gentleman like you, friend?" asked the cobbler. "Do they use burgesses for messengers in the army."

"I am not a burgess, fellow," said the man wrathfully. "I have been castellan and factor to the greatest troubadour, living or dead, and I know the viscount very well indeed, for I served him at table, and he was a friend of my master, monsenher the knight of Belgueil, Peire Vidal—the saints preserve his memory!"

"I have heard of Peire Vidal," said the cobbler, "and how there was none could sing better than he." He laid down the leather chausses he was working on and took up the boots, appraising their workmanship. "You shall have them within an hour, delivered by my apprentice here. To whom shall I send them?"

"To Jehan Porcelet, at the house of the podestat, where our leaders, the troubadours Raimon of Miravals and Gui of Cavaillon, are holding conference."

When he had gone Guilhem the cobbler began to talk again, while he slit a ragged edge from the Cordovan boots and searched among his pieces of dressed Spanish leather for one fine and thick enough to match.

"I have heard of this Peire Vidal, who was once a knight. They said he did much evil, but I know he made good songs. He made this one:

> Once, within a royal hall,
> Roundly was I praised,
> And, like a tennis ball,
> Vaingloriously raised
> Briefly toward heaven, my pride beset
> My soul, and in an unseen net
> Destroyed it, self-amazed;
> Then from that height I plunged, and all
> My glory vanished in the fall."

411

The cobbler had a rich deep voice; it filled the whole of the dim little shop with melody. Guilhem had been a jongleur once himself, but having married a town wench he found himself with a family and took to cobbling.

"I don't remember the rest of it. Once I knew many of Peire Vidal's songs, and some I still know and sing them as I tap old boots. The next part begins, 'Long then in silence . . .' but I don't remember."

The jongleur in the shadow stirred. "Yes, there was more," he said in a faltering voice. " 'Long then in silence, I . . .' " his voice, weak and uncertain, gathered strength.

> Long then in silence, I
> Wandered, stricken dumb
> As beasts that dumbly lie
> In barren meadows; overcome
> With sickness of living, my despair
> Believed no beauty anywhere
> Was ought but wearisome,
> Until my lady raised on high
> A new sun in my sunless sky.

"Ha!" cried the cobbler. "You have it! I'm glad now I fed you, for we shall sing some good songs together! That one, I do remember, was made by Peire Vidal for the great countess of Les Baux, Alazais——"

"Adélasie des Baux," corrected the jongleur.

"Alazais of Roca Martina, they called her here. Adélasie was her French name. A beautiful lady, they say!"

"A beautiful lady," murmured the jongleur in a low voice.

"Once," said the cobbler, "I made music myself, and I played upon a viol that I got at Toulouse, but hard times fell upon us, and I had to part with it, and never since then have I owned an instrument. Still, I have my voice, which God has not taken from me, and I have three children that are as hearty rascals as you'd find anywhere. It is hard for them to be kept out of the fields at this time of the year, for they will be running naked in the long meadow grass, but the saints will soon deliver us from armies, and then they can put themselves in the sun again and make posy-rings. My wife, the naughty wench, will be getting me another soon. She is big enough you could mend a boot upon her belly! What is troubling you, master jongleur, that you groan so? Are you sick?"

"I—I—yes, I am sick!"

"There is a lump of beeswax. Take it and chew it. The wax of the bee is not sweet, but it has the nature of sweetness in it and cures the humors of the blood. You have gone hungry too long. The first food is often poison then. Here! These boots are finished and as good as when Peire Vidal gave them to his castellan-what was his name?"

"Jehan Porcelet."

"Take them to Jehan Porcelet at the house of the podestat, and perhaps you will hear some singing by those great troubadours, the Monsenhers Raimon of Miravals and Gui of Cavaillon. The air will do you good, though the light is poor. They must be burning the old straw in the fields. Do not loiter, for there is much to be done."

The jongleur rose and took the boots and went through the town to the house of the podestat. There he asked to speak to Gui of Cavaillon. At first they would not admit him, but when he said it was urgent, they took it he had to make an explanation about the boots, and let him in. And when the baron, clad in mail, approached him, the jongleur said, "I am Peire Vidal."

The crusaders had invented many new and ingenious weapons and machines. Besides mangonels and esprinagles, they had dondaines that fired "Holy Water Sprinklers"—great balls of lead or iron attached to the end of an iron chain, and these could cut as many as three men in two. But their chief machine was the "Cat." It was a huge wooden tower, covered with stout sheepskin, and set on rollers. When it trundled up to the wall of Béziers, the side against the ramparts opened, and an immense beam, like a monstrous cat's paw, emerged. At the end of the beam were iron hooks. It was operated like a battering ram, but when it had loosened the wall by repeated blows, the claws took hold of the stones and dragged them into the moat. When the moat was filled up at that

413

spot, the crusaders rushed across and set up their scaling ladders, but the defenders overthrew them, and rained upon them bolts and quarrels, rocks, stones, beams, scalding water, hot pitch, boiling oil, and whatever they had at hand.

The bishops encouraged their followers, assuring them seats in paradise beside the throne of the Lord Jesus and close to the golden chair of the Lady Mary. They promised them, and the lord abbot of Citeaux himself gave his oath upon it, plenary absolution of all their sins committed from the day of their birth to that of their death, if they should make an end of the heretics of Béziers. Whereupon the besiegers, filled with fresh zeal, undermined the western barbican, piled beams and rubbish under it, and set the mass ablaze. Part of the wall fell, but a group of knights and troubadours of the town leaped into the breach among the hot stones, and their fellows rebuilt the wall behind them.

Then, for the season was one of extreme heat, the water in the cisterns of the city failed; and it seemed that God had taken sides with the crusaders. But the stiff-necked citizens of Béziers would yield neither to Simon de Montfort nor to Archbishop Fulk of Toulouse, persisting in their graceless devotion to their false prophets.

"It will be necessary," said the Baron Gui of Cavaillon, "for us to make a sally. Even though we be cut to pieces, it will show them there is plenty of spirit among us to resist them to the death, and they may leave off and go their way."

"That is true," said Raimon of Miravals, who had lately witnessed the burning of his own castle; "there is nothing to lose but our lives, and we may save the city."

Peire Vidal frowned. They were all three in armor, and they looked haggard and worn with constant fighting. He remembered some things now. He remembered the sally of the Greeks from the Galata citadel and was deeply troubled.

"A sally from a walled city is always dangerous," he said.

"There is no more water, and very little wine," said the baron. "The end, in any event, is close upon us. Let us make this desperate attempt, Monsenher Vidal, and do you remain to captain the city if we fail."

"So be it!" said Peire Vidal, sighing. "God have mercy on us all!"

Three hundred knights were chosen for the sortie. They were in full panoply of war, and each of them wore the favor of his lady, though some of these were no longer among the living. They did not make confession, that office being omitted by the Albigensian pastors, but they were fortified by the *viaticum*, pronounced in the common tongue of Provence. They rode without esquires and without gonfalons or any trappings not pertaining to their mission, and as they passed clattering through the streets of the city the people looked upon them sadly, without huzzahing.

Before the principal gate of the city, opening toward Carcassonne, the knights were assembled with the troubadours, Gui of Cavaillon, Raimon of Miravals, Peire Cadenet, and others at their head. They kept their horses quiet as the last orders were delivered to the guard at the gate for the lowering of the drawbridge. The people of the city were hurrying through the streets. They bore nothing with them other than babes in arms.

Then, from several parts of the city came the voices of the jongleurs, raised in song. In the great cathedral of Saint Nicaise and in the church of the Magdalen and in all other churches they were singing *Te Deum*.

Gui of Cavaillon, before he became a troubadour, had learned well the arts of the jongleur. He drew his sword and flung it high in the air; it spun in a gleaming arc, and descended into his hand again. Then he began to sing the part of the chanson of Roland that he best loved, and the other troubadours joined with him.

Veire paterne, ki unkes ne mentis
Seint Lazarun de mort resurrexis
E Daniel des lions guaresis
Guaris de mei l'anme de tuz perilz
Pur les pecchiez que en ma vie fis.

Our true Father, without dissimulation,
Who raised from the dead Saint Lazarus
And shielded Daniel among the lions,

415

Deliver my soul from the jeopardy
To which my sins have exposed it.

The portcullis began to creak, and the drawbridge to clank as the winches let the chains slide through the blocks. The horses, scenting the charge, began to curvet, whiffling eagerly the breath of battle, for they were all destriers of good breeding.

The gate stood open.

The column suddenly came alive. With a flashing of swords, lances, armor; with a long thunderous volley of hoofbeats on the planking of the bridge; and with a single great shout, "Au hazard, Béziers!" it swept straight into the center of the besieging army that stretched as far as the eye could see, covering the plains to the northeast, to the southwest, and to the south as far as the edge of the Cap Etang; a multitude clad mostly in white, splendid in its infinite standards, banners, pavilions; straight to where the mangonels and espringales were mounted, each one topped by a cross.

The onslaught of the party carried it almost to the pavilion of the Archbishop Fulk.

But Simon de Montfort was too good a general and crusader to be caught napping. He had been expecting the sortie. At the flanks of each gate he had stationed his most seasoned knights with the order that, in the event of a sally, they should allow it to expend its force before closing in and securing the drawbridge. The military machine worked with the utmost precision. As the charging troop was being cut to pieces, the sappers ran for the drawbridge, carrying heavy beams.

Peire Vidal commanded the bridge to be raised as the last knight passed over, but the guards, in their haste and excitement, jammed the winches. It rose part way and hung there suspended. The sappers thrust their heavy timbers upon it, and forced it down again, and crusader knights jostled each other into the moat as they rushed forward, eager to be the first in the city. The portcullis, however, dropped into place with a crash of metal. It was a heavy piece, well made by expert iron workers. Simon de Montfort viewed it, and commanded the Cat to be brought up, and at the same time he commanded a general assault to be made on all parts of the walls at once.

Meanwhile the priests among the crusaders, hearing from the city the sound of much singing, themselves burst into chanting.

> *Dies irae, dies illa*
> *solvent saeclum in favilla:*
> *teste David cum Sibylla.*
>
> *Quantus tremor est futurus,*
> *quantus Judex est venturus,*
> *cuncta stricte discussurus!*
>
> *Tuba mirum spargens sonum*
> *per sepulchra regionem,*
> *coget omnes ante thronum.*

The engineers of the Cat sang too, working with greater vigor as the machine reached its giant paw into the metal grill and dragged away a tangle of twisted iron bars.

In every street and square of the city were jongleurs who, brandishing their naked swords, sang lustily their songs of love and hate. The bells of all the churches were tolling. They were crowded to suffocation, some seven thousand in the cathedral and almost half that number in Saint Mary's.

To the tent of Archbishop Fulk came an armed priest, greatly perturbed. It was the lord abbot of Citeaux, Arnold Amalric, a man of exemplary life and of unquestioned probity.

"Reverend Father," he said, "I am greatly troubled. We are about to take the city, and it occurs to me that among the heretics and wretched unbelievers there may be a number of the true faith. How shall we distinguish between them?"

Fulk of Toulouse was clad as a prince of the church. He wore a richly fringed episcopal dalmatic, beneath which showed a tunic of Palermo silk embroidered in thread of gold; beneath them both a stole, encrusted with gems, was visible. From his left wrist depended a maniple, embroidered in sacred emblems. Over his other vestments was a cope, exquisitely worked with the Dove and the

417

Lamb, and it was fastened across the breast with a morse charged with an Agnus Dei. The prelate wore his miter, and in his left hand he held his crosier, a staff thickly overlaid with gold and gems. On a finger of his right hand he wore a ring of great beauty and value, and this hand held also his episcopal gloves, made with an opening to display the ring.

The archbishop pressed the tips of his fingers lightly together and considered the militant priest a moment, then he answered with unruffled firmness, "Slay all; the Lord will know well those who are His."

Mors stupebit et natura
cum resurget creatura,
judicanti responsura. . . .

Peire Vidal undid his coif and, standing on the sentry's walk, leaned far over the battlement, between its crenelations. There was a momentary lull in the attack, while Simon de Montfort selected the flower of his army for the dash through the gate. The troubadour's voice had regained its strength; he cried out:

"I, Peire Vidal, and all the people of Béziers charge you, Simon de Montfort, and Folquet of Marseille, and all those with you, to appear before the Judgment Seat of God and to answer for what you have done and are doing!"

The report of this citation before God, a summons feared at that time even by the boldest and strongest, was carried at once to Simon de Montfort and to the Archbishop Fulk who thereupon ordered Peire Vidal at all costs to be taken alive.

Rex tremendae majestatis
qui salvandos salvas gratis
salva me, fons pietatis.

Recordare, Jesu pie,
quod sum causa tuae viae:
ne me perdas illa dies.

Juste judex ultionis
donum fac remissionis
ante diem rationis.

The gate was wholly destroyed, the last bits of the portcullis drawn into the moat. The crusaders poured through it with an impetuosity that swept resistance before them as chaff before the wind.

At the cathedral of Saint Nicaise they found difficulty in entering because of the press of folk within. But they entered three abreast, hacking and stabbing, and clearing a larger space as they advanced toward the altar.

At the church of the Magdalen they set scaling ladders against the windows and arbalestiers mounted them. And then, with deliberation, they began firing at the huddled, chanting multitude within.

Lacrimosa dies illa
qua resurget ex favilla,
judicandus homo reus;
huic ergo parce, Deus:
Pie Jesu, Domine,
dona eis requiem. . . .

At length there was no more to be done by the crusaders. They withdrew from the city reluctantly, having set fire to it in every place; and as the flames mounted they witnessed the funeral pyre *cum ingenti gaudio.* Within the walls of what had been Béziers, there was no house left standing nor one living human being.

A notation, in the scholarly hand of Peire Cardinal, secretary to Count Raimon of Toulouse, on the title page of the work, *De Contemptu Mundi, sive de Miseria Humanae Conditionis,* written by one Lothario Conti, later to be known as Pope Innocent the Third:

"Love of God is not incompatible with hatred of one's fellow-men, nor with the taking of human life."

Chapter Thirty-four

"T HE blessed Sant Julian and the less beatific witch Venus," said Gaucelm Faidit, "have ever seemed well disposed toward him. They delivered him from many perils and the misadventures resulting from his follies, perhaps because, as it has been said, 'A fool may dance among devils unscathed.' His final deliverance was the most remarkable of all, he being one of three coming out of Béziers alive; and of what was done to two of them, no man should speak."

The troubadour's audiart, ambling on a forlorn and spindling jennet beside the patient ass of his master, paid little attention. He was accustomed to the rambling discourses of the old man. The audiart, a darkish young man in a patched, faded mantle of green brocade, was observing the little white bells of the brière, and the yellow blossoms of the plantagenet, or wild broom; but his raffish expression suggested that his thoughts were elsewhere than on flowers. From time to time he touched the strings of his lute, evoking bits of melody, to which his lips formed words.

The burden of the troubadour's ass seemed far more than one small beast could bear; the vast bulk of the troubadour rested mountainous upon the animal's back, saddled only with a piece of coarse cloth, tied about the belly with leather thongs. Patched too was the dingy habit of Gaucelm Faidit; clumsily, for the quick fingers of the wanton, Guilhelma Monjo, had long been closed in a devout posture beneath the sod. Her lord, howbeit he had but few deniers and oboles in his wallet, must still be giving candles to a wayside church, on a certain anniversary, for the better disposition of her soul, which he feared might have been held too soiled for admission to the abode of the blessed.)

"Miraculous, nothing less, was the manner of Peire Vidal's escape from the final judgment they passed upon him. He was to have been flayed, but not until he was dead; then roasted, but not until he was dead; then to have his eyes put out and his nose and ears lopped off, and if he had not then died, he was to be hung, drawn, and quartered, his body consumed in flames, and his ashes cast upon a dungheap. But they got no farther than using the rack and thumb screws when providence, in the shape of a woman, came between them and their designs.

"There was a lady, it seemed, he had once loved and who had loved him. Her name was Rambauda, and she was the widow of Lord Rostaala of Biolh, who died in the odor of sanctity and bequeathed a handsome annuity to the Church. The widow also was a most devout Catholic, having made a pilgrimage to Jerusalem at the time of Richard's crusade. From the Holy Land she brought back a precious relic, the thumb of one of the Apostles, which her saintliness had secured to her, though I am inclined to believe her own comeliness had something to do with it. At any rate, the abbot of Biolh, desiring greatly to make his church a place of pilgrimage, coveted the Apostle's thumb, and she had promised to bequeath it to him. Since she was a palmer of unquestioned orthodoxy, and since she had the thumb, her castle was not only spared by the crusaders; the lord abbot of Citeaux, Arnold Amalric, went thither immediately upon the fall of Béziers to humble himself before the sacred relic, and to beseech pardon for any transgression he might have committed in the murdering of the true believers along with the heretics.

"Madomna Rambauda then learned that they were engaged in the trial of Peire Vidal, and what they proposed to do with him. She besought the lord abbot to save him; but he said he could not, for Simon de Montfort and Archbishop Fulk were determined upon their course, and nothing could stop them. Then she made an offer of the holy thumb to the lord abbot, to be placed in the abbey of Citeaux if he would intervene. After much vacillation he yielded, tempted by the immense value of the object, and perhaps even more by her beauty. It is certain, whatever she promised him, that he has made more than one visit to Biolh since then. The lord abbot returned in hot haste to where the tribunal was deliberating on varieties of torture, and he demanded the person of Peire Vidal, alleging the man's madness, and the consequent connivance of the saints in his misdeeds.

"Simon and Fulk were wroth beyond measure; they made the counter-claim that Peire Vidal, when he uttered the citation to God upon the wall, was as sane as they. 'Nay,' says the abbot, 'on the contrary it proves his utter frenzy, for what man in his *compos mens* would summon two servants of Christ to appear before their Lord to answer for their crimes? Besides, he has suffered during his life from that fearful seizure, lycanthropy, the belief that one is a wolf; from the delusion that he was born to be an emperor; from the dementia of going naked, as in Sicily; from the *furor sexualis*, exhibited toward all females; from maniacal stubbornness, as when he stood up against the doge of Venice; from the *vertigo religionis,* or turning to one creed after another; and from the *maladie imaginaire,* the melancholia of viewing the world as a place of torment and unhappiness.' The abbot waxed eloquent and cited occasions when the condemning of a madman had resulted in all the judges being overtaken by the same form of madness. Simon de Montfort and Fulk, becoming horrified at the thought they might be found no better than Peire Vidal if they persisted, suspended judgment and delivered their prisoner to the abbot, who gave him into the keeping of Madomna Rambauda; though what she received was far from being the man he had once been, after the hours he had spent with the inquisitors."

"H'm," said the jongleur who was beginning to be bored with this lengthy recital. "The moral seems to be, to secure the good offices of many fair and noble and powerful ladies throughout one's life."

Gaucelm Faidit drew from his dirty tunic a bottle, and having tipped it to his bristly lips, continued, "The intercession of the lord abbot profited my old friend, but it did little good for the Lady

Rambauda. Her abbot, enraged that the thumb had gone to Citeaux, withdrew his protection from her, and allowed most of her patrimony to be seized upon by a rascally neighboring knight; so that for the rich and broad fiefs she held, she got in exchange the poor body of a past lover."

"That," said the jongleur, plucking carelessly at his lute strings, "consorts well enough with the Thirty-second Article of the Laws of Love, which declares: 'What one loses for the sake of love cannot be reckoned wholly lost; for the return is measureless.' Yet, for me, if there is any loss of goods to be considered, I would rather get for them the pleasures of the body than the consolations of the Church."

"Small pleasure of that sort has she got!" said Gaucelm Faidit shortly.

"Yet I knew one," said the audiart, "who gave up all his patrimony to wear a single brown tunic of coarse drugget and live on crusts and water, when he wasn't fasting. In Assisi, where I once dwelt, there was a youth of my own age, by name, Giovanni Bernardone, like this Peire Vidal, the son of a cloth merchant, and well-to-do. There never was a more gay, roistering, and spendthrift young blade than this Giovanni; and he was so taken with the songs of the troubadours that we called him 'El Francesco,' or the Little Frenchman, thinking in our ignorance that all who sang were French. He himself knew well the *langue d'Oc* and made many good songs in that tongue, which he later destroyed after he turned to piety. For a most unfortunate affliction overtook him. He came near to dying, and when he was scarce cured of his malady he began to show signs of derangement. He said that poverty should be his bride thenceforth, and he straightway began to give away to the poor not only his own belongings, but his father's as well, which so enraged the good merchant, Pietro Bernardone, that he made his son renounce his inheritance. Thereupon El Francesco went to live in a cave, and was there visited with angels, so he said, and he built a little church with his own hands, and soon he gathered some followers of like mind about him and established an order. Only last year, so I have heard, the pope, Innocent the Third, gave his official sanction to the brotherhood, and now my luckless friend, who might have made an excellent troubadour, is on the way to becoming a saint, God pity him!"

"Well," said Gaucelm Faidit, wiping his lips after another potation, "as Peire Cardinal remarks, 'The true value of a life cannot be measured until after death—and then it cannot be measured.' . . . There should be a path turning here, though the country is so changed it is hard to know the landmarks, what with the yearly crusading, and the harrying up and down the land of heretics, and near-heretics, and heretics-suspect, and relatives and kin of heretics, so that all the fields are growing up to brushland again, and the roads are only used for armies. Ah me, at the battle of Muret fell the last of our line of troubadour singers, for I count myself as no more than a traveling corpse, being borne to Italy in the company of a rascal jongleur of no morals and less pence! Have you ever heard of how Peire of Aragon came to his end? The young king defeated the Moors at Navas de Tolosa, then he hastened to the assistance of the last knights-troubadours who were standing out against Simon and Fulk; that was in the fifth year after the taking of Béziers and Carcassonne. Carcassonne fell because of treachery to Lord Raimon Roger after they had promised him safe conduct to make a treaty with the crusaders; and when the city had been taken, in November of that year Simon, who had the viscount in his keeping, gave out that he had died of dysentery; but dysentery never leaves the face black. Well, Peire of Aragon sent a sirvente to the camp of Simon, entrusting its delivery to one of his jongleurs, who was bidden to sing it to the assembled crusaders as the message of the king.

"The jongleur, a singer of great merit, was happy in his song till he came to the phrase in his lord's composition, 'For the love of my lady I am coming to drive ye out, barbarians, from that beautiful land that you have ravaged and destroyed.' Hereupon Simon de Montfort, having no ear for good music, cried out in a loud voice, 'So help me, God! I do not fear a king who comes against God's cause for the sake of a harlot!' Simon, you see, was ever of a virtuous mind and held love-making as the principal vice in the calendar of evil. He himself spent most of his years away from his wife. So Peire of Aragon was entirely defeated in the battle, and he was slain, together with what remained of the trou-

424

closed his eyes. "She will see to the proper disposal and entertainment of the ambassadors, until the emperor returns. . . ."

He lay quiet, with closed eyes, the sun giving his face the aspect of tranquillity.

"That is all," whispered Rambauda.

Gaucelm Faidit came close to the sleeper, bowed his head to the white hair, and kissed it.

"It is for you, Sordello, I am too old. It will do you honor."

Sordello took the green mantle of knight errantry from Gaucelm Faidit and placed it about his shoulders. "Madomna Rambauda," he said gallantly, "when I tell the noble Count Blacatz that I come from Peire Vidal, and that you have given his own mantle to me, he will bless you, be sure of it!"

Gaucelm Faidit held the lady's hand in his a long time. "He is no great trouble, is he?" he said at length.

"There is no trouble I would not endure to have him with me," she said. "Sometimes, for moments, he knows me, and then I know that God has been good to me."

As they rode away, Sordello said, "Blacatz will give us a good welcome, coming from his friend, Peire Vidal!"

"A very knave!" muttered Gaucelm Faidit, averting his gaze from his audiart. But the jongleur began to sing, with great gayety:

> Love will not hold me long
> If I may pay with song
> And paying, do no wrong. . . .

At a time when thirty years of crusading by the orthodox in the golden land had somewhat subdued the stubborn temper of its people and had left it less golden, an exile in Spain, writing in the *langue d'Oc*—now a despised provincial dialect—of the troubadours he had known as a youth, said this of Peire Vidal:

"He sang better than any man in the world but—*e fo dels plus fols homes que mai fossen, qu' el crezia que tot fos vers so que a lui plozia ni q'el volia*—he was one of the most foolish men that ever lived, for he believed that all things that pleased him, or that he wished, were true."

429

GLOSSARY

Glossary

ailette, a metal shoulder-plate worn on armour.

alba, a morning-song.

arbalest, crossbow requiring a mechanical appliance to bend it.

arbalestier, a crossbowman.

arras, tapestry woven in colors, showing figures or scenes.

aubade, French word for *alba*.

audiart, an apprentice in the Joyous Craft; a lower degree than jongleur, though the latter often were audiarts to troubadours.

balada, a song to dance rhythm, usually sung while dancing.

baldachin, a canopy of rich stuff.

ballista, an engine for hurling missiles, of early origin but still used in the Middle Ages.

barbican, an outer fortification.

barriers, a fence or railing dividing the justing-field.

bezant, a gold coin, in value about $2.42; in silver worth about 72 cents.

bliaut, a frock-like garment worn by men and women, with sleeves that widened out toward the wrists, usually richly embroidered.

buss, to kiss.

buss, a large two-masted vessel.

caïque, a long pointed skiff used on the Bosporus.

calends, the first day of the Roman month, still used in the Middle Ages.

camlet, a stiff fabric of camel's hair, or an imitation of it.

canzo, *chanzo*, or *canzon*, a song devoted mainly to love.

canson redonda, a round, in which the last line of each stanza becomes the first line of the next.

caparison, decorative trappings for a horse.

carros, literally, "war-car," an elaborate form of song, representing a defence of a lady against the attacks of other ladies.

castellan, keeper or commander of a castle.

castles at the cross-trees, defensive works in the tops of war craft.

433

cendal or *sendal*, a thin silken material used for dresses or banners.

chalons, slender rings of gold or silver gilt, sewn with jewels, used to orna- ·ment clothing.

chapman, a trader or merchant.

chasuble, the outer vestment worn by a priest over the alb and stole; a sleeveless mantle.

chausses, leg-harness or hose of mail.

cisclaton, brocade from Moorish Spain.

citole, a box-shaped psaltery.

close, an enclosed space about a castle or palace.

cobla, stanza of a song.

cockatrice, a fabulous serpent believed to kill by its breath.

coif, a close-fitting hood or skull-cap worn under the helmet.

comjat, a song of farewell to the lady whom the singer has ceased to love.

complines, see *Hours of the day*.

comte, a narrative or didactic song.

cope, a semi-circular mantle worn by the clergy.

cordon, an ornamental cord or ribbon for adornment; sometimes bestowed on the winner of a contest in singing.

crenelation, embrasure of a battlement.

croquepois, sticks armed with iron hooks.

dalmatic, a wide-sleeved tunic.

denier, a silver penny of small value.

descort, a song of unrequited love.

destrier, a war-horse.

devinalh, a song containing a play on words, involving constant apparent contradictions.

diaspre, cheap silk of Antioch.

domna, Provençal for "lady," or "mistress," as a title of address.

dondaine or *dondine*, an engine for hurling stones.

dromond, a large ship of war propelled by both oars and sails.

drugget, a coarse woolen fabric.

ducat, a Venetian coin of varying value up to $2.98.

el gai saber, the Joyous Craft or Science.

ell, a measure of length about four feet.

enseigne, a lady's favor worn by her knight.

escondich, a song in which the singer justifies himself to his lady.

esnecca, a swift vessel built on the lines of the Viking ships.

434

espringale, an engine similar to a ballista.

estampida, an ancient national dance of Provence, wild in character.

estoc, a short stabbing blade used by Venetians.

étangs, the lagoons of southern France bordering the Mediterranean.

fauchard, a long-handled, scythe-like weapon with a convex edge.

favel, a horse of chestnut color, valued in the Middle Ages.

florin, a coin of varying value, usually about six shillings.

fosse, a ditch or moat.

fustian, a stout cloth of cotton and flax.

galley, a vessel propelled by oars, or by oars and sails.

gambeson, a defensive coat of leather or cloth, stuffed and quilted.

gigue or *giga*, a kind of fiddle with a clear high note, for dancing.

gobbet, a morsel of cooked meat highly seasoned.

gonfalon, a small flag, pennant, or streamer attached to the end of a lance.

gerfalcon, a large falcon, highly prized.

grains of paradise, aromatic seeds of *Ammomum melegueta*, used for pungency in seasoning foods and liquors.

griffin, a fabulous creature, half lion and half eagle.

Griffon, the common French designation of a Greek.

guisarme, a scythe-like weapon.

harpe, old form of harp.

hauberk, coat of mail of interwoven steel rings.

hippocras, a cordial of spiced wine and other ingredients.

Hours of the day in the Middle Ages followed the canonical hours, beginning with *matins* at midnight, *lauds* about three in the morning, *primes* at six, *tierces* at nine, *sextes* at noon, *nones* about three in the afternoon, *vespers* at six, and *complines* at bed-time or about nine.

jennet, a small Spanish horse.

jerkin, a frock-shaped tight-fitting jacket.

joc-partitz, a dispute in song; a lyrical debate with several participants.

Joyous Craft, or *el gai saber*, the art of song and love, comprising a thorough knowledge and practice of the many forms of song, instruments, and niceties of gallantry and love-making, which formed the body of a troubadour's profession. This "science" might be personal and inspirational in its application, but the technique required years of arduous preparation and long experience to perfect.

langue d'Oc, a distinct and independent romance language common to the regions of what are now southern France and Catalonia. It was a development of provincial vulgar Latin, with a slight infusion of other tongues, Celtic and Germanic. Loosely, it was called the *roman* language.

lauds, see *Hours of the day*.

lectern, a reading desk for church services.

linsey, a cloth of coarse linen or wool mixture.

lyard or *lyart*, a silver gray or dappled gray horse, highly prized.

manchet bread, a small loaf of fine white bread.

mandore, a four-stringed lute.

mangonel, an engine used for throwing stones and other missiles.

maniple, a band worn on the left arm as a vestment by the clergy.

mark, a gold or silver coin of varying value.

medlar, the fruit of *Mespilus germanica,* hard and bitter when ripe but agreeably acid when verging on decay.

menie, the medieval household staff, including personal servants, retainers, and attendants.

messer, simple title of masculine address.

midden, dunghill or refuse heap.

minever, a mixture of furs used for trimming.

misericorde, a short dagger used to give the death-blow to a fallen knight.

miter, a headdress worn by church dignitaries from abbots to popes.

monsenher, masculine title of respectful address, implying gentility.

naves, vessels often used as transports.

nones, see *Hours of the day*.

novas, a lyrical news-letter, including also moral or didactic pieces.

obole, a small coin of slight value.

orarion, a broad stole.

organistrum, a sort of small hurdy-gurdy whose sound was produced by turning a wheel and playing the stops with keys.

orison, a devotional prayer.

palfrey, an easy-riding saddle horse, usually reserved for women.

pastorela, a simple idyllic song, generally a folk-song rather than of troubadour composition.

pectoral cross, a cross worn on the breast of the higher clergy.

pelisse, a long outer garment or mantle, usually lined with fur.

piment, a hot spiced wine containing honey.

planh, a lyrical lament.

pleasance, an enclosed garden.

podestat, Provençal form of *podestà,* a chief city magistrate.

psaltery, a stringed instrument of thirteen strings.

quarrels or *carreaulx*, great arrows or bolts of four-edged heads, discharged from arbalests.

questeaux, the common people; the lowest social grade above villeins.

quillon, an arm of the cross guard of a sword.

retroensa, a song with a refrain.

roman, a long narrative song or lay.

roncin, a common hackney horse.

rote or *rota*, an instrument of the guitar type.

routiers, free-lances, mostly from Brabant, Navarre, and the Basque districts, little better than brigands.

russet, a coarse homespun cloth.

sakkos, a tight-fitting garment, supposed to symbolize the seamless robe of Christ, worn in the Byzantine Empire.

salut, a letter in song form, in complimentary terms.

samite, a rich silk.

senher, a title of masculine address, implying a social grade above that of *messer*.

serena, an even-song.

sextes, see *Hours of the day*.

sol, a coin of slight value.

sirvente, a song of praise or censure, often with a satiric treatment.

sorb apple, the fruit of the service-tree, *Sorbus domestica*.

sticherion, the Eastern form of the alb and dalmatic.

stole, a narrow band, fringed at the edges, worn by the clergy while officiating.

surtout or *surcoat*, a cape-like but close-fitting overcoat.

tabor, a small tambourine without jingles.

talent, a unit of coinage, generally used as a term of value rather than actual currency.

tenson, a debate or duel in song between two persons.

tornada, a return to the melody of the preceding stanza.

tornimen or *tornejamen*, a tournament, or general contest in song.

trencher, wooden platter.

truye, a large war machine, armed with a ram and capable of holding several hundred men.

tunicle, a short ecclesiastical vestment.

turcople, a Saracen mercenary.

tympanum, an ancient form of drum.

urser or *usher*, a large unwieldy vessel of the transport type.

437

vair, originally a variegated gray and white fur; hence, as a color, changeful or variegated shades of gray.

vers, the oldest name for a song or poem; used loosely for any song when not particularized.

viol, a stringed instrument with six strings, played with a bow.

volta, a strong pause in a stanza, from which was derived the division of the Italian sonnet.